# A SWORD OF REIGN & STEEL

## CASTIEL A. STEELE

# A SWORD OF REIGN AND STEEL

*To Jean,*
*A muse from fleeting dreams*

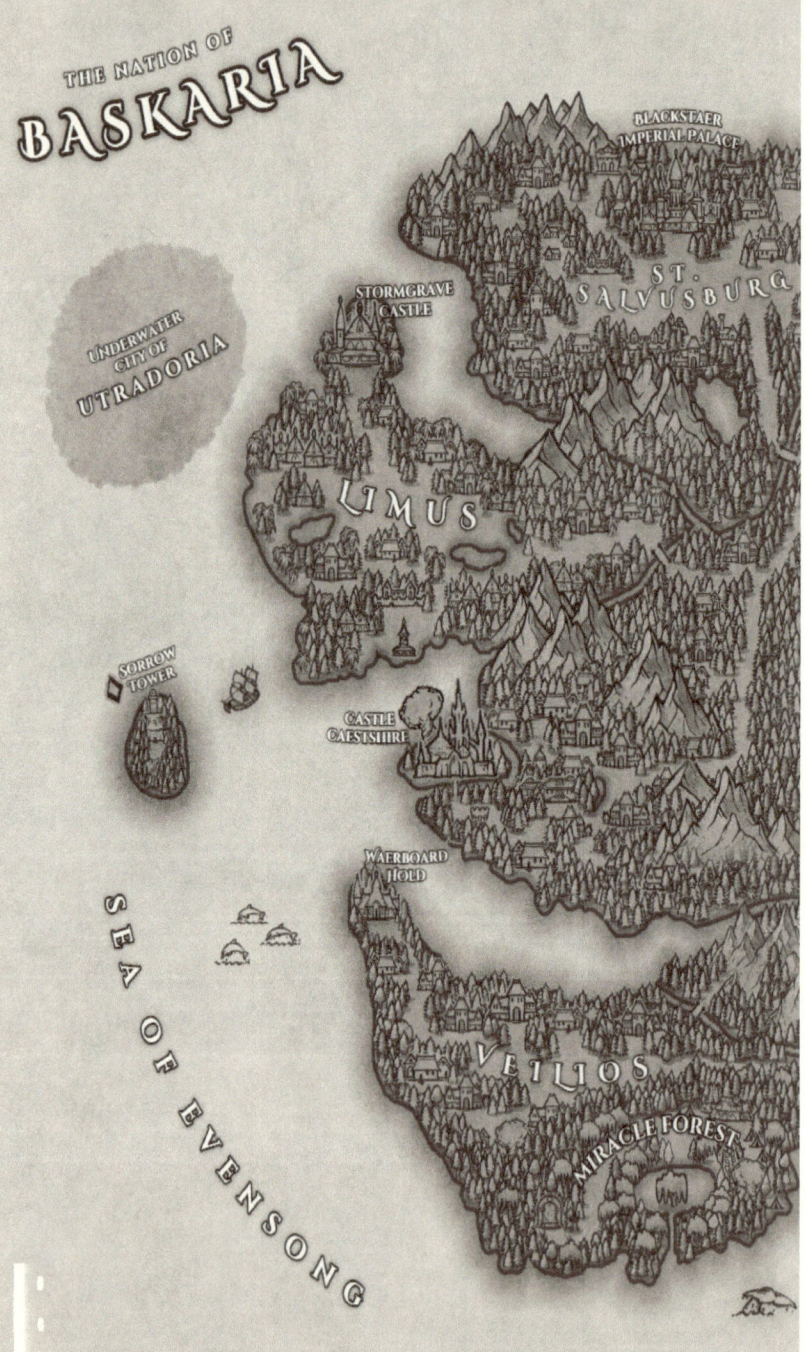

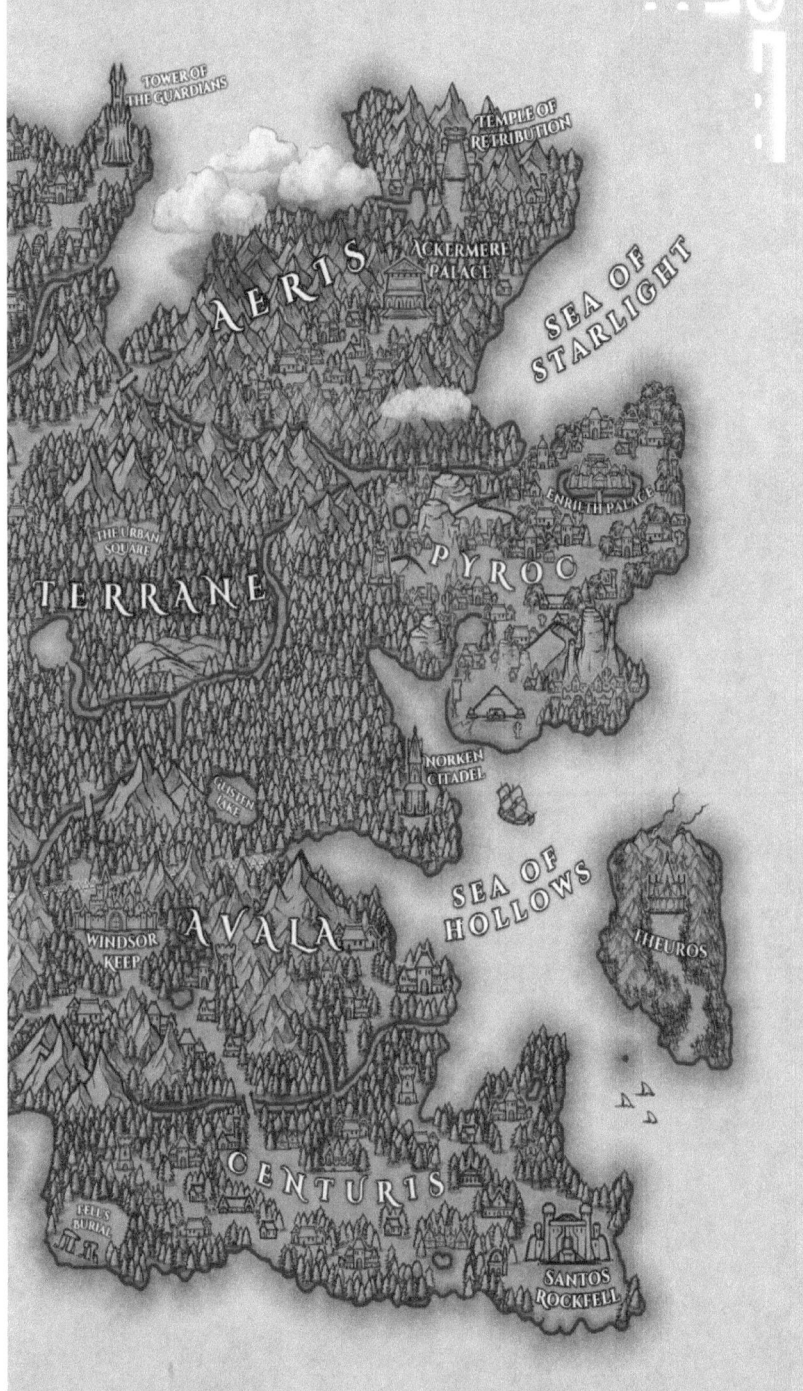

**The two moons ascended above the tallest tower of Blackstaer** Palace at the struck of midnight. Inside the palace, a hidden artifact remained, collecting dust over the years. Many have spoken of its existence, but only a few have ever laid eyes on it. The device with the ability to travel through worlds was more of a folktale than a fact, a whispered rumor spread through the Nine Lands of Baskaria.

A Glax hovercraft, the second-largest vehicle of the three models, appeared visible in the night sky. It was an ovular-shaped structure, twenty-eight feet long, with three wings spread from left to right as well as underneath, a silver color palette, and six large fans underneath to allow the vehicle's motion of flight. Citizens of Saint Salvusburg craned their necks as it zoomed overhead on a direct path to the palace.

As the vehicle landed on the ground, a group of caedose soldiers exited the vehicle. Their Insully blades and KT7 Foxsull lasers were held firmly in their hands as they marched towards the old rusted double doors of the palace. Exiting the vehicle next were their leaders: DeVault Beauchamp and Aldothfex Soulryth. The two stood side-by-side, wearing long black coats with feathered hoods to keep them warm against the harsh wind. Winter was on the horizon, and DeVault knew it was going to be a long one.

"Search the perimeters," demanded DeVault. He sharply turned to the three soldiers on his right-hand side. "You three, open the doors and search for traps. Any homeless elementals spotted in the area are to be executed on sight. Move quickly. We have a long journey ahead of us."

After forcing the doors open, the armored men quickly ran inside and began scouting. After it was confirmed clear, DeVault and Aldothfex began their steps forward.

The sound of gunfire echoed from the hall ahead. DeVault figured his men had found one of the many homeless elementals who called this decrepit palace home.

While the soldiers continued scouting the crumbling palace, DeVault and Aldothfex walked down to the underground tunnels where Emperor Stephanus and Empress Farrah had constructed their dungeon. There were three prisoners there originally, which wasn't where prisoners typically were held. However, DeVault felt it was only fitting to keep them in the mold-infested dungeon, given who they all connected back to.

Arriving, the men found a cell with a woman curled up in the corner. She had a son with her beforehand, but he was no longer imprisoned, thanks to the lack of security DeVault demanded of his caedose soldiers. The son had escaped, but he ensured that it would not happen again with six of his soldiers stationed below with them.

The woman, Stella Grantford, attempted to keep herself warm with the ripped blanket held tightly in her hands. DeVault knew that she could easily shapeshift into a wolf to keep herself warm, so instead, he had some of his best employees develop a device that would not allow a shapeshifter to transform into any creature. It brought him joy to see her suffer.

"How are we holding up this evening, Mrs. Grantford?" DeVault asked, tauntingly.

"May the Gods punish you for all eternity," Stella Grantford spat.

"Well, you've earned yourself a week closer to your execution. Do try to play nice the next time we come to visit."

The men made their way to the second prisoner, right next to

Stella's cell. There, they were met with an old friend who they believed to be an ally up until a few years ago.

"As for you, *traitor*. Are you ready to talk?" asked DeVault.

"I'm with the shapeshifter on this one," replied the man, voice hoarse and dry, like every word hurt to speak. "May the Gods punish you for all eternity."

DeVault did not show a shred of emotion. Instead, he turned to Aldothfex and nodded his head. As the prisoner received his tenth beating, the blood oozing from his mouth and eyes blue as the night sky, Aldothfex tossed the man down onto the cold concrete flooring and exited the cell.

"I'm giving you one last chance," DeVault said patiently. "Tell me where the artifact is. Or, we can have you decapitated for your children and the rest of Baskaria to witness. It is up to you."

"*Bastards*," the man groaned.

"Very well. We'll expect to see you tomorrow morning. Have your final words prepared."

As DeVault and Aldothfex began walking away, the man grunted and crawled forward, pressing up against the bars of his cell. "The East Tower..." he said, defeat heavy in his words. "I recall the Emperor holding most of his forbidden artifacts up in the tower. It's the same one he kept in that mirror."

DeVault knew very well what the mirror was. Unfortunately, the mirror had been destroyed. The only way to continue *his* work was by finding the artifact in question.

\* \* \*

Reaching the third floor, DeVault looked around the long hall. He held an electronic glass device showcasing the blueprints of the vacant property. As he continued, memories of the night during the invasion at Blackstaer Palace resurfaced. DeVault could still hear the pleas in Empress Farrah's voice.

"Something caught you off guard, DeVault?" asked Aldothfex.

"Only the memories of our enemies," DeVault responded. "These walls will be forever haunted with the death of many who defended the Bellemores."

"The Bellemores would have ushered destruction across the Nine Lands. Soon, the order will be restored. Our new ruler shall rise again."

DeVault looked down at his device. The screen revealed that both of them were close by.

"We're almost there," DeVault started. "Possibly the next door up, over there." He pointed to the third door on the right-hand side of the hall.

Aldothfex brushed past DeVault and placed his hand on the gold doorknob. There was a pause as he waited for DeVault's confirmation.

"Yes. This is the door," DeVault confirmed. "It leads up to a flight of stairs and the tower."

"Very well."

Proceeding upstairs, both men arrived at the tallest room of the palace. It was no secret that it was where Emperor Stephanus Bellemore kept the infamous mirror; the same mirror that conjured up the Shadow Lord eighteen years ago.

The room was in disarray. Dust covered every surface, and large cobwebs strung along the walls like hanging tapestries. It was clear the room had been untouched for a long time. DeVault let out a relieved breath. Aldothfex chanted "*Pyroc*," and flames appeared on the tips of his fingers to light their way around the room.

DeVault left Aldothfex as he scouted the area. Upon the left-hand corner of the room, he saw an old-looking cloth draped over a large object. Instantly, DeVault made way and grabbed hold of it. He pulled it down—disappointment filled him as he revealed a circular stone object.

"I've been deceived," DeVault said. He turned to Aldothfex. "Where could the artifact be located?"

"The Shadow Lord said that it was located in a room owned by a family enemy. If not the Bellemores, then who?" asked Aldothfex.

DeVault stood and recollected his thoughts as he mentally went down the list of family enemies in his past. All of which seemed to have been annihilated. Although, one in particular did come to mind:

Reju Tufte.

DeVault looked at Aldothfex as he shook his head. "My deceased wife... Her bastard son must have had it last. Of course, he would. That sneaky little rat." DeVault slammed his fist into the window, scattering glass along the floor. He spun around and headed out of the room.

"Reju has always been the thorn in my vine."

"DeVault, might I remind you that the Shadow Lord killed Reju weeks ago? How are we to find the artifact now?" asked Aldothfex.

DeVault had his ways. It would only be a matter of time before he found the location of the artifact. Until then, the Lost Prince would be his problem to handle.

* * *

Exiting the stairway, the men returned to the hall where they discovered two caedose soldiers arresting one of their own. DeVault raised an eyebrow at the scene.

"And what is the meaning of this?" DeVault demanded.

"We found this one scaling the rooftop of the palace. He was speaking with no one present when Vance and I walked up. Vance found a communicator device in the impostor's ear."

"A rebel?" Aldothfex hissed.

"That is our thought," the soldier said.

DeVault raised his hand, dismissing the two caedose soldiers. Once they did so, DeVault reached into his coat pocket and pulled out a shimmering green liquid in a tiny glass bottle.

Aldothfex grabbed the rebel's neck and held his face up as the innocent man's mouth opened wide. He had beige skin with tattoos visible from his neck, a muscular body structure, black braided hair, and brown eyes that revealed aggression. DeVault leaned the bottle to the middle of the man's tongue as a drop landed. Aldothfex then closed the rebel's mouth and forced him to swallow.

"We've done quite a few experiments these past couple of years to find the exact elixir that'll reveal one's true supernatural identity," DeVault explained. "If you are a supernatural being, you won't be making it out of here alive, I'm afraid."

"You're a coward," the rebel scoffed.

"A coward who seeks to destroy those who are a threat to the elemental race. To rid this planet of the ones who are destroying this planet before our very eyes. My boy, you have no idea the amount of work I've done to serve a higher purpose—to let future generations have a better way of life."

The rebel clutched his chest and started coughing violently. He fell over as his body began to twitch, eyes rolling into the back of his head.

Both Aldothfex and DeVault stood idly by, watching the transformation take hold.

The rebel's human appearance soon shifted to a huge white polar bear, then back to its regular human form once again. The rebel was a shapeshifter.

The rebel struggled to catch his breath before talking. "This is *not* a better life. This—this is a massacre to serve a darker purpose. To s—serve your outdated agenda against supernatural… beings." The shapeshifter grunted, body contorting into a painful shape. "There… is no other r—reason. Peace and h—harmony were in the heart of Baskaria… decades ago. The Bellemore family. They b— believed in a… better world. Your jealousy and hatred towards beings like me caused you to destroy that perfect paradise. Your s— system is flawed."

DeVault chuckled. He crossed his arms behind his back and began pacing back and forth in front of the shapeshifter.

"Are you familiar with the greatest lie?" DeVault asked softly.

"No… but imagine y—you'll tell me," the shapeshifter answered mockingly.

" *'He gives us hope in darkness when we can't see the light.'* For centuries, we were taught of one God who created all living things on Zorall. And yet, during our darkest days, He abandoned us. The angels He created came down from the Heavens to help mankind when our 'Creator' would not. I've seen that darkness. I've made physical contact with it. Hope is a foolish emotion used to convince someone that everything will be alright. In the end, it was that darkness that showed me and my fellow Guardians the truth—the road to paradise."

A small piece of glass fell from the shapeshifter's hand. Blood flowed across the old wooden floor. DeVault and Aldothfex exchanged looks before bending forward and grabbing the damaged object. Examining, DeVault could not help but be mesmerized by the piece.

"By the Gods... It is the last piece of the original mirror. Where did you find this?" DeVault demanded.

The shapeshifter refused to answer. Eager, DeVault reached into his coat pockets in search of a specific serum out of the four doses he had with him. Once he found the correct one, he poured the small amount of blue liquid into the shapeshifter's mouth. He was gagging at the taste. DeVault waited until the serum did its wonders: To tell the truth.

"I—I was instructed to search for remains of the mirror that conjured the Shadow Lord years ago," the shapeshifter revealed.

"By whom?"

"It was a—anonymous. I was... I was paid a hefty amount of aspar to get the job done."

DeVault wasted no more time. He reached back into his pocket and pulled out one of the liquid substances. It was blood, but more specifically, Prince Antonius' blood. He managed to smuggle some from his encounter at Glisten Lake. With a drop of the prince's blood, a large amount of black smoke began to emerge from the remains of the shattered mirror. Slowly, the smoke formed into something, or rather someone: The Shadow Lord.

"Impossible," the shapeshifter gasped.

"Marvelous. Do you have any last words, shapeshifter?" asked DeVault.

"M—may my soul rest... above the stars. You," the shapeshifter said, grinning while blood slunk from the corner of his mouth, "are no match for what is to come. The Lost Prince has been found. H—he will be your downfall. A gift from above, a true form of hope."

"Then you are a fool. Supernatural beings are not welcomed into the Arts of Heaven, shapeshifter. Remember that."

"Neither are murderers," the shapeshifter barked.

Aldothfex stepped forward, looking bored. He chanted with an intense tone, "*Pyroc*," as a massive funnel of flames disintegrated the innocent shapeshifter's body.

DeVault turned to the Shadow Lord as he bent down on one knee and bowed his head.

"My Lord, welcome back," said DeVault.

*"My time is once again limited on this world, so let me instruct your next task…"* the Shadow Lord began. *"Find me the vampyre fugitive. She can locate the artifact you seek. Her connection to the Eckwood brothers may prove useful. If all goes according to plan, I won't need the remaining Eternal Elements."*

*Act One*

# 1
## A Hunter and His Arrow

**MALAKAI**

Nightmares fell like loose cobwebs from Malakai's mind as he sat up in bed, rubbing his eyes. A cold shiver ran down his spine as he remembered the dream. He tried to convince himself that nothing he'd seen was real, and it worked for the most part. After all, it wasn't like he was back in the Dark Dimension. Those days were behind him. Four months, to be exact, since Vorkalth haunted his mind. Malakai was safe and sound here in Windsor Keep.

Beside him in bed was Prince Kelton Eckwood, his partner and dashing protector. Malakai lay back down, and the comforting scent of honey and cinnamon from Kelton smoothed his mind. Minus the obnoxious snoring, Kelton looked beautiful as he slept. Malakai couldn't help himself as he caressed his hand across Kelton's cheek. His touch seemed to have activated a response for the snoring to stop. *Good.*

It brought a pleasant warmth to Malakai to know Kelton was not enduring the nightmares he had. There were only a few occurrences where Kelton found himself in the Dark Dimension. Luckily, Vorkalth had not interfered. *I pray to the Gods it stays like that*, he thought.

The holographic clock by the nightstand showed five o'clock.

The sun had yet to rise, which allowed Malakai enough time to take a quick, peaceful moment, and then quietly hop out of bed and throw on some clothes. As much as he loved the idea of Kelton being by his side almost every hour of the day, Malakai enjoyed his space, too, and the times when he could be on his own. Malakai then gathered his hunting equipment, snuck out of the castle, and wandered off into the snowy woods of Avala.

Located on the left side of Windsor Keep, a specific pond was hidden within the mountains. Malakai had stumbled upon it a couple of weeks ago, and it became his favorite place to go. It wasn't too far from the castle or the barrier. He knew he had nothing to worry about being out here, but the paranoia was hard to shake. There hadn't been any incidents during his time in the South, but trouble had a habit of following Malakai everywhere he went.

It wasn't easy at first to find the correct time frame to sneak out. Malakai was on heavy watch after the fiasco he, Eli, and Rahaf found themselves in last month. Though he couldn't blame Eli for what he did. Eli wanted to find a way to save his mother and Orian from their unfortunate capture in the North. One of the witches made the mistake of mentioning an ancient artifact located in Fell's Burial, and ever since, Eli has made it his mission to get hold of it. Malakai didn't know much about what happened when Eli and Rahaf split off from him to go look for it; he was forced to stay behind and convince the rulers of Centuris to lend their army.

Needless to say, the Grand Empress Dowager, Maelena Bellemore, was furious when she discovered what had taken place. She claimed Eli's bad influence made those in Centuris look at Malakai differently, questioning whether or not Malakai was fit for the Baskarian throne. Malakai didn't pay mind to all that, though. In the end, they were successful in convincing the old queens, Julee and Janna Briscker, to lend their army for war.

Kneeling on a boulder, Malakai looked out to where the frozen pond resided. Winter made permanent residence here in Avala for decades, and there was no sign of the weather ever changing.

Malakai held on tightly to his metallic bow and arrows, searching the woods for any animal that might have crossed his path.

Maelena insisted that her grandson stay out of the action and not fight. It irked Malakai's soul. He felt as though her demand was a bit of an insult, like she didn't trust him to be able to fight on his own. Had he not proven himself after all he went through in the North? Granted, there had been some issues, but most of that was a result of Vorkalth interfering in the Dark Dimension. Now that he had the Eternal Element of Pyroc, Malakai wouldn't have to worry about the Shadow Lord for another eighteen years. *Bottom line, how does Grandmamma expect anyone to take me seriously if their heir to the Baskarian throne doesn't fight alongside them? What kind of example will I be setting for them?*

A flock of Enis flew past Malakai, giggling and cooing as they embraced the winds that rushed through the woods. The distraction caused Malakai's concentration to wane, and a few wildlife managed to run past him. He huffed and noticed his breath was visible in the cold. Malakai tightened the black scarf on his neck and zipped his gray coat before hopping off the boulder, landing on the edge of the frozen lake. It wasn't until he landed that he caught footprints on the snow. *Deer.*

*CRACK!*

Upon a nearby cliff, Malakai caught an abnormal set of antlers moving at a steady pace. *Could it be? Maybe...* He'd hunted plenty in the past. The poor creature must've stepped on a branch. Unlucky move.

Climbing on the rocks, Malakai struggled with his black gloves, not gripping hard enough.

Suddenly, Malakai had an idea. *I have the Eternal Elements of Terrane and Pyroc. This would be a good chance to practice using them.*

Malakai closed his eyes and emptied his mind. The woods fell silent as he reached deep into his soul and felt the rush of heat surging through his bones. Opening his eyes, he chanted "*Pyroc*" and saw a zap of fire shoot from his index fingers and clash against the icy rocks. The ice melted off, and Malakai repeated the process until he reached the second-to-last rock before he reached the deer.

"What do you plan on doing with that little creature?" a male voice shouted, voice echoing along the snow.

Malakai screamed as his hands slipped, his body ready to plunge into the snow.

"*Terrane*," the male chanted.

Vines grew from beneath the ground and wrapped themselves around Malakai's wrists, hips, and ankles, catching him before he could hurt himself. Once secured, Malakai remained in midair, dangling as he came into eye contact with Kelton Eckwood.

"Kelton, you jerk!" Malakai struggled to use his element to get himself released. "Help me out of this, please."

Kelton chuckled. "I don't know, I think I like you like this. What do you think I can do with you all tied up?" Kelton raised an eyebrow, lips quirked into a teasing smirk.

"You can watch me slowly freeze to death is what you can do," Malakai said, rolling his eyes at Kelton's flirting.

"You're killing me, Kai." Kelton flicked his wrist as the vines shrank back into the ground. He then caught Malakai and helped him stand straight, brushing off the snow he was covered in.

"When did you realize I wasn't in bed?" asked Malakai.

"Roughly fifteen minutes ago," Kelton replied. "Why do you keep coming out here? You know your grandmother is going to freak out when one of the guards catches you sneaking off."

Malakai sucked his teeth. "Please. I've studied Windsor Keep from the inside and out. The morning guards don't do anything but sleep and talk a bunch of nonsense. It's easier for me to practice in the morning while everyone has yet to wake up."

"And what is it, my precious prince, you are practicing for? Don't tell me you still want to fight in this war. There's already so much for me to worry about as it is. The last thing I need is to add you to the list."

Malakai brushed Kelton's comment to the side. He began walking down a cobblestone path back to Windsor Keep. Kelton followed.

"I'm sorry," Malakai sighed. "I just feel useless. All I do is stand

4

around and look presentable while everyone trains and makes decisions for a war on my behalf. That's not who I am. I understand the Nine Lands need their 'Lost Prince' alive to claim the Baskarian throne, but I couldn't forgive myself if I didn't fight alongside my people. It doesn't feel right."

Malakai stopped walking and turned to Kelton. The look on his face showed just how worried Kelton was now that Malakai had opened up to him. "You and I went through so much within those three days in Terrane. And those three days were such a rush, kicking ass, escaping near death, and leaving behind a massive scene for the ground kingdom to pick up. I miss that feeling."

Kelton nodded his head, processing Malakai's feelings. "I get it. You want adventure. Excitement. But you have to realize something: If anything happens to you, the Elder Guardians will have a one-up on all of us. Even if the South takes down the North, Maelena is getting old. Citizens will elect their own government, and who knows what that would look like? Entrusting anyone to rule the Nine Lands who isn't a Bellemore is a dangerous game."

"Not for nothing, but we're in this situation *because* of the Bellemores. My biological parents conjured Vorkalth through that stupid mirror and everything went to shit afterward. I saw it with my own eyes…"

Malakai shook his head and continued walking in silence. However, the silence was cut short when Kelton tugged on Malakai's wrist. Both their bodies nearly touched as Malakai looked up, seeing a petrified Kelton.

"What do you mean you *saw* it?" he asked.

*Damn*, Malakai thought. *He caught me.*

"It's nothing, Kelton. Let's just get back to Windsor Keep before the guards catch us."

"No."

Malakai's vision shifted from reality to hallucinations in between moments, making him freeze in place. He saw images from his past popping up here and there. A force of pressure rose in his head, almost like he was going to explode. Malakai couldn't recall the last time he felt like this. In the images, he saw the mirrored barrier when he first arrived. Next, he saw the crescent moon amulet that was hidden deep in his mother's dresser. Malakai heard whispers circling his mind, then he saw an image of his nose bleeding when he was at the barrier.

Suddenly, Malakai's legs weakened. He fell to his knees and began hyperventilating. His chest tightened, preventing him from breathing. *What's going on with me?* He questioned.

Kelton rushed to Malakai's aid, attempting to use his Terrane element to heal whatever it was Malakai was enduring, but it wasn't enough. Malakai turned, feeling up Kelton's arm to his face. He grabbed him and pulled him down, sealing their lips together. As he melted into the kiss, he felt the pain begin to subside, and his vision focused back to the present.

Once their lips parted, Kelton asked, "What was that all about? Are you okay?"

Malakai nodded. "I read somewhere that kissing helps reduce cortisol. It's like a hormone that helps with stress and anxiety. I guess you can say you're my anchor."

Kelton cupped his hands on Malakai's face, his thumbs gently caressing him. "You sweet idiot. If you wanted me to kiss you, I'd do it a thousand times," Kelton teased, pressing another brief kiss to Malakai's lips. When he pulled away, however, his face was more serious. "But I have to ask, is Vorkalth back? Have you started having those dreams again in the Dark Dimension?" Malakai shook his head. "Then how did you see what the Emperor and Empress did? Clearly, it was recent. You've never brought it up to me before."

Malakai held his tongue. He tried desperately not to let the stress overwhelm him once more. He wished Kelton would stop worrying so much. He hadn't been visited by the Shadow Lord in months, and that truth still stood true. The only ones who should be concerned about the Dark Dimension were Kelton and Silianna. Unlike Kelton, Silianna has been open about her encounters once in a while. Her deceased uncle, Reju Tufte, had been assisting her in helping the Lost Souls cross over into the afterlife, allowing them to find peace and resolve their unfinished business. It has become a new passion of hers, which helped her overcome her fear of the scary realm.

As for Kelton? Nothing. He never talked about his time there. Malakai worried that he might be keeping stuff from him, considering that there were some nights Kelton would wake up screaming from a nightmare. But Kelton always said he was fine, and all Malakai could do was try to believe him. *I wish he could tell me what he dreams about.*

"No. I haven't been back to the Dark Dimension since I abstracted the Eternal Element of Pyroc." Malakai stood up from the ground and began walking, wanting to put the incident behind him. "I'm not sure why I had that dream last night. The witch, Annalu La'Crox, said my memories would slowly return to me in time. Perhaps this was one of them."

"It would make sense; however, you could only see through the Emperor and Empress's perspective when you were in the Dark Dimension. Vorkalth allowed you to see that moment when the invasion occurred. If you dreamt of them again from their perspective, what's to say you weren't traveling in the spirit realm again?"

Malakai's fist tightened. "It is impossible for me to return there, Kelton. Drop it. If it's that concerning to you, I shall find Annalu later and ask her about it. Maybe she will have answers. Right now, all you're doing is stressing me out."

The two fell silent.

Peeking out from above the trees, Malakai saw Windsor Keep. The castle looked much further away than it was. The flock of Enis flew above them once more. One of them in particular separated from the flock and circled Malakai before setting herself on his shoulder.

"I haven't seen you in a while," Malakai said to the Eni. "I have yet to give you a name."

The Eni shook her head and flew back to her flock, indicating to Malakai that she was waiting to be granted a name. Even his grandmamma, Maelena, explained that once an Eni was attached to an elemental, they must provide a name. *It's been four months, and she has every right to be ticked off with me*, he thought.

"I'm sorry, Malakai." Kelton's voice cracked, breaking the tension between them. "I don't mean to stress you out. I should've given you your space and waited for you back at Windsor Keep."

"It's okay, Kelton. I get why you act the way you do. You want to protect me, but I need you to know that I can take care of myself. Once I master the elements of Terrane and Pyroc, it will be a lot harder for anyone to mess with me."

"Gods, I don't think I've ever met anyone as charming as you," said Kelton.

"*If you wanted me to kiss you, I'd do it a thousand times*," Malakai said, mimicking Kelton's voice.

The boys laughed and continued their walk, Malakai tucking away his worry to deal with at another time.

# 2
## Lost in Between

**MALAKAI**

Later, when Malakai stopped by the Windsor Keep Library, he found the elusive Princess Silianna Beauchamp twirling around the room to the sound of gentle music with a book open in her hands. The room smelled of a vanilla and cacao butter mixture, one of Silianna's signature perfumes, as Malakai carefully navigated his way through towers of stacked books on the floor. Silianna had been spending a lot of time in the library recently, attempting to study as much as she could about her newfound gift.

She spun around and spotted Malakai, and the look on her face when she saw him gave him the sense that she had news to share.

"I'm assuming you've found new information?" he asked.

"Technically, yes! But it is extremely long." Silianna paused in her movements, set the book she currently had to the side, and pulled out a large leather-bound book. Silianna polished the front of the book with her hands, scattering dust and revealing the book's title, "*A Journey into a Dark Realm.*"

"By the Gods," Malakai gasped, "you actually did it!"

"The book was written by Narkissa," Silianna said. She handed the book over to Malakai so he could observe the author's name. "Have you any idea who Narkissa might be?"

Malakai vaguely remembered a diary he had read that was written by someone named Narkissa. It was during his short time at Castle Caestshire, locked in the East Tower. If memory served, Narkissa had insights into multiple worlds outside of their planet. Malakai also recalled how Narkissa claimed to be the oldest vampyre who walked Zorall.

"What are you thinking about?" asked Silianna, her voice sounding intrigued.

"I think I'm familiar with the name," he responded. "Although I don't have much information for you other than what I read four months ago. What did the book talk about?"

"That's the problem I'm facing." Silianna grabbed the book from Malakai's hands and set it on the table. She flipped a couple of pages only to reveal they were blank. "The pages are empty. The only thing that appears is a note on the very first page. I think the book has some sort of an enchantment lock. Whoever this Narkissa is, they must've known how important this information was."

"Narkissa claimed herself to be the oldest vampyre to ever walk this world. I wouldn't be surprised if she knew someone with that kind of magic to enchant the book."

Suddenly, Malakai had an idea. If Narkissa has been around for this long, perhaps she has intel on not only the Dark Dimension but also Vorkalth as well. *He must have some sort of weakness she knows about.*

Silianna proceeded to flip to the first page of the book. A short message bled through the pages in red ink:

> *Dear reader,*
> *The contents of this book are protected. A drop of blood from its owner shall grant you access. Attempting to break the spell will destroy the book in its entirety.*
>
> *Yours truly,*
> *Narkissa*

Malakai shut the book and pushed it to the side. He knew what his next task would be. Since his grandmother wanted him to sit idly by while Eli traveled with Annalu to Veilios to convince Lord Hussayn to lend his shapeshifter army, Malakai figured he'd make use of his time and try to gain another alliance. However, it was still a surprise to everyone that his grandmother gave Eli a second chance after his little side quest last month.

The only kingdom left to seek an alliance with would be the vampyres on the island of Theuros. If Narkissa ruled over the domain, then perhaps Malakai could maneuver his way into some information about Vorkalth and the Dark Dimension. *The issue is,* Malakai thought, *why hasn't Grandmamma spoken a single word about them? Do we not plan to gather them for the war?*

The stakes were certainly high now that everything came to light. As long as Malakai, Kelton, and Silianna had a connection to the Dark Dimension, there would always be danger. It did not matter if Malakai was protected. What would happen after the next eighteen years? The protection the Eternal Element of Pyroc had on him won't be around forever. He needed to get ahead of the situation before things spun out of control.

Finding Narkissa was their best shot at understanding and controlling their dark abilities. Whomever Narkissa may be, Malakai intended to find her within the next couple of days.

"You're plotting something," Silianna said, narrowing her eyes at him knowingly. "I want in."

"I may have a way to locate Narkissa. I'm just concerned it'll be complicated to get through my grandmother. The fiasco at Centuris is really screwing me over. I need to regain her trust. Once I do, I'll let you know what the game plan is."

"Fine. In the meantime, I shall continue my research and do whatever I can. I haven't spoken to Reju in a while, hopefully, he has some intel on Narkissa."

"That would be good." Malakai was a little taken aback now that he thought about Reju Tufte. He looked at Silianna and asked, "How does someone who has used the spirit element all his life not have all the details about the Dark Dimension?"

"Your guess is as good as mine," Silianna said, shaking her head.

11

"But I suppose that's what happens when you use the forbidden element for personal gain rather than use it for good, which is exactly what I'm trying to do. Use it for good."

"I pray to the Gods that you are careful with whatever it is you're doing for the Lost Souls. If Vorkalth ever were to find you…"

"He won't. He hasn't. Regardless, I'm not the one he wants." Silianna gave Malakai a long stare, indicating she was referring to him.

Malakai would be lying if he didn't say he was concerned for Kelton and Silianna's safety. His protection was solidified for nearly two decades, but theirs wasn't. *I know I should be concerned about the fate of the Nine Lands, but I can't stop thinking about their safety.*

Silianna pulled some other books towards her and started flipping through them, refocusing on her task. As Malakai turned to leave, he saw Kelton walking towards them, covered in dirt and blood. However, there was no sign of open wounds on the visible parts of his body.

"Kelton! What happened to you?" Malakai exclaimed, rushing over to his side.

"Sorry to interrupt," Kelton started, "but I came in here to have a breather. Didn't expect it to be occupied."

"I don't mind you taking a second to yourself, but I *do* mind you getting hurt. What happened?"

Kelton groaned. "If you must know, they assigned Demetri and me to train together. He got one over on me, knocked me to the ground… I retaliated, and we just kept beating on each other." Kelton rubbed his head, frowning in pain.

"Something tells me those two weren't training," Silianna commented to Malakai. "I have a weird feeling they were fighting over pettiness instead."

"I have a weird feeling you're right," Malakai agreed. He helped walk Kelton over to a nearby chair and sat him down. "Kelton, you two have got to stop this hatred for each other. You are both brothers."

"Have either of you considered therapy?" Silianna suggested idly, not looking up from her books.

Kelton frowned. "Trust me, Demetri is the least of my concerns." Kelton gently tugged Malakai down, setting them next to each other, and pressed a kiss to his lips. "You're my concern, Malakai. If you feel I need to end this feud with my brother, then I shall do my best. You're too important for me to be the reason you're unhappy."

Malakai felt his face flush. He couldn't understand what it was about Kelton, but he was so drawn to him that no matter how stupid he could be. Malakai didn't even care for their short-lived argument earlier this morning, now that Kelton was being sweet again.

"No more fighting," Malakai said, leaning his head on Kelton's shoulder. "That's all I'm asking. I don't like Demetri either, but even I am trying to coincide with him. My grandmother seems to like him, and although I can't help but blame her old age for her delusional defense of him, I respect her in some ways. Let's just all do what we need to do and take down the Elder Guardians."

"I shall try my best, Your Imperial Highness," Kelton replied, teasingly.

"Good."

Kelton and Malakai stood up, departing the library as Silianna was left to continue her research in peace.

\* \* \*

Eli was conversing with one of the centaurs by the time Malakai walked out to the courtyard. Aside from the library, the courtyard in Windsor Keep was one of Malakai's favorite places to go. There was a sharp chromatic water fountain with glittery water that emerged from the top of the fountain. Eli once compared the water to the same shimmering at Glisten Lake. Ever since then, Malakai could not unsee it.

Eli had no idea Malakai had stumbled upon him as he snuck his way towards him.

"... And you think Lord Hussayn will agree?" asked Eli.

"I'm certain," the centaur, Qiu, assured him. "Lord Hussayn is an honorable man who will stand by us. Your story of living in the North will be compelling."

"I just want my mother and brother safe. If that means going through with this, then I shall do my part."

"Believe me, the Grand Empress Dowager always rewards those who do good deeds. Your little adventure with Princess Rahaf may have frustrated her, but she understands that you mean well, my dear boy. The Gods have it all planned out in the end."

"Thank you, Qiu. I appreciate your words of wisdom."

"I fear this conversation has reached its end." Qiu looked at Malakai as he stood behind Eli.

Eli turned around and was stunned to see his best friend appear from nowhere. Qiu left the courtyard without another word.

"How long have you been standing there?" Eli asked.

"Not long at all," Malakai replied.

Eli shrugged, pulling out some chocolate from his pocket and popping it into his mouth.

"Shouldn't you be waiting to eat that after lunch?" Malakai asked, teasing.

"Kai, I've gone through a lot of crap these past couple of months. If I want to eat chocolate before lunch, I will." Eli popped another one into his mouth gracefully. "*Mmm.* Delicious. If I were to die tomorrow, at least I'd die knowing I got to taste these magnificent treats."

Malakai looked closely at the gold wrapper that was around the chocolate. There were initials *A.B.* on them—*Antonius Bellemore.* Malakai's eyes widened as he realized Eli had been smuggling his chocolates from his bedroom the whole time.

"Eli!" Malakai shouted. "You're annoying. Those are *my* chocolates. I thought Kelton was the one stealing them!"

Eli looked down at the wrapper and back up at Malakai. He knew his deception was over as he continued munching on the candy.

"Damn," Eli whispered, mouth still full. "I was so careful the last two weeks. But you gotta admit, it was pretty clever to make it look like Kelton was taking them, huh?"

"Shut up." Malakai playfully pushed Eli to the side. "You don't need to sneak into my room to take some. Just ask, I don't mind.

14

But I will say that was pretty clever of you."

The boys laughed as they walked together into the castle and down the hall.

Princess Rahaf Soulryth passed them in the stairway as they headed up, and Malakai couldn't help but notice the way Eli's gaze lingered on her. It wasn't a secret to him that Eli had grown quite fond of Rahaf, especially since their travels to Centuris. Malakai had consulted with Kelton about the matter, but Kelton felt it was best not to interfere.

Malakai thought it was cute to see Eli having a crush. Although she was head over heels for Prince Theodosis Steelhart, Malakai couldn't help but root for his best friend, even if he didn't think his chances were that great.

"So, are you excited about flying with Annalu to Veilios tonight?" Malakai figured asking Eli a question would help him look away from Rahaf before she noticed he was staring.

"Yeah," Eli responded, his attention not fully there. "I'm excited. Hey, um, aren't you supposed to be practicing with Rahaf to master your fire element? We should get together with her before she leaves for Aeris, you know?"

Malakai nodded, fully aware of what Eli was trying to do. "I'll probably catch up with her either tonight or tomorrow. She's been keeping herself busy with Annalu's coven for quite some time."

"You don't think there's any way to change her mind and stay, huh?"

Malakai shook his head. "I'm sorry, bud. She's in love with Theodosis. People will do some crazy stuff when they're in love. Even if it means traveling through a portal with witches to get to him, she's going to do it."

Eli placed his hands in his pockets and went mute.

Entering the narrow hallway was none other than Prince Demetri Eckwood. He was wearing nicely fitted silver armor that highlighted his muscular body. He looked slightly different from the last time Malakai saw him. Demetri still had the long black hair set lazily in a bun, however, the once dark stubble dusted across his jawline was now covered with a full black beard. There was something about Demetri having a full beard that brought goosebumps crawling through Malakai's body.

Both their eyes locked, Demetri's blue eyes revealing the only gentle thing about him.

"How are the precious Lost Prince and the shapeshifter this morning?" asked Demetri. His voice sounded a bit bright, the usual heaviness in his voice was missing.

"I have a name…" Eli said, annoyed.

"And that nickname seems redundant, considering I'm no longer lost anymore, right?" Malakai responded to Demetri.

"I suppose so," Demetri replied. He looked at Eli as he said, "Do not forget we are tasked with picking up Celdric and Nehila later today. I expect to see you no later than two o'clock, got it?"

Eli groaned. "I'm fully aware. There's no need to speak to me like I'm a child. I'm still questioning why the Grand Empress Dowager thinks *you* are suited to escort the kids to and from their educational programs."

"Watch your tone with me, shapeshifter. I was asked because you two have shown just how irresponsible you can be together. Perhaps you should take some notes from me rather than whining about Her Imperial Highness' request."

Despite Demetri's abrasive attitude, Malakai couldn't help but respect his desire for efficiency and his clear regard for the Grand Empress. Demetri might be hard-headed, but he was loyal, and that was a trait Malakai valued very much.

"Right, well, Eli and I are going to have some lunch," Malakai said, breaking the tension. "I trust you, Demetri, will not influence my brother and sister with your *shenanigans*. Contrary to belief, you, too, should know what it is like to be irresponsible. Considering you're always bickering with Kelton over stupid stuff, I would say. Perhaps we *all* should take some notes from each other."

Malakai walked away dismissively, able to feel Demetri's angry gaze drilling holes into his back. Eli followed behind him as he burst into laughter.

"By the Gods, you just told him off!" Eli said, impressed.

"Demetri is a handful, but I refuse to let him get under my skin. I've got your back, Eli. Don't worry. If he messes with you today, please let me know. I shall have a word with my grandmother about him."

"Say no more. I'm *starving*."

\* \* \*

The boys sat down with their tray of food at one of the enlarged tables in the Great Hall. Eli had a pile of food on his tray compared to Malakai. It had been like this since they arrived in the South—Eli was constantly eating. When Malakai asked why he ate so much, Eli explained that shapeshifters tend to use food as a source of fuel when shifting. It explained why Eli felt weak at certain moments when he was traveling alongside Malakai and his siblings.

"So, what's up with Demetri?" Eli asked, his mouth full of food. "I've dealt with a lot of people in my time, but something about Demetri is just so… aggressive."

Malakai shrugged. "Not sure what his problem is. He once told me he didn't like me because I brought some sort of happiness to Kelton. I don't think I've told you, but the two of them had a fallout some odd years ago."

"From the way those two are always going at it during training, I can tell. But what's their issue?"

Malakai paused before speaking, trying to think of the best way to explain it. "From what Rahaf told me, the two of them fell in love with some girl named Seraphina Blackworth. She was planning on leaving Kelton for Demetri since they were having an affair, but Kelton wasn't aware of it at the time. On the day of her death, Kelton took Seraphina up to the mountains for a date. He got her flowers, unaware that there were juxure flowers in them. Seraphina put them on her face as she sniffed them and, well, I'm sure you can put the pieces together."

"But Kelton didn't know the juxure flowers were in the bouquets?" Eli asked. Malakai shook his head. "Then I don't understand why Demetri is blaming Kelton. First of all, it seems like

Demetri has a lot of his own demons to get over. Second, it's wrong that he was secretly seeing his brother's girlfriend. The dude sounds like a problem."

"Yup. And now I'm paying the price for dating Kelton." Malakai sighed, taking a bite of his sandwich. "I'm sure you're getting the shitty treatment from him because you're my best friend and you're cool with Kelton. I should honestly have a conversation with the guy, but I don't know how much good it would do. The only good thing he's done was rescue me after the Wondrous Trials. And now, I guess, taking good care of Celdric and Nehila."

Eli huffed. "There must be a motive behind it."

"Yeah?" Malakai asked curiously.

Eli shrugged. "Beats me. Maybe he's trying to build some credit for himself so when the war is over, he'll be able to claim Terrane and be on good terms with you and the Grand Empress Dowager."

"That would be a good explanation," Malakai said, considering Eli's theory. He wasn't used to the idea of people trying to get on his good side for political gain; he still felt like that same nobody boy who lived in the forest.

"For what it's worth," Eli added, "I like Kelton. I think he's good for you. You're different around him in the best way possible."

"Kelton's a good guy. He's a pain in my ass, but he's a good guy. No relationship is ever perfect, after all, or so I've read growing up. There are definitely some things we have to work on, but I'm up for the challenge."

"Uh-oh. Trouble in paradise already, huh?" Eli joked.

Malakai chuckled. "Nothing that can't be fixed."

"You know, I just realized that this is your first relationship. *Ever.* Have you two managed to say those three words yet?" Eli said, bouncing his eyebrows up and down.

"No. We haven't yet," Malakai replied tersely, feeling uncomfortable going into detail about his relationship with his best friend.

"Neither of you has said it yet?!" Eli asked, shocked. "Have you two even, you know…" Eli made an explicit hand gesture. Malakai frantically tried to get Eli to stop before anyone saw him.

"Eli, shut up! It's none of your business. I'm trying to eat my lunch, thank you very much. We are not having this conversation."

"Oh, please. You and I both know you want to—" Before Eli could finish his sentence, Malakai grabbed his tray and walked away. Eli was laughing behind him. Malakai couldn't help but laugh too, knowing if the roles were reversed, he would've said the same thing.

# 3
## Box of Deception

**DEMETRI**

The glass city was bustling during the evening as Demetri and the shapeshifter, Eli-zak, strolled downtown. It was roughly thirty minutes before Celdric and Neihla would be released from their educational activities. Eli occupied himself while he waited by making conversation with a stranger. Demetri knew better than to consult with strangers—by now, everyone in Avala knew who they were. The past four months had been a handful as Demetri and the others attempted to familiarize themselves with the glass city. Unfortunately, Malakai, Rahaf, and Eli caused a bit of a ruckus in Centuris that resulted in the Grand Empress Dowager banning Malakai and his friend from hanging around together outside Windsor Keep without the assistance of the witch, Annalu.

Last he heard, Annalu was busy gathering her strength alongside her coven, so Demetri and Eli were tasked with retrieving the kids. *It would be me to get stuck with this idiot,* Demetri thought.

"And what happens when I swallow one of these gumballs?" Eli asked.

"They have traces of Fae Dust. You'll be going on a trip within seconds. The experience can last anywhere between two to three hours," one of the fae-folk explained.

Demetri let out a sharp breath through his nose. Eli could not seriously be considering buying drugs off a sketchy fae. Intervening, Demetri gently pulled Eli away as the two walked side-by-side to another location in the city.

"Hey! I was going to buy something here," Eli complained.

"You'll thank me later, shapeshifter." Demetri's voice was cold. "Trust me, you don't want to mess with the fae-folk. They may present themselves as sweet and innocent, but they're quite the opposite."

"Whatever. I'm sure the other Eckwood brother would've bought some with me," Eli mumbled under his breath.

"I'm sure he would have," Demetri spat.

The two of them proceeded in silence, air tense.

It was clear the shapeshifter was another copy of Kelton with the annoying humor and smart comments. Like he didn't already have his hands full dealing with one.

There were only a few more minutes to spare until the kids were released. Demetri tried to kill time by looking at some of the shops. One in particular piqued his interest. It didn't have a name, but it had unique symbols with an image of a dragon flying over it. Demetri recognized the symbols belonging to the mythical Rlyrum tribes.

Without hesitation, Demetri walked inside the shop. A chime rang in his ear, followed by piano music playing in the distance, and the scent of sage wafting in the air. The shop was cluttered with artifacts, but Demetri did not mind. For some reason, the atmosphere felt comforting to him.

Eli found himself looking through some devices while Demetri trailed to the back of the shop. It was there that he came across a spectacular armor that resided in a glass case. The armor had spikes in certain areas and shades of gold and black. If his examination was correct, Demetri speculated that this armor may be made of dragon stone.

There was no price tag listed on the glass case. Demetri desperately wanted to touch it, though he knew better than to do so without purpose. He scouted around for the owner of the shop, but there was no such luck.

Suddenly, the music stopped.

"*Psst,*" someone whispered.

Demetri noticed the sound coming from upstairs. He cautiously made his way to the stairway. There, Demetri was welcomed by a woman who wore a red velvet cloak. Her long wavy red hair was visible, though it seemed to be the only visible part—the hood masked her identity.

"Good afternoon," Demetri said. "I was wondering if you were the owner of the shop. I'm interested in knowing more about the armor you have on display over there." Demetri pointed back in the direction of the glass case.

"A gift has been offered," the woman said.

Demetri furrowed his brow. "My apologies, but I do not follow. What gift?"

The woman pulled out a small box with strange carvings on it. She held it out for Demetri to take.

"The citizens of Avala offer you a gift," the woman said, still sounding ominous. "Please accept, as a 'Thank You' for your service."

"I—" Demetri felt bad, not wanting to take the gift. However, the woman seemed like she was not going to take "No" for an answer. Reluctantly, Demetri took the box and placed it into his pocket. "T—Thank you?"

"*Marked,*" she hissed.

The lights flickered above them. Within seconds, the woman wandered off. Demetri was left lost for words.

Turning around, Demetri found himself face-to-face with an old man. He had long white hair and a beard nearly eight inches long.

"What are you doing back here?" the man asked, hysterical.

"I—I'm not sure. I was speaking to a woman who was standing on the stairs. I figured she worked here," Demetri explained.

"Nonsense! Nobody works in my shop but me. You have no business being back here. Now scram before I contact the authorities and have you filed for trespassing."

Demetri held out his free hand as he said, "Please, I do not mean any trouble. I was looking for the owner, whom I presume is you. The armor you have in the glass case caught my eye, and I wanted to learn a little bit about it."

The old man looked at the glass case and then examined Demetri's appearance from head to toe, as if he was debating telling Demetri anything.

"You're muscular enough to fit in it," the old man said. "However, I doubt you could afford such a thing. No one has been able to match the price since my great-great-grandfather first opened this shop. I refuse to sell it for less than what it's worth."

"Well, how much are you asking for it?" Demetri asked.

"A hundred thousand aspar," the old man answered.

Demetri was shocked by the price, though he had a hunch as to why it was so expensive. "It's made of dragon stone, isn't it? I recognize the gold on the armor. It originated from the Rlyrum tribe, if I'm not mistaken."

"How did you know?!"

A smile creased on Demetri's face. "Let's just say, I used to study about the mythical dragon riders while I attended Cressmoore Academy."

"Cressmoore? My, you must be one of the wealthy folks, huh?" the old man asked.

Demetri shook his head. "On the contrary, I am the Prince of Terrane—Demetri Eckwood. It's an honor to meet you, Sir."

The old man's jaw dropped. It was almost like he'd never spoken to a Royal-Blood before.

The old man bent his knee and bowed his head. "The honor is all mine, Your Majesty. Please, forgive me for my tone earlier." The old man rose from the floor and straightened his fragile posture. "My name is Jaeyse Caerlight. It is not often I get customers here. Let alone anyone from the Royal-Blood family."

"Please, no worries. If I may impose, how did your great-great-grandfather come across such a unique historical artifact?" Demetri asked.

"It was something that was passed down from generation to generation. I'm not sure how our family got hold of it, but considering the Caerlight bloodline used to be one of the most powerful magic families throughout the Nine Lands, I'm not too surprised we have it."

"Used to? So, I presume you're a warlock?"

"Correct. My precious daughter was selected by the witches on the Other Side to become the Superior Witch. However, she meddled in dark magic she shouldn't have, and it cost her life. As for her sister, I have not seen her in decades. I've feared the worst since the Elder Guardians took over the North. Alas, I am what remains of the Caerlight bloodline. I've been alive for nearly two hundred years."

Demetri was not too familiar with the Superior Witch other than the fact that whoever was selected was considered the highest magical being of their era. Whether it was a witch, warlock, or wix.

"That's an incredible story, Mr. Caerlight. I'm sorry to hear about both of your daughters. My sincere condolences."

"Thank you, Your Highness."

"Please, call me Demetri." Demetri held out his free hand as Jaeyse shook it. "If you don't mind, I'd appreciate it if you held on to that armor for me. I plan on coming back to purchase it. I doubt anyone will buy it before me, but stranger things have happened in my lifetime."

"No problem at all, Demetri," promised Jaeyse.

Eli stumbled upon Demetri and Jaeyse as he informed Demetri that it was time for them to pick up Celdric and Nehila. Demetri bid farewell to the warlock and headed back through the city. The box gifted to him by the stranger was still in his hand.

# 4
## Unsettling Choices

**SILIANNA**

After flipping through countless pages, Silianna gave up on her search for today. Windsor Keep was said to house some of the most important historical texts and records; however, whoever claimed such a thing forgot to mention that there would be *nothing* that related to the Dark Dimension. The only thing Silianna and Malakai were able to gather was the following:

> *A) The Dark Dimension was created by the Gods to imprison Vorkalth.*
> *B) Lost Souls with unfinished business were stuck in the spirit realm until they found peace.*
> *C) Malakai, Kelton, Reju, and she were able to access the Dark Dimension.*

Well, Malakai and Reju *used* to.

There had been ideas floating in her head in terms of reaching out to the Grand Empress Dowager about the situation, but that would go against Malakai's wishes to keep her and Kelton's ability a secret. Malakai expressed deep concern that his grandmother may lock her and Kelton away in a desperate attempt to prevent Vorkalth from reaching Malakai.

Silianna sighed. Her only source of information was, sadly, her uncle, but even he was useless at times when it came to the important stuff.

"You're awfully busy," said a brooding voice.

Silianna perked up as she spotted Demetri in the doorway. He was leaning on the side, arms and legs crossed, with a smirk on his face.

"Not today, Demetri," Silianna said, unamused.

Demetri uncrossed his arms and legs as he sat down next to Silianna. She observed his wandering eyes as they scanned the number of books scattered across the table.

"You know, I've stood quiet for a long time," Demetri started, "and not once have I dared to ask what it is that you're looking for. But now I feel like I must."

"Demetri, I'm serious. Now is not a good time. I'm stressed and in serious need of a good night's sleep, and you prying into my business isn't going to help. I'm not sure what's going on with me, but I feel like all the energy I had was sucked out of me. All these books are giving me a headache."

Demetri looked as though he took offense at what she said. "Are we not close enough to want to express what's going on?"

Silianna didn't bother to respond. Giving him a deadly stare, she turned back to the books on her desk and began stacking them up. She then lifted them and started walking down the aisles, placing them back in their correct spot.

At the corner of her eyes, Silianna's annoyance grew as she saw Demetri carrying a stack of books and placing them on the shelves, too.

"What are you doing?" she asked.

"I'm helping," Demetri answered. "What does it look like I'm doing?"

"I feel like you only speak to me because I'm the only one who tolerates you to a certain extent. And that you're only being nice to me because you're worried that I will tell someone what we discussed a few months back."

Demetri was taken aback. "What? I'm lost. Sil, I don't come to you for anything other than being a friend. I thought when we opened up to each other about Nerumi and Malakai, we built some sort of connection nobody else would understand. I don't find everyone else as easy to talk to as I do you."

Demetri set the stack of books on the ground and put both his hands on Silianna's arms. He forced her to look straight into his sharp eyes as he said, "For whatever I did to you, I am sorry. I've thought I've been pretty good with you up until now. If you're worried, I promise to you now that our friendship is important to me, and I don't want to do anything that might hurt it."

Silianna knew the real reason she was upset with Demetri. Even though it had nothing to do with her, she feared what his reaction would be if she spoke her mind.

"I don't like how you treat the boys," she finally admitted.

"What?" Demetri said, acting clueless.

"Malakai, Kelton, and Eli. You're too harsh on them, and it hurts to see my friends fighting. I understand your frustration, given everything that has happened, but you cannot blame them for your secrecy. Your actions have consequences, and I'm not interested in being friends with someone so mean to my other friends."

Demetri paused, like he was taking in what she had said, and then nodded. Silianna almost expected some sort of sarcastic remark or push back, but Demetri's face remained very serious.

"I know somewhere in your headstrong heart that a lovely soul is aching to come out," Silianna said, teasingly. "Show some compassion. You'll thank me later."

"I wish it were that easy," Demetri said with a sigh. "I don't feel like I have a soul anymore. It was lost a long time ago."

"I don't believe that."

"Perhaps you are all alone in that department, Sil." Demetri cleared his throat. "Well, for what it's worth, I am trying. I suppose I will try harder."

Silianna wasn't sure why she did it, but she reached in and hugged

Demetri. As much as he liked to pretend that he didn't care about anything, she truly believed there was a gentle soul. A hug may not be the answer to everything, but she had hoped it would soothe the pain he endured emotionally. Once Demetri clutched his arms around Silianna, it was a clear indication that she was right.

"Thank you, Sil," he whispered.

"I know what it's like to stand on the sidelines and see someone you love with another. But if it's meant to be, it'll happen in time. You just gotta sit back and let the stars align accordingly." Silianna released Demetri and took a deep breath. "I think I needed that more than you did, honestly. My brain hurts from all this research."

"Well, as I've said, if you need help looking for something, I am more than happy to help. Just say the word." Demetri was being uncharacteristically helpful, but Silianna was too tired to examine it further.

"I appreciate it, but I think I'm going to take a break for today."

"Very well, I'll go find something to entertain myself with and stay out of trouble. I'll see you later."

Demetri departed, leaving Silianna to finish cleaning up the mess she had caused in the library. Though she did not mind it, Silianna couldn't help but feel someone or something was watching her. She should be used to it, but the chills that developed into goosebumps were too strong not to ignore.

A gust of wind flew past Silianna's short curly black hair. The atmosphere around her shifted from a warming sensation into a freezing winter chill. The sight of her breath from the cold was a clear indication that she was back in the Dark Dimension. Nothing brought her more frustration than finding herself back in this place when she was least expecting it.

Standing on a puddle of black water, Silianna raised her left foot to see a gooey liquid substance drip. Her heart sank to her stomach as she looked around.

"Uncle Reju?" Silianna called out. Her voice echoed endlessly, though there was no response.

A growling sound alerted Silianna, echoing from behind her. She was reluctant to turn around, but her instincts reacted quickly. Behind her, some sort of demonic entity emerged from the shadows. It was shaped like a mortal covered in black substances; the face was that of a bird with a black beak. A set of enlarged arms dangled with sharp claws nearly six inches long on each finger. The entity's appearance caused Silianna to shriek and step back, tipping over into a small hole and plunging into the puddle of dark liquid.

Without hesitation, Silianna chanted *"Limus."* The water slightly rose from the puddle; however, it ultimately fell flat back onto the floor. Silianna was stunned to see that her water element was rejecting her. *No, no, no,* she thought in a panic. Chanting *"Limus"* once more, Silianna saw a red spark zapping her fingers. This was not good.

The creature flew to Silianna with a horrible growl. It landed on top of her, but she managed to grab onto its wrists, holding back its claws from touching her face.

"Get off me!" she screamed, feeling tears in her eyes. "Limusic, my faithful God of Water, please rescue me!

"Your silly little God can't save you here," the creature snarled.

*By the Gods, it can talk!* Silianna thought. Suddenly, a blast of bright light caused the creature to fly off her and disappear.

Looking in the direction of the blast, Silianna saw a group of ghostly strangers huddled together, their hands locked as they repeated a language unfamiliar to her. Walking past the group, Reju Tufte appeared with a smile on his face.

"Reju!" Silianna said, her shoulders dropped as tension slid away. She picked herself up and ran toward him. "Thank the Gods you came at the nick of time!"

"Well, I'm glad to see my friends saved you from that Dravkyn Demon," said Reju.

"A drav-what?" asked Silianna, puzzled.

"A Dravkyn Demon. They are entities morphed together by the Shadow Lord's creation. He's been sending his little minions to locate the culprit behind the Lost Souls crossing over."

Silianna swallowed harshly. She was the culprit. Of course, she knew her time to save the Lost Souls was limited. It scared her to think the Shadow Lord, Vorkalth, was searching for her now. The last thing she needed was the man behind chaos across the Nine Lands to find her.

"It's me he's looking for, isn't it?" Silianna asked.

"I'm afraid so," Reju confirmed. He turned to the group of ghosts and nodded. The group vanished like smoke. Reju turned back to Silianna and said, "The work you are practicing is dangerous. If you keep drawing too much attention to yourself, you'll end up just like me. We can't allow the Beauchamp bloodline to end— especially since we're so close to breaking our family curse."

*The Beauchamp Curse*. Silianna's interest was piqued. For months, she had been dying to uncover the story behind her family's curse.

"Please tell me about our family curse," she begged. "I have to know, Uncle."

"I know you've been searching for answers. Perhaps it is time to explain it all, but first I must ask: Will you stop helping the Lost Souls find peace if I tell you the truth?"

Silianna froze. Helping those stuck in such a forsaken purgatory was a new passion of hers. She could not pursue the career of a Healer as she wanted to, so helping others differently was the closest thing she could do. It was in her nature. *I cannot turn away from who I am*, she thought. Silianna knew the choice she would make, and she knew her uncle would not be too pleased by it.

"I'm sorry, Uncle Reju," Silianna said, torn between her sense of duty and her desire for information. "But I can't do that. I guess I'll have to keep searching for answers on my own. I will not stop helping these poor souls find peace."

"I understand," replied Reju. He was in no mood to argue with her. "Do your friends know what has been happening to you?"

"Malakai knows. And, I suppose, Kelton and Rahaf know a little bit. But that's about it."

"I'm not talking about your spiritual element. I'm referring to the fact that your body is beginning to reject your water element."

Silianna's body went numb. She feared the worst had finally come to pass. There were speculations, but her uncle finally confirmed it. A part of her wanted nothing more than to cry, but she did not.

"H—How do I stop it? There must be a way to keep both of my abilities."

"I'm afraid not. It is extremely rare for an elemental to obtain more than one ability. Your vessel, unfortunately, cannot withstand both. Limusic, God of Water, is beginning to strip you of your water element. You must choose to release one before it is too late."

"How much time do I have?" asked Silianna.

"From the looks of it, you have until the next full moon," Reju answered.

"And what happens if I try to fight it? What if I manage to keep both of my elements?"

Whispers surrounded Silianna and Reju. They were inaudible, but Silianna understood that the spirits were trying to warn her. Reju was responding to the whispers in the same unknown language from earlier. Once the sounds stopped, Reju looked Silianna straight in the eyes.

"Death." The singular word dropped from Reju's mouth. There was no further explanation. The message was clear now.

With a blink of an eye, Silianna found herself back in the real world. She was no longer in the library where she had last stood prior to the Dark Dimension. Instead, she was now standing in the middle of her bedroom.

On the floor, there were loads of papers filled with drawings of the same thing—an image of a crescent moon amulet, an anklet, a sword with wings, and a chalice. There were written words on the paper, though Silianna was unaware of what they meant. *Is this the same language the spirits were speaking?* As she examined the drawings closely, she realized that blood was used to create them.

Silianna cupped her hands and nearly gagged. She quickly gathered all the drawings and threw them into the trash. *How did I get back into my room? Where did these drawings come from?*

# 5
## An Alliance

**MALAKAI**

Nehila was circling her hands inside the pond as a flock of fish followed her movements. Malakai was eyeing her while she did so, ensuring that she was not about to hurt herself. Ever since her arrival, she's found the weirdest things to be fond of. Fish was one of them. Malakai figured if his sister had the choice, she'd most likely pick the water element as her ability rather than the ground.

On the opposite side of the greenhouse, Celdric was practicing wielding his sword with Eli. The two were going at it intensely, dodging and clashing their weapons against each other. Though Malakai was not entirely sure why Celdric was so eager to fight, he assumed it was merely a phase he'd get out of. *I hope he doesn't think he's going to fight in this war,* he thought.

There was time to kill before Malakai got to see Kelton later tonight. He received a message from his glass communicator a few minutes prior, instructing him to wear something nice for their date. Whatever Kelton had in store, Malakai was looking forward to it. Anything to take his mind off his chaotic life.

Malakai was still reminiscing about their first date. They explored the city of Avala for the first time, and Kelton had snuck Malakai into an abandoned clock tower where they walked nearly thirty flights of stairs before reaching the top. There, the two discovered a rusty hovercycle, and Kelton somehow got it to work. The two flew through the night skies before authorities stopped them in their tracks and demanded they return to Windsor Keep. Malakai thought about that night fondly, from the adrenaline rush to the feeling of clinging to Kelton's back on the hovercycle.

Walking over to one of the flowers, Malakai decided to practice using his Terrane element. He was doing okay, but he needed to be great. If he were to prove himself worthy of the Baskarian throne, Malakai would have to master all four elements and show he was serious about his claim.

The flowers were just the start. They were similar to the juxure flowers, but not. The juxures were a purplish-glittery beauty, whereas the ones in front of him were a glittery mixture of red and orange. They weren't poisonous to everyone, yet they were surely poisonous to shapeshifters. *Muloore*, they called it. Malakai had questioned why his grandmamma would keep such a thing in her greenhouse, though she did not answer. Malakai assumed it had more to do with keeping them as a backup in the event the shapeshifters ever stepped out of line. It was odd, but Malakai did not dare question his grandmother's intentions. Not now, anyway.

Luckily, Eli seemed to be fine in the greenhouse. Malakai suspected the flowers had the same effect as the juxures, where they required contact with the skin to be considered life-threatening. As long as Eli kept his distance, all was safe.

Nehila dried her hands with the water and walked towards Malakai as he focused his concentration on the muloore.

"Do you remember how to do it?" Nehila asked innocently.

"I think so," Malakai replied. He faced the palm of his hands in front of the muloore. "I focus on the flower and then I chant to the God of Ground, Terranequrk."

"That's right!" Nehila giggled.

Malakai took a deep breath and let the element take control of him as he chanted, *"Terrane."* Suddenly, a large rock emerged from underneath and nearly clashed with Malakai's face. Nehila was quick to pull her brother away as Malakai fell to the floor. The circular rock flew up in the air before plunging.

Celdric intervened as he shouted, "*Terrane.*" The rock returned to where it came from, but the flowers that once resided there were now destroyed.

"By the Gods, Kai, you have to be careful!" Celdric said, concerned.

"Sorry," Malakai apologized. "I thought I had it."

"You're going to need some more practice," Eli commented. He helped Malakai up from the floor and dusted off the soil on his clothes. "There's no need to rush, you know? You have to learn four elements, and it's not like you're going to achieve it overnight. Just take your time."

"I don't have time, Eli. There's too much pressure on me right now, and I cannot let the nation down."

"But you're not. You're doing the best you can, and that's all that matters. You cannot force a miracle to happen. You were put in a shitty predicament, and no one can blame you for that."

"Language!" Nehila reminded Eli.

"Sorry, Nehila. It won't happen again." Eli was lying, but Nehila wouldn't be able to tell.

Malakai thought about what Eli said. He technically wasn't supposed to be here in the South until he was twenty-one. His grandmother said so herself. Whatever was planned, it was clear the Gods had other intentions. Like his father used to say, "*Life isn't how you plan it. We make plans and the Gods laugh.*"

Two people walked into the greenhouse as Malakai debated whether to practice again. However, Malakai was stunned to see it was Demetri and Kelton, talking amongst themselves. It seemed that whatever they were conversing about, they were not fighting, which was a first.

Malakai brushed Eli and his siblings to the side as he made his way over to Kelton.

"What brings you two here?" Malakai asked.

"We're 'attempting' to make peace," said Kelton, sounding

relieved. "It was long overdue, but I'm glad we can move forward."

"I agree," was all Demetri said.

Malakai did not bother to question Demetri's short response. Instead, he focused on Kelton's emerald-green eyes and nearly fell into a daze. The two shared a quick kiss and then held each other's hands.

"I missed you," he told Kelton.

"I missed you, too," Kelton replied.

Demetri intervened and said, "Alright, the lovey-dovey show is over. We're here to check up on you and see if there's any progress with your element."

"Well, perfect timing because Kai almost killed himself with a huge rock," Celdric said.

Malakai frowned. "Shut up, Celdric."

"Is this true?" Demetri asked.

Malakai sighed. "Yes. I'm working on it, okay? But as for my fire element, I've gotten the hang of it. Rahaf thinks I'm a natural at it. I wish the same could be said about my ground element…"

"Perhaps I should train with you one-on-one," Kelton suggested.

Eli huffed as he shared this opinion. "I doubt that's a good idea. The two of you together are a ball of distraction. Kai's best bet at focusing is if he trains with Demetri. As much as I hate to admit it, he's the better alternative."

Malakai looked in Demetri's direction, though Demetri was staring out into oblivion, like he didn't hear a word Eli had suggested. Malakai didn't understand at that very moment as to why he felt a little bummed regarding Demetri not responding. Did he not want to help train?

"Absolutely not," Kelton detested.

"No," Malakai said, swallowing his pride. "I think Eli is right. As much as I love being by your side, Kelton, I'm just going to get distracted. I think Demetri could help me with my Terrane element."

Kelton didn't bother to argue. Malakai suspected that their conversation earlier in the forest had sunk into his brain. *And this is why I love being with Kelton*, he thought.

"What do you say?" Kelton asked Demetri.

"About what?" Demetri said, tuning back into the conversation.

"Would you like to help Malakai master his Terrane element?"

Demetri paused. His blue eyes looked back and forth from Kelton to Malakai before speaking. A part of Malakai felt impatient, somewhat anxious to hear the final verdict.

"Okay."

*Okay.* He agreed. A sense of relief flowed through Malakai. He loved Celdric and Nehila, but Malakai knew that they wouldn't be able to help him as much as he'd wished. Demetri would suffice. *Soon, I'll achieve Terrane and Pyroc.*

Abruptly, the alarms went off in the greenhouse. The group huddled close to each other as they tried to figure out what was going on. The intercom informed everyone currently in Windsor Keep to report to the Great Hall immediately. The group did not hesitate as the Eckwood brothers guided Malakai and the others out of the greenhouse.

* * *

The Great Hall was packed with all sorts of individuals when Malakai and the others arrived. There was so much commotion going on that Malakai could not immediately gather what the emergency was. Through the crowd, he spotted Silianna and Rahaf waving their hands. He instantly knew they were signaling for him and the others to walk over to them. Once they pushed through the crowd, Malakai was welcomed by Rahaf's pet bobcat, Aleek, who managed to maneuver his way between Malakai's legs.

"There you are, Aleek!" Rahaf said enthusiastically.

"Please, control your pet," Malakai said, trying to calm himself. "I nearly had a heartache just now."

"Oh, hush. Aleek is harmless," she replied defensively.

Behind Malakai, he overheard Kelton comment under his breath, "Didn't that beast rip someone's head off?" Even though Rahaf didn't hear it, Malakai did, and he was laughing.

"Well, if we're done being immature," Demetri began, sounding irritated as he continued, "what seems to be the emergency?"

"Nobody knows," Silianna answered. She hugged her arms, a clear indication that she was overwhelmed.

Malakai held Kelton's hand as he looked around the crowd, trying to figure out what was going on. Across the Great Hall, the two of them saw the Grand Empress Dowager appear with the centaur, Qiu, and her robotic servant, Celsa. The three of them stood in front of the crowd as Qiu prepared the microphone for what Malakai assumed was a speech.

Kelton made the first move, swerving through the crowd, as Malakai continued holding his hand. The rest of the group followed. Luckily, the crowd was easy to get through with Kelton at the helm.

Once they stood by Maelena's side, Her Imperial Highness adjusted her microphone to her height and ensured it worked with a few taps. "Good evening," she began. "We appreciate you all reporting to the Great Hall promptly. I'm afraid DeVault Beauchamp and the remainder of the Elder Guardians are just about ready to make their preparations and deliver a long-awaited speech to those in the North. Our team has been able to capture a broadcast of the live event, which we will showcase momentarily."

A holographic projector appeared behind Malakai and the others. In the visuals, there stood DeVault, Aldothfex Soulryth, King Alistair Eckwood, and Queen Viktoria Eckwood.

Malakai and Kelton exchanged looks, both on the same wavelength that something messed about was about to go down.

"Something seems off," Demetri commented.

From the broadcast, everyone watched DeVault step forward to the podium, where he pulled out a glass clipboard.

"Citizens of Baskaria, our nation has faced a threat like no other these past few months. We fear the smulders that walk deep in the forest have managed to evolve into something much more deadly, one of which resided here in the kingdom of Terrane. Unfortunately, two of our fellow Elder Guardians have fallen at the hands of said-smulder. We mourn the four-month anniversary of Yamina Eckwood and Bliss Steelhart. May the Gods have mercy within their souls." DeVault paused, flipping the page of his speech.

Malakai, from the corner of his eye, examined Kelton, who was struggling to control the quivering of his lips. Kelton let go of Malakai's hand, shielding himself against the sudden rush of emotions he felt. Taking the time to process what was said, Malakai could not help but feel slightly offended that DeVault would blame Yamina's death on him. *Sure, I killed Bliss Steelhart*, he thought, *but I didn't even get to meet Kelton and Demetri's grandmother. Whatever they're plotting, they're clearly trying to make me look dangerous.*

"…And we do not doubt that the smulder has managed to reach the South. We can only conclude that the rebels are experimenting and using these smulders to their advantage. We must be ready to strike back when the time is right. The South currently imprisons the following Royal-Blood heirs: Demetri Eckwood, Kelton Eckwood, Rahaf Soulryth, and my precious granddaughter, Silianna Beauchamp." DeVault swiped to the page and continued. "Make no mistake, the rebels have no intention of returning the hostages. The North falls into jeopardy without the Royal-Blood heirs to claim their rightful titles to their thrones. Without them, our economy shall plummet."

Demetri made some inappropriate comments in the background.

Arriving with her coven was Annalu. Malakai speculated their tardiness was due to some training they were participating in.

"What have I missed?" Annalu asked Demetri.

"A bunch of bullshit," Demetri spat.

"Ah, so nothing has changed. Splendid."

Malakai stopped eavesdropping on the conversation and turned his attention back to the live broadcast.

DeVault continued, "With the passing of Yasmina Eckwood, I would like to officially announce the next Elder Guardian of Terrane to be none other than Alistair Eckwood. As for the Terrane throne, Queen Viktoria shall temporarily hold her title until we retrieve Prince Demetri and Prince Kelton. As for the Elder Guardian of Aeris, we have yet to hear a word from King Keon Steelhart. If we do not hear back within the week, we shall assume the air kingdom has claimed independence and will be considered an enemy to the

North just as much as those in the South. You have been warned."

Annalu approached Malakai's grandmother as she said, "Your Imperial Highness, I can assure you that my coven and I are just about charged and ready for our departure. Since King Keon has yet to respond, we have a fighting chance to convince the air kingdom to join the rebellion."

Malakai was well aware of how Annalu and her coven planned to travel to Aeris. With twelve of them together, they could conjure a portal. Malakai was eager to see the process in action when the time came. Although, he'd be lying if he said he wasn't a tad bit jealous that Rahaf would be traveling with them. It was all she talked about since it was first brought to her attention.

The broadcast ended.

"Kelton," Malakai whispered.

"Don't," said Kelton, tense. "I...I think I need to be alone right now."

Kelton stormed off, leaving Malakai to remain with his friends and family as they discussed the information from the broadcast. *I guess we won't be having a date tonight*, he thought.

Malakai's grandmother stepped forward, speaking into the microphone. "Now that we have confirmation that Aeris has claimed independence from the North, we will send our witches to the air kingdom tomorrow morning with confidence that they will join our alliance." Maelena looked at Annalu and her coven within the crowd. "My fellow witches, get some sleep these next two nights. You will have a long journey ahead of you. As for those remaining in the South until further notice, we will need confirmation from Lord Hussayn and his shapeshifter tribes in Veilios that they will fight alongside us. So far, we have a guaranteed army from Centuris."

The crowd roared with excitement. The revolution was taking form.

Annalu walked over to Eli as Maelena said, "I trust you will keep the shapeshifter in check in case he falls out of line, Annalu." Maelena gave Eli a wary look. "We wouldn't want a repeat of previous events in Centuris, do we?"

"Certainly not," Annalu responded. "Especially since his partner in crime will remain *here* in Avala while we make our travel over there."

Malakai was about to argue why he should go, but he was quickly cut off by his grandmother, who gave both Eli and him a warning look. "Mr. Vakloon, you are to do as Annalu instructs. Do I make myself clear?"

"Yes, Your Imperial Highness," Eli said, nodding.

As everyone in the Great Hall departed, Malakai pulled Eli to the side and said, "You better hope you know what you're doing, Eli. I won't lose another family member."

"Don't worry, Kai. We're not in the North. Remember?" Eli patted Malakai's back shoulder. "Besides, Veilios is where the majority of my people are. If anyone can convince the shapeshifters to lend their tribes, it's me. I'll just butter them up and tell them my story living in the North."

Malakai was concerned. "I sure hope you're right."

# 6
## Expressions of the Mind

**MALAKAI**

Although Malakai tried to hide it, seeing DeVault on the broadcast brought forth a wave of uncomfortable memories from his time at Castle Caestshire, and he felt his stomach churn in distaste. He hadn't properly sat and thought about everything he went through at the castle and how much it all affected him. Those memories, on top of the false accusations being thrown around by DeVault, unsettled him to his core. Everyone in the South knew they were lies, of course, but the people of the North? They would easily believe it, and those words would color their thoughts of Malakai forever.

The corridors were silent as Malakai walked, trying to shove away the thoughts. He had other things to focus on right now, like taking care of his siblings. They walked next to him on either side, but the silence was tense as they headed towards their rooms. Nehila didn't seem to notice the awkward air, too busy playing with her teddy bear. But Celdric was squeezing his hands together and his eyes were darting every which way.

"Something bothering you?" asked Malakai, turning his attention to Celdric.

Celdric stopped twirling his thumbs and looked at Malakai like

41

he had been caught doing something wrong. "Who? Me? I'm not bothered by anything." The tone in Celdric's voice was a clear indication that he was lying.

"I hope you're not expecting to pursue a career in acting, your lying skills are pretty terrible if you ask me."

"Well, then, it's a good thing I'm not asking."

Malakai dropped the conversation, seeing that it was going nowhere. He had an idea of how to maybe pursue it further, but first, he would have to ensure Nehila returned to her bedroom before he acted on his plan.

As Nehila entered her room, Malakai helped her put her pajamas on and get ready for bed. Once tucking her into bed and kissing her forehead, Malakai turned off her lights and closed the door shut.

Celdric was waiting in the hall, thumbs flying across his glass communicator.

"Who are you messaging?" Malakai asked.

"No one." The short answer irked Malakai, and he was almost tempted to just take the communicator from him. However, he decided not to choose violence. "Can I go to my room now?"

"Not quite yet." Malakai leaned against the wall alongside Celdric. "Why are you being so cold with me? Have I done something wrong?"

"No. It's just..." Celdric struggled to speak. Something was holding him back from expressing himself. Malakai desperately wanted him to spit it out.

"If you're worried about telling me something, just know that I can handle it. We've gone through the worst of the worst. I doubt whatever it is you need to say will be *that* bad."

Celdric groaned right before turning off his communicator and placing it into his back pocket. There was a shift in his demeanor as he cleared his throat and stood up straight. "Malakai," he began, "there is no easy way to say this, so I'm just going to do it: I want to join the Resistance and fight in the war."

Malakai felt the world tilt on its axis. Of all the things he expected Celdric to say, that was not even close. The uneasy feeling took over him again, tingling along his skin, along with a sinking sense of dread. After all they had been through, after all the violence and danger, why would Celdric ever want to do something so unbelievably stupid?

"So? What do you think?" Celdric said, waiting for Malakai's answer.

Malakai took a deep breath, steadying himself. "No. I don't know what gave you the impression that fighting in the war was a good idea, but I refuse to watch something bad happen to my little brother. You're fifteen. It's not safe. You have so much ahead of you, Celdric."

Celdric sucked his teeth with attitude. "It doesn't matter what you think, Kai. The law in the South is that you must be at least fifteen to enlist in the army. I'm old enough to make that decision. Besides, Demetri thinks I would be an excellent fighter. He's trained with me in the past."

*Demetri.*

Suddenly, everything made sense. Of course, it would be Demetri behind this ridiculous idea. If there was anything Demetri was good at, it was getting on Malakai's nerves. *And to think, I was okay training with that idiot,* he thought furiously.

Malakai did not bother continuing his disagreement with Celdric. He knew it would amount to nothing if he escalated the situation. Rather, he nodded his head and told Celdric to head to bed. He needed to get away from his brother before he lashed out and strained their relationship further.

There was only one thing on his mind as Malakai stormed down the corridors: *I need to kick Demetri's ass.*

* * *

There was no easy way to handle Demetri. Malakai knew that for a fact as he stood at the front of his bedroom door. He debated whether or not he should knock or barge in. In either situation, the result would simply end in an argument.

Malakai decided Demetri didn't deserve his manners.

As the door swung open, Malakai stumbled upon Demetri, who

was standing by the balcony and staring off into the night sky. The two moons bathed him in a bluish hue, his black hair gleaming underneath the light, almost shimmering.

Turning around, Demetri locked eye contact with Malakai. His gentle blue eyes showed pure innocence. Malakai reminded himself to stay focused as he marched his way over to the balcony.

"You're Imperial Highness," said Demetri. He bowed his head and bent his knee. His tone was sarcastic rather than serious. "To what do I owe this visit?"

"I'm here to bash your head into a wall," Malakai threatened.

"I've always admired your tact and way with words. If you're looking to start a fight for some reason, I'd rather you wait till morning. I already have enough of a headache without you attempting to follow up on your threats."

"Good. Then this should be quick. You're not allowed to speak to my brother and sister moving forward."

Demetri seemed puzzled by the demand and almost hurt. Though Malakai could not understand why he would feel that way. It wasn't like Demetri enjoyed watching them...did he? Regardless, Malakai had to stand his ground.

"And why am I not allowed to speak to them? I thought Celdric and Nehila had grown quite fond of me. Did I say something to them?" asked Demetri, tinged with something Malakai couldn't identify.

"Yes. You encouraged Celdric to fight in the war. I don't want my little brother putting himself in that kind of danger. I did everything I could to keep him alive after the death of my parents. I did not go through all that just to see something bad happen to him. He's too young for that sort of stuff."

"He turns sixteen next month, Malakai," Demetri said calmly. He took a few steps forward, invading Malakai's space. "That's only a three-year difference from you. If he feels that is what he wants to do, then who am I not to encourage him? He has great fighting skills from what I have seen. I think he's capable of doing an amazing job if given the chance."

"This isn't a matter of opinion. What I say goes, and I'm keeping what I have left of my family safe. I may not be adjusted to this whole royalty crap, but I can sure put my foot down and use my title to my advantage when I say: *I want you nowhere near my brother and sister.*"

Malakai turned sharply away from Demetri and went to leave, but his foot caught on the edge of something on the ground. He stumbled slightly and looked down, looking at a box with strange carvings along the surface. Malakai shook his head and stepped over the box, still fuming with anger and ready to leave.

Just as he made it to the doors, a sharp pain ripped through his brain. Malakai screamed, grabbing onto his head as though he could protect himself from the feeling. His eyes rolled back into his head, and suddenly his vision was taken over by a string of visions.

\* \* \*

*Turning to face the opposite side of the room, Antonious saw a boy around his age, maybe older, standing near the fireplace. The boy had pure black hair with blue eyes. He couldn't remember the boy's name, but he knew this was a childhood friend of his.*

*"There isn't much time to explain," said the boy. He pointed to the fireplace. The same fireplace that once led them down to the stables, where they played hide-n-seek. "Remember when I guided you down? It'll lead you to the stables and you can hide there."*

*"I—I haven't seen you since Yal's death," Antonius said.*

*"We don't have time, Antonius. The Elder Guardians are here to assassinate the Bellemore bloodline. I overheard my mother and father talking about it the other night. I am trying to save you!"*

*The boy activated the secret passageway. Once Antonius stepped inside the fireplace, the boy deactivated the entrance and stayed behind on the other side. Antonius was left in darkness.*

\* \* \*

The fireplace. The boy. The assassination.

Malakai took a deep breath. His chest tightened as he tried to regain his strength, blinking back the memory.

Demetri was standing next to Malakai, with a hand on his back and his chest, helping him remain standing. The closeness of

Demetri only made Malakai feel more unsettled, like the floor was being ripped out from under him.

"What just happened?" asked Demetri, concern lacing the words.

"I'm fine. You don't need to help me," Malakai said, shaking his head. "Annalu said my memories would come back to me here and there. I just didn't think they'd come to me so intensely."

"What memory did you have?"

"Why does it matter to you?"

"Because I worry about you," Demetri said. "As shocking as it is to any of you, I actually do care."

Malakai frowned. Demetri was such a confusing man, going between helpful and hurtful in the same breath, at once antagonistic and sympathetic. Malakai didn't know if he could trust anything about him.

"You weren't intentionally trying to encourage Celdric to fight in the war to get some sort of sick revenge on me, were you?" asked Malakai, giving voice to a paranoid thought in his brain since Celdric had confessed his desire to fight.

"Why would I do that? I've already hashed things out with Kelton—it's water under the bridge. If I had known it was going to upset you, I would've never voiced my opinion to your brother."

Malakai crossed his arms and tilted his head before asking, "Is this your way of an apology?"

"The closest you're gonna get, *Your Imperial Highness.*"

Malakai sighed, still unsure but at least willing to give Demetri the benefit of the doubt. "The memory was of some boy. He helped me escape the night of the invasion. I've been trying to remember who he was, but my memory is not fully there yet. I suppose in time it'll come back to me."

Demetri swallowed, shifting on his feet. Malakai noticed how nervous he became after he explained himself.

"I think you'd better go, now. I'm sure Kelton is waiting for you in your room." Demetri said, clearing his throat. "Let me know if there is anything I can do to help with the pain."

Malakai nodded and awkwardly turned away from Demetri,

aiming for the door leading out of the bedroom. The only sound was a gush of wind coming from the balcony as he walked off.

# 7
## No Matter What Comes Next

**SILIANNA**

Silianna and Rahaf found themselves on the dancefloor surrounded by a bunch of vampyres at a nightclub. It was a new level of weird for them, considering they never encountered vampyres in the North before. Rahaf came up with the idea to celebrate her last night in Avala by dancing the night away. Silianna was reluctant to do it, but she wanted to respect Rahaf's last wish before she traveled with the witches to Aeries. There was no telling when she would get to see her best friend again, so she wanted to cherish the time they had together.

The nightclub was buzzing with electric music and flashing lights in a multitude of colors. Silianna let herself relax, throwing her body back and forth to the music and taking shots of liquid courage. Normally, Silianna was the quieter, innocent one of the group, but the atmosphere of the nightclub lulled her into a sense of fun. Maybe this was what she needed to de-stress. A night of no expectations where all the burdens she carried with her could be danced away.

"Are you having fun?" Rahaf shouted.

"Yes! I can't believe I've never been to a club before!" Silianna shouted back.

"Technically, we did, back at Reju's club a few months ago."

Silianna chuckled, nearly spilling her drink on her heels. "That doesn't count, silly! We were there to handle business. There was no partying involved with us… *Or* alcohol."

Silianna looked Rahaf up and down, admiring her choice in outfit. She wore a short black leather dress and knee-high boots, with her hair set up in a long ponytail. Silianna had chosen a shimmering blue dress with an open back and a pair of silver heels. She knew, objectively, that she was attractive, but always felt that it was Rahaf who really stole the show every time.

Two vampyre men slithered their way through the crowd to try and dance with Silianna and Rahaf. The tall one had neon blue hair and dazzling, bright brown eyes. He had many tattoos covering his face and cascading down his arms. They were both acting slightly odd, especially the one who was dancing with Rahaf, almost like they were on Fae Dust or something.

"Are you enjoying yourselves?" asked the tall vampyre.

"I *was*," Silianna responded. "Go bother somebody else, we're not interested."

"You don't like what you see?"

"Definitely not. I like women, and my best friend has a boyfriend. I suggest you get lost while you still can, buddy."

"Oh, come on. If you're not gonna dance with us, then let us have a taste of your blood. We've been itching to get our hands on some elemental blood. You ladies seem to be willing to help the cause. What do you say?"

"Yeah, no thanks." Silianna grabbed Rahaf's hand and dragged her away from the two creeps, shooting distrustful glances over her shoulder as she moved. "Can you believe those two? I don't get what wasn't clicking in their brain-dead heads."

Between one blink and the next, the vampyres were standing in front of them, looming ominously. Before Silianna could open her mouth to threaten them again, Rahaf stepped past her and lit a ball of fire into her hands, head cocked towards the men. Both vampyres tensed, eyes darting between the girls and the steadily growing ball of fire, before they ran off.

Once the two left, Rahaf grabbed onto Silianna's arm and steered them both out of the nightclub, grabbing their coats on the way out to help against the chill outside.

"By the Gods, those idiots sure know how to ruin a good time!" Rahaf complained. She chanted "*Pyro*" and created a ball of fire for her and Silianna to huddle around to keep each other warm. "Did you have a nice time, Sil?"

Silianna nodded. "I surprisingly did. Makes me question if I'm becoming just like my uncle."

"Gross. Why would you think such a thing?"

Silianna shrugged. "I don't know. Considering my ability to connect with the Dark Dimension and now realizing how much I liked it there... It just seems like I'm going two-for-two. What's next? I wonder."

Rahaf groaned. "Don't think like that. Besides, you're too pure to be anything like him. Reju was a con artist. You're not using your element for your own personal gain. You're actually doing some good, or, at least, I *hope* you are."

"I am! There are just some things that I'm working out." Silianna did a horrible job pretending like she had everything under control. Her voice wobbled on the obvious lie, and she could tell Rahaf caught on immediately. *Damnit.*

Rahaf stopped in her tracks and faced Silianna as she went into interrogation mode. "Silianna, you better tell me what's going on before I wreak havoc. I'm leaving soon, and I do not want to leave knowing you're going through trouble that I could've helped prevent. Spill."

Silianna felt the palms of her hands sweat. There was no easy way to explain to Rahaf that her body was starting to reject her water element. The God of Water, *Limusic*, was not happy, and Silianna had to decide whether to keep her water element or her spiritual element. If she had her way, she would've kept both, but that was not an option.

Naturally, Silianna caved in and went into full detail about the entire situation. The Lost Souls, Reju Tufte, Vorkalth, Limusic's fury, Malakai and her searching for answers, and her encounter with her fingers zapping. The two were walking back to Windsor Keep while Silianna explained it all. As she was finishing up the story, Rahaf looked concerned, and Silianna could already tell that she had a lot to say on the matter.

"So… What do you think?" Silianna asked nervously.

"I just don't understand why you're still holding on to a forbidden element. If there is a way for you to get rid of it, then do it! Why would you want to lose your water element over something so dangerous? You saw the outcome of your uncle when he was meddling with that stuff."

"I—I don't know, Rahaf! It just makes me feel good to know I'm helping people. Alive or dead, I have a chance to do something nobody else has managed to do."

"I get that, but you're deliberately making yourself a target. You said it yourself. Vorkalth is looking for the culprit behind the Lost Souls passing through the Dark Dimension. Does Kelton or Malakai know about this?"

Silianna went mute.

Rahaf's eyes widened. "Sil! You have to tell them. Nobody knows more about that creepy place than they do. If you don't tell them what's at stake, I will."

Silianna gasped. "No! Okay… I will find them when we get back, and I'll come clean. I just don't want you going to Aeris with any worries about me."

"I'm always going to be worried about you guys. I may not show it sometimes, but it's the truth. You need to be careful, Silianna."

Suddenly, Silianna and Rahaf were thrown forward as something slammed into their backs. A heavyweight landed on top of them, and they struggled to escape whatever it was. Rahaf conjured a ball of fire, the light revealing that the same vampyres from earlier were attacking them. Rahaf increased the size of the fire and flung it behind her, searing the vampyres faces. They both stumbled back, clutching at their burning skin.

Silianna used her water element, manipulating the molecules

from the snow to create a water shield nearly six feet tall. She pushed the shield forward, and a wave of water clashed on the vampyres, their bodies slamming up against one of the glass structures. Silianna pulled her arms down; however, a sharp electrical pain radiated throughout her arms and fingers right after, making her cry out in pain

"What's going on?" Rahaf said, turning towards Silianna. "What can I do?"

"I don't know!" Silianna screamed. "It hurts! Make it stop!"

Rahaf held onto Silianna's arms, but the gesture brought no comfort. Silianna saw red sparks dance at the end of her fingertips as the pain increased.

"It's Limusic," Silianna stated, her voice shaking. "He's upset with me. The more I use my water element, the more my body starts to act out."

"We have to get you to the infirmary, Silianna." Rahaf placed Silianna's arm around her shoulder and started to carry her. "Come on, we're not that far from Windsor Keep."

Aiming for the glass bridge that led to the security gates, Silianna and Rahaf stumbled along in the direction of the infirmary. Before they made it too far, a strange woman passed in front of them. She wore a long red velvet cloak with black boots peeking out from the bottom. Her long auburn hair hung down on either side of her shoulders, but her face was obscured. The woman held a scent mixed with lavender and mint. For some reason, Silianna felt she recognized the woman, though given the state of her condition, she wasn't entirely sure what she was seeing was real.

"Rahaf?" Silianna murmured.

"Yes, Sil?" Rahaf responded.

"You see the weird lady too, right?"

"Yes. I do."

The woman came to a halt in front of them, blocking their path. She pulled out a black pouch from her pocket and loosened the strings. Before either Silianna or Rahaf could do anything, the woman moved mere inches from them at an alarming speed. She faced Silianna, raised her hand to reveal a small pile of sand nestled in her palm, and then blew, scattering the sand across Silianna. In the next blink, she was gone, vanished into the night as Silianna started to sway unsteadily on her feet.

"Silianna!" Rahaf shouted. She quickly pulled Silianna up as her body started to weaken, nearly falling to the floor. "By the Gods, what is going on?"

Rahaf proceeded to carry Silianna to the gates. Silianna barely saw Rahaf wave down a group of guards, who flanked the two girls and began escorting them back to the Windsor Keep.

* * *

Entering the west side of the castle, Silianna felt her strength start to slowly restore itself. She wasn't sure how, but whatever that stranger did to her helped simmer the pain.

Assisting them was the Grand Empress Dowager's robotic servant, Celsa. He was leading the way when Malakai's best friend, Eli, stumbled upon them. He was shirtless, yet he wore black sweatpants and black shoes. It was evident that he was finishing a workout session with all the sweat on his body. Both Silianna and Rahaf observed the six-pack abs he managed to gain during his time training these past few months.

"Master Vakloon," said Celsa, cheerfully. "Wonderful to see you. I trust you've had a splendid evening?"

"I did. Thank you, Celsa." Eli looked behind Celsa and noticed Rahaf carrying Silianna on one shoulder. "What's going on over here?"

"Nothing," said Silianna, straightening her posture and clearing her throat. "I wasn't feeling good, but I've started feeling better."

"It doesn't matter. You should get tested just in case," Rahaf argued. She turned from Silianna to Eli and Celsa. "There was a stranger outside the security gates who blew a weird substance in Silianna's face. I'm not sure what it was, but it can't be good."

"Why would anyone do that?" asked Eli.

Rahaf shrugged. "We went to this club tonight, and some vampyres were messing with us. Maybe that woman was with them?

She ran fast like one. I wouldn't assume otherwise."

"*Vampyres?* You two are crazy to be messing with those bloodsuckers," said Eli, both disgusted and concerned. "Either way, I'm glad to see you're doing okay, Silianna. But I agree with Rahaf, you should go get tested."

Silianna felt defeated. "I suppose. Let's go see if any of the Healers are in the infirmary."

Celsa continued guiding the ladies down the hall, passing Eli as he walked in the opposite direction.

On the right-hand side, Silianna caught a glimpse of a green neon light emerging from the cracks in a bedroom door. It was instantly that she knew who the room belonged to: Demetri.

"*Save Prince Demetri,*" a ghostly voice whispered in her head, echoing against her skull.

Silianna's arms broke out in goosebumps as she understood that the spirits on the Other Side were warning her. Whatever the green neon light was, it was not good. Her body flung forward as she aimed for the doorknob. Celsa and Rahaf were right behind her, reaching out to try and grab her. Silianna barged through the bedroom door and found that the room was empty.

"Silianna, what has gotten into you?" Rahaf asked, frantic.

"I—I'm not sure," Silianna said, struggling to speak. "Do you not see the green light? The spirits are trying to warn me of something. They said Demetri was in trouble."

"I see the green light, however, I'm more concerned about the voices you're referring to. I thought you could only communicate with them when you're in the D—" Rahaf caught her tongue, realizing that Celsa was still standing with them. "*Hmmph.* You know what I mean. Regardless, if that's the case, what's to say that the substance that vampyre gave you isn't making you hear things?"

Silianna felt overwhelmed. There was too much going on in one singular night. She took a moment to right herself, closing her eyes and emptying her mind. Once she opened them, Silianna traced her eyes to where the green light was beaming. There, underneath Demetri's king-size bed frame, there was a box with strange carvings and the Arajibac language. The box glowed green.

"*Evil*," a ghostly voice whispered.

"*Save Prince Demetri*," another whispered.

It was happening again. Silianna was conflicted about whether she should grab the box. Before she could make a final decision, Celsa volunteered and pulled it out.

Silianna and Rahaf hovered behind Celsa and examined the weird box.

"Dravkyn Demon," Rahaf read out loud. "W—What does that mean?"

Silianna gasped. It was the same entity that attacked her earlier today. But why was the box labeled "Dravkyn Demon" in Arajibac? More importantly, why did Demetri have it of all people?

"They're creatures not of this world," Celsa responded. His eyes lit up a light blue, followed by an image that was conjured up through his eyes like a projector. "They were created in Vorkalth's image while he's held prisoner in the Dark Dimension. They were designed to locate the Superior Witch. Over time, their purpose became something much more—to wreak havoc on anyone who attempted to reach those who were trapped in purgatory."

"That doesn't sound good," Rahaf said.

Outside the bedroom door, there was a commotion. Silianna rushed out into the hall and found Eli and Demetri fighting each other. It seemed Demetri had already broken their promise from earlier not to antagonize her friends.

"Demetri!" Silianna cried out.

"There's something wrong with him!" Eli shouted. He managed to push Demetri against a wall, pinning him in place with an arm across his neck. "I think he's possessed or something. His eyes are pitch black!"

Silianna and Rahaf exchanged looks.

"Celsa. You don't suppose that box would cause a Dravkyn Demon to possess Demetri, do you?" said Silianna, torn between moving forward to help or waiting for more answers.

Celsa ran calculations. "There may be a high probability. The box seemed to originate from the pyramid located in Pyroc. It is an ancient artifact from the Old World. The box was designed to house dark energy—Dravkyn Demons included."

"Do you think that is why he's been acting out today?" asked Silianna.

Rahaf shook her head. "He's a douchebag on a regular given day. You can't blame us for not realizing something was off sooner."

Demetri managed to get the upper hand, dislodging Eli's arm and landing a strong punch to his face. His mouth was turned down in a frown, and his eyes were dark black. As Eli went down, Rahaf moved forward, grabbing onto Demetri's arm and pinning it behind his back so she could shove him back against the wall.

"I have to tell him," Demetri mumbled, face pressed into the wall. "Please, you have to let me go. I have to tell him before it's too late."

"Tell who what?" Rahaf asked.

"Antonius…" Demetri started breathing heavily, struggling against Rahaf's grip. "I have to find Antonius. He has to know the truth. Please, I have to tell him. I can't do this anymore."

*By the Gods,* Silianna thought. *Those demons are screwing with Demetri's mind! They're making him relive the torment he endured with Malakai. I have to do something.*

The room around her fell silent as Silianna reached inward, focusing on the pull of dark energy. In a matter of seconds, Silianna was back in the Dark Dimension. There, where Demetri was pinned to the wall, Silianna saw a Dravkyn Demon latched onto his body.

"Spirits," Silianna started, "if you're here, please show me guidance and protect my friend. I cannot fight this entity on my own. Please."

Whispers surrounded Silianna as she stood in place. Emerging from the shadows was her uncle, Reju, who did not seem pleased to see his niece return.

"I told you it would become dangerous if you continued to meddle around here," said Reju, furious. "Vorkalth has identified that you are behind the Lost Souls crossing over. He's sending his creatures to go after your friends."

"Okay! Fine. I'll stop helping the spirits. Just, please, save Demetri from the Dravkyn Demon," Silianna pleaded, desperate. "I beg of you."

Reju chanted words along with the spirits. Silianna caught the same bright light from an earlier clash with the Dravkyn Demon. The entity turned into dust, flowing away from Demetri. Silianna felt the tightness in her chest ease, knowing it was over now.

"Thank you, Uncle," said Silianna.

"Don't thank me. You need to be careful. Whatever happened in the Dark Dimension can latch onto you in the real world. You need to brace yourself for the inevitable."

"So, what are you saying? Should I let go of my spiritual element? I don't understand you. You're the reason I have this ability now. Why give it to me if you were going to ask me to release it in the end?"

"Because I thought my niece would know better to think strategically and use her gift to her advantage, not for the advantage of others. The Shadow Lord has you marked." Reju lowered his voice as he continued. "Try not to return to the Dark Dimension moving forward. You are no longer welcome back. In the meantime, the spirits shall guide you in the real world whenever you need it."

\* \* \*

When Silianna returned to the real world, she was lying on the floor. Celsa, Rahaf, and Eli surrounded her as they lifted her. Silianna wasn't sure how long she had passed out, but nothing in her body hurt when she returned. The only thing that did hurt was knowing her uncle was furious with her, and that she was not wanted back in the Dark Dimension.

Silianna brushed off the helping hands surrounding her, too focused on trying to make sure her mission had been successful.

*Demetri.*

Looking down the hall, Silianna caught Demetri slowly walking towards an open window. The curtains surrounding the window were blowing in at a heavy rate, snow falling inside and landing on the floor. Outside the window, Silianna caught a silhouette of what looked like a person holding out their hand.

"Guys, I need you to stop what you're doing and look over there," Silianna said, pointing in Demetri's direction.

With everyone redirecting their attention, Silianna was able to get a closer look as she realized it was the mysterious woman from earlier. She still wore her red velvet cloak and black boots. Everyone was shouting for Demetri's attention, but it was evident that he was hypnotized by the woman.

There was only one other person Silianna recalled who possessed such long, auburn, reddish-brown hair: Seraphina Blackworth. The same woman who caused the devastating rift between the Eckwood brothers. There was no chance it could be her, was there?

Suddenly, Silianna heard a roar and spun around. Entering the hall, there was a white polar bear that made its presence known. It charged at Demetri, closing its mouth around his shirt and pulling him away from the window. Then, a gust of wind blew through, pushing the mysterious woman over the edge and closing the window shut. Silianna saw the Grand Empress Dowager herself, Maelena Bellemore, as she stood at the end of the hall.

"Welcome back, Prince Demetri!" Celsa said in his robotic voice.

"W—What happened?" Demetri asked, clutching at his head and stepping back from the window.

"I would like to know the same thing," Her Imperial Highness said, anger in her voice. "I want someone to explain what is going on in my domain, and I want an explanation *now*.

"We're not sure you'll believe us," Rahaf said.

"Oh, trust me. You'd be amazed to see how easily I can get answers, especially when that *somebody* is expected to travel with my witches to Aeris. Now, if you wish to reunite with your lover, I'd start talking, Princess Rahaf."

Silianna was appalled by the Grand Empress Dowager's blackmail. Rahaf had been dying to reunite with Theodosis for quite some time now. Her only hope was that Rahaf would cut out any information that pertained to Silianna and her connection to the

Dark Dimension.

Fortunately, the conversation shifted when Demetri uttered a few simple words. As his eyes rolled back and he fell against the wall, the words that passed his lips were, "Seraphina is alive."

# 8
## Eternally Yours

**MALAKAI**

One thing Malakai enjoyed most about Windsor Keep was the bathing rooms located underneath the castle structures. There were caves updated with white marble flooring, air conditioning, and floral perfumes to create a relaxing atmosphere. After his encounter with Celdric and Demetri, Malakai was itching for a break and some place he could cool his head.

The tubs were circular-shaped, made of onyx rocks, dotted with small bits of crystal that sparkled under the low lighting. Malakai recalled that the Insully blades were made of a unique crystal material, too, that originated from caves, leaving him to wonder if there were the same sort. Inside, the tub was filled with clear blue water and naturally forming bubbles. Malakai sank into the water. He let out a relieved sigh, feeling the stress melt off his body.

There was a charcoal bar of soap that Malakai brought with him. He slowly began to wash himself. By the time he got to his arms, he found himself spacing out as he looked at the scar on his hand. Now that he knew the scars' origin, back from his childhood as Prince Antonius, and that it was connected to his memory of that mysterious boy, it left lingering thoughts of his identity.

\* \* \*

*Abruptly, a young Malakai tripped over some sort of metal object. That did not work to his advantage as he used his hands to catch his fall, which resulted in his left hand landing on something sharp. Malakai shrieked in pain.*

*The boy with black hair and blue eyes rushed to keep Malakai quiet as they were in the middle of a game of hide-n-seek. The boy observed the cut on Malakai's palm and acted fast. The boy used his Terrane element to grow a peculiar leaf. There were oils visible on the leaf as the boy gently placed it on Malakai's palm.*

*"I'm sorry this happened to you," said the boy, remorsefully. "The leaf will heal your wound, but it won't get rid of the scar."*

*"My parents won't be too pleased to see it. Could I not go to one of the Healers and have the scar removed?" asked Malakai.*

*"The oils prevent it. You'll always have it unless you want to go see one of the magic-folks. They can cast a glamour spell, but they can be kind of weird to talk to."*

*"It's okay. Glamour spells are temporary. I'll just tell everyone it's a battle scar!" Malakai laughed.*

\* \* \*

The memory played on a steady loop in Malakai's mind. Truthfully, he'd been thinking about that same boy again and again, like an itch he couldn't quite scratch. He managed to remember everything about Yal, his childhood friend, but when it came to that particular boy, it was like he didn't exist. Whatever that witch, Annalu, did to his memories was extremely effective.

The bar of soap slipped from Malakai's hand, submerging to the bottom of the tub. Malakai let it go, turning his hand to watch how the scar caught the light. He knew it was unhealthy to do such a thing. *Why was I stupid enough not to seek a Healer? Was the game of hide-n-seek really that important?* Malakai sighed. There was no point in dwelling on a different outcome.

"It is imperfections that make the beauty within a soul." Kelton appeared, grinning widely. He wore a nicely fitted black and white suit, which complemented his dark, dirty blond hair. Those emerald, green eyes struggled to stay on Malakai's face and not wander lower. "How is my angelic boyfriend doing tonight?"

"I'm managing." Malakai wet his hair and slicked it back, looking over at Kelton coyly over his shoulder. "Did you come for a sneak peek?"

"*Mmm*," Kelton purred. "Tempting. However, that's not why I am here. Did you already forget what I had planned for tonight?"

Malakai dragged a hand across his face, feeling like an idiot. "Kelton, I'm sorry. I assumed you needed space after that broadcast. You never had a chance to mourn your grandmother's death, and I didn't want to overbear you. Then Celdric and I had a little argument, which resulted in Demetri and me having an argument. I'm just swamped at the moment."

"Hey, it's okay. I hear you. Nothing that involves Demetri is ever stress-free." Kelton snorted, his laugh making Malakai's heart flutter in happiness. "And I was mourning. Thank you for giving me time to heal."

Behind Kelton, a familiar presence emerged, radiating blue light.

"You know, you don't need to shadow me around everywhere I go," said Malakai. He chuckled and held out the palm of his hand. "Come along, now."

The Eni that found Malakai by the barrier showed herself as she flew toward him and sat on his palm. The funny thing about Enis was that even if they were made of blue flames, touching one did little to no harm. They just felt like a vibrating rush of water.

"We should really give you a name if you're going to keep following me around for the rest of my life," Malakai said to the Eni. "I assume it would be cliché to call you 'Blue' because of your blue flames, huh? Maybe I can alter the spelling. Perhaps 'Bluu' with two U's might work."

The Eni jumped in glee. She seemed to approve of the name.

A few weeks ago, Malakai was learning about the Enis and their purpose. As his grandmother explained, "If you take the time to know your Eni, it won't be hard to see into her soul and understand her. That attachment will develop a special bond. Once the bond is locked, she will transform into your spirit animal. Mine is a polar bear, and Rahaf's a bobcat. The first step, of course, is to give her a proper name. There's no rush. It's not like your Lustris element is going anywhere anytime soon." *Lustris*. It was a rare element only a few could obtain, and it would allow an elemental to claim an Eni of their own.

Though his memory was fuzzy, there was another flashing image of his grandmother that appeared. He was young, perhaps nine or ten. His grandmother was using her Lustris element to shape her Eni into a dancing polar bear of sorts. A young Prince Antonius lived for those silly tricks.

Kelton waved his hand in front of Malakai's face, trying to get his attention. "Hello? Did you zone out or something?"

Bluu rose from Malakai's palm and flew away, leaving the two to their privacy.

Malakai blinked. "S—Sorry. I was just in memory land, it's not important." Kelton had moved to sit on the edge of the bath while Malakai was lost in thought. "Are you going to just sit there, or are you going to come join me?"

"I suppose we can count this as a little date. What do you think?" Kelton asked, teasing.

"By the Gods! Get in here already."

"Your wish is my command, Your Imperial Highness."

Without further discussion, Kelton jumped into the onyx tub with his clothes still intact. Malakai's lips pressed into a thin, bloodless line at the idiocy of the move, but couldn't help finding Kelton's silliness charming. Kelton moved forward, caging Malakai against the wall of the bath and leaning in for a kiss. Malakai responded eagerly, chasing the familiar taste of Kelton on his tongue.

Suddenly, Kelton pulled back. Malakai felt the frustration as it burned through his bloodstream.

"What's the matter?" asked Malakai.

"Nothing. I just…" Kelton paused. It was clear from his facial expression that something was bothering him.

"Kelton, come on. Don't do this to me now. If there's something you need to say, then just say—" Malakai started, but Kelton cut him off.

"—I'm sorry." The words echoed across the room. Malakai was puzzled as to what Kelton was sorry for. "I'm sorry for the way I behaved this morning. I don't mean to upset you."

Malakai was puzzled. "Do you honestly think that I care about this morning? There are a million other things for me to be upset about, and trust me, that isn't one of them. You're fine. We're fine." There was an awkward pause between the two. "We're fine, *right?*"

Kelton nodded. "Right. We are! I just tend to feel guilty about the stuff I do. Whether it's towards you, Demetri... *Anyone.*"

Malakai placed his hands on both sides of Kelton's cheeks and pulled his face a bit closer to his. "That's because you have a big heart. There is nothing wrong with that. You should give yourself some more credit."

"There's something else I've been wanting to tell you for a while."

"By the Gods, what else do you have to say?"

"I love you." Those three words, eight letters, slipped from Kelton's mouth. He was the first to say it between the two, and yet *that* was what managed to shut Malakai up for once. "It's been four months, and I can't wait any longer to say it. The words have been dying to come out of me forever, and I have no regrets saying it now. I love you to the moon and back, Malakai Thorns. From the moment I laid eyes on you in my dreams, and then again in real life. I knew there was something special."

Malakai was breathing faster than normal. He was speechless, though he struggled to find the right words. Why was it so hard to say it back? Malakai was just ready to explode when he finally blurted it out, "I love you, too."

Kelton stood up inside the tub and quickly undressed, tossing his clothes every which way so they floated in the water. He then sat and pulled Malakai close to him, wrapping an arm around his shoulders and relaxing into the tub.

Kelton proceeded to hold Malakai's hand, his thumb tracing the scar on his palm. "You know, I wish nothing more than to live a simple life with you."

"Well, what's to stop us?"

Kelton chuckled. "Do you see the predicament we're in? I fear we are destined to live a life that is beyond simple. It's like we're cursed."

Malakai set his head on Kelton's shoulder, feeling overwhelmed by the sheer amount of emotion in his chest.

"Well, we officially reached the '*I love you*' stage in our relationship. We have plenty of time to reach that simple life," Malakai said.

"Gods, you make me have wild thoughts. I'm eternally yours." Kelton guided Malakai's body and had Malakai sit on his lap. The two spent the remainder of their night enjoying each other's company.

* * *

The next day, Malakai and Kelton strolled down the hall holding hands as they followed Celsa, who was ramping up speed. Celsa had woken them up very suddenly in the morning, ruining their peaceful moment by telling them there was urgent news to share. Malakai wasn't mentally prepared to hear more about this war his grandmother was planning, but he figured attending would prevent her from giving him a long lecture about how important it was for him to claim the Baskarian throne. *Blah. Blah. Blah.*

Celsa made a sharp turn, leading to the west side of the castle. Malakai was perplexed by Celsa's direction, given the fact that the conference room was located on the north side.

"Celsa, excuse my question, but where are you taking us? I thought we were going to the conference room," said Malakai.

"My apologies, Your Imperial Highness. I should've been clearer in my wording! Indeed, you and Prince Kelton are requested to meet with the Grand Empress Dowager; however, she is not there. She and the others are located in the infirmary."

"The others?" Kelton questioned.

"Yes. Your fellow friends are with the Grand Empress Dowager. We could not locate the two of you last night, so I figured I would wait until the morning to retrieve both of you."

Malakai and Kelton exchanged looks. It was true that they weren't back in their rooms until three hours ago. They'd spent most of the night fooling around and lost track of time.

Clearing his throat and his mind, Malakai proceeded to ask, "What happened last night? Are Celdric and Nehila okay?"

"Your brother and sister are perfectly fine in their rooms. As requested by the Grand Empress Dowager, they are to remain in Windsor Keep and miss their educational studies for today. If you have questions as to why, I believe that is for Her Imperial Highness to answer."

Malakai shrugged off his worries and continued following Celsa. As long as Celdric and Nehila were okay, it didn't matter to him what this meeting was for. It only further confirmed his theory that it was related to war. Although he was still confused as to why the meeting would be held in the infirmary.

Celsa turned right as the three of them stumbled upon the enlarged double doors. Above it, there was an infirmary sign.

"Who got hurt?" Kelton asked, his face twisted with worry. Malakai looked at Kelton with his eyes wide open. "What? Was it wrong to ask?"

"Maybe."

The double doors opened. Inside, Malakai saw Eli, Silianna, and Rahaf huddled together with cups of coffee in their hands. On the opposite side, his grandmother was occupied with one of the Healers reading a holographic chart.

As Malakai looked beyond them, he noticed someone was lying on one of the infirmary beds. He stepped closer to see that Demetri was there, various wires leading from him to a monitor beeping at a steady rate.

"Oh," said Malakai, guilty for feeling a small bit of relief. "It's just Demetri."

"Figures," Kelton mumbled. He turned to Eli, Silianna, and Rahaf. "What did he do now? He pissed one of the guards off or something?"

"Actually, it's much more serious than that," said Eli. He

uncrossed his arms and handed Malakai a cup of coffee. "You might want to sit down for this."

"By the Gods, can someone just tell us what's going on already?" Malakai said, impatient.

Maelena Bellemore walked over to the group. She nodded her head to Rahaf—a clear signal that she was approved to do or say something.

"Last night, Silianna and I stumbled upon Demetri's bedroom," Rahaf started, "and we found a box that was under his bed. This box originated from Pyroc, most likely ancient, from the Old World. It is a cursed box and was housing a demonic entity—a Dravkyn Demon. Her Imperial Highness has ordered a lockdown until the guards determine it is safe."

"I don't understand. Where did this box come from?" Malakai asked, his tone shifting from annoyance to horror.

The room fell silent. Everyone besides Malakai and Kelton knew the answer. Still, nobody wanted to speak up. *What was all the secrecy for?*

Eli rolled his eyes. Taking the initiative, he said, "They think that the girl, Seraphina, gave him the box. The same Seraphina whom Demetri and Kelton were in love with." Eli gave a death stare to Kelton. "The girls filled me in on the details last night."

Malakai didn't dare look in Kelton's direction. He wasn't sure how he felt about the idea of Seraphina being behind this, especially since he was informed by practically everyone in his life that she was dead. How could she still be alive if the juxure flowers melted the skin off her face? Was everyone lying to him the entire time?

Eli went on to say, "Rahaf and Silianna don't necessarily agree with me, but I believe the box was meant for you, Kai, rather than Demetri. However, since she gave it to him, I think she was hoping the box would find its way to you. I just have a weird feeling you were a target."

"It doesn't make sense," Rahaf chimed in. "Seraphina didn't know who Malakai was back then. She wouldn't have a reason to target him. If anything, she's probably bitter about the fact that she ended up with neither of the Eckwood brothers."

"Exactly my point," Eli added. "She has neither of the Eckwood brothers. And yet, Malakai is with Kelton. What if she's jealous? What if she wants Malakai out of the picture so she can have them both for herself? Given everything you two have told me about her, she sounds deranged. And the fact that she faked her death? Pretty diabolical if you ask me."

Malakai tilted his head and crossed his arms. "Nobody could ever survive an encounter with the juxure flowers. Why would Seraphina be an exception?"

Rahaf turned to Silianna, who was sitting quietly. "Silianna and I went clubbing last night and found ourselves dealing with some vampyre drama. There was a woman in a red cloak who blew some weird substance in Silianna's face. I'm not sure what it was, but it helped whatever weird headspace she was in." Rahaf's bobcat, Aleek, casually walked into the infirmary and rubbed himself on Rahaf's leg. Rahaf started petting him as she continued speaking. "At first, we didn't know who the woman was. But once Demetri started acting out and attacked Eli, we realized that the same woman from earlier was lingering by the window, watching. Demetri confirmed it was Seraphina before he was knocked out."

Kelton finally spoke, voice ice cold as he said, "He could've been hallucinating if he was under the influence. This cursed box must have played tricks on his mind. I saw Seraphina with my own eyes up on that mountain. Her entire face melted off in my arms. I'm one hundred percent certain that she is dead."

Rahaf looked back at Silianna and then at Kelton. "Well... That's what I was trying to get at. The woman was following us after that club with the vampyres. She had a crazy amount of speed, *just like a vampyre*. Eli, Silianna, and I saw her for ourselves by that window."

"Are you telling me my dead girlfriend somehow came back to life as a vampyre?" Kelton asked, anger coloring his words.

*Ex-girlfriend*, Malakai thought, wanting to correct him. There was a sudden form of jealousy that stirred Malakai's emotions. Though as much as he tried not to let it bother him, he couldn't shake the feeling that Kelton was hoping the theories were true about Seraphina's survival.

"Did she *really* come back to life if she's a vampyre? Technically, they're already dead," Eli said, trying to be funny. Nobody found it funny. "S—Sorry. Poor timing. I'll just shut up."

Malakai's grandmother was occupied with Demetri's results. She stood by his bedside with a worrisome look on her face. Malakai found it strange how glued she was to Demetri. Why did she like him so much?

"Grandmamma, what do you think about all this?" Malakai asked.

Her Imperial Highness shrugged. "It's hard to tell. But what I will say is that if she had vampyre blood in her system before she died, that would have resulted in her transformation. With severe damage to her face, the blood in her system would've taken weeks, perhaps even months, before she fully transitioned. No one would've known by the time she was buried."

"She seems like the type of girl to take vampyre blood," Rahaf said. Silianna bumped into her arm and mouthed for her to shut up. "What? It's true!"

"I have to ask you all a serious question," Maelena said, sounding tired. "Is this woman going to be a threat to my grandson?"

Eli did not share his input, nor did Kelton, but Rahaf and Silianna were quick to agree that Seraphina Blackworth was a threat to Malakai as long as he associated himself with either of the Eckwood brothers. Maelena did not speak another word. Instead, she dismissed everyone and remained with the Healer as they spoke amongst themselves regarding Demetri's status.

Malakai didn't bother speaking to Kelton. Instead, he grabbed Eli's arm and pulled him away from the others.

\* \* \*

"I wish I could go with you to Veilios," said Malakai. The two of them were walking side-by-side in the garden, making conversation. There was a hint of warmth that flowed through, which was refreshing, being that they were in the coldest kingdom throughout

69

the Nine Lands. "Are you ready to see what life is like over there with the shapeshifters?"

"I think so," Eli admitted. "It will be good to go somewhere where elementals and bloodsuckers aren't trying to kill my best friend."

Malakai burst into laughter. "You're not wrong."

"How are you feeling with all that back there? I know it must've drawn some distance between you and Kelton."

Malakai jumbled through his head to find the right words. He feared if he spoke without thinking that Eli would start to treat Kelton differently.

"It's whatever. I have Kelton, and that's all that matters. He's good to me. We're good. I haven't seen this Seraphina girl, but I've dealt with far worse before, and I'm not going to let her mess with Kelton."

Eli raised his hand. Malakai reached for it and gave him a high-five.

"Spoken like a true badass!" Eli said cheerfully. He pulled out his glass communicator and showed it to Malakai. "Listen, I'll only be gone for a few hours. If you need to contact me, you have my information. And I mean *anything*. Even if you're having boy-trouble, I'll listen to you complain. I doubt it'll take long to convince Lord Hussayn to lend his army to fight alongside us."

"Screw my boy problems. I just want you to be safe while you're there. You'll have Annalu traveling with you, so I shouldn't be too concerned. But after everything that happened in Terrane, I have to mentally prepare myself for the worst outcome."

Eli chuckled. "I'll be alright. Now, let's talk about the fact that you and Kelton slept together last night."

Malakai stopped walking in his tracks, his jaw wide open. "W—What... H—How do you know about that?!"

"Who do you think told Celsa that you guys were missing? I went looking for you guys after Demetri beat the crap out of me. I could *hear* you guys from a mile away." Eli pointed at his ears and then his nose. "Shapeshifters have pretty good hearing *and* a killer sense of smell when I'm in my wolf form."

"Are you implying that you *smelled* sex off of us? *Eww!* Gross, Eli." Malakai gagged at the thought of Eli stumbling upon any of that.

"Hey! The second I realized what was going on, I left you two to your thing. There's no shame. My best friend finally got some action! *Woooahhh!*"

Malakai, embarrassed, playfully shoved Eli away from him and started walking away. He was not entertaining their conversation any further. However, Eli's laughter could be heard in the distance.

# 9
## Lord Hussayn

**ELI**

The flight to Veilios wasn't as bad as Eli expected. Dodging mountains and trees, it was his first time flying in his owl form for a long period of time. Annalu estimated that the flight would take around two hours. With Eli hoping his calculations were correct, they may have been in the air for an hour and thirty minutes. *Only half an hour to go*, he reminded himself.

Annalu was enjoying the breeze with her arms spread out and her eyes closed, a smile stretched across her face. It had been a while since Eli saw a witch, let alone a witch who could fly. Seeing Annalu fly without having to shift into an animal was fascinating. The South was so free and open that any supernatural being could live peacefully without fear of being killed for simply existing. Annalu's enjoyment was a reflection of that freedom, and Eli felt it in himself, too.

Down below, there was a stretch of colored trees that shimmered in the sunlight. A slight scent of sweets and cinnamon caught Eli's attention because it was coming from the colorful trees.

"The domain down below is Miracle Forest," said Annalu. "I can imagine the smell and colors have piqued your interest. It does for everyone who stumbles upon it. Miracle Forest is home to the fae-folk. Most of them don't typically like to live outside their domain. The kingdom of Veilios was at war between the shapeshifters and fae-folk long ago; however, they settled on a treaty where they would each keep their share of the kingdom."

Eli wanted to respond to her, but it wasn't possible while he remained in his owl form.

Some substances grew from below and into the sky. Within seconds, the substances blew up into sparks of confetti.

"Don't be afraid," Annalu instructed. "They're just daylight fireworks. The fae-folk like to throw celebrations in the afternoon. I never really cared about learning why, but it's part of their culture, and I tend to mind my business."

Since he was little, Eli was told by his parents to stay clear of the fae-folk. They can be tricky when it comes to getting what they want. Even when he lived in Aeris, the fae-folk would cause a ruckus with the shapeshifters and magic-folk. Eli wasn't sure why they acted the way they did, but perhaps one day he could get the answers to it.

During the last few minutes in the sky, Eli caught a glimpse of unique building structures in the distance. They were made of brass, copper, wood, bricks, and cast iron. The materials used were endless. Lots of steam clouds were all around Eli and Annalu, though it did not stop them from their travels. *A kingdom filled with such technology and buildings*, Eli thought. *Malakai would've loved this.* From the countless books he'd catch Malakai reading, there was always an interest from Malakai when it came to fictional stories set in such a world. Eli didn't understand the fascination until now.

With so much wonderful architecture, Eli wasn't sure which one was the castle they called "Waerboard Hold."

Annalu went up ahead, Eli following at a steady rate behind her.

"We shouldn't be far now!" Annalu shouted.

Without warning, Eli was struck, electricity running through his body. He tried to flap his wings, but it was like his muscles were frozen in place from shock. His owl form started falling from the sky at a rapid speed. The only thing visible from his view was Annalu flying as fast as she could with her arms reaching out. The pressure of the air was causing Eli's head to bob up and down.

*BOOM!*

Another lightning bolt struck. This time, it nearly hit Annalu. Fortunately, she was able to dodge the collision. Annalu proceeded to reach her hand out to Eli before successfully grabbing hold of his wing and hugging him close to her chest. Annalu fixed her position as she continued straight for the brass and copper city.

"That was a close one," said Annalu, her voice tiresome. "Let's land somewhere and take a second to regroup."

Annalu flew towards the ground and managed to find a safe spot within an alleyway. She gently set Eli down on the cobblestone pavement. Annalu then tossed Eli's bag filled with clothes next to him as he shifted back into his mortal form.

"What the heck was that all about?" Eli shouted, furious. "A bolt of lightning hit me. I might as well have been as good as dead—fried chicken!"

"Relax. That was no ordinary lightning. If it were, you would've been dead. Those were actually electric shockwaves created from the towers that guard the city. They knock down any sort of energy that is unauthorized in their domain. It was designed to protect against any threats from the sky. I forgot that they were there."

"*Forgot?* That's not something anybody would casually forget! Especially if we're *flying*."

Annalu ground her teeth, her jaw twitching. "Look, we can stand here all day talking about the towers, or we can shut up and continue to Waerboard Hold on foot. What do you think?" Annalu crossed her arms, tapped her foot repeatedly, and waited.

Eli was too traumatized to fly back up into the sky. The last thing he needed was another electric shockwave to hit him. Walking would have to do.

The two continued their travels, walking amongst those who lived in the city. Eli caught the wafting scents of the nearby restaurants and felt his stomach rumble.

"Annalu, you don't suppose we could stop somewhere quick to eat, do you?" asked Eli, trying to seem casual with his request but hoping they would be able to stop.

Annalu sighed. "Only because I know how much energy the shockwave could've affected you, I will allow it. But we are only staying for twenty minutes, max. Don't get any ideas, shapeshifter."

Eli didn't need to hear her twice. His stomach rumbled again, and he ran towards a nearby restaurant, eager to get something to eat.

\* \* \*

As he took a bite of his sandwich, Eli let an exhale escape him. He was sitting alone in the back corner of the restaurant while Annalu was conversing with the owner. Though he did not mind being alone, Eli was curious to know what the two were talking about.

The restaurant was dim inside, decorated with black walls and gold pillars. However, a purple crystal ball that floated at the circular ceiling allowed for light inside the establishment. Some birds chirped and flew around the ball. When Eli asked Annalu what the purpose of the ball was, Annalu explained that it was an energy source that allowed for engineering equipment to run on its own, and in return, steam would be conjured up from the metallic chimneys. The crystal ball was an energy source that once resided on a planet long forgotten. The Old World used to use these techniques, but most kingdoms in Baskaria moved past the practices. Veilios seemed to be the only kingdom that continued the old ways.

At the table next to him, there was a peculiar man who was also eyeing Annalu and the restaurant owner. After careful examination, Eli realized that the man was one of the fae-folk. He had orange skin, unique wavy tattoos that started from the side of his pointy ear and slithered their way to his neck. The faerie then turned to Eli and smirked, revealing a pair of silver eyes that locked with Eli's. His heart was pounding as he questioned what the stranger's intention was. *On second thought, how did a faerie manage to get into the city?*

Contemplating whether he should try to notify Annalu, the faerie beat him to the punch as he jumped from his chair and aimed for Annalu with a knife.

Eli shifted into a wolf and lounged for the stranger.

The faerie raised his hands, like he was about to be arrested. A group of men circled him and Eli.

"We don't do fighting here," said the muscular man. "You can take that nonsense outside."

Annalu intervened. "Please. The wolf is with me. We were just on our way to speak to Lord Hussayn on behalf of the Grand Empress Dowager, Maelena Bellemore. We mean no harm."

Eli shifted back into his mortal form and quickly got himself dressed. Once doing so, he said to everyone, "Screw that! That faerie was about to attack you. He was eyeing you for quite some time while I was eating."

"A faerie?" the muscular man questioned.

The faerie growled and twisted a silver ring on his finger. A beam of light circled him. Annalu gasped. However, Eli wasn't sure what was so special about a stupid ring and the light.

"A glamour ring," Annalu said, surprised. She looked to Eli and asked, "But how did you manage to see past the faerie's disguise?"

Eli shrugged. "Not sure. I just kind of did. Does nobody typically see through a, what is it called? A glamour ring?"

Annalu shook her head. "Not any shapeshifter I've ever met. You would be the first."

"The Orb of Fell's Burial," the faerie hissed. "You came into contact with it, didn't you? You ought to stay away from things you have no business messing with, *boy*."

Eli's eyes widened. He was shocked to know this random fae-folk could tell he messed around with the Orb of Fell's Burial. It had been a month since he traveled with Malakai and Rahaf to Centuris. Everyone told him not to, and yet he still went ahead and looked for the orb. It was meant to show him images of what his heart desired most; however, if he broke eye contact before he could fulfill his desire, then there would be side effects for weeks. Perhaps seeing through a glamour ring was a side effect.

"Is that why the Grand Empress Dowager was upset with you?" Annalu asked, disappointed. "I warned you! That type of magic draws the fae-folk. It heightens their craving and not in the best way."

"Yes. I smelled the scent of the witch, but it is clear now that this shapeshifter was the origin of the smell." The faerie hissed, his mouth watering like he desperately wanted to take a bite out of Eli.

"By craving, do you mean like…eat me?" Eli asked, wrinkling his nose in disgust.

"Indeed," Annalu responded. She turned to the faerie and chanted, "*Araictum Padlarbus.*" Within seconds, the faerie's eyes rolled into the back of his head. Annalu seemed frustrated with the situation she found herself in. She looked to the men that surrounded them and said, "Well, my friend and I shall be going. The faerie should be unconscious for about an hour. That gives you boys enough time to carry him as far as you can back to Miracle Forest."

"You're too generous," the muscular man said. "We don't take kindly to their people roaming around here trying to kill one of our own. He's going to be held accountable for his actions."

"Accountable in what way?" Eli asked.

Annalu pushed Eli away from the group and waved goodbye to them as they left the restaurant.

"Hey! That was pretty cool what you did back there," Eli complimented.

"I will never understand how you managed to become best friends with Prince Antonius. *You* are making a simple task more complicated than it has to be."

"For the record, we wouldn't be in this predicament if you didn't forget about those stupid energy shockwaves. For someone who is the leader of her own coven, I will never understand how *you* managed to get the title."

Annalu continued walking in silence. Eli felt accomplished in getting her to shut up. But even though she remained silent, a part of Eli felt guilty for saying what he said. *Maybe I went a little too far*, he thought, remorseful. *Shit. I'll have to apologize to her after we meet with Lord Hussayn.*

* * *

The steps to Waerboard Hold were incredibly long and high up. To avoid the walk up, Annalu and Eli flew to the top of the steps where they were welcomed by two guards. They wore funny long black feathered hats, metallic gold staffs with a yellow electric ball on top, and long green robes.

"My name is Annalu La'Crox," Annalu introduced herself. "My companion here is Eli-zak Vakloon. We request to speak with Lord Hussayn on behalf of the Grand Empress Dowager, Maelena Bellemore."

The guards were mute, but they nodded at the same time to indicate their approval. Behind the guards, the double doors slowly opened. The guards then held out their arms, signaling them to walk inside. As Eli did so, he was met with a marvelous castle heavily made of brass, copper, and iron. The walls and flooring were made of repurposed industrial elements, like pipes, gears, and cogs. The inside smelled of pinecones and cherries, which was exactly how Eli remembered it smelling back in Aeris when he was younger.

There were guards at every corner of the castle. Not only that, but some animals roamed freely, too. Eli speculated that the animals could have been shapeshifters rather than actual animals. It would be hard for someone to sneak in here and try to do something malicious, which was lacking back at Windsor Keep.

Making a sharp turn, Eli stopped in his tracks as he and Annalu waited for the guards to open a door in front of them. There was an awkward pause as they waited. Once the music started to play, that was when the guards opened the door and ordered them to walk inside.

Eli's heart started to race as he realized that he was entering the Throne room of Waerboard Hold. This was where his family was meant to be after the Elder Guardians assassinated the Emperor and Empress. If it hadn't been for Thaddeus Thorns, perhaps Eli and his family could've made it to the South. Or they could've ended up dead like the unfortunate ones in the North. Fate was a strange thing, and yet Eli had to put all his trust into the Gods that things would work out in the end. After what he went through with the Orb of Fell's Burial and the warning the Lady of Glisten Lake gave him, all he could do was hope at this point.

There was a man at the end of the room who sat on an iron throne. He looked to be in his mid-sixties, maybe older. The man had long white dreadlocks, a white beard, and dark skin. *This must be Lord Hussayn*, Eli thought.

Lord Hussayn wore a green robe similar to the guards, although his robe had unique gold designs. As he stood from his throne, Eli estimated that the man could potentially be around six feet tall. He was way higher than Eli, but then again, almost everyone was taller than Eli.

"Welcome to Waerboard Hold," said Lord Hussayn. His arms were spread out in a welcoming manner, followed by a smile. Eli spotted that his arms had tattoos that were common for tribes within the shapeshifter community. "To what do we owe the pleasure of your visit?"

Annalu took the initiative to speak first. "We have been asked by the Grand Empress Dowager, Maelena Bellemore, to seek your army in joining us to fight the remaining Elder Guardians. The Lost Prince, Antonius Bellemore, has returned, and he is preparing to reclaim the Baskarian throne. We cannot accomplish this without getting all the help we can."

"I would not mind discussing the idea of lending my army. I'm a little thrown off to see you standing before me and not the Lost Prince himself. I must say, I find it a bit insulting. Is there a particular reason for Prince Antonius' absence?"

"Yes. There is an enemy within our domain who is attacking those closest to him. Until we catch the culprit, Prince Antonius is to remain on lockdown at Windsor Keep until further notice. We would have hoped that us being here today would be more than enough, given everything Maelena Bellemore has done for Veilios."

Lord Hussayn observed Eli from head to toe. "And you think bringing a shapeshifter here would help convince me in the absence of the Lost Prince?"

"Not at all, My Lord," Annalu said. She cleared her throat. "Eli-zak Vakloon is Prince Antonius' best friend. He wished to travel with me to see what it is like among other shapeshifters."

"Well, if he wanted to do such a thing, why had he not come sooner? I trust he's been in the South for years now. Why am I to trust either of you that this boy is who you claim him to be? You must understand my hesitation."

Eli knew that Annalu wanted him to remain quiet. It was pretty obvious she wanted to handle the conversation. One thing about Eli, however, was that whenever he felt he had to do something then he was going to do it. Lord Hussayn was talking a lot of nonsense just to stall time, and it was clear to Eli.

"If I may," Eli finally spoke. "I lived in the North all my life. My family managed to stay in hiding for years after the invasion thanks to a wonderful man named Thaddeus Thorns. He was the one who kept Prince Antonius Bellemore safe—treated him like his own son, too. I have the pleasure of being Antonius' best friend. We hunted together, lived in the poorest area of Terrane, and we would scrape by in the wintertime. Antonius goes by another name—Malakai Thorns. We went through a great ordeal to reach the South after the death of our parents. Well, my father was killed, but my mother and brother remain captured in Saint Salvusburg. If you care for your fellow shapeshifters as much as you claim to, then you will lend your army to fight alongside us. With the Elder Guardians' defeat, we can restore what Baskaria once was and save my family."

Lord Hussayn stood there as he took a moment to consider what Eli had said. During that time, Eli just prayed that his speech would show that there was some good in this old man to stay on the right side of history and help take down the Elder Guardians.

"Very well." Lord Hussayn said, and Eli felt relief flood through him. "But I would like to travel to Avala in the coming days and meet with the Bellemores myself. Surely that could be arranged?"

Annalu nodded. "Consider it done."

"Marvelous!" Lord Hussayn said. "In that case, why don't you two join us tonight for a festive celebration? After all, there is so much for this young shapeshifter to learn. You were part of the Vakloon tribe, am I correct?"

"Yes. I am," Eli responded with pride.

"Well, it is an honor to see one of my grandsons survive the brutal killing sprees up in the mountains of Aeris. Would you care to accompany your grandfather for some tea?"

Eli felt his mouth drop open in shock at the revelation. He turned to face Annalu, who looked equally surprised at the news that this man was Eli's grandfather. Eli swallowed, suddenly feeling like, rather than coming to a nice conclusion, things had only just begun.

# 10
## Hearts of Wolves

**ELI**

There was a storm brewing as night ascended. Annalu suggested it would be best that they spend the night in Veilios until the storm cleared in the morning. Eli was still slightly in shock and decided to use the time to get as much information as he could. In this case, he was on his way to the Great Hall to meet with Lord Hussayn and his extended family.

Annalu requested that she be left alone so she could recharge her energy for tomorrow. Eli understood that she was going to have to use every ounce of her energy to conjure the portal tomorrow with her coven, and he didn't want to do anything that would jeopardize that.

While strolling the hallway, Eli took it upon himself to contact Malakai with his glass communicator. The connection was pending for a few seconds before Malakai finally answered.

"Eli, where are you?" Malakai asked, his voice was worrisome. "They told me you should've been back by now. Is everything okay over there?"

"Relax, Kai. Everything is fine. I managed to persuade Lord Hussayn to lend his army. But there's a catch…"

"There always seems to be one," Malakai said, rolling his eyes through his holographic projector. "What does he want in exchange?"

"He wants to meet with you and your grandmother in Avala. Since you couldn't come to him, he doesn't mind going over to you."

"I don't see why that should be an issue."

"Yeah, well, considering you got the Eckwood brothers' crazy ex-girlfriend lurking in the shadows, I'm worried she might make you look bad if she tries anything."

"Don't remind me about that. I'm concerned about Kelton. First, he was reminded of his grandmother's passing, then his father joined the Elder Guardians, and now he's found out that Seraphina may still be alive. It's been very stressful here."

Eli wanted to ask a big question that he'd been thinking about since the meeting in the infirmary. However, he wasn't sure if he wanted to spike Malakai's insecurities higher than they already were. It seemed to be odd that Seraphina was out there, but it was also odd how Kelton reacted to the news. He worried about what actions Kelton might take if Seraphina was truly alive, and how those actions might affect his relationship with Malakai.

Strategically, Eli decided to step back from his poorly timed questions and change the subject.

"Just talk to Kelton when he's cooled down. He seems like a mellow, easy guy to talk to. Don't overthink it. But, back to the bigger issue at hand…"

"By the Gods, there's more?" Malakai asked.

"Dude, I'm sorry! I have to tell someone because I'm freaking the heck out myself. But apparently, I'm related to Lord Hussayn."

"Hold up, I think I misheard you for a second there. Did you say *related*? Like, you guys share the same bloodline?"

"Yes! I told him I was part of the Vakloon tribe, and I guess that rang a bell in his head. He called me his grandson. I'm heading over to him and my supposed extended family right now. I'm nervous, Kai."

"Woah. I'm actually shocked. Who would've thought you and I both came from royalty?"

"That's what I'm saying!" Eli exclaimed. "We were really out here living in the forest, holding on for dear life, when we could've been living lavishly. I think we were robbed of a perfect life."

"And your parents never told you none of this before?" Malakai asked, puzzled. "I mean, I get why my parents never said anything, but why didn't yours? I would've imagined if they knew you guys were trapped in the North, then Lord Hussayn would do everything in his power to save his family."

Eli shrugged. "I'm not sure what exactly is going on, but I intend to find out tonight."

"Well, I wish you the best of luck. Keep me posted!"

"Will do."

The connection was cut off.

Eli continued until he reached the doors to the Great Hall. Two guards waited for his arrival as they opened the doors for him.

Entering, Eli was welcomed by a vast wooden table that spread out about twenty feet long. Countless people sat on both sides of the table, serving themselves plates of food from the trays in the middle.

There on the ceiling, loads of green light bulbs floated in midair, with no sort of wires that activated them. It was magical, to say the least.

"Ah, look who finally decided to show up!" said Lord Hussayn, who shouted from across the table as he sat at the far end. There was an empty seat next to him that he patted down. "Come along, child. Come sit next to me."

Eli slowly walked over to him, nerves tingling. A few people along the table waved as he passed them, seemingly excited to see him.

Setting himself down on the chair, one of the servants placed a plate in front of Eli along with some silverware. Eli wasn't sure whether he should reach for some food now or wait.

"So, how are you liking Waerboard Hold?" Lord Hussayn asked.

"Um, I'm not sure. It's the second castle that I've been to in my whole life. It's very... *metallic*." Eli wasn't sure how else to describe it. "I, uh, like those enchanted green light bulbs you got floating around."

"Those are emerald crystals. They're very hard to come by these days. Most of the emeralds that exist on this planet are here in Waerboard Hold. The energy from them allows for inspiration, balance, patience, and wisdom. Once you accept that energy, you will start to feel a shift within yourself." Lord Hussayn placed the palm of his hand on Eli's chest. "That acceptance starts from the heart."

Eli was unsure of how to respond, so he just reached out to start loading his plate with food. At least eating would give him something to do rather than sit there awkwardly.

On Lord Hussayn's left-hand side, there was an older woman around the lord's age. She was staring at Eli. It was a bit off-putting, but he tried to ignore her while he moved to start eating his food. The peace did not last, sadly, when the woman reached in and jabbed her knife into the table, blocking Eli's spoon from the plate.

"Where are your mother and father?" the woman asked.

"I—I'm sorry. Who are you?" Eli responded.

"*Your grandmother.*" The woman responded with sass. "You're not Orian. I'm going to assume that Darren and Stella had a second child."

"No, ma'am. Orian is my older brother. I am the youngest."

"Do you have any other siblings besides Orian?"

"Not that I am aware of. Just us two." Eli raised his eyebrows and tilted his head. Something did not seem right. "Did you not know that I existed?"

Lord Hussayn intervened. "Your mother and father cut contact with us some odd years ago. We did not approve of their marriage, but we still would visit and see Orian before they moved away. I assumed they moved to Aeris with some of the other shapeshifters. We had no idea of your existence, unfortunately."

"Which one of my parents is related to you two?" Eli looked in both his grandparents' directions.

"Stella was our daughter," the grandmother answered. "We were not too fond of your father, Darren. He used to get Stella and himself into a lot of trouble. He participated in some sketchy business for Reju Tufte when he was younger. We did not want Stella in any part of that. But, of course, she did it anyway. She was in love with the man, and we couldn't change her mind."

Eli released the spoon from his hand and leaned forward from his chair to better look at his grandmother. "Whatever your view is of my father, keep it to yourself. He was a great man and an amazing father to Orian and me. He did the best he could for us and showed loyalty to those who kept us safe. You dare speak of my parents with such hate when none of you bothered to come to search for us when the barrier was set in place. You should be ashamed of yourself." Eli turned to everyone at the table. "*All of you.*"

Eli stood from his chair, filled his plate with food, and began walking out of the Great Hall.

Turning back to everyone one last time, Eli said, "And these emerald crystals clearly don't do anything. Inspiration, balance, patience, and wisdom? My ass."

Eli left the Great Hall, not caring about the scene he made.

* * *

Rain was pouring down heavily as Eli roamed the city. He wore a hood to cover his head, which did little to nothing to protect him from the rain. Anger was consuming him, and he did not know how to handle himself. He knew most of his anger stemmed from the reality that his father was dead and his mother and Orian were held captive in Saint Salvusburg. To hear anyone, especially those supposedly part of his family, speak so poorly of them irritated Eli.

In his pocket, Eli felt his communicator vibrate. He pulled it out and saw that Malakai was trying to get a hold of him. Eli answered the call.

"Hey! How's everything over there?" Malakai asked.

"I don't know. I'm pissed. I think I might have blown our chance at getting Lord Hussayn's army."

"Oh no. What happened?"

"They were being disrespectful about my parents. My grandmother told me that she did not approve of my parents being together and that my father used to help Reju Tufte with stuff that I didn't know about. There was a reason my parents lost contact with them, and now I understand why."

"Hey, it's okay. If they really cared, they would've never said that stuff to you. I'm sorry you had to hear all that crap."

"You're not mad at me for blowing everything?" Eli asked.

Malakai chuckled. "Dude, no. I could never be mad at you for speaking your mind. You did the right thing. If they are as honorable as they present themselves to be, they'll apologize to you and stand on the right side of history by fighting alongside us."

Eli groaned. "There was so much more I wanted to tell him, but I knew it wouldn't have changed how they felt about my parents. Especially my father. I just want to get back to Avala and forget I even met them."

"How bad is the storm?" asked Malakai.

A thunderbolt struck within the night sky. Malakai was quick to realize he had gotten his answer by the look on his holographic face.

"I'm just going to go back to Waerboard Hold and hide in the guestroom for the remainder of the night," said Eli.

"Don't get comfortable. The reason I called you was because I had a feeling something might happen, so I have a hovercraft coming to get you and Annalu."

Eli was thankful. "Bless you, Kai. You are a lifesaver."

"Always here to help. Okay, I'll call you when the hovercraft arrives. Bye!"

The connection was cut off.

Eli shifted into his wolf form, grabbed his clothes with his mouth, and sprinted for Waerboard Hold.

* * *

Annalu wasn't pleased with Eli after he broke the news to her. He tried not to bother her, but there was no way to explain why a hovercraft was coming to pick them up without explaining what had happened at the Great Hall.

They were waiting up by the rooftop where flying vehicles came and went, trying to avoid the pouring rain.

Annalu was standing there, arms crossed, as she shook her head

87

repeatedly. "And how long did Prince Antonius say before they got here?"

Eli shrugged. "Not sure. He said he would call when they were close by."

"Wonderful."

A group of guards arrived on the rooftop. Behind them, Lord Hussayn followed. Eli frowned, expecting the worst.

"I would like to speak to my grandson for a moment if you don't mind," Lord Hussayn told Annalu. She granted them their privacy and walked towards the guards. Lord Hussayn then turned to Eli with a nervous smile. "I'm sorry for how Wanda spoke to you at dinner. It was never my intention to cause an argument."

"I appreciate the apology," Eli said, his voice battling between peace and anger. "I'm assuming my outburst has cost us your help fighting with the Resistance, huh?"

Lord Hussayn burst into laughter. "Not by a long shot. I will gladly lend my army. Anyone who is a threat to my people is an automatic enemy to me. But I still hold firm on my request to see the Grand Empress Dowager and the Lost Prince. Your grandmother will not be in attendance, I'll make sure of it." Lord Hussayn winked, followed by a smirk.

A smile creased Eli's face. He tried desperately not to, but a part of him felt seen and heard by his newfound grandfather.

"Why don't you fly back with us to Avala? We are expecting a hovercraft any minute," Eli recommended.

"My dear boy, why do you think I have my guards here with me? Surely you don't think I brought them here just to speak to you and the witch." Lord Hussayn patted Eli on the shoulder. "Speaking of guards, I have sent some of my best warriors to travel beyond the barrier and rescue your mother and brother. We will hope for the best and pray to the Gods that they do not get caught in their mission."

Hope consumed Eli's heart as he heard those words come out of his grandfather's mouth. There was a chance his mother and brother would be saved, and he was thrilled to hear that something was finally getting done about it.

A Glax hovercraft hovered over the group as it slowly parked on the rooftop.

# 11
## Box Around the Sun

**MALAKAI**

After so much of his life spent with Eli at his side, Malakai often found that their time apart left him feeling anxious and uncertain. Before everything happened, Eli was always a constant shoulder he could lean on, a steady presence to soothe his nerves. So maybe he had been a bit rash by telling Eli to come back so soon after things went south with his grandfather, but he couldn't stop the wave of excitement that washed over him when he saw Eli's hovercraft land.

Malakai was surprised to see Lord Hussayn by his side as well, considering everything that had happened. Eli, looking frazzled and tired, waved away Malakai's questions and promised they would talk in the morning. Several hours later, Malakai was lying in bed, wide awake, unable to go to sleep.

Kelton decided to sleep in his room for the night rather than Malakai's, which left Malakai feeling all sorts of emotions. A sinister mix of paranoia and jealousy was churning in his stomach. Did this have something to do with Seraphina's return? Despite his best efforts, his mind ran wild with awful possibilities. This anxiety was the very reason Malakai had been so reluctant to say those three words to Kelton. It was like opening a door to chaos. Malakai had read enough books to know where relationships could go wrong.

Kelton was his first for everything, and Malakai was terrified of getting his heart broken. It almost felt like he was a box spinning in orbit around the sun, and he had no way of seeing what was going on in that ball of fire while trapped inside.

As the thoughts continued to wreak havoc in his head, Malakai rolled out of bed and got to his feet. There was no use just lying around if he wasn't going to be able to sleep anyway. He itched to get more information, find answers to his questions, but since they were on lockdown, his options were pretty limited. He was left with really only one avenue: Demetri. He'd been there when Seraphina appeared again. Maybe he knew more than he was letting on, and Malakai wanted to be there when he woke up.

When he entered the infirmary, Malakai was met by Rahaf and Silianna, who were sitting down next to Demetri's bedside. Demetri had yet to wake up from his coma, unfortunately.

A Healer injected a serum into Demetri's arm and cleaned him up afterward.

"How long do you think he will be like this?" Malakai asked the Healer.

"We don't have an estimate, I'm afraid," the Healer admitted. "But ideally, it would be later tonight if everything goes smoothly. We shall see."

"Thank you."

The Healer excused herself as she left the group alone.

"How are you two doing?" Malakai asked the girls, settling in beside them.

"It could be better," Silianna murmured. "Rahaf is leaving me after today."

"Oh, that's right! I completely forgot about that." Malakai looked to Rahaf and said, "Are you excited to be traveling to Aeris? I'm sure Prince Theodosis will be ecstatic to see you."

"Not as ecstatic as I will be. I miss him so much. I cannot wait to feel his arms wrapped around me," Rahaf said, looking wistful. "By the Gods, I'm ready. All my stuff is packed. I love you guys so much, but I think four months is more than enough time being around you. I'm ready to see Theo."

Silianna started to get emotional. She reached over and hugged Rahaf. "I don't want you to go!" she cried. "I'm going to be left with all these boys and their problems."

Malakai's mouth fell open. "Hey! I don't think we're *that* bad. Well, for the most part."

"No. You're manageable," said Silianna, clearing the tears from her face. She then pointed at Demetri and said, "It's this dumbass and Kelton that I'm more concerned about. Rahaf would set them in their place quickly. With her gone, it'll be a nightmare."

The doors to the infirmary swung open.

The three looked at the same time to see Kelton walking in. His clothes were all dirty, and his hair was a mess.

Malakai got to his feet, startled.

"What happened to you?" Rahaf asked, disgusted.

"I was training by myself. Needed some time to think," Kelton answered.

"Think about what?" Silianna said.

Kelton looked at Malakai as he said, "Can I have a moment with you? We should talk."

Malakai's heart sank to his stomach. Those words never sounded good in the same sentence, especially when Kelton said it in a serious tone.

Reluctantly, Malakai exited the infirmary. Kelton closed the door behind them.

"What do you want to talk about?" Malakai questioned.

"First, I need to say how sorry I am. There was a lot that kept happening, and there was no time for me to process any of the information. With my grandmother dead, my father stepping in as the new Elder Guardian, Demetri in a coma, and now Seraphina, I can barely breathe. I feel like I'm going insane around here."

Malakai grabbed Kelton's hand and held it. He hoped the comforting touch would ease Kelton's frustration.

"I get it. I've been there. But you have to remember that you are not alone. I'm here to support you in whatever it is that you're going through. Shutting me out and leaving me in my room all alone is not the answer, Kelton."

"That's why I wanted to apologize. I've never been one to handle my emotions well. Since Seraphina, life has been different. And not in a good way. I'm just worried about ruining what we have."

There it was. Malakai knew that if he did not take this opportunity to ask the question, he would regret it for the rest of his life. He had to know what was going through Kelton's mind. He needed that confirmation.

"Do you still love her?" Malakai blurted out.

"What?" Kelton looked confused.

"Do you still love her? Seraphina. I have to know—I need to know the truth."

"I—No. I don't love her. She tore a wedge between me and my brother, faked her death, and is possibly conspiring to hurt you. Why would I love a woman like that?"

Malakai's lips pressed together. The answer helped ease some of the weight off his shoulders, and he felt the tension seep through his body. All his worries were completely alleviated, but they were settled for now.

"Was there anything else you wanted to ask me?" Kelton asked.

Malakai shook his head. "No, I would just like you to open up to me more often. And stop apologizing for everything you do."

"Sorry. It's a force of habit."

"There you go again!" Malakai playfully complained. "By the Gods, you're lucky you're cute."

"Do you want to take a shower with me?" Kelton made a flirtatious facial expression.

"As much as I would love to, I cannot. I have to meet Lord Hussayn in a bit. Go get washed up, and I'll see you after the meeting."

Kelton smiled. "I love you."

Malakai kissed Kelton. Once their lips parted, Malakai whispered, "I love you, too."

As Kelton left, Malakai decided to return to the infirmary and spend time with Rahaf and Silianna before his meeting.

* * *

The thrones at Windsor Keep were made of glass. When sat on, the thrones lit up with a gentle blue light, similar to how the Insully blades worked when activated. Malakai only ever sat on it once, which was the day the Grand Empress Dowager introduced him to the South.

His grandmother was making herself comfortable as she approached the throne and took a seat. Malakai followed her example and did the same. Those down below the steps that led to the throne had bent their knees and bowed their heads.

"Rise," the Grand Empress Dowager ordered.

Everyone rose from the ground.

Celsa entered the Throne room to present their guests. "Entering, Lord Hussayn, Ruler of Veilios. Accompanying him is his grandson, Eli-zak Vakloon."

Malakai's grandmother turned to Malakai and leaned forward from her throne. "Since when was your friend related to Lord Hussayn?" she asked, surprise coloring her words.

"Since last night," Malakai shrugged.

"Fascinating."

Lord Hussayn and Eli walked side-by-side down the aisle. Malakai and his grandmother stood up from their thrones and bowed their heads.

"It is wonderful to see you again, Lord Hussayn," said Maelena.

"Likewise, Your Imperial Highness." Lord Hussayn's eyes beamed in Malakai's direction. "My Heavens... He looks just like the late Emperor and Empress. May the Gods show mercy on their souls."

"T—Thank you?" Malakai said, unsure of himself. "It's a pleasure to finally meet you, Lord Hussayn."

"I sent my best witch and shapeshifter to meet with you in Veilios. Instead, they brought you back here. It is a surprise, though I am pleased. I trust you understand my reasoning for sending them to your domain?" the Grand Empress Dowager asked.

"Indeed. I shall lend my army to fight with you and the Resistance when the time comes. I am merely here to set my eyes upon the infamous Lost Prince and ensure that he is, in fact, alive. There have been many stories circling his existence. But as someone who is relying on the last remaining Bellemore to rule the Baskarian throne, I must see proof that he is capable of ruling. Has the Lost Prince mastered his four elements?"

Malakai gulped. Not a lot of people outside Windsor Keep knew of his dilemma. What if he learned the truth and decided Malakai was not fit to rule the Nine Lands? So far, Malakai had obtained two of the four main elements. Ground and fire. And out of those two, Malakai was most successful in fire. The element of Terrane had yet to be accomplished.

"Prince Antonius is still training," his grandmother spoke for him. "He lived in the North under a false identity for eight years. Antonius was under the impression that he was a non-elemental and could not conjure any of his four elements. But he has been doing well with his Terrane and Pyroc elements."

"Sounds promising," Lord Hussayn said, hopeful. "May I see a demonstration?"

Malakai stiffened in place.

The Grand Empress Dowager turned to Malakai and nodded her head. Malakai knew there was no way out of this. He had to show something rather than nothing.

"Here?" Malakai asked his grandmother.

"It'll be fine," she answered. "We can restore the damages as long as you don't shatter anything made of glass."

Malakai walked down the steps. Eli stepped forward as the two faced each other.

"I will be your demonstration," Eli offered. "Try not to burn my face, will you?"

"No promises," Malakai replied, petrified.

Taking a deep breath, Malakai started with fire. He chanted "*Pyroc*" as a ball of fire shot straight for Eli. Eli was able to dodge the attack and land on the floor. Malakai then placed the palms of his hands onto the floor. Chanting "*Pyroc*," fire shot through his palms, and he floated off the ground. Malakai then swung his body toward Eli and landed on top of him.

Malakai moved to use his Terrane element, although he worried about the results. There was barely any time for him to practice some more before he met with Lord Hussayn. This would either make or break him.

Chanting "*Terrane*," a pillar of rocks emerged from the ground and slithered its way towards Eli. His legs and arms were locked, with nowhere for him to escape.

Suddenly, Eli shifted into an owl and escaped from the rocks. Eli's clothes fell to the ground in the process.

Malakai gritted his teeth, trying to think of an alternative plan. He looked at his surroundings and saw a huge vase with flowers on both sides of the doorway.

Using his Terrane element once again, the vines from the flowers grew and were raised high up to the ceiling, where Eli flew. The vines wrapped around the owl and pulled him back down.

"I think I've seen enough," said Lord Hussayn.

Malakai exhaled deeply, releasing any steam in his body. The amount of energy he used to conjure those vines took a toll on him.

"Well, color me impressed. But I would like to see you use your water and air element the next time we meet. If you have any chance of taking down the Elder Guardians and proving to the Nine Lands you can rule the nation, you're going to have to prove you can master all four elements."

"Yes, sir." Malakai bowed his head.

The Grand Empress Dowager walked down the steps and stood alongside Lord Hussayn.

"While our grandsons get themselves freshened up, why don't you and I discuss how Eli is related to you? Shall we?" Maelena said. Their conversation faded as they left the Throne room.

"You did good!" Eli said after getting dressed. "You used your Terrane element with no complications. How did you do it?"

"Pressure?" Malakai suggested. "I'm probably going to need

more of it if I have any chance against DeVault and Aldothfex."

"Yeah. Well, let's get cleaned up before Rahaf and the witches leave."

Malakai chuckled. "You want to say goodbye to your 'girlfriend' before she leaves, huh?"

"Shut up," Eli said defensively. "Rahaf is *not* my girlfriend."

Malakai knew that. But he just wanted Eli to confirm that it was Rahaf he was crushing on and not someone else. *Poor Eli*, he thought.

## 12
## Eytros

**SILIANNA**

With an hour or so to spare before Rahaf's departure, Silianna took it upon herself to research the demonic box they'd found in Demetri's room. The carvings left an impression on her when Rahaf revealed that they were in the Arajibac language. With that crucial piece of information, it shouldn't be challenging for Silianna to look in the right section and get some answers.

Silianna came across an aisle that was dedicated strictly to Pyroc and the fire elementals. If there was one thing Silianna loved most about Windsor Keep's library, it was one of the most extensive keepsakes of knowledge known to Zorall.

The Grand Empress Dowager explained to Silianna and the others that there was a treaty set in place between Saint Salvusburg and Avala long ago, where Avala would store copies and ancient artifacts that would help society progress. Literary works regarding technologies, energy, elements, tales/folklore, historical landmarks, and much more resided in the library. It was the reason Silianna and Malakai figured there may be information pertaining to the Dark Dimension. However, even four months into exploring the depths of the library, she had still only scratched the surface of what it had to offer.

Luckily, within the aisle filled with tomes relating to Pyroc, Silianna was able to find an enlarged black leather-bound book titled "PYROCIAN MYTHOLOGIES" that stood on one of the higher shelves. Once she climbed the ladder and pulled the book out, Silianna made her way to one of the tables and opened it. Dust flew around her as she opened the book, making her cough.

"Alrighty, Silianna. Let's find some Dravkyn Demons."

Opening the book to the first couple of pages, Silianna was able to brush up on some well-known information regarding Pyroc.

> *The desert kingdom houses many historical landmarks dating back centuries of the Old World. Before our Creator sent an asteroid to plague fifty percent of the planet's population, civilians referred to themselves as the Thakailan tribe. They worshipped our Creator so much that they built the famous pyramid in their honor, which allowed them to generate cosmic energy to help our planet communicate with other worlds beyond ours. It is the only one to remain to this day, as the others built across the world have sunk underwater after the asteroid. The pyramid that resides in the kingdom of Pyroc is said to house many dark objects. A symbol is used to warn those whether an object is cursed or not.*

Silianna looked at the photos of multiple symbols and recognized one that was the same on the box Demetri had. She knew at that moment that the cursed object originated from Pyroc's pyramid.

Continuing to flip through countless pages, Silianna managed to come across a specific chapter dedicated to creatures that lived in the depths of the spirit realm. Silianna's heart started racing as she adjusted herself in her chair and read the material.

> *Foretold in the early days of the New World, there were special beings that referred to themselves as the "Eytros." They were first discovered in what was once*

known as "Thakail," the desert land which was later changed to "Pyroc" in honor of the God of Fire.

"Eytros," the spiritual element, was the fifth element to be created after the main four: Pyroc, Limus, Terrane, and Aeris. The Eytros elementals were able to communicate with those who had passed away; however, these rare beings went extinct slowly as the New World evolved. Legend says that Vorkalth, the son of Pyrocian, was behind the extinction. Spirits warned that once there was no one to protect the gates between the spirit and the real world, Vorkalth would return and wreak havoc on the elementals for his banishment. Those who still roam Zorall with the element of Eytros are said to be in grave danger.

Though the Dark Dimension was created to hold Vorkalth prisoner, the Gods mistakenly created a purgatory in the process for the Lost Souls who have not found peace or closure before their passing. Because of the Gods' reckless creation, their sister Goddess, Eytrosus, had no choice but to offer her gift to the mortals in hopes they would keep Vorkalth contained. These special beings were known as the Gatekeepers.

Vorkalth uncovered Eytrosus's clever tactic. To eradicate her precious elementals, Vorkalth created entities referred to as "Dravkyn Demons." These entities were designed to attack Travelers between realms. He took the Lost Souls and transformed them into these deadly creatures. Vorkalth was mostly successful in his mission, as he was the cause of the Eytros' waning numbers; now, very few remain.

The element of Eytros is rarely taught in current educational studies.

A zap caused Silianna to jolt up from her chair. There was something about the book that caused an electric shock, though she didn't understand why that was. She proceeded to walk forward, her hands shaking rapidly with uncontrollable force. Silianna started panicking.

"By the Gods," she gasped, frantic.

Suddenly, water burst through the walls and began circling her like a snake. Whispers came from all directions from where Silianna stood, echoing against the walls.

"I haven't used the spirit element today!" Silianna cried out. Though she was speaking to no one, she didn't know what else to do. Clearly, she had angered the spirits. "Please. Just give me until the full moon. I'll pick my Limus element, I swear. I just need some time."

The library faded into a grayish tone, the colors melting away from Silianna's vision. Then, within seconds, the world went pitch black.

* * *

Silianna stood in the center of what looked like it was a bedroom. The walls were painted red with dark wooden flooring to complement the style. On the red walls, there were gold stripe patterns. The style felt so familiar to Silianna, however, she could not place why.

As Silianna traced her eyes, she caught a holographic photo of Nerumi Steelhart and her cousin, Theodosis, standing next to each other when they were younger.

"Where am I?" she asked under her breath.

Suddenly, she remembered. This was Nerumi Steelhart's room—her crush from Cressmoore Academy.

Turning around, Silianna found a grown-up Nerumi standing by the door. Her beauty remained impeccable—hair pink in tones with a mixture of purple, blue, and gray by the tips. Her skin was pale, opposite to Silianna's. Nerumi had a concerned facial expression, her monolid-shaped, grayish-blue eyes wary.

"Nerumi? What's going on?" Silianna asked.

"No... You're in grave danger," Nerumi said, shaking her head. "You shouldn't be here."

"I don't understand. Do you have the element of Eytros too?"

"You're too late. They've found you."

The room fell silent. Then, in the blink of an eye, Nerumi was surrounded by Dravkyn Demons. There were about ten or so as they started to eat away at Nerumi. Screams followed, though Silianna did not dare to stick around and try to see Nerumi as she screamed, "Go! Run!"

And so, Silianna ran.

The walls to the bedroom opened like a door, leading Silianna to a field of white roses. Located a few feet away, Reju stood with a group of spirits. He held out his hand.

"Reju!" Silianna cried out.

She held her arm, desperately trying to grab onto her uncle's hand. From every step she took as she ran, the ground disappeared into oblivion behind her. Silianna refused to look back. She knew one slip-up and she would be joining the ground and disappearing, too.

"You're almost there!" Reju shouted, attempting to encourage her.

Silianna felt her breath starting to give out. She wasn't sure how much energy she had left. *Keep going*, she encouraged herself. *You have to do this!*

She grabbed Reju's hand.

Relief hummed through her body. She managed to escape the Dravkyn Demons, but she knew this safety was only temporary.

"I promise, I didn't come here on purpose," Silianna said, hoping her uncle believed him. "I was just trying to do some research on the box. And suddenly I ended up here."

"There are many things you could do to upset me, but this was merely an accident. It is okay," said Reju. His voice was strangely calm. "The text you found will not provide all the answers you seek. If you're looking for information on the box, the spirits may be able to help you."

Silianna looked behind Reju and made eye contact with one of the spirits. She was old in age, possibly in her nineties. She walked forward and held Silianna's hand.

"You have a lot of bravery in you for such a young woman," the old woman said. "By now, you know that your elements are fighting each other. Your body cannot house both, and it is a matter of time before it kills you. I'm sure you know what choice you will make by the next full moon."

Silianna nodded. "I believe I've made up my mind." She looked at her uncle and sighed. "I will release my Eytros element and continue to live my life with my water element."

"Very well," said the old woman. "In that case, we shall give you whatever information you need to help you and your friends."

Though Silianna wanted answers to the box, she felt she was not quite done with the previous topic. "If I am to release my Eytros element, who will be the Gatekeeper? Reju was the Gatekeeper before me, and Malakai is protected from the Dark Dimension now that he has one of the Eternal Elements. Won't Vorkalth escape his prison and come for Malakai?"

Reju intervened. "It's not that simple. Vorkalth would need to receive one of the Eternal Elements to do so. He can kill all the Gatekeepers he wants; it will not change the fact that one of the Eternal Elements is what stands in his way."

"Not to mention that the prince of Terrane houses the element of Eytros as well," the old woman reminded them.

"You're referring to Kelton. Aren't you?" asked Silianna. The old woman nodded in response. "Do any of you know how he's able to obtain the elements of Terrane *and* Eytros, but I cannot without it killing me?"

"He was born with it," Reju answered. "Just like I was born with it. It is rare, but some elementals can house two elements as long as they are born with them. It is why DeVault and the other Elder Guardians passed laws to kill anyone who possesses more than one element. They fear anyone born with Eytrosus' gift would get in the way of Vorkalth. Unlike Prince Kelton and me, you inherited it through me. I passed the family curse down to you."

*The family curse.*

Silianna was intrigued to know about the Beauchamp Curse for so long. It was now or never to get answers before she was unable to communicate with Reju again.

"Please, tell me about the block," she said, pleading. "I need to know."

"Very well." As Reju was getting ready to explain, a flash of images emerged from the night sky. A crescent moon pendant, a sword with wings, an anklet, and a glowing chalice. Those were the images, and Silianna only recognized two of them.

"What is that?" asked Reju.

"The pendant is the one Malakai has," Silianna said, amused. "It had the Eternal Element of Terrane. And that anklet belongs to Rahaf, which also housed the Eternal Element of Pyroc."

"So that sword and the chalice must have the last two Eternal Elements," said Reju. He looked Silianna dead in her eyes. "You must relay this message to Prince Antonius. Vorkalth knows what objects house the last two Eternal Elements. He is warning you. He knows where you are. Wake up, Silianna."

"But the Beauchamp Curse!" she cried out.

"Never mind that. Once you get rid of your Eytros element, it won't matter. You know what you must do by the next full moon. Do not hesitate when the time comes." Reju walked over to her and placed his hands on her shoulders. "And whatever you do, do not trust Prince Kelton Eckwood. Seraphina Blackworth is working alongside Vorkalth. She managed to get her hands on that box from Aldothfex Soulryth. Destroy it with fire."

Silianna was overwhelmed by the information thrown her way. She wasn't able to process it all as a bright light emerged and blinded her vision.

# 13
## This Quiet Violence

**MALAKAI**

After a long day, Malakai was feeling rather accomplished. They'd managed to convince Lord Hussayn to lend his army, and Malakai had managed to use his Terrane element in combat without any issues. He was eager to practice some more and test out the full control he had over the element, but he would have to wait. Silianna mentioned earlier that she would be going to the library to do some research about the box, and Malakai wanted to follow up with her as soon as possible in case she found anything.

Entering the library, Malakai was shocked to find Silianna lying on the floor. The chairs and table were flipped over next to her. She was mumbling something under her breath with her eyelids closed, though Malakai couldn't comprehend what she was saying.

Malakai elevated Silianna's head on his lap as he attempted to wake her. He shook her gently and called her name several times, but she did not respond. Just as Malakai was considering trying to get some help, Silianna slowly opened her eyes.

"Thank the Gods," Malakai said, thrilled for her condition. "You had me worried for a second there."

"*Mmm.* My head hurts." Silianna rubbed her head. "W—What happened?"

"You fell to the floor and passed out. I was so close to slapping you, but luckily, I no longer have to resort to that." Malakai helped Silianna up from the floor and set her down gently on one of the chairs. "Care to explain what happened? Have you been eating? Drinking lots of water?"

Silianna shook her head. There was an obvious worrisome look on her face that told Malakai everything he needed to know—she was keeping something from him. Malakai frowned. He pulled up a chair next to her and waited for an explanation.

"Okay!" Silianna shouted. "*Ugh*. I ended up in the Dark Dimension again. I thought I had it under control, but it's clear to me now that I'm far from managing it."

"So, that's what I looked like when I'm knocked out and traveling through there." Malakai chuckled. Then, his smile simmered. He realized that there was more she was withholding. "That's not the only thing you want to say, is it?"

Silianna shook her head. "There's been a lot of stuff that I've been keeping from you. I already know what your thoughts are going to be if I told you, so I figured it would be best to stay quiet."

"And now look," Malakai held Silianna's hand and comforted her. "It's okay. I've had my fair share of making stupid decisions. Now, tell me, what's been happening?"

Silianna went on to explain everything that has occurred these past few weeks. Starting from the fact that she was helping the Lost Souls find closure and peace—which Malakai already knew about—and now Vorkalth sending his Dravkyn Demons after her for helping the Lost Souls escape his domain.

The entire thing caught Malakai off guard. Of all the things he expected her to do, this wasn't one of them, but he understood why she did it. The two spent a good chunk of time together, and Silianna opened up to him about how she wanted to be a Healer. Sadly, her dreams were taken from her when her older brother, Dallec, was killed. Whatever she was doing to help the Lost Souls, it was clear she did it as a way to substitute her passion for healing.

Silianna continued telling her story, informing Malakai of the ultimatum she was given: Keep her Limus element or her spiritual element. And if she decided to keep both, it would kill her in the end.

"Are you mad at me?" asked Silianna.

Malakai shook his head. "Not in the slightest. Less mad, and more concerned. Have you decided what you plan on doing?"

"Well, I have no choice but to give up my spiritual element. My body is fighting back every time I use it. I fear I have overstayed my welcome in the Dark Dimension."

"It's probably for the best." Malakai looked around the library and caught sight of the book that belonged to the oldest vampyre. "I suppose there's no point in searching for Narkissa if you're going to give up that part of you, huh?"

Silianna gagged. "Are you insane? Have you forgotten that Kelton can travel through there, too? Regardless of whether I have the spiritual element or not, we're still finding Narkissa. Plus, she might have some information on Vorkalth if we're lucky."

Malakai took a deep breath. He knew bringing up the idea of traveling to Theuros would upset his grandmother, but it had to be done at some point. He figured he would do so after Rahaf's departure.

Luckily, he wouldn't have to worry about Silianna's safety once she released her ability.

"I'll let you know if I can convince my grandmother," Malakai told her. "There's no promise it'll work, but it's certainly worth a shot."

"I'm glad to hear it," said Silianna, an obvious weight lifted off her shoulders. "Let me know."

"I will. And you need to do the right thing and get rid of your spiritual element *pronto*. I fear by the sounds of it, you're running out of time."

Silianna pouted, but she seemed to listen to his word's crystal clear. All he could hope for was that she made the right choice.

* * *

Later that night, Malakai took it upon himself to visit Kelton in his room. He wanted to make sure that he was okay and handling everything. His only wish was that they didn't end up arguing. Despite Kelton's reassurances, Seraphina's return still had Malakai on edge.

Malakai opened the bedroom door and slipped inside, trying to be quiet if Kelton was asleep. His caution was in vain, however, as Kelton was not in his room.

Clothes were scattered all across the floor, and the room was in a general state of disarray. Almost on autopilot, Malakai walked around the room and picked up the discarded clothes, folding them and putting them on top of Kelton's dresser.

A breeze slipped through the cracks of an open window. Malakai felt the chill and walked over to close it shut. However, he stopped in his tracks as he came across a photo that wiggled in between the cracks of the window. He reached over to take a look. To his surprise, the photo was of a teenage Kelton kissing a teenage girl.

"There's no way," Malakai whispered.

Turning the photo around, there was a label "Seraphina Blackworth" and a date when they made their relationship official.

Malakai became sick at the sight of the photo. It was one thing to see Kelton with an ex and the wave of jealousy that flooded over him, but it was another to see that Malakai looked so much like Seraphina.

Demetri's voice suddenly echoed in Malakai's head. At first, he didn't pay attention to it. But the more he stared at the photo, Malakai gave in and recalled what Demetri once said to him at the Masquerade Ball.

\* \* \*

*"You look very much like someone we once knew," Demetri said. "And it irks me to know who he saw in you. Anyone with half a brain can see there's more to you than meets the eye. Unfortunately, my brother is too stupid to see that."*

*"And who is it that I remind you two of?" Malakai asked.*

*"We both seem to have found ourselves thinking of two different people. Nevertheless, I have my suspicions. You have no idea what you found yourself in for, smulder."*

Malakai gasped.

Demetri knew from the very beginning why Kelton was interested in him. Malakai didn't see it before, but he saw it now. He felt a creeping numbness start crawling across his chest, threatening to overwhelm him.

Malakai crumbled the picture and tossed it into the metallic trash bin. Tears started running down his face, his stomach tightened like a knot. There were voices in his head that came from all directions, ones from Demetri, Silianna, and Rahaf, all talking about Seraphina at one point in time. Malakai begged for the memories to stop. He didn't want to think of them anymore.

The noises got louder, and his head spun faster. Losing control, Malakai yelled and picked something up from the nightstand. He wasn't sure what it was, but he threw it across the room and heard it shatter into many pieces. The sound of shattering glass overrode the voices, and Malakai was able to focus back on reality. He looked over to see that he had destroyed a glass picture frame of him and Kelton on their first date.

"Oh no," he said under his breath.

Malakai cupped his hands and tried cleaning up the mess, desperate to undo the damage.

Another memory surfaced in his mind. This one was when he and Kelton traveled to Reju Tufte's nightclub and came across the Mirror of Gold.

* * *

*Only moments later, the glass exploded outward. The shards shot towards the two bouncers, piercing their bodies. Malakai would have met a similar fate if not for Kelton stepping in just in time and tackling him out of the way. The tinkling sound of glasses rained around their bodies.*

*Disoriented, Malakai clung onto Kelton's body on top of him, arms wrapped around his shoulders. He could feel Kelton's breathing, but couldn't tell if he had sustained any injuries.*

*"Kelton? Please tell me you are alright," Malakai said, turning his face against the side of Kelton's head.*

*"I'm fine," Kelton said quietly, giving Malakai a reassuring squeeze. "Are you okay?"*

*Kelton lifted himself from on top of Malakai, checking to see if there were any cuts on Malakai's face.*

*"I'm alright, Kelton. I am mostly worried about you. Turn around and let me see if you got hurt."*

*"I don't think that's a good idea. Let's get you out of here before anyone shows up to find out what happened."*

*Malakai stopped Kelton from moving another muscle. "Why won't you let me see? What are you hiding, Kelton?"*

*"I'm not hiding anything!" Kelton shouted, impatient and annoyed. "Malakai, we need to go. What don't you get?"*

*Malakai grabbed onto Kelton's shirt, wrapping the material tightly in his fists and using it to pull Kelton down until their faces were only inches apart.*

*"I'm the most stubborn person you're ever going to meet. I would rather get caught by those damn caedose soldiers than continue with the secrets and lies. Let. Me. See."*

*Kelton glared back, but eventually admitted defeat and slowly turned his body around as Malakai examined him. Kelton's shirt had holes and rips, though no blood or pictured wounds were visible. The glass had clearly struck him, but had not left any marks on his skin.*

*"What?" Malakai asked, confused. He touched the unmarred skin and felt Kelton shiver underneath his fingertips. "How are you not hurt?"*

*"I don't know. Like I said, I have been this way since I can remember. Please, Malakai. We have to go before they find us," Kelton begged, nodding his head up towards the ceiling where movement could be heard.*

\* \* \*

Malakai didn't know how to feel, but it was evident that Kelton was keeping more secrets than just Seraphina. The real question was whether or not Malakai had it in him at the moment to confront Kelton about any of it, but he had a feeling he would not.

# 14
## Departure

**RAHAF**

As she shut her suitcase, Rahaf was greeted by her bobcat, Aleek, who purred as he rubbed against her leg. Rahaf petted his head and scratched his ear with a smile on her face.

"I guess it's time for our next chapter, Aleek," Rahaf said excitedly.

Today was the day that she'd finally get to see the love of her life, Theodosis Steelhart, again. All her hard work would pay off once she felt his arms wrapped around him. Aside from the fact that she'll reunite with him, the instructions given to her by the Grand Empress Dowager were clear: Arrive at the rooftop no later than noon, ensure she had everything packed, and convince the Steelhart family to join the Resistance. With Theodosis by her side, it shouldn't be too difficult to accomplish.

There was a knock at the door that prompted Rahaf to stop petting Aleek. She opened it and was delighted to see Silianna standing there.

"Come to say goodbye?" suggested Rahaf.

"Not just yet!" Silianna said. She offered to assist Rahaf in carrying her belongings. "We will have a proper goodbye when we get to the rooftop. It's only fitting I get to walk my best friend down for her departure."

"Sil, I don't do well with emotions, but you're seriously going to make me cry," Rahaf said.

"Oh, I know. But it won't be a forever-goodbye. Just a, well, I-will-see-you-soon-goodbye."

Rahaf couldn't help herself. She reached in for a hug. A part of her wanted to take Silianna with her, get her away from the madness in Avala. But she knew where Silianna's heart resided. There was a mission she intended to handle, and Rahaf would be damned to get in the way of that—no matter how dangerous that mission may be.

"Have you told Malakai about your situation?" asked Rahaf.

"I did, not too long ago." Silianna rubbed her arms and ducked her head. "He found me having an episode. It's not looking good, Rahaf."

"Well, you know where I stand on the situation. But even I can tell you're evolving into a new person, which means you're willing to face challenges you never thought you would before. I have to respect that. I'm just worried that a month from now, I'm going to receive news that my best friend ended up dead, and I'll beat myself up for not doing something about it."

Silianna pouted. "You can't think like that. I'll be fine. I know what I have to do. The full moon will be here in a matter of days, and I will release my Eytros element."

"Eytros?" Rahaf repeated, confused.

"It's the name of the spiritual element. I learned about it recently." Silianna brushed over the conversation and shifted topics. "There's something more important I have to tell you about. I don't entirely trust the witches to relay the message." Rahaf nodded her head, waiting for Silianna to continue. "While I was in the Dark Dimension, there was an image of a crescent moon pendant, an anklet, a sword with wings, and a chalice. If my understanding is correct, I believe that the sword with wings might house the Eternal Element of Aeris. I don't know much about it, and I stupidly forgot to inform Malakai of this information, but I'm asking you to find it and have it brought here. I trust no one with this information other than you since you are traveling there."

Rahaf did not bother to ask further questions. She knew what she had to do. She simply told Silianna, "Okay," and kissed her on the forehead for one last goodbye.

* * *

Celsa and Eli escorted Rahaf and Silianna to the rooftop. Once they arrived, Rahaf saw that the area was packed with guards and armored centaurs. Even though she should feel excited, Rahaf's emotions were anything but that right now. The only thing on her mind was finding this sword with wings. Her friend's life depended on it, and she had to step up to the plate before the Elder Guardians got their hands on it.

In front of a circular stone gate stood Annalu and her coven. From what Rahaf was told, the gate was where the portal would be when activated.

Rahaf set her belongings down between Eli and Celsa as she adjusted her lavender dress. Aleek stood by her side, purring to soothe her frazzled nerves.

The Grand Empress Dowager arrived with Lord Hussayn by her side. She began her speech as she said, "Ladies, you'll be traveling to the Aeris kingdom today. I must remind you of the severe danger you may find yourselves in while on this journey. The North will be watching as King Keon Steelhart has yet to declare where his people stand in this political war. I want each of you to keep an eye on the sky for any suspicious activities. Saint Salvusburg and Pyroc are more likely to attack as they are closer. Do whatever you must to keep the air elementals safe—show them that they can trust us."

Maelena Bellemore paused, turning to look directly at Rahaf. "Princess Rahaf, you are closest to the Steelharts and Prince Theodosis. We are counting on you to convince them as well. Negotiate a peace treaty with them, and you all shall be greatly rewarded. Fail in your endeavors, well, I only fear the worst for the nation of Baskaria. May the Gods be with us."

"May the Gods be with us," the crowd repeated.

The witches bent their knees, bowing their heads.

Joining everyone on the rooftop was Malakai and his blue Eni. Malakai looked upset, frowning and running a hand through his messy hair. As much as she wanted to know the backstory behind it, she knew there wasn't enough time.

A few moments later, Kelton entered the rooftop with two guards escorting him. Rahaf noticed he also looked rather upset. Though it was merely speculation, Rahaf guessed Malakai and Kelton might have fought prior to their arrival.

The Grand Empress Dowager walked over to Annalu. "I'm counting on you. Be the best warrior you can for Baskaria. I hope for your swift return."

"I will not let you down, Your Imperial Highness," Annalu promised. "I will accept the consequences if I fail you."

The coven gathered around the stone gate and began chanting in a strange language. Seeing a slight opening, Rahaf took it upon herself to speak to Malakai and Kelton one last time before her departure. She debated who to speak to first since both of them were far apart from each other. However, she ultimately picked Malakai. There was something that drew her to him for a simple reason: She felt slightly guilty—guilty for taking her time for granted with him.

Malakai, or rather Antonius, was Rahaf's childhood best friend way before she met the Eckwood brothers. When she was left to believe her best friend was murdered at the hands of the Elder Guardians, it left an impact on her. *It felt like a horrible string of bad luck*, she thought. *First, Antonius, then my mother, and finally my sister.* It was never-ending.

Now that she had discovered her childhood best friend was alive and well, thanks to her mother's involvement, Rahaf wasn't sure how to process the news. She never thought in a million years she would be in this situation, and yet she was. Everything that was going wrong in her life was now changing for the better. First, she escaped her arranged marriage, then she reunited with Antonius, and now she was going to be with Theodosis again.

Considering the time she took for granted, Rahaf did feel a little better knowing she did get to spend a week with him and Eli during their trip to Centuris—even if it ended poorly with Eli's side quest. Regardless, she had fun with those two idiots, and she would do it again in a heartbeat.

"Princess Rahaf," said Malakai.

"I want to say something to you before I leave," she started, her voice a little dry. "A long time ago, you and I were best friends; close enough to say that we were brother and sister. I know you have not regained all your memories of your past, but for years, I was left to believe you were dead. I'm still in awe at the fact you're standing here in front of me. I guess what I'm trying to say is… I hope when all this madness is over, you and I can rekindle our friendship like we once had. Of course, we're grown up and have lived different lives, but that shouldn't mean anything." Rahaf sighed. "I wish you the best of luck, Malakai. You deserve so much in life for everything you've been through."

Malakai pulled Rahaf close and wrapped his arms around her. She returned the hug, feeling overwhelmed with emotion.

"Thank you, Rahaf. I hope that in time I regain my memories of our friendship. My only wish is that you understand none of that should change the fact that I do appreciate our friendship *now,* and the time we *did* get to spend together will be cherished. Right now, you should go to Theodosis. We got nothing but time, yeah?"

"I suppose so. Goodbye, Malakai."

The witches were still casting their spell, which gave Rahaf enough time to speak with Kelton. She snuck over to where he was standing, thankful for the Grand Empress Dowager's distraction.

"I'm not sure what you two are fighting about, but I have a weird feeling it has more to do with you than it does him." Rahaf shook her head, disappointed, and crossed her arms.

"I could never get past you," Kelton admitted. "I did do something stupid, and I'll have to fix my mess like usual. Just try not to worry about us too much, will you? Enjoy the reunion with Theo and forget about all the nonsense here. I love you, Rahaf. Stay safe."

Rahaf gave Kelton a farewell hug before walking back to Annalu and the witches.

Eli stood a few feet away, staring at Rahaf. She felt there was something he wanted to tell her, but he was struggling to find the right words. *By the Gods*, she thought, *this guy looks like he's going to throw up. What's wrong with him?*

A blue ball of light emerged from the stone gate, followed by a gust of wind. Rahaf's heart started to race with excitement. It was time. She grabbed her belongings and joined the coven as they formed a line. *I can't believe it; I'm finally going to—*

*BOOM!*

Cement and glass flew from all corners as Rahaf fell to the ground and covered her head.

A screeching sound roared, causing the floor to vibrate.

Slowly looking up, Rahaf was petrified to see a demonic entity with enlarged claws attacking Kelton. Malakai was nowhere to be found, nor was the Grand Empress Dowager or Lord Hussayn.

Screams were coming from the guards as they joined together to attack the creature. There was only one thing that came to mind as Rahaf observed: There was a Dravkyn Demon that managed to escape the Dark Dimension.

"My fellow coven, we don't have much time!" Annalu shouted. She pointed at the blue portal. "Enter now before it closes. We will not have this much power for seven days. Quickly!"

Rahaf began to panic. It didn't feel right to want to leave knowing that her friends were under attack. All her thoughts were cluttered, stumbling over each other to take control of her mind. The witches were jumping into the portal one at a time, giving Rahaf only a few seconds to make a final decision.

*Stay or go.*

*Stay or go.*

*Stay or—*

It no longer mattered what her choice was, because it was made for her in the end. One of the witches grabbed her hand and pulled her into the portal. With the amount of chaos and smoke that blurred her vision, Rahaf assumed she was pulling her belongings into the portal along with her.

Instead, she felt her hand close around a warm wrist and heard the sound of a startled yelp before she was pulled away.

## 15
## Aftermath

**ELI**

Before getting sucked into the portal, Eli saw the great demonic creature get shot by a device one of the guards was using. Then, Eli felt Rahaf's bobcat scratch across his leg before it jumped into the portal. Eli hissed in pain, stumbling backwards, then felt a hand close around his wrist. By the time he realized what was happening, it was too late—he was joining Rahaf and the witches as they traveled to Aeris.

They all landed on a rocky mountain with nothing but mountains and clouds visible from the great height. Eli picked himself up off the ground, dusting himself off, and recuperating the strength he had lost.

The witches were getting themselves straightened out while Rahaf knelt on the ground, staring at the area where the portal used to be as it vanished. Her back was hunched, and her eyes barely blinked. It was evident that the girl was still in shock.

"Are you alright?" Eli asked, feeling stupid. Of course, she wasn't alright, but he didn't really know what else to say.

"I just saw one of my best friends get attacked by a Dravkyn Demon," Rahaf replied, numbed.

*Shit. She's definitely in shock*, he thought. "Kelton will be alright,

Rahaf," Eli said. "The South has access to a lot of medical remedies that the North doesn't. If they can heal Demetri, they can surely heal Kelton."

Rahaf's face twisted into a nasty scowl, and she got to her feet, sticking her hands out in front of her. Fire gushed forth from her palms as she screamed. Her yell echoed all around the mountains, loud and terrifying.

"It's not just Kelton!" she hissed. Eli swore he saw fire blaze through her eyes. "Silianna is in danger, Malakai is in danger, both the Eckwood brothers are in danger, and where am I? Here, getting ready to reunite with my true love. I'm selfish! I don't deserve these friends. All the while, I mistakenly pulled Malakai's best friend into the portal, and now I have to worry about *your* safety, too."

"Princess Rahaf," Annalu interfered, attempting to calm Rahaf down. "Perhaps now is not the time to waste your energy. We have a long journey ahead of us. Once we get to Ackermere Palace, we will contact the Grand Empress Dowager and get an update about Prince Kelton and the others. You mustn't let your emotions get the best of you."

"Speaking of," Eli started, "how far are we from the palace? I thought the portal was supposed to take you all straight there."

"You aren't wrong, shapeshifter. However, when the Dravkyn Demon attacked, we all lost our focus. We are in Aeris, but not where we *need* to be."

"And there is no way for me to get back home?" asked Eli, concerned.

"I'm afraid not. You are stuck with us until we gather the strength to conjure another portal."

Eli sighed. "Are we to fly there then?"

Annalu shook her head. "Our bodies are all out of resources. We'll have to walk. If you want to be useful, you can be our guide and shift into an owl." Annalu pointed to West in their direction. "Ackermere Palace should be there."

Eli turned to Rahaf one last time. Her frustration left him wanting nothing more than to comfort her. He understood her pain, more than he cared to admit. For so long, he tried to deny his feelings for her. And now he would be forced to watch Rahaf and Theodosis be together. Eli figured that once she left that it would be easier to lose those feelings. Now that he was here with her, he knew there was zero chance of that happening. *I wish I could relive those moments with her in Centuris*, he thought.

A part of him was grateful to hold his tongue back at Windsor Keep. He nearly blurted out his feelings for her when she stood next to him on the rooftop. Perhaps the Dravkyn Demon interfering was meant to happen. Eli would've felt awkward expressing himself and then having to travel alongside her.

"If we get a move on, we should arrive at Ackermere Palace by tomorrow morning," Annalu said, examining the holographic map in her hand.

"Tomorrow morning?" Eli exclaimed. "You've got to be joking…"

"I'm afraid not. Start shifting and keep an eye on the sky. Alert us of any danger ahead. It would be much appreciated."

Eli groaned. "Whatever. Just please hold onto my clothes for me. I didn't get a chance to pack for the occasion."

Eli shifted into his owl form and took flight.

# 16
## And Then We'll Be Alright

**MALAKAI**

Malakai blinked smoke out of his eyes, stumbling forward through the destruction. All around him, he heard moans of pain and soft crying. He moved forward a few more steps, swatting the air in front of him like the action would dispel the smoke, until his foot hit something. He looked down to see Silianna, hunched over on herself and coughing harshly.

"Silianna!" Malakai said, relieved. "Are you okay?"

"No. I think I swallowed something," she said, gagging.

Malakai searched the area as he shouted, "I need some help! Please. Quickly."

One of the guards arrived and pulled Silianna away. Malakai followed them into the hallway, where Silianna was forced to sit on a bench and drink some water. *Okay*, he thought, *Silianna is safe. But what about Eli and Kelton??*

The Grand Empress Dowager appeared, using her Aeris element to blow the smoke away. As the silence set in, snow began to fall once more. His grandmother's Eni stood by her side, in its polar bear form, muzzle dripping with a black substance.

"Are you hurt?" his grandmother asked.

"I'm fine, Grandmamma. What is all that stuff?" Malakai pointed at the black liquid.

"It was a Dravkyn Demon. I think we've underestimated just how many might be lurking these halls."

With the smoke gone, Malakai was able to properly scan the area. He saw many people, but not the two he was looking for. "Where are Eli and Kelton?"

"We're not sure. We will find them. But right now, we need to get you inside and away from danger. Come." Her Imperial Highness tugged at Malakai's sleeve, though he resisted.

"I'm not going anywhere until I find Eli and Kelton!" Malakai argued.

A group of guards rushed through the hall and out onto the rooftop. Malakai took a couple of steps back. The guards circled the perimeter and found a couple of individuals lying on the floor. Malakai couldn't tell whether they were dead or unconscious.

The guards shouted at one another and worked together to help move the injured people.

Malakai's grandmother was holding him back as he leaned over to keep looking. However, it didn't take long for him to stop resisting his grandmother. One of the guards managed to find Kelton on the floor. There was dried blood on his shirt, yet no cut, like back at Terrane when that mirror exploded, and Kelton was left without a scratch. Malakai was still unsure as to how Kelton could heal, but it wasn't something he could worry about right now.

"Kelton!" Malakai yelled, pulling towards Kelton.

The Grand Empress Dowager released Malakai as he ran over to see him. There were multiple guards that worked together to help pick him up. Malakai began hyperventilating. More concern engulfed his chest as he realized that Eli was still missing.

Silianna appeared and cleared her throat. "Eli isn't here. I saw what happened, Malakai."

"What do you mean you *saw* what happened? Where is he?" Malakai asked, frantic.

"It was Rahaf. I'm not sure what happened in those final moments, but I think she accidentally dragged him into the portal.

Eli is currently in the air kingdom as we speak."

Malakai took a deep breath, trying to steady himself as his panic threatened to overwhelm him.

* * *

Malakai sat next to Kelton's bed in the infirmary. He wrung his hands nervously, glancing between the two unconscious Eckwood brothers. They had placed Kelton on an infirmary bed next to Demetri's, and looking over their still bodies, Malakai felt a wave of dread.

Entering through one of the cracked open windows, the Eni, Bluu, appeared and flew toward Malakai. She set herself down on Malakai's shoulder and began cooing.

"You enjoy hanging out there on my shoulder, huh?" Malakai asked. Bluu nodded in response. "Well, I figure at some point you're going to transform into my spirit animal. You got any idea what you'll be?" Bluu shook her head. "I wouldn't mind a bobcat like Rahaf if that's what you decide to be."

Bluu flew off his shoulder and started circling his head. From the noise she made, it was clear that a bobcat was *not* something she was looking forward to.

Malakai held out his hands and said, "Alright! I get it. You don't want to be a bobcat. I can take a hint."

Bluu made a chiming sound and then flew back out from the window.

A groaning noise alerted Malakai, and he spun around, hoping to see Kelton awake. But unfortunately, it was Demetri, using his arms to push him into a sitting position.

"By the Gods, who are you talking to?" Demetri asked, annoyed and half asleep.

"Woah…" Malakai's jaw dropped. "Y—You're actually awake!"

"Yes? Why do you sound so surprised?"

Malakai jumped off his chair and rushed over to Demetri. He looked at the holographic charts and examined his health. It seemed everything was green—good. Although, to be honest, Malakai wasn't sure he knew what he was looking for.

"I'm afraid you've been in a coma for a while," said Malakai. "Someone gave you a cursed box, and you were possessed. But it looks like you are doing much better now."

"I know who that *someone* was. I remember seeing her standing by the window when it happened. That bitch," Demetri muttered, disgusted.

"You're referring to Seraphina Blackworth, aren't you?" Malakai asked, concerned. Demetri nodded. "I was worried you would confirm it. A part of me was simply hoping it was just an illusion. I don't know how to feel about the whole ordeal."

"Why do you say that?"

"Because the second it was brought to Kelton's attention, he started to act weird. Granted, it didn't help being reminded that your grandmother passed, then seeing his brother fall into a coma, and now discovering the woman he loved was still alive."

Demetri chuckled. "You're jealous."

"I—I am *not* jealous!" Malakai said, defensive. "Why would I be jealous?"

"You said it yourself. She's the woman he loved."

"*Loved*. Not anymore. Kelton made it pretty clear the other night that he's in love with me."

Demetri fell silent. Malakai wasn't sure what part of his sentence caused him not to respond.

"Can I ask you something?" Malakai's voice softened, almost like he was whispering. He wasn't even sure he should say what he wanted to say, but the thought had been weighing heavily on his heart. "Do you think Kelton is only with me because I look like Seraphina?"

Demetri hesitated. "Do you honestly want my input?"

Before their conversation could go further, the robotic entity known as Celsa entered the room. He walked over to Malakai with a digital envelope in his hand. Malakai reached over and grabbed it.

"This is a letter sent from Annalu," Celsa explained. "It seems Eli-zak Vakloon won't be arriving anytime soon. The witches will have to gather their strength to reopen a portal, and they won't be doing so until they've successfully convinced King Keon to join the rebellion. I'm sorry to inform you of such terrible news, Prince Antonius."

The sadness Malakai felt earlier vanished as rage took over. He threw the digital device on the floor, glass scattered across.

"I do not accept that. You expect me to sit around while my best friend is stuck in the North, where they *kill* shapeshifters for sport? I refuse to wait for his return and risk him getting killed. If there is one thing I've gathered during my time in the South, it's that there is a loophole for anything. My best friend is no exception. You will relay my message to the Grand Empress Dowager and Annalu if you must. You are dismissed, Celsa."

Celsa nodded and exited the infirmary.

Malakai turned back to Demetri who was in shock. Malakai wasn't sure he'd ever seen Demetri in that way. He couldn't tell if he was scared or impressed.

"What?" Malakai spat. "Did I do something wrong?"

"N—Not at all. I just like the way you handled Celsa there. Very assertive."

"Have you not seen me assertive before?" Malakai asked, puzzled.

"You have your moments, but that was a different level of assertive. Personally, you gave off the energy of someone ready to rule the Nine Lands. You're coming into your own, *Prince Antonius.*"

Malakai rolled his eyes and headed back to Kelton's bedside. He placed his hand gently on Kelton's forehead and felt the warmth rush through his palms. Malakai desperately wanted to fix whatever it was that was happening between them. He just didn't know where to begin.

"What happened to Kelton?" Demetri asked.

"There was another attack. Rahaf and the witches were getting ready to depart when a Dravkyn Demon appeared. According to Silianna, Rahaf accidentally dragged Eli into the portal. The Dravkyn Demon then got a hit on Kelton, and he fell unconscious. A few guards were killed during the attack."

Demetri was flabbergasted by the info-dumping Malakai dropped. "Wow… Sounds like I missed quite an event. Surely I won't miss the next one."

Malakai scowled. "Leave it to you to make an emotionless comment about something serious."

"Hey, there are only a few things that I care about in this world." Demetri raised his arm and stuck his index finger out. "First, it's ensuring that my friends and Kelton are safe at all costs. I may not show it, but I do care for their well-being." Demetri then held out two fingers. "Second, it's improving my fighting skills and preparing for this war. I have a habit of not losing, and I don't plan on breaking that streak."

"And I'm assuming there is a third on your list?" Malakai said, already growing tired of Demetri.

Demetri's silence regained Malakai's attention, turning his head to look at him. Demetri's gaze was on the bedspread before him, heavy and unreadable.

"The third is you," he answered softly. "There's nothing else to say on the matter."

Malakai stood there, not knowing how to respond. Demetri was always a wild card—unsure whether he was worth trusting or not. But now he understood. Demetri didn't know how to express himself. He struggled with the concept of being nice. Yet, Malakai somehow understood that. *I just need to be patient with him*, he thought. *Demetri will have his moments*. Malakai then reminded himself that he shouldn't take anything that Demetri said to heart.

"If you want," Demetri started, "I'd be more than happy to take you to the city tonight. I think I might have a solution to getting your shapeshifter friend back. But we'd have to be sneaky about it."

Malakai snorted. "The two of us are going to visit the glass city together? That sounds like a disaster waiting to happen if you ask me."

Demetri disregarded Malakai's comment. "Couldn't be worse than the crap you got yourself into with your friend and Rahaf. So, what do you say, Lost Prince? Are you game or not?"

Malakai contemplated for a brief second. He figured there would be consequences for his actions, but temptation gave in as he finally asked, "Fine. What do you have in mind?"

# 17
## Midnight City

**MALAKAI**

It was nearly midnight, and Malakai was nervously pacing back and forth in the hallway, waiting for Demetri's arrival. He wasn't sure how tonight was going to play out, but he was desperate to get Eli back to Avala safe and sound, even if it meant putting his trust in the dark and brooding older Eckwood brother.

Demetri's plan wasn't entirely out of the realm of possibility. He simplified it for Malakai: They would sneak out of Windsor Keep, head to the city, locate an antique shop, and consult with the owner, who happened to be the father of a once-powerful witch. Demetri was certain that the old man might have information as to how they could conjure a portal. Though Malakai thought the plan may be a waste of time, he had no other options other than to wait for Annalu and her coven to return.

The sounds of footsteps caught Malakai's attention. He faced the end of the hall only to find Celsa with one of the guards. Paranoia set in as Malakai questioned what they'd ask if they saw their precious Lost Prince roaming without supervision.

"Prince Antonius!" Celsa said enthusiastically. "I'm so pleased to see you. However, I am concerned to see you out and about by yourself. Are you in need of any service?"

Malakai shook his head. "No, thank you, Celsa. I am simply taking a moment for myself. I was going to visit Kelton before bed. Was there something you wanted to inform me of?"

"Not at all! We are simply securing our nightly run through the castle and checking for any suspicious activities. Do return to your bedroom as soon as you can. We wouldn't want anything to happen to our heir to the Baskarian throne, would we?"

From behind Celsa and the guard, Malakai caught a glimpse of Demetri making his way down. However, Demetri halted and quickly hid behind one of the pillars. Malakai quickly dismissed the two and said, "I appreciate your concern, Celsa. I shall visit Kelton and then return to my room pronto. Thank you for your hard work, and I'll see you in the morning. Have a safe night."

"Likewise, Your Imperial Highness," Celsa replied.

As Celsa and the guard departed, leaving Malakai alone in the hallway, he rushed to join Demetri in hiding behind the pillar.

Demetri wore a black cloak and handed Malakai a navy blue cloak.

"We'll need to disguise ourselves," he said.

"How far is this antique shop?" Malakai said.

"Possibly ten minutes or less. It's in the same area where Celdric and Nehila go for their educational studies."

Malakai wasted no time. He placed the cloak over himself and tightened the string. Once he covered his head with the hood, the two of them headed for the fourth floor. Though he wondered why they were heading upstairs instead of down, Demetri explained that he had checked the parameters earlier after he got discharged and saw lots of security, especially in Malakai's favorite escape route to the woods.

Reaching the fourth floor, Demetri led Malakai to an exit door as they reached a balcony. There was a hovercycle waiting for them.

"How did you manage to get one of these?" Malakai asked, thrilled.

"Bought it last month on the East side of Avala," answered Demetri. He sat down on the hovercycle and turned on the engines.

"You coming on or what?"

Malakai was pleased that he'd get to ride yet another hovercycle. The last time he did, it was on his first date with Kelton. The two had strolled through the city after their dinner and came across an abandoned clock tower. At the top of the building, there was a discontinued hovercycle collecting dust. Kelton was able to get one working, and the two flew around the city at night. It was a magical experience that he'd never forget. The only thing he felt weird about at this moment was that instead of Kelton, he'd be riding Demetri.

"Try not to kill us," Malakai said.

"No promises."

As Malakai settled down and wrapped his arms around Demetri, the vehicle zoomed off the ground and flew out.

\* \* \*

In a shocking turn of events, neither of them argued while on their travels. Demetri reached the glass city and parked the vehicle in front of the antique shop.

Malakai took it upon himself to examine the area for anything out of the ordinary. Luckily, the coast was clear.

The store did not have a name, but it had unique symbols with an image of a dragon flying over it. Malakai recognized that it was the same dragon Demetri had a tattoo of on his arm. *The Rlyrum tribe*, he thought. *I would've loved to have met a dragon rider.*

When entering the antique shop, Malakai and Demetri were welcomed by an old man. Malakai presumed this was the person Demetri was referring to earlier. He was old and fragile looking, very much like the antiques that surrounded him. The boys peeled back their hoods, revealing their identity. It didn't take long for the old man to smile, showing recognition and happiness.

"I haven't seen you in a few days," the man told Demetri.

"I got myself in some trouble," Demetri replied. "Been recovering from an injury. But I was fortunate enough to have some of the best Healers help me."

"I'm glad to hear that. I'm assuming if you've come back here, then you must've made up your mind about the armor, huh?"

"There are two reasons why I returned, actually. The armor is one of them, yes. But I have some questions, my companion and I hope you can help answer."

*My companion and I.* Malakai's face flushed red. He tried to make it stop, but it was out of his control. There's something about the way Demetri introduced him that was... *Why is my body heated right now?* Malakai wondered.

The man looked Malakai up and down before saying, "And what is your name, companion?"

Malakai shook the old man's hand. "Malakai Thorns. But everyone else knows me by another name—Prince Antonius Bellemore."

"B—By the Gods..." The man bent a knee and bowed his head. "Please forgive me, Your Imperial Highness. I thought the closest I would get to coming across royalty would be Prince Demetri. I'm not one to check the news, so I was not familiar with your face. I only hear the gossip I am told by customers. It is an honor and a privilege to be standing here in front of you."

"Malakai, this is Jaeyse Caerlight," Demetri introduced them. "He's been around for a very long time."

The fragile man struggled to get up. Demetri assisted him.

Malakai smiled. "It is nice to meet you as well, Jaeyse."

"Please," Jaeyse said, holding his arms to allow the two of them to sit on some chairs. "Have a seat. I will be more than happy to get you some herbal tea."

"That won't be necessary," Malakai said.

"Speak for yourself," Demetri intervened. He looked at Jaeyse. "I would love to have some."

"Very well. I shall be right back!" Jaeyse exited the room and headed to the back.

Malakai shook his head and made eye contact with Demetri.

"What?" Demetri asked.

"You're a dickhead. You wanted to come here for some armor, didn't you?" Malakai asked.

"I—Yes. *But* I also came to ask about the portal. I swear it. I figured I could kill two birds with one stone. I should've told you. I'm sorry."

"*Hmmph.* You and your brother have been saying 'sorry' a little too much for me lately. Whatever this armor is, it better be worth the hassle."

"I will attempt to be as entertaining as possible, Your Imperial Highness," Demetri said with a smirk.

Jaeyse returned with the tray of tea. He handed Demetri a cup and placed the tray down on a glass coffee table.

"So, we've established you wanted to purchase the armor," Jaeyse started, "but we haven't covered the second reason for your return, Prince Demetri. Care to ask me the dire question?" Jaeyse settled down next to them.

"I was wondering if you know anything about conjuring portals, or whether there may be any that are still working behind closed doors," Demetri responded. "You see, Malakai's friend was sucked into a portal and we're trying to bring him back before something terrible happens. The friend is a shapeshifter and, well, needless to say, he won't make it on his own, stuck in the North."

"By the Gods," Jaeyse gasped. "I'm sorry to hear that. Unfortunately, I may be of no use. Decades ago, authorities forced all magic-folk to destroy any portals we may have had. There were laws set beyond our world. Celestial beings from across the galaxy wanted to stop those who could travel between worlds. Even though most portals we cast were only from our world, they feared one could slip up and connect to a different world. If a portal was conjured recently, then you might be facing severe consequences with the Celestial Ones. You'd best hope it slipped their radar. Otherwise, I fear for your safety."

"Trust me, it's not our safety we're concerned about," Demetri assured him. "The portal was created in hopes of gathering more alliances. We'll handle whatever 'celestial ones' come our way. But as of right now, we have bigger stakes at hand."

Jaeyse minimized his eye contact with Malakai and Demetri. Malakai could tell that the old man was withholding information. It didn't take a genius to gather that. Malakai then exchanged a look with Demetri, signaling that he had caught on to it as well. Malakai debated whether he should be the one to bring it up, but given the dire nature of their situation, there wasn't enough time to play coy.

"You're not telling us something," Malakai said.

"What gave it away?" Jaeyse asked.

"Your facial expression." Malakai stood from his chair, standing over the old man. "Please. If there is anything you can tell me, it will be greatly appreciated. There must be something you'd want in return."

"I'm afraid you cannot give me what I want, Your Imperial Highness."

"Why not?" Malakai felt defeated. "Give me a price. Is aspar what you want? I have more than I can manage. I shall pay you if that is the case."

"It's not aspar he wants," Demetri said from behind. Malakai looked back, puzzled. "If there's anything he wants in this world, it has to be his daughters. I remember what he said. It's an impossible request, I'm afraid."

Malakai understood. He gave up and returned to his seat.

"Trust me, some things are best not to be messed with," Jaeyse said to Malakai. He then faced Demetri and raised an eyebrow. "Are you still interested in the armor?" Demetri nodded in response.

The three of them headed to the back of the store. It was a little hard to get through due to all the clutter Malakai passed. But once they reached the back, Malakai was left in awe by the sight.

There was an enlarged glass case that held the beautiful gold and black armor Demetri talked about. It had spikes in certain areas and shimmered like shifting scales. The shade of gold resembled that of Rahaf's enchanted anklet.

"What is the armor made out of?" Malakai asked.

"That is made of dragon stone," Jaeyse answered. He rubbed the glass case, almost like he was mourning the fact that it would no longer be in his possession. "It is extremely rare. The material originated from those who were part of the Rlyrum tribe."

"The dragon riders?" Malakai questioned.

"Correct." Jaeyse flicked his wrist, and the glass case opened by itself. "I suppose you have a thousand aspars for me, Prince Demetri?"

Demetri stepped forward. He pulled a bag filled with coins and handed it over to Jaeyse.

"I added in some extra aspar if you feel the need to count it," said Demetri, winking at the old man.

"I believe you. I shall have it shipped to you early tomorrow morning," Jaeyse responded.

"I appreciate it."

As Demetri and Jaeyse were saying their goodbyes, Malakai took it upon himself to wander around the front of the store and look through some other artifacts. There was a peculiar bookshelf with a small silver pyramid device collecting dust. Curious, Malakai reached for it and accidentally activated the device. A mini holographic projector screen emerged, showcasing a family from what looked to be decades ago. Above the photos, there was a caption that read "The Caerlight Tree."

Malakai touched a button on the device. The hologram swiped to the following photo. He kept swiping until he came across two women, possibly in their early twenties. Behind the young ladies, there was a man with gray hair. As Malakai looked closer, he realized it was a younger version of Jaeyse with his daughters.

Malakai swiped to the following slide. This time, the screen showcased one of the daughters by a lake. However, Malakai knew better than to assume that it was an ordinary lake. In fact, he recognized the shimmering glow from the water that he had come across four months ago. That was Glisten Lake, and the young woman was the infamous Lady of Glisten Lake.

"By the Gods…" Malakai said under his breath.

"Her name was Damaris Caerlight," Jaeyse said from behind. "She vanished a long time ago. I fear she may have been killed in the North."

Malakai shook his head. "No. She's very much alive, Sir. I saw her with my own two eyes. It was four months ago when my friends and I fled Terrane and fought the Elder Guardians. If it weren't for her guidance, I would not be alive today."

Jaeyse's eyes began to water. His lips quivered, uncontrollable emotions taking control.

"I—It cannot be true," Jaeyse gasped.

"Malakai is telling the truth," Demetri said, stepping up beside Malakai. "Supposedly, she was cursed to reside in Glisten Lake for as long as Bliss Steelhart remained alive. Malakai killed the Elder Guardian, which resulted in your daughter's freedom."

"If that is true, then why has she not returned to me?!" Jaeyse asked, voice wet and uncertain.

"I'm not sure," Malakai said, saddened. "The last I saw of her, she flew off into the night."

Malakai's glass communicator rang in his pocket. Pulling it out, he saw that Silianna was trying to get in touch with him. He denied the call and resorted to messaging as he asked what was wrong. Silianna wasted no time responding and informing him that the Grand Empress Dowager had learned of Malakai's absence.

"Great," Malakai fussed.

"What is it?" asked Demetri.

"My grandmother figured out I'm not at Windsor Keep. We need to get back before she learns I'm in the city."

"Very well."

As the two were about to depart, Jaeyse begged them to wait. Malakai felt bad to leave him alone after such a reveal.

"If you can find my daughter, I will give you any information you need to reach a portal. There's one in Miracle Forest, but I know a way to sneak in without getting caught. Find Damaris, and I will help you."

Malakai straightened his posture and shook Jaeyse's hand. The agreement was set. The boys then hopped on the hovercycle and returned to Windsor Keep.

# 18
## A Fiery Friend

**MALAKAI**

Malakai managed to sneak out of Windsor Keep early in the morning to practice, but more so to burn off some steam. Of course, sneaking out was not easy for him. There were more guards than usual and extra security measures ordered by his grandmother.

Malakai had finished practicing his fire element, where he conjured a ball of fire and burned a pile of wood to a crisp. He was by the shore of the frozen lake while he practiced. Once he got the hang of it, he decided to move on to his ground element. Malakai was well aware he had to practice more in that department than in fire. He wasn't sure how he accomplished his performance in front of Lord Hussayn recently, but he did, and he wanted to do it again.

Although fire came naturally to Malakai, he hoped the same could be said once he got the elements of Aeris and Limus, but judging by how his Terrane element was going, the outlook didn't look so great.

Without much progress, Malakai turned his attention towards the metallic bow leaning against a nearby rock. He always had more success with physical training, but before he could reach for it, Bluu flew in a quick circle around his head. Malakai was confused by what she was trying to convey to him.

"What's the matter?" he asked.

Bluu used her tiny fiery arms to showcase something growing. Then, she used her arms to pretend like she was shooting an arrow.

"You want me to shoot something while moving?" Malakai questioned, unsure.

Bluu cooed and flew around in the air, giddy.

"Alright," Malakai said.

Closing his eyes, Malakai focused on the vibration from underneath the ground. He softly chanted "*Terrane*" numerous times. Eyes still closed, he imagined roots from underneath the ground wrapping themselves around the enlarged rocks nearby.

Looking up, Malakai saw three six-foot pillars made of ground roots. On top, some rocks resembled target practice for him.

"*Woah*," Malakai gasped. A smile creased across his face. "I—I actually did it again."

Bluu flew over to the metallic arrows and circled them.

Malakai walked over, grabbed the bag of arrows, and strapped it onto his back. Once adjusted, he picked up his bow and pulled an arrow from his bag. As he pulled the string, Bluu quickly intervened, and she blew on the tip of the arrow. Malakai was confused, but then he saw what she was trying to have him do. *She wants me to use my Pyroc element to light up the arrow*, he assumed.

"*Pyroc*," Malakai chanted. Suddenly, the tip of his finger enflamed the arrow. His eyes widened, and he looked to Bluu. "Nice on! We did it, Bluu."

Malakai aimed the tip towards the rock farthest to the left. Then, he released the arrow. He watched as the rock exploded into tiny pieces. Malakai stood there, astonished.

"H—How was I able to do that?" he questioned.

He had never seen a Pyroc elemental do something so unique before.

There was an applause that rang out from behind Malakai. He slowly turned, only to be shocked by the appearance of his grandmother, Maelena, and Celsa. Neither looked mad, but rather amused.

"Grandmamma," Malakai said.

"Well, it's no secret that I've known about your little 'getaway' for quite some time. I typically am not one to worry as long as you have one of the Eckwood brothers to keep an eye on you, but considering their recent ailments, I figured I'd come along with Celsa to see what it is you tend to do out here all alone."

There went Malakai, thinking he was clever enough not to get caught. There was no point trying to talk his way around this one, he'd been caught red-handed.

"It's the only place I can go to clear my head," Malakai replied. He examined the white woods and sighed. "It helps me to forget about my problems back at Windsor Keep."

"I understand." Maelena walked over to Malakai and examined his creation with the pillars and the rocks. "I am pleased to see you are doing marvelously in your Terrane element. Surely with your Eni's assistance, she has helped you improve along the way."

"Her name is Bluu," Malakai corrected.

"You've given her a name?" "Is there something wrong with her name?" he questioned.

"Not at all."

Bluu flew toward Malakai and sat on his head. She occupied herself by playing with Malakai's hair. Malakai couldn't help himself as he laughed. The feeling was ticklish. He was surprised that even though her tiny, fiery hands were touching his hair, his hair did not light up into flames.

"Do you remember what I told you about naming your Eni?" Maelena asked.

Malakai recalled what she was referring to: Once he and Bluu bonded, she would transform into his spirit animal. His grandmother's Eni was a polar bear, and Rahaf's was a bobcat. The first step to reaching that goal was to give his Eni a proper name—which is exactly what Malakai did. *That's the beauty of the Lustris element,* he thought. *Even though I still have no clue what a Lustris element is.*

"Grandmamma. Is it weird to ask you how many elements I was born with?" Malakai said. "I understand that the Bellemores can obtain all four: Terrane, Pyroc, Limus, and Aeris. However, I can't help but question how you and I can have a Lustris element as well. I've gathered why I had that spiritual ability—because of Vorkalth's curse when I was an infant. It would mean I can hold six elements. But to learn of this Lustris element... Has that even been done before?"

Maelena cleared her throat. "I was so sure you would have five elements before your birth. I saw your charts when Farrah did her weekly check-ups, and I knew you would inherit a rare element that only I and three others in the Bellemore bloodline have managed to achieve." She paused. There was hesitation to continue speaking.

"When I learned of the Shadow Lord's temporary escape from the Dark Dimension, I was fearful for your safety. The Great Warlock, Wulissek Noire, may have sacrificed himself to send Vorkalth back, but he wasn't able to stop him from bestowing a curse on you. Six elements were alarming. No one has ever had more than five throughout history. Stephanus, Farrah, and I collectively agreed that the best way to protect you was to locate the Eternal Elements."

"Why did you have Annalu take away my elements? It was bad enough that she took my memories, but to take my elements away too... It was torture during my teen years. You couldn't have at least left me one?"

Maelena shook her head. "We all have to make sacrifices in life for a better outcome. Annalu did not take away your elements. She simply suppressed them. To reawaken them, you need the Eternal Elements. Not only did it protect you from the spiritual element, but it would give you what was hidden in return. I did what was best for you. And considering that you're here now, alive and well, I would do it again in a heartbeat."

Malakai held his tongue. He felt the rush of anger getting the best of him. He decided to take a moment to collect his thoughts before engaging with his grandmother.

"So, what can you tell me about the Enis and the Lustris element that I don't already know?" he asked, diverting from the previous topic.

"Very well." Maelena signaled Celsa to come forward. Celsa uses his robotic eyes to create a holographic image of the universe. "Everyone knows of the four Gods, but little is ever talked about when it comes to the Goddesses. There were two who presented themselves to the mortals—Eytrosus and Lustrisqull. They were angels crafted by our Creator to represent two types of spiritualities: Death and Guidance. Eytrosus is the Goddess of Death, and Lustrisqull is the Goddess of Guidance.

"In terms of Lustrisqull, her ultimate goal was to allow a mortal and an Eni to bind each other for guidance and protection. Both of these Goddesses were selective of who could possess their elemental gifts. Lustrisqull, rather than selecting specific mortals, created Enis. Those tiny creatures would be the ones to choose their owner. Once they are attached, the Eni would transform into the embodiment of one's true soul—a spirit animal. And with that, they provide guidance and protection. It is why you see your friend, Princess Rahaf, at every corner with her bobcat. He protects her."

Malakai gently grabbed Bluu from his hair and held her in the palm of her hand. He smiled as he wondered what his spirit animal would be. Whatever it was, it would reflect his soul.

Bluu jumped off Malakai's hands and started flying around, playing with the snow as it fell from the sky.

"So, I assume I have the element of Eytros and Lustris?" Malakai asked.

"Indeed. The older Eckwood brother, Demetri, informed me of your test results the day he saved you at Castle Caestshire. You had six different colors. Each one represents the six elements you have."

Demetri.

Hearing his name brought a weird feeling to Malakai's stomach. He'd tried to forget last night in the city. For the most part, it had been working—until now.

Malakai glared and said, "Grandmamma, do you trust Demetri Eckwood? I mean, considering everything that has happened thus far?"

His grandmother chuckled. "My dear boy, I trust Demetri more than I trust my guards. There is so much you do not know about him. Unfortunately, it is not my story to tell. But from what I've learned from him, the man does care for your well-being. Under that dark façade, he portrays himself there is a gentleman inside. Just give it some time." Malakai's grandmother winked and kissed him on the cheek. "Enough chitchatting. I'll return to Windsor Keep and leave you to your practice."

Curiosity swirled through Malakai's head. Both of them had had a private conversation, and he wished to know what it was. *Why do I care so much?* Malakai groaned. *What is it about Demetri Eckwood that makes me so... confused?*

## 19
## House of Steelhart

**RAHAF**

The kingdom of Aeris was located high up in the mountains. The altitude was different from below, which caused Rahaf to have a couple of nosebleeds during her travel. Luckily, she had finally adjusted to the change as of about half an hour ago.

Eli was flying in his owl form, scouting the area, while Rahaf held onto his clothes. She couldn't help but find it humorous that Eli had to get naked every time he shifted, and she'd be lying if she said she hadn't taken a peek or two at his shirtless form and enjoyed what she saw. There was surely a tiny bit of guilt, but she rationalized it was almost impossible not to see, given how often Eli shifted forms.

Annalu was leading the group when Eli came flying toward them. He landed on the surface as Rahaf tossed the folded clothes in his direction, avoiding any contact with his unclothed body.

"Are we close by?" asked Annalu.

"Ten minutes and you'll be able to see the gates to the city," Eli answered, dressing himself quickly.

"Good. Then let's keep moving forward."

As the group continued, Rahaf found herself walking next to Eli. He was quiet, but given the facial expression he had, it was clear there was something on his mind. Rahaf was curious to know what he was thinking, but she ultimately held back from asking anything.

*Theodosis.*

Yes, that's exactly what Rahaf needed to focus on. Ackermere Palace was in the far East of the city. She knew it would be another hour before they could reach it. Regardless, she was eager to see Theodosis, to feel his arms around her again, to hear him breathe, and to smell the fresh scent of cherry blossom from his hair.

Yes, she was looking forward to seeing Theodosis again. Whatever thoughts she may have had for Eli, it wouldn't matter. *I'm just missing the feeling of being with someone*, she convinced herself. *Once I see Theodosis, it'll be back to normal.*

* * *

The city's gates were made of titanium. Rahaf observed the material as she and the group arrived. Possibly twenty feet tall, the bars had fancy curves and decorations, giving the kingdom of Aeris an extravagant air. Guarding the gates was a group of caedose soldiers; however, their outfits were very different from what Rahaf remembered. They used to have white suits with blue lights that beamed throughout. Now, the suits were black with white lights beaming. *Something is not right here*, she thought. *Have the rulers officially cut ties with Elder Guardians and opted for their own version of authorities?*

"We're here to speak with King Keon and Queen Seona," Annalu stated, head held high. " My coven and I have traveled from Avala to negotiate a peace treaty."

The guards consulted with each other. One of them used their communication device to contact someone, nodding along to the information he was given. Then, the guard held up a thumbs-up to signal for the gates to open.

Rahaf felt a sense of calmness ensue as Annalu led them into the city. Four caedose soldiers followed behind, keeping a close eye on them.

"I'm freaking out right now," Eli whispered.

"Just relax," Rahaf responded. "We can't show them any sign of weakness."

"That's easy for you to say. I'm a shapeshifter in a specific area

143

where we're killed for sport. Relaxing is *not* an option for me."

"I hate to break it to you, but you don't have much of a choice. Besides, you're surrounded by twelve witches. You're not the only one at risk." Rahaf looked at Aleek, who was glued to her side every step of the way. "Even Aleek is a threat based on his supernatural existence. So, yes, *relax*. I know the Steelhart family. They'll give us grace."

Eli did not respond.

* * *

There were an estimated one hundred and fifty steps that led up to Ackermere Palace. It was easier for the Aeris elementals to travel, simply flying with the gush of air they conjured. But for those without the element of air? Well, Rahaf was trying to catch her breath by the twentieth step.

Ackermere Palace had a different structure compared to the other castles throughout the Nine Lands. A ten-floor square temple building with a triangular rooftop. The roof was red, along with the pillars. However, the rest of the structure was a cream color with countless windows.

Waiting at the top, King Keon and Queen Seona stood patiently. Rahaf wiped her face quickly, hoping to make a good impression. By their side was Theodosis' cousin, Nerumi Steelhart. Nerumi still had her vibrant, colored hair. The top was pink, whereas the rest was a mixture of purple, blue, and gray. However, her hair was a bit longer than Rahaf had last recalled.

"Welcome to the House of Steelhart," King Keon said, holding out his arms in a welcoming gesture. He looked directly at Annalu as he went on to say, "We've been looking forward to meeting you. I assume you are here on behalf of the Grand Empress Dowager, Maelena Bellemore?"

Annalu nodded. "Yes. We come in peace, in hopes of setting whatever feud you may have with the South aside so we can work together to restore peace across the Nine Lands."

Annalu reached inside her bag and pulled out a holographic device belonging to Maelena Bellemore. She handed it to King Keon as he activated it. There, a letter appeared. Rahaf was unable to see what was written, though she could guess it had something to do with asking for their alliance.

Once King Keon finished, he handed the device back to Annalu. "Maelena was always persuasive with her words. Nevertheless, we shall see where this goes tonight." He shifted his focus from Annalu to Rahaf and Eli. "I sure hope you all are hungry. We have quite the feast for you tonight."

Rahaf didn't care about food—she wanted to see Theodosis, but knew she would have to wait. She followed the group inside, watching as Eli eagerly moved up the stairs towards the promised feast.

\* \* \*

Aleek cleaned himself while Rahaf observed her reflection in the mirror. The room that was provided for her was luxurious—much better than what was offered to her in Avala. The flooring was made of marble, similar to what it was like for her back home in Pyroc. The walls were painted in a beige tone with black swirls and gold striped patterns.

The dress Rahaf wore was short and white, with a hint of iridescent shine. Her shoulders were covered with a puffy sleeve attached to the dress. The back of the dress was open, revealing her smooth olive skin. Rahaf completed the look with some white heels and a set of pearl earrings.

Even though she wore it constantly, Rahaf felt it was best to keep her enchanted anklet in a small purse of hers for safekeeping while in uncertain territory.

Entering the bedroom, Rahaf grinned widely at seeing Theodosis there, waiting for her.

Theodosis' black hair had grown out a bit since Rahaf last saw him, giving a shaggy sort of look. It fell teasingly over his monolid grey-blue eyes. The black and white suit he was wearing accentuated his muscular build, and Rahaf felt overwhelmed by seeing all of him in person again.

"You don't know how badly I've missed you," Theodosis said,

his voice was deep, rumbling pleasantly, a familiar rhythm that made Rahaf instantly feel at home.

Rahaf rushed over to him. The two wrapped their arms and held on tight, like they might be ripped apart again. Then, their lips locked with a kiss, and Rahaf felt relief wash over her, knowing none of her feelings for Theodosis had dulled in their time spent apart.

"I've been wanting to kiss you for so long," Rahaf said softly.

"Promise me we will never be separated again."

"I promise."

Theodosis' eyes began to water. Rahaf quickly grabbed a box of tissues that resided on top of her dresser. She used one of the tissues to clear the visible tears on Theodosis' face.

"What's the matter?" asked Rahaf.

"I was just so scared when I heard the announcement—your marriage to Quill Dorrel. I thought I had lost you forever. I wanted to come to you right away, but I was forced to remain here. A lot is going on behind the scenes that you don't know."

"It's okay, Theodosis. Demetri, Kelton, and Silianna saved me. Demetri made it his mission to get me out because you are his best friend—his brother, I dare say. Even though he's a pain in my ass, he wanted to make sure he did right by you."

"May the Gods bless him. I don't know what I would do without Demetri. Ever since the death of Dallec Beauchamp, all I had left was you and Demetri, who are close to me."

"Well, we'll never have to be separated again. It's you and me against the world. You got that?"

"Yes, my love. Us against the world."

Theodosis reached in and kissed Rahaf. This time, the kiss lasted much longer. Things started to get heated between the two, and Rahaf knew if she didn't stop things now, then neither of them would be arriving at dinner on time.

Rahaf pulled away and cleaned herself up. "Sorry, Theo. But we really should get to dinner. I don't want to give a bad impression by being late."

"I understand," Theodosis said with an embarrassed laugh. His hand remained on the side of his pants, holding onto something. "I do have to tell you… I sort of told my mother and father about us a couple of weeks ago. I think my love for you is what convinced them to give you and those witches a chance."

"You told them?" Rahaf said, panic seizing her body.

"Yes. I did. Naturally, there were some consequences for choosing to be with you. For one, I will no longer be able to rule the kingdom. But I'm okay with that. If it means I get to be with you, nothing matters. They seemed to be accepting of that."

Rahaf calmed down. He gave up the throne for her. She didn't think it was possible to love him more than she did right now. However, it did beg the question as she asked, "If you won't inherit the throne, then who will?"

"Nerumi. She was born for the throne. I feel my parents knew it, too. Considering my aunt and uncle passed away and my parents raised Nerumi as their own, it's almost like she was going to get the throne regardless of my existence. I'm okay with that."

"I love you, Theodosis. I know I've already said it, but I do. I really do."

Theodosis chuckled. "We can stand around here all day being lovey-dovey, but let's not forget that we have a dinner. It was you who wanted to make a good impression, right?" Theodosis smiled, being playful in his question. "Besides, you can catch me up on your crazy adventures afterwards. I would love to hear about the Lost Prince, too."

"Well, you might need a bottle or two of wine for the story I got for you tonight. It's a good thing I picked this dress out."

"Speaking of, where did you get that dress? You look so gorgeous in it." Theodosis purred, followed by a wink.

"One of the servants offered me a few dresses. I picked this one in the end."

"You'll definitely woo my family tonight." Theodosis held out his hand. "Shall we head out for the evening, Ms. Soulryth?"

Rahaf giggled. There was no hesitation as she grabbed his hand, and they walked out of the bedroom.

* * *

The twelve witches and Eli were already seated by the time Rahaf and Theodosis arrived. King Keon was eyeing the two heavily as Theodosis directed Rahaf to her seat. Rahaf caught sight of King Keon's observation, and all she could do was hope that he liked her enough to approve of the relationship with his son.

"I'm happy to see you and Theodosis have reunited," said King Keon. He took a bite from his plate before continuing to speak. "I feared my son would never find love. And yet, he found it during his educational years all along. Many of the Royal-Bloods tend to be concerned about their children inheriting the throne, but not my wife and me. We simply want Theodosis to be happy."

"Thank you for that, King Keon. It means a great deal and I am grateful to be here," Rahaf replied.

King Keon redirected his focus to Annalu, who was sitting at the far end of the table. "I trust very little that these news outlets have to share about the state of the world," he began, "so I'm intrigued to learn what the truth is when it comes to the South. Annalu, is it?"

Annalu collected herself. "Yes. I am the leader of my coven, and we've worked alongside the Grand Empress Dowager since before the Bellemore assassination. To get straight to the point, this 'smulder' that the Elder Guardians are making a fuss about is not true. In all reality, the one they're referring to is the Lost Prince, Antonius Bellemore. Since he returned to his grandmother, we've been gathering our alliances and building an army to take down the Elder Guardians and restore what Baskaria once was. We'd hope that you would join us, given that you chose not to partake in the Elder Guardians' reign and segregated your people to remain here in Aeris."

"Fascinating." King Keon seemed pleased. "I must say, I was wary about allowing my soldiers to fight alongside you without a Bellemore claiming the Baskarian throne. But if it is true that the Lost Prince is alive, then I will do everything in my power to ensure we take down DeVault Beauchamp and Aldothfex Soulryth. Make no mistake, my mother, Bliss Steelhart, did not speak for us during her time as an Elder Guardian. Seona and I fought religiously to stop her from making reckless laws. We could never understand how she would choose hate and violence over peace for Baskaria. We strive to bring that peace back to our world. And if the Lost Prince is the key, then who am I to deny my soldiers?"

Rahaf knew the reasoning behind Bliss's sudden shift to create horrifying laws in the North: Vorkalth.

"If I may interject," Rahaf said, "I spoke with the Lost Prince. I was there the day that he fought the Elder Guardians. He did not kill Yamina Eckwood like DeVault claimed, but he was behind the death of Bliss. You see, the Shadow Lord found a way to get inside the Elder Guardians' heads. It is why they are the way they are. He's the puppet master, and the Elder Guardians were doing his bidding. Mala—" Rahaf caught herself. "Sorry. *Prince Antonius* realized that there was nothing he could do to break the control the Shadow Lord had over them. We're unsure how they came across his compulsion, but we're aware that it is strong enough to cause great damage."

"That would explain a lot," Queen Seona chimed in. "Farrah Bellemore, Roslynda Soulryth, and I were very close. Close enough that she opened up to us about the forsaken act she performed to contact the Shadow Lord. I would imagine that the mirror somehow came into the Elder Guardian's path at one point in time. It surely would make sense why Bliss had a sudden change of heart, too."

Annalu redirected the topic back to her goal. "At the end of the day, all of this has to do with Vorkalth and his influence on our government. Once we take the remaining Elder Guardians down and have Prince Antonius reclaim his right to the Baskarian throne, we can ensure peace. All I need now is confirmation that you will lend your army so I can notify the Grand Empress Dowager, and we can dethrone the corrupt."

"You have my word," King Keon said.

Rahaf felt comfort in knowing that there would not be a conflict with Theodosis and his family. Everything was falling into place, and she knew she would finally get the happy ending she desperately deserved.

Theodosis stood up from his chair and reached into his pocket. It was the same pocket from earlier where he was touching something unknown. It wasn't until he pulled out a small black box that Rahaf figured out exactly what was about to take place. She's envisioned this moment countless times, but never did she think it would ever become a reality.

Theodosis kneeled down on one knee. He opened the box. Rahaf cupped her mouth and started to cry.

"Rahaf Soulryth," Theodosis started, his voice shaking. "Will you do me the greatest honor and marry me?"

*Yes.*

That's what she wanted to say without hesitation, but the words stuck in her mouth. She couldn't understand why. That is, until she finally looked across the table and saw the shapeshifter who had been hanging with her for the past few months. Eli-zak Vakloon. He looked so heartbroken to see the engagement ring. A part of Rahaf wanted this moment to be over with. To see Eli in that state brought a sense of guilt.

"Rahaf?" Theodosis asked.

She blinked. Rahaf wasn't sure how long it had taken since he popped the question, but she knew it would look bad if she waited any longer.

"Yes," she breathed. "I will marry you."

## 20
## Lord of Shadows

**KELTON**

The fog was heavy as Kelton attempted to walk towards an unknown destination. He knew where he was, but no matter what he tried to do, he couldn't find a way to wake up. Screams were echoing all around him, sending shivers down his spine. The Dark Dimension was an unsettling realm to be in, but over the years, Kelton had become used to it.

A part of Kelton wanted to tell Malakai the truth; however, the fear of his reaction held him back. There was always speculation that Kelton's ability to fly, heal, and gain an extensive amount of strength stemmed from the Dark Dimension. The only ones who knew the truth about this were his parents and Demetri. Kelton had successfully suppressed those urges over time, but something about meeting Malakai seemed to have reactivated that urge once more. As desperately as he tried to control it, it was only getting worse. So much so that he could not wake up from this horrific nightmare.

Screeching sounds roared from Kelton's left-hand side. He puffed his chest and clenched his jaw, expecting to prepare for a fight. *The Dravkyn Demons must be near*, he thought.

The last thing Kelton recalled, he was on his way to say his goodbyes to Rahaf. Then, a Dravkyn Demon managed to escape the

151

spirit realm and attack him. How was it possible? Kelton had a feeling he'd learn the truth momentarily.

In the distance ahead of him, a shadow-like castle was visible. It was the castle where Vorkalth resided. The Dark Dimension was his domain, so it would be fitting that the Shadow Lord would create a castle out of literal shadows.

There was a river with green liquid that led to the castle. White balls of energy were seen floating through the green river. It was at that moment that Kelton figured out this was where the screams were coming from. The Lost Souls were enduring excruciating pain in that river, and there was nothing Kelton could do. It ached his soul to want to jump in and save each and every one of them. But at what cost? He'd just end up like them if he did such a thing.

By the shore, a wooden dock resided with a small boat. Kelton took it upon himself to investigate the area. Once there, he was welcomed by an older man. He had shackles that chained him to one of the pillars. The elderly man had a long white beard, long straightened white hair, and a blue velvet robe around him. There was an aura around him that sparkled with miraculous shades of silver and gold, giving the illusion that he was magical—or perhaps he was.

"Y—You cannot be here!" the old man shouted, horrified. "I sacrificed my life to protect you and the prince years ago. Leave this place before he finds you!"

Kelton examined the old man closely. For some strange reason, he felt he recognized him. He certainly had never met him before, but Kelton swore the man looked familiar.

"Why do I know you?" Kelton asked, curious.

"You foolish boy. I am the Great Warlock, Wulissek. I am the one who sent the Shadow Lord back to the Dark Dimension in exchange for your safekeeping—along with Prince Antonius. Sacrificing my life will mean nothing to the Nine Lands if you manage to release him from his Prison World!"

*The Great Warlock.* Kelton had heard stories whispered around by the spirits who roamed outside the river freely. He was young at the time, and he didn't understand what it all meant until he was much older. Although the adults around him tried to cover up the truth regarding why the Elder Guardians did what they did to the Bellemores, the spirits did not sugarcoat the truth to Kelton. He knew much of the lore when it came to the night of Prince Antonius' birth.

"I don't know how to return to the real world," Kelton told the warlock. "You must help me find directions."

"You'd best find a way before it is too late. Riding on this boat will do you no good. I suggest—" Before the warlock could finish, his mouth appeared to be sewn together with stitches. He struggled to detach them, but it was no good.

Rising from the green river, a cloaked figure appeared and chuckled. Vorkalth had found him.

*"Pardon the interruption, but we have much work to do."* Vorkalth's voice sent chills running down Kelton's spine as a beam of bright light emerged. *"Time to wake up, my special boy!"*

Everything went quietly.

# 21
## Flickers

**MALAKAI**

The infirmary was silent while Malakai sat in a chair beside Kelton's bedside. He was occupying his time by reading a book regarding Enis and the studies researchers have done on them. As interesting as it was, his attention kept being redirected to Kelton every few moments.

Suddenly, Kelton's eyes shot open, and he began screaming. Malakai nearly fell off his chair as he stood up and rushed to Kelton's aid. Sweat was all over Kelton's face when Malakai grabbed a cool towel to dab at his forehead. Malakai reached out, snagging one of Kelton's twitching hands and holding on tight. At the contact, Kelton seemed calm, breaths beginning to even out.

"It's okay," Malakai said calmly. "I'm right here. I got you."

Kelton took a deep breath. "Malakai... I'm so sorry about everything. I feel like a broken record apologizing all the time. I don't mean to be a screw-up. I should've told you from the beginning."

Malakai chuckled. "Tell me what? What type of nightmare did you have this time?"

"It was awful." Kelton looked into Malakai's eyes, and Malakai could see something in his gaze crumble like an eroding tide. "It's Vorkalth. I've been traveling through the Dark Dimension whenever

154

I sleep. It's been going on for a while now. I thought I had it under control, but I'm not sure I do anymore. Kai, he found me. He found me, and I'm worried about what's going to happen next."

Malakai stood there, silent. He wasn't sure how to respond or what emotions to process first. Concern, sadness, or rage. Although he had suspicions that Kelton may still be traveling through the Dark Dimension, he'd hoped it wasn't true. It was foolish of him to assume such a thing. Malakai pushed away his anger for now; it wasn't productive, and because the only one he should be mad at was himself for not helping Kelton when he needed it.

Concern was his next emotion on the chopping block. There was no telling what Kelton meant by Vorkalth finding him. All he could assume was that it was something bad. He'd need to find Silianna soon and see what could be done to stop Kelton from traveling there.

Finally, sadness. Malakai couldn't help but feel a wave of emotion as he stared into Kelton's scared eyes, screaming out for help even as his lips could not form the words. Malakai wrapped his arms around Kelton and hugged him tightly. He refused to let go and felt a few tears slip down his cheeks.

"I'm so sorry," Kelton choked, clinging to Malakai.

"It's okay," Malakai replied, his voice cracking. "It's okay. We'll get through this. We can find a way to stop Vorkalth from hurting you. I promise."

"There's no way to block it. I've tried for years. There's only one way to steer clear of the Dark Dimension, and I refuse to stand in the way of that. Not while you're still in danger."

Malakai gathered quickly what Kelton was referring to—the Eternal Elements. The Eternal Elements gave Malakai protection from the Dark Dimension, but if he were to give Kelton the Eternal Element of Pyroc, then he would lose his fire element and any sort of coverage it provided. Given the fact that the Eternal Element of Terrane's protection has expired, there was only one solution.

"When we locate the next Eternal Element, I will give it to you," Malakai finally said.

Kelton looked at Malakai like he was insane. "*No.* I forbid you to do such a thing. You need to restore all four of your elements. The Bellemore bloodline must continue with all four so you can restore the Baskarian throne. I refuse to stand in the way of that."

"There is no world without you in it, Kelton. If something bad happens to you, I will never forgive myself. In dark times like these, sacrifices have to be made—including this one."

Kelton shook his head. Yet, Malakai did not care. He had already made up his mind. As long as Vorkalth remained a threat, neither of them would be safe. Luckily for Silianna, she didn't need an Eternal Element to protect herself. From what he gathered, she would release her spirit element and default back to her water element. Unfortunately, Malakai and Kelton did not have that luxury. Once Kelton was protected, Malakai would make it his mission to vanquish Vorkalth so neither he nor Kelton lived in fear once eighteen years had passed. That was how long the protection lasted, and Malakai had had enough of living with a ticking clock until a new threat came for him.

"You're still going through with your idea, aren't you?" asked Kelton, concerned.

"I've decided," Malakai answered. He overlooked all the consequences that could follow and simply smiled. "We'll just have to kill Zorall's greatest evil before he kills us. It's you and me forever."

"I love you, Malakai."

"I love you, too."

Malakai leaned forward. Both their lips locked as they shared an intense kiss. However, the moment was short-lived as Demetri entered the infirmary.

"*Awh,*" Demetri said mockingly. "Look at the two lovebirds."

Malakai groaned. "Way to kill the mood. Don't you have anything better to do?"

"Of course I do." Demetri raised a tray of food over his head. "I brought you some food. I'm sure there's enough for Kelton, too. Sorry, little brother. Wasn't expecting you to wake up so soon."

Kelton developed a puzzled look.

"Malakai," Kelton started, "could you catch me up on what I've missed? For starters, why is my brother being awfully nice to you?"

Malakai exhaled. "It's a long story."

"A long story?" Kelton questioned, worried.

"Oh, come on," Demetri chuckled. "Your Loverboy and I had a little adventure last night. You see, while you were sleeping, Malakai's shapeshifter friend got sucked into a portal with Rahaf and the witches. So, I offered to take Malakai into the city and search for answers regarding a portal."

"*Are you insane?*" Kelton said, raising his voice. "You'd be that idiotic to risk Malakai's life when Seraphina is wandering out there? She gave you a cursed box, caused Dravkyn Demons to roam the vicinity, and might have a—"

"—Relax. I would never let anything happen to our precious prince," Demetri said dismissively. "Besides, if I see Seraphina anywhere knew Malakai, I'll be sure to take care of it."

Malakai's eyes widened. He was surprised that Demetri was ready to defend Malakai from Seraphina, considering their history. There was a rush of heat that flowed through his face, causing his cheeks to redden. He had to admit, it felt nice to have Demetri be so protective of him.

"I agree. We can't let her get close to Malakai, no matter what," said Kelton. He tried to fix his posture on the bed, but he struggled tremendously. Malakai helped him adjust. "Thank you."

A part of Malakai battled whether or not to ask a dire question floating in the back of his head. Seeing Kelton awake and speaking of Seraphina, he felt the words forming on the tip of his tongue.

"Do either of you still have feelings for Seraphina Blackworth?" he asked. Instant regret and embarrassment flowed through his mind.

Demetri was quick to respond, "No."

Kelton, on the other hand, took a little longer to answer before saying, "I loved the version of her I imagined in my head. Whatever this true version of her is, I don't have an ounce of love for."

Malakai inhaled and exhaled. Calm washed over him, and although Kelton's answer wasn't as solid as Demetri's, he still felt like a large weight of insecurity had been lifted.

"I'm sorry if my strange behavior alerted you in any way," Kelton told Malakai. "There was just a lot of information happening. Including the stuff in my dreams… I needed a moment to think."

"I get it," Malakai assured him. "We'll need to work on our communication skills moving forward."

"I'd love nothing more."

Demetri grunted. Malakai was quick to take mental notes whenever he and Kelton were affectionate toward each other, and Demetri was bothered. *I'll have to address his issues in the coming days*, he told himself. *Right now, I need to focus on Eli and the portal. Then I can check the progress with Silianna's well-being. Baby steps.*

"Demetri, could you give us some privacy?" Kelton asked.

Demetri set the tray of food on the nightstand and exited the infirmary. Malakai proceeded to sit down on the chair and share some food with Kelton.

"I understand your insecurities when it came to Seraphina," Kelton started. "I hope you can understand mine when I say your little friendship with Demetri is giving me déjà vu when he stole Seraphina from me."

Malakai placed his food down and crossed his arms. "Are you implying I would do the same thing Seraphina did to you guys?"

"No, I'm not saying—"

"—Stop. I'm going to say this in the nicest way possible: Demetri and I will *never* happen. I love you. There is no competition, and I would never stoop so low as she did. What Seraphina did to both of you was not okay, and you deserved so much better."

Kelton smiled. "That's reassuring to hear. I'm sorry for implying such a thing. It won't happen again."

"See? Communication is key." Malakai stood from his chair and wiped his hands. "And stop saying sorry. By the Gods, you and Demetri are getting on my nerves with that. Nobody is perfect. We make mistakes. Let's learn from them and move forward."

Kelton nodded in agreement.

Malakai checked the time and realized it was nearly seven o'clock at night. He hadn't checked on his siblings in several hours, too distracted by his worry about Kelton.

As he was getting ready to leave, there was a sudden shift in temperature in the room. The lights flickered on and off. Then, a brush of wind passed Malakai and caused him to shiver. The infirmary became cold and hollow. Malakai only recalled one place it felt like that.

"No," he whispered.

A sinister laugh caught Malakai's attention. Turning in the direction of the sound, he found himself facing Kelton. His eyes were black, and his body floated in midair.

"He's coming," Kelton said, though it wasn't his voice.

"W—What's happening?!" Malakai questioned, petrified.

"I will burn you and the Nine Lands to the ground. The dead shall rise. There is no rest for the Nine Lands."

The doors to the infirmary made a loud banging sound. Something was trying to get in—or someone.

With a few pushes, the doors flew wide open.

Malakai fell to the floor. In the blink of an eye, everything returned to normal.

It was Demetri who was trying to push his way into the infirmary. He found Malakai lying on the ground and ran to him. Demetri checked all over his body for injuries, but there were none.

"What happened?" he asked.

"I'm not sure," Malakai admitted. "But I think I'm running out of time."

"Running out of time for what?"

Malakai swallowed heavily, regaining his bearings. When he looked past Demetri, he saw Kelton sleeping peacefully in his bed, like nothing had ever happened.

"It felt so real," Malakai said under his breath. "I don't understand."

"Malakai, you're scaring me. What happened while I was gone?"

"It was Kelton. For a split second, his eyes turned black, and he was… *flying*. I can't tell if my mind was playing tricks on me. It was almost like I was back in the Dark Dimension, but I knew it wasn't. It was real. I was *here*."

Demetri held back from speaking any further. The look on his face said it all: He knew something he didn't want Malakai to know. Instead, Demetri reassured him and escorted him back to his room without further discussion.

## 22
## She's Come Undone

**DEMETRI**

Demetri knew the truth behind Kelton's episodes. He wanted to explain it all to Malakai, but he also knew that it wasn't his story to tell. Whenever Kelton was ready to, he'd explain it to Malakai. Although it killed Demetri not to say anything, he knew Malakai would continue to push him on the subject in the days to come. All he could do was remind himself that the situation was between Kelton and Malakai.

*Don't repeat the past.*

*Don't get involved.*

*Protect the prince.*

*Protect his siblings.*

It was a simple task, and he would force himself to follow through on it no matter what the circumstances were.

Entering his room, Demetri paced back and forth while stewing in his thoughts. He knew Malakai was with Celdric and Nehila. There would be no worries about his safety as long as he stayed away from the infirmary.

Demetri desperately wanted to confide in Silianna about everything he was going through emotionally, mentally, and physically. Only she knew the truth about his feelings for Malakai.

Those feelings were ever-growing, and he wasn't sure how to stop them from getting out of control.

Unfortunately, it was late at night. He knew Silianna would be asleep at this time. *Perhaps I could bother her tomorrow*, he thought.

There was only one thing that could get his mind off all of it— Seraphina. The moment he saw her standing by that window, he knew everything that had once been was a lie.

It was pretty clear what he wanted from her: Answers.

*How did she survive? Did she fake her death? Did she love him like she said she did? Was he and Kelton just a game to her?*

If the chance came to see her again, he wasn't entirely sure what he would do, but his instinct said it would be violent. There was no mercy for the wicked. She deserved as much for what she did, for dividing him and Kelton. However, Demetri would never put the full blame on her for the conflicts he and his brother participated in. Demetri selfishly put a woman before blood. That was his choice. No one else.

Setting himself onto the edge of his bed, Demetri felt a gush of wind as the windows to his left-hand side came crashing inward, letting in a swirl of snow. Demetri, annoyed, pulled himself back and rushed to the windows, closing them. While doing so, he could hear a *swooshing* sound in the distance.

"Wow. Don't you look as delicious as ever?" said a feminine voice.

Goosebumps emerged across Demetri's arms. There was no doubt the voice belonged to none other than Seraphina Blackworth herself.

She stood at the entrance of the balcony, smiling in his direction. Still wearing her red velvet robe, Seraphina's pale skin was visible; her freckles barely noticeable since her transition into a vampyre. Those long, auburn, wavy locks of hers were perfectly intact. Seraphina was undoubtedly similar to Malakai, almost like they were twins. Aside from the fact that one was male, and one was female, along with Malakai having a tan skin complexion, they were surely identical. Demetri wondered how it was possible.

"If there's one thing that you're good at, it is poor timing." Demetri grabbed a wooden stake from under his bed and pointed the sharpened end in his direction. "Word on the street is that you're a vampyre. Do you mind if I put it to the test?"

"Ouch," Seraphina said mockingly. "Someone's a little aggressive tonight. I'd say it has to do with me, but we both know that's not true."

"Why are you here?"

Seraphina sucked her teeth. "I found myself in a bit of trouble with the vampyres. Ever since I angered off the Vampyre Queen, Narkissa, I've been on the run. There's a bounty on my head and I have nowhere else to go."

Demetri couldn't stop himself from letting out a dry laugh, bitter and heavy. "This is perfect. So, let me get this straight: You fake your death, turn into a vampyre, don't bother to say anything to anyone, flee the North, get yourself caught in some vampyre mafia drama, and you expect *me* to help you?"

"What part of that summary was funny to you?"

"All of it."

Demetri walked over to his dresser and pulled out a tiny dagger. He used it to sharpen the wooden stake, taunting Seraphina as she remained by the balcony. He was curious as to why she hadn't charged after him yet.

"You can't come in?" he asked.

"No. I'm a vampyre, remember?" she answered, face twisted into an annoyed frown.

"Ah! That's right. You bloodsuckers need to be invited in. By the Gods, this just gets better and better."

Seraphina hissed; her vampyre teeth were visible with her mouth open. Demetri wasn't fazed by her mindless threat.

"So, let's skip the chitchat and get into the nitty-gritty," said Demetri, still sharpening the stake. "Are you behind it?"

"Behind what?" Seraphina said, tilting her head to the side.

"The summoning of the Dravkyn Demons. Conveniently, they appeared around the same time you showed up."

"That wasn't me, and you know it."

"Do I? Do I know anything about you?" Demetri questioned, defensive. He gritted his teeth and shook his head, refocusing. "Then why were *you* by the window the night I got possessed? You wore the same cloak that the stranger wore when I was given the box. Don't play dumb with me, Seraphina."

"There is a lot you don't understand." Seraphina's voice darkened. "I am at risk, and I have nowhere to go."

"I'm sure the North will welcome you with open arms. After all, you're a Blackworth. Have mommy and daddy pay to keep you safe. Oh! That's right… They're under the impression that you're dead. Kelton and I had to endure harsh publicity from the media because your parents accused us of your death, and all the while you were gallivanting around with the vampyres being a whore."

"Okay. I get it," Seraphina said, waving a hand lazily through the air in a dismissive gesture. "You're upset."

"Upset? Ha! That doesn't even scratch the surface of how I feel," Demetri stomped forward, a few inches from where Seraphina stood. "Why are you here? The last thing any of us needs is you meddling in our problems. Just go back to wherever you came from. The Seraphina I knew has been gone for a long time, and I plan on keeping it that way."

Seraphina sighed. It was evident that whatever plan she had to manipulate Demetri was not working out to her advantage. Instead, she resorted to a tiny bottle in her cloak pocket. The bottle was filled with a peculiar liquid substance that looked almost like poison.

"You want to know what happened that day in the mountains?" she asked, holding out her hand with the bottle. "Take a sip of this. You can see for yourself."

Demetri shook his head. "You're crazy if you think I'm going to take a sip of that garbage. For all I know, it's some sort of poison."

Seraphina shrugged. "Then I suppose you'll never know the truth. I can see it on your face—you want answers. *How did I survive? Did I fake my death? Is my love for you true?* Blah, blah, blah. You can see what happened through my perspective—my memories."

"How?" Demetri questioned, intrigued by her offer.

"I may or may not have stolen some potions and blood from the oldest vampyre throughout the Nine Lands." Seraphina continued holding the tiny bottle in her hand. "If you're going to drink it, don't drink it all. I have a very limited amount on my hands."

Demetri took a dim view of her direction. "Please tell me the Vampyre Queen doesn't have a bounty on your head over a stupid potion."

Seraphina was unmoved by Demetri's snarky question. "You got one last chance before I leave here. I won't offer again."

Demetri held his tongue. He knew she was right. In the end, nothing she said about him was a lie. He wanted to know all those things. Closure. That's what it was.

Leaning forward, Demetri grabbed the bottle and took a tiny sip. After a few seconds, his mind started to vibrate. Seraphina grabbed the potion back from him and watched as the substance took its course. What followed next was Demetri's vision fading to black.

\* \* \*

*Seraphina Blackworth had been experimenting with an unusual liquid for quite some time. Seeking to preserve her beauty as she got older, she traveled through the City of Terrane in search of Reju Tufte. Up to this point, she had not expressed her desire to look young to any of the Eckwood brothers. As a matter of fact, she had not shared this secret with anyone.*

*Meeting Reju, Seraphina was offered the elixir of beauty with a catch. "In exchange for the elixir, I request a drop of your blood," said Reju Tufte.*

*"Why do you need my blood?" Seraphina asked.*

*"There is a particular entity on the Other Side that seems to be fond of your beauty. She is willing to provide the ingredients for the elixir in exchange for your blood."*

*"This spirit isn't going to, like, haunt me or anything if I give her my blood, is she?" Seraphina's tone did not sound a bit concerned, more curious and intrigued than anything else.*

*Reju shook his head.*

*Without further explanation, Seraphina made the deal. She did not care to know about the identity of this entity, nor did she care what her blood would be* needed for. Beauty was all that crossed her mind. No wrinkles, no aging spots, none of that.

After a few minutes, Reju was able to conjure up the elixir of beauty. The bottle was a tiny glass filled with a reddish liquid inside.

"You are to drink this at midnight under the pale moonlights," Reju instructed. "Once you do so, all your imperfections will be a memory as you awaken the following morning. Do not drink the elixir before or after midnight. And whatever you do, do not die within twenty-four hours of consuming this liquid."

"Die? Why would I die?" asked Seraphina.

"The Gods work in mysterious ways. Avoid death at all costs. Stay inside if you must. This elixir will not be your friend if you do not make it out alive before the twenty-four mark. Do you understand?"

Seraphina understood. Although, there was a slight problem. She had plans to go on a date with Kelton tomorrow. It was the day she planned to break up with him so she could be with his brother, Demetri. The plan had been set for quite some time now. No elixir would hold her from finally moving forward. Besides, the chances of something bad happening to her were slim.

Departing the club, Lé Rouge, Seraphina headed home. She waited until the clock struck midnight. Once the time came, Seraphina went out into the woods and faced the pale moonlights as she began to drink the elixir.

The liquid tasted of metal—almost like blood. It left a bad taste in her mouth, though she did not care.

Come morning, she would be a perfectly young woman forever.

"By the Gods," she prayed, practically begging as she landed on her knees, "please do not fail me. Please, let this work. For I deserve perfection."

\* \* \*

The memories faded.

Demetri found himself standing in his room once again, his vision clear as day. Seraphina remained on the balcony, looking at her red almond-shaped nails, unaware that he had returned to the present day.

"You did all that crap just to keep your beauty?" asked Demetri, not in the slightest bit shocked by her arrogance.

"Oh, please. You would've done the same. How was I supposed

to know that I would die the following day?"

"You're a disgrace," Demetri muttered.

"Come on. You know you miss me. I am the love of your life, you said so yourself. Many times…"

"You're delusional."

Seraphina squinted her eye, a suspicious frown tugging at her lips. "I wasn't your first love, was I?" Seraphina paused, examining Demetri's demeanor. "*Mmm.* Your heart jumped when I asked the question. So, it's true. You weren't in love with me because of me, huh?"

"What are you implying?" Demetri asked, feeling like he was quickly losing the upper hand in the conversation.

"Malakai looks just like me." Seraphina giggled, putting the pieces together. "Now this is rich. I should've known by the way you looked at him in the city. You and Kelton are always around him. You must've known Malakai when he was younger. Prince Antonius Bellemore."

"*Enough,*" Demetri growled

"Your blood flow is rushing. I'm going to go out on a limb here and guess that Malakai is the one you're in love with. I'm a little offended that you wanted me simply because I looked like him. But I'll let it slide." Seraphina played with her auburn hair, twirling her finger around it. "The heart wants what the heart wants, I suppose."

Demetri clenched his fist in one hand and tightened his grip on the wooden stake in another. She had one more comment before he shoved the weapon through her dead heart.

"I think it is best that you leave," Demetri said, his teeth grinding. The veins on his neck and arms were visible.

Seraphina held both her hands up in truce. "Fine. But this won't be the last time you see me. If I don't get the help I need, then I'll continue coming after you, Kelton, and Malakai. I have nothing else to lose when the world wants me gone."

Demetri charged after her, but before he could jab the stake through her heart, she vanished without a trace.

# 23
## Resemblance

**MALAKAI**

Malakai had quite the task ahead of him as he sat in his room. He managed to find a piece of paper and pen as he jotted down a list of what he needed to accomplish by the end of the week.

1) *Locate the Lady of Glisten Lake and reunite her with Jaeyse.*
2) *Travel to Miracle Forest and locate the portal.*
3) *Check up on Silianna's well-being.*
4) *Check up on Rahaf and bring Eli home.*
5) *Locate the next Eternal Element and give it to Kelton.*

Difficult, but not impossible, especially with how determined Malakai was to get it done. He had no intentions of stopping until he was able to complete his tasks. The only thing he had to worry about was his grandmother getting in his way.

Folding the list and placing it in his back pocket, Malakai strolled down the halls in search of Demetri. It was a little past one-thirty in the morning. He hoped Demetri was still awake by the time he got to his room.

The halls were silent with no guards in sight. It was strange, considering the Grand Empress Dowager hired more security to roam Windsor Keep. Was there something that occurred tonight he wasn't aware of?

A small green light appeared from the corner of Malakai's eye. Shifting his attention to the light, he was welcomed by a flowing ball of green flames.

Without his consent, his feet began following the ball. He tried to jerk himself in another direction, but when he did, a bolt of pain laced through his brain. No matter how hard he tried to resist, he helplessly followed the light.

*Why can't I stop following it? Why can't I speak either?*

Malakai felt his lips were glued shut. Something was controlling him, and he couldn't tell what it was.

Malakai found himself wandering out into the courtyard. The two moonlights beamed toward a tree covered in snow. A stranger stood by the tree, though their back was turned. The stranger wore a red velvet cloak and had a strange scent of peppermint, like his grandmother.

The green ball of light suddenly stopped in its tracks and vanished into thin air. The stranger turned around only to reveal herself. She had long, wavy auburn hair that was exactly the same as Malakai's. Her eyes were chocolate brown, as Malakai's were. And to top it off, her facial structure was uncanny to him. If Malakai had known better, he'd say that this woman was his twin. The only difference between the two was the fact that Malakai had a tan skin complexion, whereas the woman was pale white, like a corpse.

The feeling of his lips glued shut slowly simmered away. Malakai finally spoke as he said, "W—Who are you? Why do we look so much alike?"

The woman giggled. "Come on. You seriously can't guess who I am? The Eckwood brothers sure have a type when it comes to dating."

"Seraphina," he said, the name heavy on his tongue.

"Yay! We can finally get past the introduction and jump to my next topic."

"Which is what?" Malakai asked, anger simmering inside of him.

"I've heard the stories about you and believe me, none of them have been good."

"You've heard a one-sided story about me. Am I really a bad person for loving Kelton and Demetri? The heart wants what the heart wants. I can't control that."

Malakai wanted to dissociate from this conversation. But given the situation he found himself in, he figured he'd play along. "Can we just skip the nonsense and get to the part where you tell me what it is that you want? I have other important matters to attend to."

In the blink of an eye, Seraphina used her vampyre speed to run behind Malakai and pull the folded note from his back pocket. Seraphina then sped back to her original spot by the tree and began reading the paper.

"Ah, yes. These are all very interesting matters you must attend to," said Seraphina. However, by the tone of her voice, it was evident that she was mocking him. "You'd risk putting this nation on the brink of disaster to save a shapeshifter and a damaged elemental? Tsk, tsk. I expected more from the Lost Prince of Baskaria. But I can't say I'm surprised. All you Bellemores are the same—always thinking about yourselves without considering the repercussions for your actions. Just like you've heard stories about me, I've also heard stories about you and your family bloodline."

"If you're here to seek something from me, you're doing a really good job at persuading me not to," Malakai responded, annoyed. "I'd be careful about the next words that come out of your mouth."

Seraphina held out her hands, calling for a truce. Though, it didn't matter, considering Malakai was already heated with rage just having to stand in front of her.

"Look, it'll be nearly impossible to find the Lady of Glisten Lake, especially with the predicament you're in. That old warlock is never going to guide you to Miracle Forest without seeing his daughter. If a portal is what you need, I'd be more than happy to assist you in that department. For a fee, of course."

Malakai squinted his eyes. "I think I'll take my chances and look for the Lady of Glisten Lake. Any deal with you is like making a deal with the Shadow Lord. I'd be a fool to listen to whatever bargain you want."

Malakai was finally able to move his body freely. He turned his back on Seraphina and headed inside; however, Seraphina started to speak, which prompted Malakai to stop walking in his tracks.

Seraphina said aloud, "I have a device that allows me to conjure portals. It was something passed down by generations of the Blackworth family. No one knows of its existence, and I'd hope you continue to keep it that way."

*Bingo.*

Malakai couldn't help the laugh that forced its way out of his throat. "You faked your death and managed to escape by conjuring a portal? I can't believe you. You really are something, huh? Those two boys have been neck-and-neck on each other's throats because you wanted to have your cake and eat it too. The emotional damage you've caused is remarkable."

Seraphina raised an eyebrow and frowned. "I never said I was perfect. You're lucky to even know someone who can activate a portal. Without me, you'd be wasting your time looking for a woman who doesn't want to be found."

Malakai knew she wasn't lying. He figured finding the Lady of Glisten Lake would be difficult and would take a good amount of time that he didn't have to spare. The last time he saw her, she flew off into the night sky. There was no telling where she could be. Was it worth risking his chances traveling through the North and South to find her? Then again, was it worth trusting a vampyre who burned a bridge between the Eckwood brothers and faked her death?

Malakai sighed and gave in. "What is it that you want from me in exchange for the device?"

Seraphina smiled, looking both eager and sinister. "I'm in a bit of a situation with the Vampyre Queen herself, Narkissa. Long story short, she wants me dead. I pissed off some vamps, so I need to ensure I'll never have to worry about my safety ever again."

"So, what is it that you're implying?"

"I need you to kill the Vampyre Queen. In exchange for her cold black heart, I shall hand over the device, and you can continue with your endeavors to save your precious shapeshifter and your Loverboy, Kelton. Oh! I'll know if you give me a fake heart, so don't pull that stunt on me. Her scent is one of a kind."

Malakai's anxiety kicked in as he finally heard her request. To kill the Vampyre Queen would be a death wish.

Suddenly, Malakai had a thought. If he were to travel to Theuros and meet with the vampyres in their domain, he could potentially gain their army to help fight alongside them in the war. Moreover, Malakai could get some answers regarding the Dark Dimension. *If I'm able to find a way to get Kelton to cut ties with the Other Side, then I won't have to worry about sacrificing one of the Eternal Elements. More importantly, if I can find a way to trick Seraphina into thinking I killed the queen, then I can get access to Eli, and life will temporarily be as good as new.*

"Okay," answered Malakai, nervously. "I'll *try* to kill the Vampyre Queen. But I want you to leave me and those closest to me alone once everything is finished. Do we have a deal?"

Seraphina smirked. "It sounds like a bargain to me. Once you return from Theuros, I shall come to find you. Until then, I wish you the best of luck, Lost Prince."

Malakai felt a cold breeze brush through his spine. A part of him wanted to ask whether or not she was behind the Dravkyn Demons invading Windsor Keep before they went their separate ways; however, by the time he thought about it, Seraphina had conjured a portal with a circular device and disappeared.

## 24
## A Dangerous Reflection

**MALAKAI**

The portal device was real. Malakai had seen it with his own eyes. The only thing he'd need to be concerned about was convincing her that he killed the Vampyre Queen. But how? It would be next to impossible to kill the one person who has been alive longer than any being in Zorall. Let alone, the oldest vampyre to ever exist. To kill Narkissa would add more enemies to the flame, and Malakai intended to stay clear of more conflict if possible, especially since he was trying to gain allies, not make new enemies.

Returning to the halls of Windsor Keep, Malakai was welcomed by Demetri, who was running toward him, sweat beading along his forehead. His blue eyes were panicked, and Malakai was momentarily taken aback by seeing such raw emotion on Demetri's face.

"By the Gods," Demetri said, panting. He took a moment to catch his breath. "I was beginning to worry that something bad had happened to you. I went to see you in your room, but you weren't there. I was close to waking everyone up and gathering all the guards. I would've wreaked havoc if something happened to you."

Malakai developed a puzzled look. The way Demetri sounded was too familiar to how Kelton would sound if he were looking for him. Then again, Malakai figured it was just some sort of Eckwood family trait of theirs, being so overprotective. It was rare to see Demetri so concerned about Malakai's safety. The last time he did anything remotely close to that was when he saved him after the Wondrous Trials.

"I'm okay," Malakai said, his voice softened. "I'm a little surprised to be alive, but I'm okay. How come you were looking for me? I was actually on my way to see you."

"Seraphina showed up on my balcony earlier tonight."

"Oh!" Malakai said, trying to sound surprised but failing.

"*Oh?*" Demetri repeated. "What is that supposed to mean?"

Malakai took a step back and crossed his arms behind his back. He wasn't sure how to break the ice, but it seemed there was no point in wasting time. So, he cut to the chase and gave a recap of everything that occurred in the courtyard.

"Absolutely not," said Demetri, coldly.

"W—What? Why not? It's the only chance we have!" Malakai argued.

"Malakai, she's taking advantage of your desperation. Nothing about Seraphina ever leads to good."

"But I saw the portal!" Malakai exclaimed. "She had some device and activated it. She's not lying about that."

"I don't care. You're not going to Theuros. If you try to leave, I'll notify the Grand Empress Dowager and Celsa. You're taking big risks here, and you need to think strategically."

Malakai huffed, feeling a familiar annoyance fill his body. Everyone was always treating him like a child, like he didn't know what he was doing and couldn't take care of himself. It seemed as though Demetri was all for taking risks when it suited him, going out into the city and breaking the rules. What had changed?

*Seraphina.*

Malakai rolled his eyes. "This is about her, isn't it?"

"What do you mean?" asked Demetri.

"Four months ago, you were at your brother's throat because of Seraphina. Then, all of a sudden, Seraphina is evil, you're cool with Kelton, and now you want nothing to do with her. Why?"

Demetri struggled to speak. It drove Malakai mad. He wanted to know what the fuse was all about, and he felt Demetri wasn't being honest, more so with himself than with others.

"Please, Demetri…" Malakai sounded exhausted. "I just don't understand why you act the way you do. All I ask is for honesty— for the truth. What is this all about?"

"You really want to know?" Demetri said, his voice was more uncertain than Malakai had ever heard.

"We don't have a lot of time, Demetri. Whatever it is you want to say, just say it!"

"It's y—" Demetri caught his tongue and furrowed his brow. "She came to my room not too long ago. That's why I came to find you. But she obviously beat me to it since she found you."

"What did she tell you?"

"She explained how she survived that day on the mountains, then went on to threaten me, Kelton, and you. It's why my views of her have changed. At first, I assumed she faked her death. But now I'm convinced she never cared about either of us. She left Kelton and me to believe she was dead just to run off doing who knows what. That wasn't love. It never was."

Malakai wasn't sure how to respond to that. He reached out, pulling Demetri into a hug. He'd known, in theory, the damage Seraphina had done to both of the brothers with her unfaithfulness and untimely departure. But he hadn't been able to fully see the effects until now.

After a second, Demetri pulled his arms closer and squeezed Malakai tightly, burying one of his hands in Malakai's hair. The hug was comforting, grounding, and somehow strangely familiar.

Flashing images of his childhood popped into his head. His younger self was being chased by a young boy—black hair and blue eyes. Then the images of Malakai's scar came to mind. The boy with black hair helped heal it, but the scar remained. Another image appeared, but this one was of Malakai four months prior. He was attending the Masquerade Ball with Kelton. Demetri grabbed Malakai's hand and questioned the scar.

*"I knew it," Demetri said ominously. "You have the same scar on your palm. I can't believe you're alive. Where have you been all this time? I've spent countless nights praying that the Gods would bring you back to me."*

Malakai pulled away.

Demetri looked him over, eyes lingering on Malakai's frown.

"Is something wrong?" Demetri asked.

Malakai shook his head. "Not at all. I—I'm just starting to feel a little tired. I think I need some rest." He lied, and it killed him to do so. What he really wanted to say was, *Did I know you when I was younger? Are you the boy from my memories?"*

"Okay," Demetri said, dropping the matter. "Do you want me to escort you back to your room?"

"That won't be necessary. But thank you for the gesture." Malakai said, feeling suddenly overwhelmed.

He proceeded down the hall, leaving Demetri where he stood. However, nothing ever came easily for Malakai, especially when it related to Demetri.

"There's no convincing you not to fly out to Theuros, is there?" Demetri asked, in a tone that suggested he already knew the answer.

Malakai turned around and shrugged. "It's not just the portal I'm after. Silianna and I found intel on the Dark Dimension. Narkissa is the only one who can provide answers to it. I'm doing this for Silianna, Kelton, and myself. Surely you can understand."

"So, your game plan is to get information on the spirit realm, kill the Vampyre Queen, and get the portal device from Seraphina?" Demetri asked, trying to gather what was going through Malakai's head.

"Pretty much. Well, I don't plan on killing Narkissa. I'll have to figure out how to trick Seraphina on that one." Malakai laughed, feeling more than a little crazy when hearing the plan said out loud. "What can I say? I'm stubborn and do what I want. You should know that by now."

Demetri sighed. "Very well. If that is the case, then I shall join you as your protector. I won't risk anything happening to you."

Those last two sentences alarmed Malakai. Something was

forming in his heart, and he wasn't capable of comprehending what that feeling was. Possibly because it may lead him to dangerous consequences if acted on. Malakai simply smiled in Demetri's direction and wandered back to his room.

# *Act Two*

# 25
## The Sword of Aerislark

**RAHAF**

The wedding was set for tomorrow, and Rahaf had a lot to prepare in a short amount of time. Luckily, she'd been dreaming of her wedding day since she was a little girl and already had so many ideas of how she wanted it to go. Spending the night with Theodosis had only solidified her love for him and motivated her to make sure everything went perfectly.

One of the servants had arrived a little while ago to inform Rahaf that Queen Seona would like to give her a tour of Ackermere Palace, where they could arrange how they'd like to perform the ceremony. Rahaf wasted no time getting herself ready while Theodosis remained asleep in bed. It warmed her heart to see him sleeping peacefully, knowing that their love was accepted by his family. *If I cannot be accepted by my family, at least I will be accepted by Theodosis' family.*

Rahaf set her brunette hair into a ponytail and wore a long, flowy purple dress. The long sleeves were see-through, but given how warm it was inside the palace, she had no concerns about being cold from the outdoor weather.

As she left her room, Rahaf was welcomed by her bobcat, Aleek. He seemed to be a little irritated, possibly because he was locked out last night while she and Theodosis had a splendid time together.

"Don't give me that look," Rahaf said, pointing at Aleek. "You know very well how much I missed Theodosis. You and I are together almost all the time. Surely you can't be mad at me for this *one* time."

Aleek growled and walked away, leaving Rahaf to remain in the halls, standing by herself. She did not bother thinking much of it, especially if she was able to find him some treats to forget about last night.

Arriving in the courtyard, Rahaf met with Queen Seona and Nerumi Steelhart. The courtyard had a beautiful metallic water fountain at the center, where a statue of a man with wings held a peculiar sword in his left hand. The handle of the sword included wings, which automatically lit a lightbulb in Rahaf's mind. Like Silianna had explained, "If my understanding is correct, I believe that the sword with wings might house the Eternal Element of Aeris." *This must be what Sil was talking about*, thought Rahaf. *I have to learn more about it.* While she continued to observe the statue, Rahaf couldn't help noticing that Queen Seona and Nerumi were praying it with their heads bowed in respect.

Petals from the cherry blossom trees fell on Rahaf's long, brunette hair. A gust of wind had blown by, causing the trees to sway.

Rahaf speculated that the statue in question may be the God of Air, Aerislark, which would explain why the two women were praying. Rahaf, unsure what to do with herself, awkwardly stood by until they finished.

The servant from earlier appeared and offered a glass of water. Rahaf graciously took the glass and gulped it down.

"Thank you," she whispered, attempting to be respectful during the prayer. The servant bowed his head and proceeded back inside the palace.

Once the women finished, Queen Seona was the first to rise from her knees. Nerumi followed after. The Queen walked over to Rahaf with a welcoming smile on her face.

"For so long, I worried that my son would never find the love of his life. But then he told me about you, and I couldn't be happier."

Queen Seona reached in and hugged Rahaf. "Tomorrow, you will officially be my daughter-in-law. If your family will not accept you and my son, then we will."

Rahaf felt her eyes get misty. For so long, she waited to hear those words from her father, but she knew how he viewed her. If he found out about her marriage to Theodosis, he would wreak havoc. Luckily, she knew that the Steelharts would fight if King Bastille retaliated against the Aeris kingdom. And yet, even though she knew that she had all the love and support, it still left a stinging sensation in her heart that her father refused to see his daughter happy. *He left my mother to die*, she thought, *and he allowed my sister to waste away in Sorrow Tower. A man like him should never be allowed to rule Pyroc—or any kingdom, for that matter.*

*Jacqueline…*

Today was meant to be an amazing day for Rahaf. She was to plan her dream wedding, but seeing the way Queen Seona treated her, and seeing Nerumi standing by her side, it broke Rahaf's heart knowing that her sister, Jacqueline, could not be by her side and walk her down the aisle. If there was one thing she would focus on once Malakai reclaimed the Baskarian throne, it would be to rescue her sister from Sorrow Tower. There was so much healing and trauma her sister would have to unpack.

"Thank you for your kind words, Queen Seona," said Rahaf, voice thick with emotion.

"Please. You may call me 'Mother.' The Gods must know how much you miss your mother. I never agreed with how they treated Roslynda. May she rest in the Heavens." Queen Seona mourned.

As much as Rahaf would love to open up about how she was feeling, she knew it was too early to express all of that to her new family. Besides, there was much to plan and very little time. She quickly pulled herself together and smiled.

"So, is this courtyard where we'll hold the ceremony?" Rahaf asked.

Queen Seona nodded. "Correct. We thought it would be nice to have the ceremony surrounded by the cherry blossoms and have

Aerislark standing guard to approve the wedding."

"I wasn't sure that that statue was who you were praying to. I had suspicions, but I did not want to assume," Rahaf said politely. "I've heard the stories of how the Gods looked. They were monstrous creatures with wings. However, this statue depicts a man with wings. Not at all what I imagined."

Queen Seona gasped. She held Rahaf's hand and looked deep into her eyes. "By the Gods, please tell me you have heard the story of Aerislark and his angelic sword." Rahaf looked at Nerumi and back at Queen Seona. She was clueless, and the queen could tell.

Rahaf took this as an opportunity to get some more information on the sword. "No, I do not. Please elaborate."

"Very well," said Queen Seona, excitement seeping through her voice. "Aerislark, the God of Air, came down from the Heavens long ago. He bestowed a sword that would house one of the four Eternal Elements. There was a treaty created by the four Gods that they would create four objects where they would store their angelic energy. Aerislark told his fellow elementals that the sword would reside in the mountains deep within a cave. Many speculate that the mountain in question is located in the Temple of Retribution. According to legend, there are three tasks that one must go through to retrieve the Sword of Aerislark."

Rahaf's heart nearly dropped to her stomach. She knew she had to locate the next Eternal Element for Malakai, but she did not expect to get the information she needed so early on. All she needed to do now was figure out where this mountain was, and she'd venture over there. *The Temple of Retribution*, she thought to herself.

"Are you okay, my dear?" asked Queen Seona, concerned.

Rahaf snapped back into the present and shrugged it off. "Yes. I was just thinking, that is all. I find the tale of Aerislark to be quite fascinating. Especially the sword he crafted."

Queen Seona chuckled. "Oh, I could go on for days about the stories told to me as a child. But we'll focus on our top priorities at the moment. Now, back to the wedding arrangements—"

"—Please, forgive me," Rahaf interrupted, eager to gain more information. "Has anyone who entered the Temple of Retribution ever returned?"

"Not a soul," Queen Seona said, shaking her head. "Time runs differently inside there. So many lives were lost in hopes of gaining that much power that we ultimately had no choice but to close it off to the public. We have guards stationed out there to keep anyone from sneaking in. It would be too dangerous to venture there. Especially with the fate of the world in the Lost Prince's hands, even I would not suggest he go in there."

At the corner of her eyes, Rahaf caught Nerumi squinting her eyes. For some strange reason, Rahaf left as though Nerumi were catching on to the plan she was slowly developing in her head. Malakai may not be able to venture into the Temple of Retribution, but Rahaf could. Either she postponed the wedding and traveled there tomorrow, or she got married tonight and traveled there in the morning. Either way, she was going to that temple even if it was the last thing she did. For her mother. For Jacqueline. For the Nine Lands.

"What do you think about having the wedding tonight?" Rahaf questioned.

"I—Why the sudden change of heart?" Queen Seona asked, confused.

"I've waited a long time to be married to Theodosis. Why wait any longer? I'm sure he will be *thrilled* to perform the ceremony here tonight. There is so much for us to get through, so why not get the wedding out of the way?"

Queen Seona seemed shocked, glancing at Nerumi. In the end, she agreed to the idea. Though Rahaf did feel a little guilty as she knew that her suggestion was not genuine, but rather created for her own personal motive, one that may get her killed.

"Well, if you're okay with the courtyard, then we can move on with the other arrangements! I will have our servants gather as much stuff for tonight. We will make this a night to remember, my darling." Queen Seona excused herself and went inside the palace.

Rahaf was left with Nerumi. Nerumi took a couple of steps

forward, scouting the area to ensure no one would overhear their conversation.

"Do not be stupid, Princess Rahaf," Nerumi said, her tone strict and firm. "I know exactly what you're thinking, and I won't allow it."

"I don't have a choice, Nerumi. The Nine Lands are in jeopardy. There's a lot you don't understand. There is an evil entity lurking in the spirit world that is threatening my friends. He's controlling the Elder Guardians, and if we do not get the Eternal Elements, we will not be able to defeat him and reclaim the Baskarian throne."

"I don't care. This is not your journey to handle. You have already endured so much pain and suffering. If anything were to happen to you, Theodosis will be destroyed. Everything he'll sacrifice will go down the drain if you die."

*This is not your journey to handle.* The sentence haunted Rahaf because, truthfully, it was her journey to handle. Rahaf's mother, Roslynda Soulryth, risked everything to save Prince Antonious that night the Bellemores were assassinated. If her mother were still alive today, she would've made it her absolute goal to retrieve that sword if it meant saving Zorall from destruction.

"Then I won't go alone," said Rahaf, choosing not to argue with Nerumi. "It's been a while since we last saw each other, but I can assure you that no harm will come to me."

Nerumi snorted mockingly. "And who do you think will be stupid enough to join you in your suicide mission?"

Rahaf's bobcat, Aleek, randomly appeared and sat next to her side. She petted him behind the ear as she responded, "I got Aleek, who will rip heads off my enemies. I also have a shapeshifter who is willing to do anything for me. And by the end of the night, I'll have a husband who will be happy to join me in my crazy mission. I won't be alone if that's what you're worried about."

Nerumi huffed. "You're missing the big picture here. I was willing to sacrifice my chance at rekindling a relationship with an old friend in pursuit of yours and Theodosis' happiness. Where will that leave me if both of you end up dead? I refuse to let you put my cousin at risk for your silly little games. My aunt may believe that the Sword Aerislark resides in the Temple of Retribution, but I believe differently."

Rahaf refused to waste another breath. Instead, she reached down to her ankle and unhooked the gold anklet. With one woosh, she was able to activate her enchanted anklet as it formed into her elegant gold whip. Nerumi took a startled step back as Rahaf released her weapon. Rahaf whipped it around in a circular motion and hit some of the blossom trees, the branches snapping off and landing on the ground.

"How do you have a magical object?" Nerumi asked, astonished.

"It was a gift from my mother. I was sworn to secrecy, but given the state of the world, I don't think it matters much anymore." Rahaf set her enchanted weapon back into an anklet form and cuffed it back on. "The reason I showed you is that this anklet housed the Eternal Element of Pyroc. I never knew I had it the entire time— nobody did. Prince Antonius was able to obtain its powers and restore his fire element. The witch I arrived with cast a powerful spell, one that ultimately prevented the Lost Prince from gaining his elements for the past eight years. The only way to retrieve all four is by getting the Eternal Elements."

Rahaf took a breath from the heavy dialogue she spoke. She then continued, "As it stands, Prince Antonious now has the powers of Pyroc and Terrane. If we plan to defeat this evil entity, then we have no choice but to get that sword. I understand you risked a lot, and I know what I'm putting myself through to get that sword. For so long, I've been selfish, but I'm now working on being selfless. Even if that means losing my life for the entire planet of Zorall, at least I know I tried."

Nerumi stood there, observing Rahaf's serious facial expression, and a smile tugged at the corners of her mouth. "You are a brave warrior," Nerumi said, complimenting her. "I admire a princess who is so passionate and able to fight for what she cares about."

"I'm sure you do. Just like you admire Silianna." Rahaf raised an eyebrow.

"I'm not sure I follow?" Nerumi said, voice ticking up in an obvious lie.

"Please, let's not waste each other's time. I know Silianna is the 'old friend' you were referring to. I overheard Silianna and Demetri having a conversation a while ago. She is still in love with you." Rahaf reached out and took Nerumi's hand. "You know what I think? I think you shouldn't let this chance pass you by. Believe me, as someone who thought I might never be able to see Theodosis again... Don't live your life with any regrets. If you care about her, *go* to her. Tomorrow is never promised, especially with the times we are living in. You have to seize every moment."

Nerumi's lower lip wobbled, but she held her chin high and gave Rahaf a tight nod.

"Now, if you'll excuse me," Rahaf added, "I have to find my fiancé. We have a short amount of time to get things done."

Rahaf winked, then walked off to find Theodosis.

## 26
## Break the Cycle

**ELI**

The announcement was made a little over an hour ago—Princess Rahaf Soulryth and Prince Theodosis Steelhart would be married by the end of the night. Eli was going through a spiral of emotions, and the only solution he figured would work was to get as far away from Ackermere Palace as he possibly could. A part of him knew it was coming, he just expected it to happen a bit later down the line. *I shouldn't have been so delusional enough to think I ever stood a chance*, he thought. *Stupid, stupid, stupid.*

Eli was strolling through the city of Aeris, attempting to jog his memories from childhood. His family used to live within the mountains alongside other shapeshifters. The city was not too far away from that place. He couldn't help noticing so many differences when it came to building structures and technology that were all around. Personally, he preferred the upgrades.

A part of him desperately wanted to venture beyond the city walls and take a walk through memory lane, but with Annalu and her witches breathing down his neck to ensure his safety, it seemed almost impossible. *I'm lucky to even be wandering through the city right now.*

As he was walking, Eli noticed an alleyway that crept down a peculiar path. Curious, Eli walked through it and discovered at the end of the alleyway, a pebble pathway led to a cliff with a view of endless mountains. He embraced the feeling of the breeze blowing through and watched the birds as they glided by.

The thought crossed his mind to shapeshift into an owl and join them, but he didn't want to risk letting any of the elementals catch him doing so. The King and Queen of Aeris may be okay with him wandering around, but there surely were some civilians who saw supernatural beings like himself as a threat and would proudly notify authorities in the homeland.

Eli turned his focus from the flock of birds to the West of the mountains. He knew from where he stood that the homeland was West. The urge to risk everything to travel over to Saint Salvusburg and rescue his mother and brother threatened to overwhelm him. If he was going to steer clear of his thoughts for Rahaf, then he was going to focus it on his family.

Memories crept up on him, making new homes in his head.

*"Your mother and brother are very much alive,"* the voice of the Lady of Glisten Lake echoed. *"The caedose soldiers took them as prisoners. The only one who perished in that explosion was your father. The remainder of your family is currently being held in a cell in Saint Salvusburg. The Elder Guardians are planning to use them as leverage in exchange for the smulder. Do not fall for their tricks. You have a very important task, shapeshifter. You must identify the Lost Prince of Baskaria and notify the Grand Empress Dowager. Once he is reunited with his grandmother, the path to retrieving your family will be straightforward."*

Straightforward. *Right.*

Nothing about these past four months has felt straightforward. From being on the run, to seeing what occurred with his family, then taking care of Celdric and Nehila, and finally reaching the South, only to learn his best friend was the heir to the Baskaria throne... It was insane and nowhere near straightforward. And then there was the disaster in Centuris, where he'd stupidly allowed himself to get caught up in the moment and catch feelings for Rahaf. The cherry on top was meeting his grandfather for the first time and being told he was part of a royal family.

Whatever it was that the Lady of Glisten Lake said, he hoped that she meant to say, "The path to retrieving your family will be *complicated*." Because complications seemed to be the new normal for him.

"What are you doing here?" someone asked from behind. When Eli turned around, he saw that it was Nerumi Steelhart, looking annoyed with her hands on her hips. "I was told by my guards that you wandered off without supervision. I decided to come find you myself."

"I'm surprised to see Annalu didn't cause a scene and send one of her witches to retrieve me," Eli said, jokingly.

"Believe me, that woman was *furious*. That is why I offered to come find you. She takes her job a little too seriously, so I felt volunteering would give her a better understanding that we do not mind."

"I appreciate you coming to find me, but I can tell that you take your job a little too seriously as well." Eli was referring to last night at dinner. Theodosis was stepping down from his role to rule Aeris, and Nerumi picked up the mantle. He noticed that she was not too pleased about the arrangement, though he couldn't pinpoint why exactly that was. "The way you stood last night, so *mighty* and *brave*. It was obviously all for show. I can sense you're holding yourself back, but I don't understand why."

"Ouch," Nerumi said, face souring slightly. "You're very opinionated, I fear."

"One of my many amazing qualities," Eli sarcastically said. "So, I might as well rip the band-aid off and ask you why you weren't so...*engaged* with last night's reunion. Are you not happy for your cousin to find the 'love of his life?'"

"You say it like you don't condone their engagement." Nerumi crossed her arms and raised an eyebrow, implying she was suspicious of Eli. "Don't tell me that you've caught feelings for the fire princess."

Eli's mouth opened, ready to speak. Yet, he held his tongue. He had an idea where Nerumi was going with this, and it was a classic tactic to deflect her own problems. *She's not diverting from my question,* he told himself.

"No. We're not doing that," he said, feeling cocky. "I will gladly head back to Ackermere Palace only if you tell me why you were so off last night."

Nerumi shook her head. "That's none of your concern."

"You don't condone their engagement, and I want to know—"

"—*BECAUSE!*" Nerumi's voice echoed beyond the mountains. She took a deep breath as all her energy went to that one scream. "I'm struggling through my past, and the only logical way to cope with it is by distracting myself. Picking up the mantle seems like the best way to not think about it."

Eli used his shapeshifter abilities to listen closely to Nerumi's pulse. It was rushing with adrenaline.

"I'm sorry," he said softly. "I guess you can say I'm going through the same situation. *Kind of.*"

Nerumi pulled out her glass communicator and checked the time. She then placed it back in her pocket and plopped onto the grass. She hugged her knees and faced the view of the mountains as another flock of birds flew by.

"I wish things could be different," Nerumi said, frowning. "If the throne wasn't an issue, if I were just a simple commoner along with the one I've fallen for, then perhaps life would be less stressful. But here I am, torn between being selfish or selfless. I'm damned if I do, and I'm damned if I don't. I'm drained, shapeshifter. You have no idea how much I think about it."

"My name is Eli for the love of the Gods… And also, why does it feel like none of you Royal-Bloods want to claim your birthright and rule the throne for your kingdoms?" Eli asked.

"I *do* want the throne. It's all I ever dreamt of. I just wish I could share that goal with the person I've come to love." Wind came gushing toward Nerumi, blowing her multi-colored hair. "I wanted to confess my love to someone special during my educational years at Cressmoore Academy, but I knew that as long as Theodosis and Rahaf are together, and the laws set in place for a mixed elemental wedding, there was no winning in whatever choice I made. So, in the end, I chose the throne over her..."

*Her.*

"I may not know much about love," Eli started, "but seeing how my best friend has managed to find it in the strangest way possible, I believe you can find it, too. And there doesn't need to be a choice either. If you want more than one thing, you can have it. You just gotta put in the work to get it. Nothing is clear-cut in life, and that's a tough pill I had to swallow." Eli held out his hand to help pull Nerumi up from the grass. "Break the cycle, Nerumi. It can't be worse than seeing the person you've fallen for get married to someone else."

Nerumi smiled. She grabbed his hand and pulled herself up. Once she adjusted her shirt, she went on to say, "You're right. I need to see her as soon as possible. I've been having these constant nightmares with her in them, and I can't make them go away." Nerumi took a deep breath, collecting herself from the little venting session they had. "I think I know how I can get to her, and it's probably going to be insane that I'm considering it. But I'm going to take your advice."

As Nerumi started heading back to the alleyway, she stopped mid-walk to confront Eli. "Also, I called it. You've for sure fallen in love with Rahaf."

"Shut up," Eli groaned.

Nerumi giggled. "*Hmm.* Do I sense a newfound friendship blooming between us?"

"Eh, take it easy. I'm very careful who I welcome into my inner circle of trust. I just hope you can prove yourself trustworthy and not tell Rahaf *or* your cousin about this."

Nerumi held out her hand, and both of them shook on it. The deal was set, and Eli was hoping that she could keep her promise not to blab to either of them. The last thing he wanted was to feel embarrassed.

"Before we return to Ackermere Palace, I need to speak to you about a very serious topic," Nerumi started, her voice sounding urgent. "I fear Princess Rahaf may be plotting to go on a journey that may get her and Theo killed. I need you to try your best to convince her otherwise."

"What kind of journey are you talking about?"

"She wishes to travel to the Temple of Retribution. I have heard horrifying stories of those who ventured in and never came back out. There is a myth that the Sword of Aerislark resides in that temple. She wants to get hold of it for Prince Antonious Bellemore."

Eli's eyes widened. There was a part of him that wanted to side with Nerumi in stopping Rahaf, but even he knew just how high the stakes were to not try getting the next Eternal Element. If Rahaf were to venture into that temple, Eli would join her, regardless of whether she followed through with the wedding tonight. He'd put his pride aside for Malakai in a heartbeat. *If Malakai doesn't get all the Eternal Elements and put a stop to this madness, then I might as well accept my mother and Orian's fate*, he thought.

Eli played it smart and decided to make Nerumi feel as though he was siding with her in the matter.

"Okay," he said. "I'll convince her not to go."

## 27
## Heaven Wears Your Halo

**SILIANNA**

*The four artifacts.*

The images from her most recent dream floated in her mind, driving her out of bed and onto her feet. Silianna felt like a fool for not mentioning them to Malakai last time they had spoken. She got dressed quickly and headed out the door, eager to find Malakai. Silianna figured the infirmary would be the best bet, considering Malakai had seldom left Kelton's side during his recovery.

She felt good to finally get the weight of her secret about the Dark Dimension off her chest, but she'd completely forgotten to mention the other information she'd received. She hoped Malakai would be able to forgive her for her lapse in focus.

Silianna was speed-walking through Windsor Keep, searching for the Lost Prince while she kept repeating in her mind the four artifacts:

*The amulet.*

*The anklet.*

*The sword.*

*The chalice.*

The voices from the spirits were still lingering in her head. There was no telling whether or not they were real or just from her memories. Either way, it sent chills down her spine hearing them.

There were a couple of things she wanted to get done today aside from notifying Malakai of the four artifacts. She had to try getting some answers regarding the Beauchamp Curse, try communicating with Rahaf and see if everything was okay, and do some research regarding Narkissa.

Silianna had accepted the fact that she would have to let go of her spiritual element on the next full moon, but that was not going to stop her from getting answers to help Malakai and Kelton. The ability may have been passed onto her, but the boys were born with them. If there was any way of saving them from that darkness, she would do whatever it took.

As she made a swift turn down the hall where the infirmary was located, Silianna was lucky to run into Malakai, who was just closing the doors behind him. *Thank the Gods.*

"Silianna!" Malakai said joyfully. "Did you get any rest last night?"

"Yes. I was fortunate enough to get some sleep," she responded, though her tone revealed a bit of worry. "I wanted to come find you first thing this morning. I'm not sure if the spirits are trying to give me a message, but I had a dream about these four artifacts, and it reminded me of something else that happened last night."

Malakai's eyes widened. "You mean there was *more* that happened?"

"Well, yes and no. It was during the time you found me on the floor. I was so focused on everything that I guess my brain was not processing every little detail. But my uncle, Reju, was there, and we saw images of these four artifacts. An amulet, an anklet, a sword, and a chalice." Silianna took a deep breath before continuing. "The moral of the story, Reju and I believe that the remaining Eternal Elements may be housed in a sword and a chalice. Reju wanted me to relay the message, and I feel the spirits wanted me to do the same as well. So, here I am."

Malakai smiled, then leaned in to hug her. "I'm sorry you have to endure such a constant headache with the Dark Dimension. I wouldn't wish it on my worst enemy," Malakai paused, second-guessing his comment. "Actually, I lied. There are a couple of people I wish it on. But that's not the point. I just want to thank you, and I hope that you remain safe until the full moon. I'll be by your side whenever you need it, okay?"

Silianna nodded. "Thank you. I appreciate that. And as of today's plans, I'm going to do some research regarding Narkissa."

"Don't bother. I'm heading over to speak to my grandmother about her. I have low expectations that she'll agree to me traveling there, but even if she doesn't, I'll find a way to get to Theuros."

"Leave it to you to rebel against your own best interests," Silianna said, jokingly.

Malakai's smile slowly faded into a more serious expression. He cleared his throat and frowned. "As for the artifacts, I think I know exactly what you're talking about. Kelton and I visited Reju's nightclub the night he died. He had a gold mirror that spoke to me and said something about those exact items. It has crossed my mind a few times."

"Oh! Well, as intrigued as I am about a talking gold mirror, I'm relieved to know this all worked out perfectly. I should also add that I told Rahaf about the sword. If my hunch is correct, she's probably already figured out where to locate it. I planned on getting a hold of her as soon as possible."

"*Pfft*. Don't waste your time," Malakai replied, disappointed. "I've tried contacting Eli on numerous occasions. The connection between Aeris and Avala is terrible. My grandmother is trying her best to get in touch with Annalu as well. Sometimes the connection goes through, and most times it doesn't."

"Well, I shall keep trying until I get something. Regardless, I wish *you* the best of luck convincing your grandmother to fly out to Theuros. I'm going to visit Kelton and see if everything is alright with him since I'm here."

Silianna and Malakai went their separate ways. There wasn't a reason why she felt the way she did, but when she got close to the infirmary doors there was a sense of darkness that clouded her vision. Everything in her body alerted her to stay away, but she ignored those feelings as she continued inside.

* * *

Kelton was sitting up straight in his bed, staring off into the distance. Silianna questioned why Malakai would leave him unattended in this state. Something seemed off as she walked over to his bedside.

"Kelton?" she said, worried. "Can you hear me?"

"Yes," Kelton responded, coldly. "I'm just thinking."

"Thinking about what?" Silianna pulled up a chair and sat down. She leaned over and held Kelton's hand. "By the Gods, you're freezing!"

"I don't know why I feel this way… It's like I can't control it."

"Feel like what?"

Kelton's eyes watered like he was about to cry, and his mouth was set in a firm frown. Silianna was concerned and desperately wanted to understand what was going on inside his head.

"Kelton, it's okay," she reassured him. "Talk to me. There's nobody in the room but you and me."

A sinister grin grew on Kelton's face. The tears stopped, and his eyes suddenly turned into pure darkness.

"Did you decide on what you'll do with your spiritual element?" Kelton's voice was different. It was almost like it was someone else's voice entirely. "You only have until the next full moon, you know? So much could happen until then."

Silianna was scared and confused. Did Malakai tell him about what happened to her last night? Moreover, why were Kelton's eyes black, and his voice sounding possessed? Silianna started to second-guess her coming into the infirmary alone as she sat there, her body slowly trying to pull away from him.

"What's the matter, Sil? You look like you've seen a ghost," Kelton said, tauntingly.

"I'm not speaking to Kelton, am I?" Silianna asked, voice shaking.

"What gave you that impression?"

"Just a hunch. Are you a Lost Soul controlling him?"

Kelton started chuckling. "Darling, I'm no Lost Soul. In fact, I've had a bone to pick with you for quite some time."

Silianna's eyes widened, and she jumped out of her chair. Her heart began pounding intensely, her body heating.

"Vorkalth," she gasped. "H—How can you control him?!"

"You've caused a bit of an issue for me, and anyone who gets in my way needs to be handled accordingly."

Kelton leaned forward and grabbed Silianna's wrist. A burning sensation grew, and for a split second, Silianna could have sworn she saw steam. She screamed in agony as she felt her skin burn.

"Get off me!" she pleaded.

"*No.*"

Kelton pushed Silianna against the wall, though it wasn't a hard surface that she clashed with. Her entire body felt like it had gone through a liquid portal. She stumbled over a pile of skeletal bones. An awful rotting stench followed, causing her to cover her mouth.

Looking around, she realized that Kelton, or rather Vorkalth, had sent her into the Dark Dimension.

Spirits appeared all around; their mouths moved, but Silianna wasn't able to gather a word they were saying. She could only imagine that they were warning her to run. But where was she to go? It was pointless.

A figure in a black cloak rose from the floor like a flower growing from the soil. His grey hands and sharp nails brought goosebumps across Silianna's arms and legs. After months of hearing about Vorkalth, she was now facing him for the first time.

"*You no longer have until the next full moon, my precious water princess,*" Vorkalth said, pointing at her burnt wrist mark. "*That mark has set the clock. You have forty-eight hours to decide whether to keep your spiritual element. And if I see you meddling in places you ought to be in, I'll make what happened to your uncle look like child's play when I'm done with you.*"

Silianna fell into oblivion. In the blink of an eye, she found herself back in the infirmary room like nothing had happened. She found Kelton still standing there in front of her, his eyes shifting from black to his natural green eye color. Then he fell to the floor, unconscious.

# 28
## The Decision

**MALAKAI**

A heavy sense of nervousness overwhelmed Malakai as he walked down the narrow halls, the palms of his hands starting to sweat. He knew that asking his grandmother to travel to Theuros would be risky, but he had no choice in the matter. As much as he wanted to explain to her the real reason for his trip, he knew that he couldn't. *Keep it vague and short*, he thought. For her to learn that all this connected back to Vorkalth would automatically ruin any chance of her agreeing to let him go.

Two guards escorted him into the glass elevator. Malakai wished he had Eli by his side right now. Kelton and Demetri were... Well, it was complicated. And Silianna was too close to the Eckwood brothers for him to confide in her about them. The only one he felt comfortable talking to was Eli.

It wasn't just the upcoming task that was on his mind. Malakai was still processing what happened to Kelton last night. Something sinister was at play, and there was no way he imagined that, like he was told. However, Kelton was in a normal state this morning, resting. It had Malakai second-guessing when he ran into Silianna.

On the other hand, Malakai was also thinking about his theory of Demetri. The idea of the dark and brooding prince having crossed paths when they were younger was a bit of a stretch, but given everything thus far, perhaps it wasn't out of the realm of possibilities.

The elevator stopped, and the three of them exited. Malakai went ahead, opening the doors that would lead to the conference room. He hadn't been back here since he first woke up and presented himself to the citizens of Avala. It still felt like a strange dream, one he had yet to wake up from.

His grandmother, Maelena Bellemore, was in the same spot she was last time, close to the skyscraper windows, as she observed the glass city in all its snow-covered beauty.

The guards closed the door behind Malakai, leaving just the two to themselves. Malakai played with his fingers nervously and swallowed, secretly praying to the Gods that they'll be on his side for this once.

"How are you today?" Maelena asked.

"I'm managing," Malakai said, attempting to put forward a calm air. "A lot has been happening these past few days, and I'm trying to gather my thoughts."

"That's good. When life throws distractions, it's best to keep your mind focused on the importance of things." Maelena headed to one of her seats. Adjusting herself, she pointed at the chair across, indicating she wanted Malakai to sit across from her. "I sure hope that you are not planning on traveling outside Windsor Keep in the middle of the night like last time."

Malakai chuckled. "No, Grandmamma. I have no intentions of going against your wishes anymore. However, there is something that I wanted to run by you."

"Oh? And I suppose I may have an answer. Go on."

Malakai took a deep breath to steady himself. He tried not to think of the worst-case scenario, but rather the positive side of things. Although the face his grandmother currently had was only making the nervousness worse. It was almost like she was annoyed at him, like his presence was irking her.

"Are you okay?" he asked.

"Yes. Why do you ask?" she responded.

Malakai shrugged. "You seem a little annoyed. I can't tell if it's because of me that you're feeling that way."

And just like that, his grandmother's facial expression changed, morphing into something more apologetic.

"I'm sorry if I made you feel that way," she said. "I could never be upset with you, no matter what. I'm simply anxious because I haven't heard back from Annalu. I'm beginning to worry something may have happened."

Malakai understood. He stood up from his seat and walked over to her.

"I wouldn't worry about it. I've been so fixated on Eli's safety that I tend to forget he's a pretty tough guy." Malakai was lying through his teeth. He was certainly worrying about Eli's safety, but he couldn't let his grandmother know that.

*If she figured out the reason for my travel to Theuros was to somehow fake Narkissa's death in exchange for a device that could conjure portals*, Malakai thought, *she would lock me away for sure.*

"Besides," Malakai continued, clearing his throat, "our army is growing by the second. We have those from Centuris, we have the shapeshifters, we have the loyalists here in Avala, and we'll soon have those from Aeris. The Elder Guardians will have no idea what's coming to them."

"I agree, but it won't be enough," Maelena replied. "We have to corner them when we reach Saint Salvusburg. To do so, we'll have to take control of Terrane. That is why I've kept the Eckwood brothers around. One of them will have to claim the throne and turn their soldiers to the homeland. But it won't be enough. Even if we have Terrane and Aeris, we can be blindsided by Limus and Pyroc. The water and fire kingdoms are the most unreliable, and they will do whatever it takes to protect the homeland."

Malakai's grandmother pulled out a holographic device and activated it. The map of Baskaria was shown, and there were pinpoints of an ideal outcome if they were successful in taking control of the kingdoms.

"If we were to somehow take Pyroc, it wouldn't matter much

when it came to Limus. Two kingdoms against seven? They might as well join us by the time we reach the homeland. But if we were taking Limus and not Pyroc, Pyroc could easily sneak behind our army and attack. If we were to split our focus, we'd have fewer soldiers to fight and defend the homeland. It's too risky."

"Then how do you propose we take Pyroc?" Malakai asked.

Maelena looked lost. "I'm not sure. I know Princess Rahaf will wed Prince Theodosis, which will mean we cannot rely on her. She would not be able to rule the Pyroc throne if she married another elemental that wasn't her own."

"And what of her sister? She had an older sister. Do we know much about her whereabouts?"

Maelena pressed a button on the holographic device. An image of Jacqueline Soulryth appeared, followed by her entire profile revealing confidential information.

"King Bastille tossed his eldest daughter and wife in Sorrow Tower long ago. Rahaf was his only hope to keep the Soulryth Dynasty from falling. Queen Roslynda was killed for helping you escape the night of the invasion. She was loyal to your mother and father until the very end. May the Gods have mercy on her soul." Maelena scrolled through Jacqueline's file and pointed at a specific paragraph. "As for the eldest daughter, she was sent to Sorrow Tower because she had an ability outside of the four natural elements. She was deemed a danger to herself and others because she could not control it—her mind started to go mad. She claimed to hear demonic entities encourage her to massacre her family."

Malakai perked up at those words. The story sounded too familiar, but could it be true? Was there somebody else who had the spiritual elemental out there?

"Grandmamma, you don't suppose she had the element of Eytros, do you?" he asked, curious.

Maelena shook her head. "No. From my understanding, she could conjure more than just regular fire. Her flames were black, and if she had enough energy, she could even create thunderbolts and control them from the sky. No one had heard of anything like it, but the Royal-Bloods collectively agreed to keep it from public knowledge. We've learned of all sorts of elemental abilities, but not this one. No historic textbooks had an answer for it."

"If Rahaf and her sister cannot claim the Pyroc throne, then how do you suppose we take over?" Malakai asked. "The fire kingdom needs someone to follow."

"There must be a connection to the Soulryth bloodline somewhere. Perhaps a distant cousin? Maybe a bastard child? The only other alternative would be to kill the king, and I'm not sure any of us are ready for the consequences of doing that." Maelena looked puzzled and stressed by the endless ideas.

Malakai closed Jacqueline's profile and went back to observing the map of Baskaria. It took him a few moments to try to come up with a clever plan, but when he got it, he got it. Just across the ocean from Pyroc resided Theuros.

"I got it!" Malakai said enthusiastically. "If we can convince the Vampyre Queen, Narkissa, to lend her army, we can have the vamps sneak up on the fire kingdom at night and take over. It's a perfect plan, don't you think, Grandmamma?"

His grandmother frowned, seeming hesitant at the idea.

"What's the matter?" Malakai asked.

"I don't trust the vampyres. I see how they act out there in Avala. I'm willing to let them wander freely like any normal civilian in the glass city, but the fact that they only allow their own kind to set foot in Theuros is what concerns me. I fear they might be doing things illegally that they don't want anyone to see."

"How can you be so certain?"

Maelena shook her head. "You don't understand. I've sent my best men over there to ally once before. They never returned. I speculate Narkissa just wants her and the nightwalkers to remain alone. If there are vampyres who want to travel beyond the island and live amongst us in the South, she does not stop them. But she does not like outsiders who aren't nightwalkers. I've respected that decision and have left her alone since."

He hadn't asked the big question yet, and Malakai already knew what her answer was going to be. Time was running out, and he couldn't bring himself to lose out on the one chance to ask before it was too late.

"I want to travel to Theuros," he blurted out. "Your 'best men' may not have been very convincing, but surely she could reconsider in the presence of the infamous Lost Prince. If she truly wants to be left alone, then she will have to join us. The reality is that the vampyres either fight with us or die alongside us because once the Elder Guardians finish with us, they'll come for them next. Nobody is safe. Narkissa would be foolish not to reconsider an alliance."

"You remind me too much of your father," the Grand Empress Dowager commented. "Not sure if that's a good thing or a bad thing, but you certainly have his stubbornness."

"I'll take it as a compliment." Malakai turned off the holographic projector and stood from his chair. "You and I both know that we have no chance of taking Pyroc without the vampyres. I'm willing to travel with whomever you want to come with me, but I have a feeling I can convince her. I've done it with the queens of Centuris, I've done it with Lord Hussayn, and I can do it with Narkissa. Please, Grandmamma."

Maelena Bellemore sat there, presumably thinking about all of the scenarios in her head. In the end, she looked up at him, worried, but determined.

"Okay," she said reluctantly. "But you are to have either one or both Eckwood brothers by your side. I can count on them to keep you safe."

Malakai looked puzzled. "I understand Kelton, but why make that remark for Demetri as well?"

"My dear, let's not pretend. I know why both of them will go to the end of the world to protect you. If there's anyone I trust, it is them. Now, start packing. We'll have a hovercraft ready for you in thirty minutes."

# 29
## Drifting

**MALAKAI**

Malakai never thought in a million years that his grandmother would allow her own grandson to travel to the most dangerous kingdom throughout the Nine Lands—or so everyone seemed to claim.

The plan was to fly out there, meet with Narkissa, do whatever he could to convince her, and then somehow figure out a way to trick Seraphina into believing he killed the Vampyre Queen. What could go wrong?

Malakai zipped his bag as he finished packing. A knock came from his bedroom door, and he opened it to see Celdric and Nehila.

"Hey!" Malakai said, surprised. "You guys are done with your class assignments already?"

"No," Celdric replied. "We were in the library doing homework, and we overheard one of the guards talk about how you're going to the vampyre island. Is it true?" Malakai nodded his head. "That's so cool. Can you try bringing me back a souvenir?"

Malakai laughed. "I'll try my best, but only if you promise not to join the Resistance to fight."

Celdric rolled his eyes. "Whatever. I'll just die of boredom with these class assignments…"

Malakai playfully shoved Celdric away from him. He proceeded to Nehila and bent down on one knee, keeping eye contact with her.

"How are you feeling?" he asked her.

"I don't want you to go," she said, lower lip trembling slightly.

"It'll be okay, Nehila. I'll be back before you know it. Would you like me to bring you back a souvenir too?" Nehila nodded her head. "Very well. I'll get you both something. But just promise to behave while I'm gone."

\* \* \*

Once Malakai walked Celdric and Nehila back to the library, he went upstairs to the fourth floor. The hovercraft should've been waiting for him by now. Of course, that wasn't the only thing waiting for him when he arrived. Demetri was packed and ready to go, too. He was dressed in dark blue denim jeans, a black turtleneck shirt, and a black leather jacket. His long black hair was down, which Malakai rarely saw, considering his hair was always placed in a bun whenever he saw him.

Demetri's fierce blue eyes scoured Malakai's body from head to toe, then a smile grew across his face.

"Looks like you did it after all," Demetri said, impressed.

"Did you doubt I wouldn't?" Malakai replied, a grin tugging at his lips.

*Stop.*

Malakai caught his tongue. He was getting a little too comfortable speaking to him in a teasing manner. *Kelton*, he thought. *Focus on Kelton*. The last thing Malakai needed was to prove Kelton's insecurities right.

"Did you get to visit Kelton before you packed?" Malakai asked, diverting the topic.

"Yes and no." Demetri was vague in his response, though it was clear that he was doing so intentionally.

"What is that supposed to mean? Did you or did you not?"

"I saw Kelton, but he wasn't in the infirmary," Demetri explained. "I guess they decided to release him an hour ago. He was in his room when I found him."

"Really?! How come I wasn't informed of his release? I saw him earlier this morning, and he was still resting. I didn't think they would be releasing him so soon."

Kelton suddenly appeared in the hallway with a filled backpack slung over his shoulder. He looked healthy and more handsome than ever, minus his heavy bags under his eyes.

Kelton wore a grey long-sleeve shirt and black denim jeans—the opposite of Demetri's style.

Seeing Kelton stand there with a smile brought butterflies in Malakai's stomach. He couldn't help himself as he rushed over to give him a hug and kiss him on the side of his face. His hair smelt of honey and coconut, a mixture that brought Malakai a sense of comfort.

"By the Gods, it feels so good to see you back to yourself," Malakai said softly in Kelton's ear.

"You didn't think I was going to let you leave Avala without me, did you?" Kelton said, cheerfully. "The second I heard the Healers talking, I unhooked myself from those wires and got dressed fast."

"Are you telling me that you weren't officially released from the infirmary?" Malakai asked.

"Yup. But I feel great. It's been a while since I've felt like this." Kelton turned his focus onto Demetri, who stood behind Malakai, pretending not to eavesdrop. "And you? Are you ready for our little 'vacation getaway'?"

Demetri's demeanor earlier simmered away as he went back to his cold, dark self. "Let us pray that we don't end up having a detour like last time we flew to Pyroc."

Kelton raised both his arms jokingly and said, "Hey, at least if the hovercraft goes down, we can say neither of us was responsible for making sure it was charged."

Demetri did not respond, but his lips did twitch up with a small smile. Malakai was shocked to see Demetri smile at a joke Kelton made. He never thought he would see the day.

Outside, the Grand Empress Dowager and a dozen of her soldiers waited by the hovercraft. Malakai felt a mixture of excitement and nervousness. There was no telling how today would turn out, but at least he would get the chance to visit somewhere new, with people he cared about beside him.

Malakai continued looking around in search of Silianna; however, she was nowhere to be found.

"Did either of you happen to talk to Silianna before you got here?" Malakai asked the Eckwood brothers.

"I did not," Demetri answered.

"I saw her," Kelton admitted. "She expressed her interest in coming to Theuros with us, but we thought it was best she stayed put to keep an eye on Celdric and Nehila. I figured since Demetri and I were coming with you, and Eli was in Aeris, Silianna seemed like the best person we could trust to watch them."

Malakai wasn't sure why he felt uneasy about Kelton's response. He did not recall seeing Silianna in the library when he dropped Celdric and Nehila off, which was her go-to place in Windsor Keep.

"Okay," Malakai said, uncertain. "I just wish I could've seen her before we left... She and I have been invested in getting answers on the Dark Dimension for quite some time."

Kelton held Malakai's hand. "Don't worry. We'll catch her up when we get back. Now, they're waiting for us. Let's get a move on."

## 30
## An Old Friend

**SILIANNA**

The last thing Silianna remembered was screaming for help, so why couldn't she remember what she was screaming about? Her memory was foggy. She recalled vivid images of a hallway, a chair on the floor, and then nothing.

*Who was the last person I saw?*

Then again, Silianna wasn't sure how she was lying down on her bed either. Her head was pounding, and the air was so thick that she struggled to get some proper air.

Pulling the silk cream sheets off her body, Silianna pulled herself together and searched for her shoes. There were some black boots by the corner of her vanity. Putting them on, she observed herself in the mirror and saw a burn mark on her wrist.

"How did that get there?" she asked under her breath.

The door to her bedroom slowly opened. Silianna walked over cautiously and swung the door fully open, though there was nobody in the hall. It was silent—too silent. *Something is wrong here.*

Suddenly, her memories came flooding back. Kelton was possessed. Vorkalth somehow got control of him. She then remembered the meaning of her burnt mark—Vorkalth had given it to her.

*"That mark has set the clock,"* Vorkalth's voice echoed. *"You have forty-eight to decide whether to keep your spiritual element."*

"No, no, no," Silianna pleaded. She started to panic, rubbing at the burn mark like she could wipe it away. "This can't be happening."

The sound of footsteps caught her attention. It was coming from her right-hand side. Silianna needed to find somebody as soon as possible to tell them what she saw.

At the end of the hall, a bright light was shining. Silianna chose to follow it, hoping it might be a sign of some sort. As she followed it, she found herself going from hall to hall until she made it down to the doors that led to the library.

The doors opened on their own, and the bright light continued floating into the library until it reached the center of the room. In the blink of an eye, the light vanished into smoke. *This has to be some sick trick by Seraphina,* Silianna thought, trying to make sense of the supernatural occurrence.

"Even after we graduated, you still look flawless," said a familiar voice.

The hairs on the back of Silianna's neck perked up, causing her body to go cold. She would recognize that voice anywhere, but she wanted to believe it wasn't real. Silianna's hand started to shake uncontrollably. If the voice didn't scare her already, the signature scent from this particular person surely would solidify her fears. A pistachio mint perfume.

"N—Nerumi?" Silianna questioned, though she refused to turn around.

"I risked a lot to come see you," Nerumi's voice said.

There was no chance any of this was real. Silianna concluded that she must still be stuck in the Dark Dimension. If Seraphina wasn't behind this, then it was Vorkalth.

"This isn't real," Silianna cried out. "Vorkalth, if that's you, please *stop*. I have no control over when I end up in the Dark Dimension. I'll let go of my spiritual element, just leave me alone!"

"I'm not Vorkalth. I promise you, it's me, Nerumi."

Silianna did not trust her, or rather, *him*. But there was no getting out of his little games. So, she decided to play along as she turned around and came across Nerumi in her full beauty. Starting from her hair, three inches from the start of her roots had pink tones, whereas the rest blended in with a mixed purple, blue, and gray.

Silianna's eyes wandered to Nerumi's neck, where she wore a unique black crystal necklace. The crystal shimmered in the low lighting of the room.

Finally, Silianna made eye contact and felt her heart thunder in her chest. Nerumi's enchanted grayish-blue eyes were what Silianna fell in love with all those years ago, and the feelings stayed true now more than ever.

"I can't tell if this is real or not," Silianna admitted.

"Last time I checked, I'm pretty real," Nerumi said, confused. "I spoke to your little shapeshifter friend. What was his name? Eli?"

*Eli*. Silianna was relieved to hear that name. It was true, Nerumi was real. But how did she manage to get here?

"Did Annalu open a portal for you? Where's Eli? Wait... How did the witches gather strength to conjure a portal so fast?" Silianna asked rapidly.

"Slow down," Nerumi said, holding up a hand. "I'll get to your questions shortly. For now, let's just celebrate the fact that I'm *here*. I've longed to see you since the last conversation we had. I would be lying if I said it did not remain in my head every day, haunting me."

"It haunts me, too," Silianna admitted. "But it also gave me the courage to fight when we were under attack. What was it you always said? *'Kneel for no man.'*"

Nerumi huffed. "I wish I had taken after my own advice. I fear I've fallen victim to pleasing others, but not myself. That's why I'm now taking a risk. Eli and I had a meaningful conversation, so I decided to go through crazy obstacles to come see you."

"What kind of obstacles?"

Nerumi reached into her pouch and pulled out a cement circular artifact. It had strange carvings all around it, filled with glowing blue light.

"What is that thing?" Silianna asked.

"It's called the Disk of Wisdom," Nerumi answered, handing it to Silianna to hold. "The lights you see are stardust particles. This device is extremely rare. It allows you to create portals and take you wherever you want to go."

"You've had this thing with you all this time and never bothered to come see me?" Silianna's voice cracked, emotion beginning to choke her throat. "My brother died, my chances of being a Healer were taken from me, and Rahaf was being forced into an arranged marriage. You could've helped stop the wedding. You could've come to see me while I was in mourning. Why didn't you?"

"It's complicated, Sil. The Disk of Wisdom was locked away deep under Ackermere Palace. Our family had guards keeping watch for decades, ensuring no one ever got their hands on it, not even us. I went through a great ordeal to get it, and I'm not sorry. I had to see you."

"Can I ask you… What did you and Eli talk about?" Silianna asked, reluctantly.

"We talked about breaking the cycle and doing what's best for our own self-interests. I finally came to terms with the fact that I've been in love with you from the very beginning. I allowed my ego and my pride to take over, resulting in me denying how I felt for you." Nerumi looked away. "I wanted Theo and Rahaf to be happy. But their happiness would result in giving up mine to claim the Aeris throne. For me to have the throne would mean I could not be with you. We're two different elementals. You and I both know how Royal-Bloods feel about that."

Silianna's heart ached. A part of her understood where Nerumi was coming from, but she was also hurt by knowing the truth behind her actions. No one should ever have to go through such pain. Releasing her anger towards Nerumi, Silianna walked over to Nerumi slowly and placed a hand on her cheek. It almost didn't feel real, holding her like this, after so long spent apart. Cautiously, she leaned forward, giving Nerumi a chance to move away if she didn't want this. When Silianna saw no hesitance in Nerumi's eyes, she closed the rest of the distance between them and kissed her lightly on the lips.

The kiss was like its own sort of magic, gentle and kind, the sort of kiss Silianna had been dreaming about for a long time. As their lips parted, Silianna smiled, feeling calmer than she'd felt in years. Then, she handed the Disk of Wisdom back to Nerumi.

"That was everything I wanted and more," Nerumi said, grateful. "I'm sorry it took me so long."

"It's okay. Better to happen now than never." Silianna paused, still finding it hard to believe all of this was real. "By the Gods, it *is* you. I'm sorry for acting so crazy when you first showed up."

"Don't be sorry," Nerumi assured her. "I seemed crazy when I was interrogated by a group of guards outside Windsor Keep. A robot also showed up named Celsa and started asking me all these questions, and I'm sure my answers didn't make much sense. But I was invited in, and the rest was history."

"Well, it's a good thing you're here now. I'm in some really deep trouble, and I'm not sure what to do, especially since it involves Kelton's safety."

"Tell me what happened. Maybe I can help you."

Silianna explained the whole situation to Nerumi, starting from when she traveled to Pyroc to save Rahaf and ending it with her meeting Nerumi there in the library.

"I'm just a little confused why you guys would waste your time with Narkissa," Nerumi said.

"Why do you say that?" Silianna questioned.

"Narkissa may have been around for a long time, but the fae-folk quite *literally* have a door that allows them to communicate with the spirits on the Other Side. It's common knowledge in Aeris. That's why a lot of us don't trust them, especially because they don't share that access. Lord Liri most certainly knows a lot, and I can bet you he would be able to get you answers regarding the Dark Dimension and Vorkalth."

"You truly believe Lord Liri could offer his help? I mean, I know they haven't been very pleased with the elementals since the

Emperor Stephanus and Empress Farrah Bellemore locked Lady Jariliz in the Sorrow Tower. We could be risking a lot going there."

Nerumi frowned. "Yeah, but even before they could attempt to kill us, we have this at our disposal if they don't want to cooperate." She held the Disk of Wisdom up in the air. "We could travel to Miracle Forest on a hovercraft and open a portal to get back here if things get off track. That is, if you think it would be a good idea."

"I'd rather find Malakai first and let him know what's going on," said Silianna. "I'm sure he'll want to come along since he was planning on speaking to the Grand Empress Dowager about flying out to Theuros."

"I hope you're not referring to Prince Antonious, Sil. I don't think you have that luxury anymore, especially if what you say about Kelton's possession is true. I fear there may be more than one person in jeopardy tonight," Nerumi said, tone worried.

"Wait. Why are you saying that?" Silianna asked.

"Because I could've sworn when I arrived that I saw Prince Antonious fly off with both the Eckwood brothers on a hovercraft…"

# 31
## Heart of Flames

**ELI**

Nightfall arrived, and the ceremony for Rahaf's wedding would commence in an hour or so. Eli was still debating whether or not to attend. After the conversation he had with Nerumi, he felt he owed it to Rahaf to be a "good friend" and support her, even if it wasn't what he wanted.

He was wandering the outskirts of Ackermere Palace, avoiding the garden area where the wedding would be taking place. His hands were in his pockets, and he occupied his time by kicking small pebbles with his feet, then following their trail only to kick them once more. It was a good way for him to keep his mind off things.

The sounds of guests arriving steadily got louder as time went on, indicating to Eli that there were lots of people coming to attend the event at the last minute.

Eli was wearing black dress pants, black dress shoes, and a white button-down shirt tucked in, but he didn't really care about his appearance. Who was he trying to impress anyway? There was only one girl on his mind, and it was her wedding night.

Violin music wove through the air, romantic and sweet. Eli looked up to see a violinist playing from the balcony. The melody was pretty, but he wasn't interested in being entertained. If anything, it encouraged him to wander further from Ackermere Palace. He thought about shifting into an owl and flying off like earlier, but he also didn't want to hear Annalu scold him for the billionth time—or so it felt to him, anyway.

So, he walked.

He walked in his mortal form and kept going without a destination in sight. By the time he stopped zoning out, he found himself stumbling upon the forest. He turned around and saw Ackermere Palace in a far distance. *Did I really walk that far?* Eli then turned back, hoping to still make it to the wedding on time. But why did it matter if he did or didn't? It wasn't like Rahaf would notice.

*CRACK!*

Eli's head shot up, alerted by a nearby presence. He scouted the area and was stunned to find none other than the fire princess herself, Rahaf Soulryth. She was more beautiful on her wedding day than he could have ever imagined. Her hair was set into a bun, long white crystal earrings dangled from her ears, and her make-up was expertly applied with long swirling swoops of color fanning out from her eyes. Rahaf's dress was long and made of silk, fitting her frame like a glove.

"What're you doing out here?" Eli asked.

"I should ask the same," Rahaf responded. She rubbed her arms up and down, looking off to the side. "I needed to get some air. All my life, I've dreamt of this moment, but it feels like... I don't know."

"Do you love him?"

Rahaf looked at Eli. Her expression was difficult to read, a mixture of guilt and confusion battling for dominance on her face.

"What are you asking me?" Rahaf said, voice a little too shaky to be genuine.

"Do you love him?" Eli repeated. "It's a simple question."

"Yes. Of course, I love him! I wouldn't be doing this if I didn't. Why would you ask such a silly question?"

Eli shrugged. "Why else would you be second-guessing the wedding?"

"I'm not—" Rahaf caught her tongue. "I'm just scared of the

outcome. I fear for what will happen to innocent lives who will be put at risk because I'm marrying Theodosis. The moment word gets back to my father, he'll burn anything in his wake out of rage. Could you imagine the lives lost because I was being selfish?"

"You're not selfish. You're just choosing to listen to your heart. At least, I *hope* that's the case. You've been through so much, and most of it was at the expense of your ruthless father." Eli paused, taking a moment to fight off the urge to voice his real thoughts. "Do you truly believe a war would break out because of this wedding?"

"Oh, I *know* there will be one. He was willing to let my mother die and lock my sister away for good. I don't think he would hesitate to start a war with the air kingdom."

"If a war were to happen, it wouldn't be your fault," Eli said. "Your father has been itching to cause trouble against Aeris for quite some time now. That falls on him and him only. Don't let any of this affect your choices."

Against his better judgment, Eli leaped forward and kissed Rahaf. There was an emotional static that took control as he lifted her up, their lips still connected, and pressed her body against a tree. Rahaf wrapped her legs around his body. The two were so entwined that nothing was stopping them from nearly ripping off each other's clothes. However, Rahaf decided to take the initiative and let him go.

"No," she gasped. "This is wrong. We can't, Eli. *I* can't."

Eli fixed himself up. "I—I'm sorry. I don't know what came over me. I just needed to know."

"I think we both needed to know," Rahaf agreed. "But now that it's happened, we need to drop it before it becomes too damaging."

Eli nodded his head. His mind was still swirling with thoughts of Rahaf's lips locked on his. There was something about it that made him want another taste.

"So, you agree. There is something there between us?" asked Eli.

"Yes. But it doesn't matter. If I don't follow through with this wedding, I might risk the South losing an alliance. I'm sorry, Eli. I truly am."

Rahaf began heading back to Ackermere Palace, but Eli was quick to pull her back to him. They shared an intense stare at one another, though their bodies remained at a distance from touching.

"I just want you to say it once," Eli said, whispering gently. "Say it once, and I'll leave you alone. You'll never see me again. I want you to say those three words, eight letters."

*I love you.*

It was simple, and he was desperate to hear her say it. Unfortunately, she did not. Even when her mouth quivered, struggling to let the words slip from her lips, she did not say it in the end.

Eli had his answer. And so, he shifted into an owl and flew off into the night sky, leaving his clothes to lie there on the dirt.

# 32
## The Island of Theuros

**MALAKAI**

Staring out the window, Malakai observed the sharp mountains that surrounded the island. In the distance, there was an extensive amount of smoke coming from behind a castle-like structure. Curious to know why that was, Malakai asked one of the guards who was flying him and the Eckwood brothers across the ocean.

"There has been an active volcano there for centuries," the guard explained. "It's always smoking, no matter what. A lot of the locals in the Glass City gossip about how the vamps will get rid of elemental and non-elemental bodies by tossing them into the volcano."

"Why would they do such a thing?" asked Malakai.

"Well, you wouldn't keep a body lying around if it's drained of its blood, would you? The bloodsuckers have to dispose of the body somehow."

"That's barbaric. I thought there were laws in place to prevent vampyres from killing."

"Unfortunately, Your Imperial Highness, the rules don't apply to anyone who sets foot on their territory. Many individuals who risked traveling there were never seen again. It's why the Grand Empress Dowager had twelve of us come with you. If they try anything funny, we're ordered to kill them instantly. No mercy."

Malakai took a deep breath. The closer they got to the island, the more overwhelmed he felt. Luckily, Kelton sensed his anxiety was through the roof and gently placed his hand on his lap. Malakai put his head on Kelton's shoulder to try to calm himself down.

"It'll be okay," Kelton whispered.

"I know," Malakai replied, trying to convince himself.

The hovercraft started to go down. Malakai knew in a matter of minutes they would land and be introduced to the vampyres. He clutched onto Kelton's hand and tried to stay focused.

Once the hovercraft landed, everyone unbuckled their seats and began exiting the vehicle.

The guards escorted Malakai, Kelton, and Demetri. The island smelled of burnt wood, though that was expected considering the view from above. Malakai gathered that they were located by the shore on the South side of the island. Burnt trees were visible from left to right, with a path in the middle that he presumed led to the castle he had seen earlier.

The guard gave instructions for everyone to stay close to each other. Malakai wasn't worrying too much since he was sandwiched between Kelton and Demetri as they started their walk.

"I can't stand being here," Demetri muttered.

"Be nice," Malakai said, elbowing his side. "They have good hearing."

"So?"

"*So*, we need to be on their good side if we want them to be our ally. Just keep your eyes on the prize and hold your tongue if you have nothing nice to say."

Demetri groaned. However, Malakai found satisfaction in knowing that he actually listened to him.

Kelton leaned over and whispered, "I give it five minutes before he makes a snarky comment."

"I give it two," Malakai snorted.

* * *

The walk lasted half an hour before they finally stumbled upon civilization. There was nothing but mountains, dead trees, and skeleton bones for miles.

Shortly after, Malakai saw a man approaching them from a far-off distance. He looked to be in his forties, bald, with sunken eyes. The man also wore a long black trench coat with spots of red liquid on his sleeves. *Blood.*

The guards went ahead of Malakai, Kelton, and Demetri. They held out their KT7 Foxsull beams and aimed the weapon at the man. Malakai was shocked to see them using brand-new weapons created by the caedose soldiers four months prior. *Thank the Gods, Demetri brought one to the South for them to replicate.* Malakai only wished he'd been informed of their completion, however.

"Don't come any closer," one of the guards ordered. "We mean you no harm. We simply want to request to speak with the Vampyre Queen, Narkissa."

"You mean me no harm, and yet you stand there pointing a deadly weapon in my direction," the bald man snarled, baring his pointed teeth.

"We come from Avala at the request of Prince Antonious Bellemore. He has joined us in our travels, and he wishes to speak with the Vampyre Queen directly. Do we have permission to proceed forward safely?"

The bald man was speaking in a different language, though he wasn't speaking toward them but rather someone on a headset located in his left ear. Once he finished communicating, he turned his direction back onto the guard and nodded his head.

"The Vampyre Queen has accepted your visit." The man held out his arm in a friendly gesture. "Come along. You have quite a walk ahead of you."

"Damnit," Kelton complained. "Not more walking."

"Suck it up," Malakai said. "We are short on time."

The guards proceeded, Malakai and the Eckwood brothers following their path.

\* \* \*

The castle had eight floors to it, and its rooftop was shaped like a circus tent. Malakai noticed the structures were of obsidian material, which would be expected given the location of the volcano was behind the castle.

The vampyre who led them down the path opened the enlarged double doors. "Before we enter Gancaster Stronghold, you all must wear a gold bracelet. This will notify our vampyres that you are not to be touched and will be protected under Narkissa's request."

Each of their party was provided with a gold bracelet and placed on their wrist.

"Now, I shall give you a proper introduction," said the man. "My name is Destlyn. I have been the Queen's right-hand commander for over a millennium and will continue to serve her for as long as I live. You are not to separate from the group without being instructed, and you may not venture underground. Gancaster Stronghold has eight floors above, and the castle has twenty floors below. If you go below, there is no guarantee you will return. Understood?"

Everyone nodded their heads.

"Good. Now follow me to the Throne room," Destlyn instructed.

As they walked through the halls of Gancaster Stronghold, Malakai was appalled by the vampyres who were openly feeding on innocent lives. The doors to some of the rooms revealed their grotesque activities, and others were straight up sucking people's blood in the middle of the hall. A couple of the people looked to submit willingly, and some struggled to push back from the puncture wounds.

There was blood oozing from the vampyres mouths, enjoying the taste. Malakai wanted to gag, but he knew it would be disrespectful to do so. He tried to focus on following Destlyn, but it was hard when there were vampyres in every corner doing something unusual.

In one corner of the hall, Malakai caught sight of an enormous bat with wings. The bat was somewhat mortal shaped, with grayish skin and pointed ears.

"Are those vampyres?" Malakai asked Kelton, hoping he was

quiet enough for them not to hear.

"I—I think so?" Kelton said, unsure. "We used to study about them in Cressmoore Academy, but I never paid attention. I probably should have."

"Great."

Destlyn intervened in the conversation. "Some vampyres can transform into bat-like creatures. The older you are, the more abilities you obtain. And before you bother to ask, yes, Narkissa and I can turn into one."

"Noted," Malakai responded, unpleasantly.

Destlyn stopped in front of a glass door. There was a fingerprint scanner he used to identify himself before the door could open.

"Prince Antonius Bellemore may proceed, but the rest of his party must remain outside the glass door," Destlyn said.

"You're out of your damned mind if you think we're letting him go alone," Demetri barked, body tense.

"The Queen would only like to speak to the Lost Prince, I'm afraid," Destlyn challenged.

Malakai sighed. He turned to Kelton and Demetri and said, "It's okay. I'll be alright. Just wait here while I speak to her. I promise nothing bad will happen to me."

"If she tries anything, you shout for our help, okay?" Kelton said, grabbing onto Malakai's upper arm and giving it a reassuring squeeze.

"Screw that," Demetri said, annoyed. "If she tries anything, I'll kill her in front of everybody. And you," Demetri pointed at Destlyn. "If I see *one* scratch on him, I promise I will feed your corpse to the wolves and burn everyone in this castle where they stand."

"We have no intentions of harming the Lost Prince," Destlyn told him.

Malakai stepped forward and walked beyond the glass door. Destlyn closed the door behind him, and the two walked down a long red carpet that led to a crystal throne. There, a woman with pale skin and long platinum braided hair sat in a yellow dress with legs crossed. Her nails were about five inches long, sharp, and painted in a black shade of nail polish. As Malakai got closer, he saw the woman's eyes were green like emeralds. *She has Kelton's same eye color*, he thought, amused. The woman's jawline was sharp and perfect; the moonlights that shone above her revealed no flaws about her whatsoever.

Malakai stood awkwardly with his arms crossed behind his back as he waited for her to speak. He was still getting used to the fact that he was royalty himself.

Destlyn stood a few feet behind Malakai and bent a knee, bowing his head after. Malakai wasn't sure whether to do the same or stand still.

"You're the prince that everyone has been fussing about, huh?" Narkissa said, unimpressed.

"Y—Yes, Your Majesty," said Malakai. "I am Prince Antonius Bellemore, but I prefer to go by Malakai Thorns."

"Interesting. You prefer your fake name over your real name?"

"I have more memories regarding my false identity than I do my true identity, unfortunately. Malakai just seems fitting to me."

"*Hmmph.* I respect it." Narkissa adjusted her posture and sat up straight. "Before we continue further, I do have a situation that must be dealt with first. You see, I've been keeping my eye on you for a while since you arrived in the South. There is a fugitive who goes by the name 'Seraphina Blackworth' that my people have been trying to hunt down."

Queen Narkissa pulled out a holographic projector and played a video. The video depicted Malakai and Seraphina talking in the courtyard.

"There was surveillance footage of the two of you consulting outside Windsor Keep," Narkissa went on to say. "Though the footage could not pick up on audio, I wish to know what it is you were consulting with her about."

Malakai closed his eyes and felt a moment of defeat. There was no point in lying to her. "She offered me a chance to travel through a portal and retrieve my best friend in exchange for your assassination. But please know that I had no intention of bringing harm to you."

Narkissa smirked. It was a facial expression that showed she was pleased he told the truth instead of lying. The expression flashed her sharp fangs.

"I appreciate your honesty, Malakai Thorns. And I acknowledge your bravery in doing so. In exchange, I will offer you whatever it is you seek of me, with a limit, of course."

"I'm not sure where to begin. You see, my friends and I have found ourselves latched onto the Dark Dimension. We've been trying to understand how it works and how to stay away from it, but it's been getting worse. Not so much for me, but rather for my boyfriend and my friend. I'm worried the longer they get sucked in, the chances of them getting killed are higher." Malakai reached into his bag and pulled out a book to show the queen. "This is a book Silianna and I came across. It's called '*A Journey to a Dravkyn Realm*' and it was written by you. But we could not read the source material without a drop of your blood."

"I have no problem providing you with answers that you seek," said Narkissa gleefully. "But if I'm being honest, the book is a fake. I only put that note there to mess with readers who stumble upon it." Narkissa snapped her fingers. A servant appeared with a glass bottle filled with a black glittery liquid. "If you want answers, you'll have to drink this potion and wander through memories from the past."

"What is it made out of?" Malakai asked.

"It is a mixture of ingredients found spread across the Nine Lands. Without a drop of my blood, it will not achieve what it is intended for. Since I withhold the information in my head, you'll need a part of me to get those answers."

Malakai was taken aback by her response. "You're not going to turn me into a vampyre, are you?"

Narkissa giggled. "No, Your Imperial Highness. The ingredients mixed into the potion prevent such a thing from occurring."

After a moment of worry, Malakai reluctantly agreed to drink the substance. It wasn't like he had a choice.

Destlyn passed the bottle over to him to drink. Nervously, Malakai swallowed the position. Then, his vision began to fade until there was nothing.

## 33
## Origins of Darkness

**A MILLENIUM AGO...**

A young adult in his late teens with platinum blond hair, emerald-green eyes, and fair skin sprinted through a field of flowers with a group of teens from his village. They were in the midst of playing a racing game to test who was the fastest of all of them. In the end, it was none other than the pretty blond boy who reigned supreme, reaching the end of their chosen finish line with ease.

He speculated that perhaps some of his friends may have gone slower on purpose just to allow him to win because they were so infatuated with him. He had sharp cheekbones, a bit of a pointy nose, and pointy ears. Those features were unusual for those who lived in the village, and ever since he had first met all of them, they had made their admiration and curiosity known.

The world of Zorall had been adapting to a new way of life since the asteroid fell from the sky and shattered the planet. Over fifty percent of the population had perished—the survivors struggled to rebuild civilization back to what it once was.

The boy's purpose since the age of sixteen was to travel to uncharted lands in hopes of finding survivors and bringing them to the homeland of Baskaria—Saint Salvusburg. Baskaria was in the early stages of forming a nation, and the current land the boy found himself in was his next opportunity to have them join his current rulers. He was now eighteen and had proven to be one of the best at locating and reforming the scattered population.

Before the current land he resided on, the boy had come across roughly three villages. But there was something about this specific one that persuaded him to stay longer than he intended to. Or rather, *someone*.

Her name was Anikstasha. She had a wave of freckles that swooped along her nose and cheeks. Her long auburn hair always caught the moonlight with an otherworldly glow, angelic and untouchable. Her smile was as bright as a star, casting warmth over anyone lucky enough to be caught in its path. He made it his mission to know more about her, even if it went against his task to gather as much civilization as possible.

Anikstasha's family also traveled far. They originated from a place called Norken, which was further deep South by the oceanside. Her family's intentions were to find civilization since Norken was running out of resources. It wasn't clear to the boy why Anikstasha's family decided to stay instead of returning to Norken. Her father managed to develop a trading system with the fellow chiefs of the village, Gust and Farley. They kept order in their domain, but they were also friendly to the outsiders. The trading system between the men allowed Norken to continue working smoothly, thankfully.

The boy was heading back to his temporary home when he saw Anikstasha walking alongside some of her newfound friends. She looked to be getting ready for an event. *I know exactly what*, the boy thought. Time was running out, so he decided not to bother her and continued on home.

This particular boy managed to go above and beyond for the village as he provided knowledge and miracles no one had ever seen before. He grew trees, plants, and vegetables, and created a stream of water with a single flick of his wrist. There was no need for labor when he could just simply *do it*.

These gifts were of angelic properties that the boy performed, something that was never seen even in the Old World. Magic could only do so much compared to what the boy was capable of—and it was anything but magic.

Zorall's Creator was not too fond of the influence supernatural beings brought through portals from other worlds. They were not intended for them, and it infuriated the Creator, nonetheless. Four angels, now heralded by those in Baskaria as their Gods, came down from the Heavens and took it upon themselves to restore Zorall after their Creator failed to obliterate every living being on this planet.

It was said that one day they would return when the time was right and select one individual to obtain their four powers.

Although, the boy knew it was not magic. His mother used to say that his "special gift" came from beyond—almost implying that his abilities were God-like. This led him to believe that the Gods would be selecting him since he'd already proven to make good of his abilities. The Gods intended to find a way to ensure Zorall became a healthy planet again and keep it maintained.

*I have to be the one*, he thought. *The others are just as gifted, but not like me. I'm different.*

"Vorkalth!" an older man shouted.

Turning around, the boy saw the man who graciously housed him in his humble cottage wave in his direction. The man, Mr. Kelf, was nearly bald with white hair growing on the side of his head. He wore a puffy cream button-down shirt and black pants. He had a black cane in his left hand that he used to help him stand. The man was fragile, and Vorkalth felt obligated to watch out for him.

"Good afternoon, Mr. Kelf," Vorkalth replied. "Sorry for leaving this morning. I had to help with the crops earlier."

"No worries, my boy. I'd just like to know where you're off to. I want to make sure you are staying safe."

"Yes, Sir!"

Mr. Kelf was like a father figure to Vorkalth. He never knew his biological father. No matter how much he tried to ask his mother for answers about him, she always refused to give him any details. It frustrated him, considering all he had done for her.

It had been roughly a year or two since he last saw her. Many back home said Vorkalth was a spitting image of his mother: Fair skin, intense green eye, and brilliant platinum blond hair. But Vorkalth felt as though those features were slowly fading the longer he was separated from her. He noticed everything about him getting darker. Skin, eyes, and hair.

"Don't you forget about the ceremony being held in Saint Salvusburg," said Mr. Kelf. He pointed at Vorkalth, eyes unusually serious. "The rulers want you and that Norken girl to travel together."

"Yes, Mr. Kelf, I know. I'm just making sure everything here is in order before my departure." Vorkalth looked at the area around him. He knew his time here was coming to an end, and by nightfall, he would have to begin his travels back to the homeland if he expected to be able to participate in the ceremony.

"I wish I could bring you along with me," Vorkalth said to Mr. Kelf.

"Ah, my boy. I am old. My traveling days are behind me. But I surely hope to see you return to us when you finish the ceremony."

Vorkalth smiled. Sadly, he knew there was a chance he would not be returning after today. There was one other thing he was tasked with while on his journey.

*"The Gods looked to choose who would be the best candidate to rebuild this world and rule the nation of Baskaria," his mother once explained. "Better days are ahead, and soon we will have an Emperor or Empress with angelic blood running through their veins who possesses the four natural gifts: Water, fire, ground, and air. That special someone will participate in what they call 'The Wondrous Trials.' Three will perish, and one will come out on top. That will solidify our new ruler."*

Three will perish.

There was a chance Vorkalth would not make it, but given the three he's come across, he felt his chances were high. Especially since his mother was different as well, it allowed a boost in his abilities to be much more advanced than the others.

There was only one problem…

Vorkalth turned around and saw Anikstasha continuing to

consult with her friends across from Mr. Kelf's home. The Norken girl Mr. Kelf was referring to was Anikstasha. He hated the idea that she would die, mostly because he held her in such high regard. There was something about her charisma, her angelic light, that drew him in. If the two somehow managed to make it to the end of the Wondrous Trials, Vorkalth made a pact with himself that he would allow her to win.

"Have you told her?" Mr. Kelf asked.

Vorkalth turned around, puzzled. "I'm not sure I follow. What was I supposed to tell her?"

Mr. Kelf chuckled. "I know young love when I see it. There's something between you two. I think you should tell her before you two travel off together."

Vorkalth shook his head, a sad smile tugging at his lips. "There's no point. We can never be together."

"Nonsense! You two are keen on each other. Go to her before that young fella beats you to it."

Vorkalth observed the man who was approaching Anikstasha. His name was Daymion Bellemore. He had jet-black hair slicked back and wore a dirty white t-shirt with ripped cream colored pants and black boots. There was nothing out of the ordinary with him, which left Vorkalth with very little room to feel concerned.

Out of the blue, there was commotion that came from behind him. Vorkalth quickly turned away his attention from the two and stormed inside the house. When he saw what had happened, he nearly lost all will in his body.

Mr. Kelf lay on the floor, bleeding to death.

There were two vampyres and a faerie huddled over him; their mouths covered in blood.

"W—Who are you? How did you get into the house?" Vorkalth demanded.

"The old man invited us in a long time ago," one of the vampyres revealed. "He was extorting goods from our people. We warned him to stay away, but he didn't listen. You'd best stay in line before you end up the same."

Vorkalth was never one to feel such hatred in his bones, but something but seeing Mr. Kelf's lifeless body brought the worst out in him. Vorkalth crafted a wooden stake out of thin air and used it to massacre the three supernatural beings. It happened so fast that he had no recollection of it when he finished. *My first kill*, he thought.

At the doorway, Anikstasha and Daymion were staring, mortified. There was so much shame and guilt that consumed Vorkalth. He screamed at the top of his lungs, demanding he be left alone.

* * *

By nightfall, they rode in a silent carriage. Vorkalth was railing in the image that resurfaced on repeat of Mr. Kelf's untimely death. The supernatural beings who took advantage of an old, fragile man… It irked his soul. He should've been there for him, and instead, he was too focused on Anikstasha and Daymion Bellemore.

Vorkalth felt the world was slipping from his grasp. Everything that made him unique was slowly drifting, and he needed the world in his hands—to be worshipped as he had when he arrived in all those villages before.

Anikstasha was staring out the window, avoiding eye contact with him. It was evident that she felt his anger and mourning.

"I apologize for my silence," he said.

"Don't be. You lost someone valuable to you. I would feel the same if the situation were placed on me." Anikstasha continued looking out the window.

"But you wouldn't have resorted to violence."

Anikstasha huffed. "Then perhaps you don't know as well as you think you do." She finally looked him straight in the eye. "I would do anything for the people I love. That also means death."

Vorkalth smiled. "What do you think the Wondrous Trials are going to be like?"

"I don't know. I try not to think about it. Whatever happens will happen. But you know what I do know?" Anikstasha leaned forward and gave Vorkalth a gentle kiss on the lips. "We have tonight to embrace each other. Let's make the most of it."

Vorkalth felt the tension between the two heat up. It wasn't long before their impulses took over, and they undressed each other.

* * *

Vorkalth, Aelmon, Huleve, and Anikstasha.

These were the four Prime elementals in question. One would be victorious, and the others would die.

Vorkalth understood that the Gods would be watching, keeping a close eye on each individual. Everyone would be watching.

The ceremony was being held in the mountains between Saint Salvusburg and Ackermere. There was an old circular arena where barbaric fighting had taken place before.

From Vorkalth's understanding, he and the others were to be put into a sleep-like state where they were to journey through a series of tasks to pass. If successful, this would be the method used to determine what element future mortals would claim as their newfound ability. The Gods would offer their elemental gifts to the world once the Emperor or Empress had been selected.

Vorkalth was in a room, isolated from the others. He was with his mother as they waited patiently to be called on.

"You remember what I told you?" asked his mother.

"Never flinch. Never fear. Never fall," Vorkalth repeated, digging his nails into his palms.

"Very good. Today will be a new beginning, and I have high hopes for you. I do not wish to see you die, my love. You were a gift from the Gods, and I've prayed to our Creator that you will prove worthy of the second chance we've been given. I cannot fathom the thought of losing you if I am wrong."

Vorkalth held her ice-cold hand in comfort, a smile curved across his face. "Even if I die, it is for the greater good, Mother. Don't be afraid."

Two of the guards arrived, ready to escort Vorkalth to the arena. Vorkalth felt a sense of anxiousness as he walked alongside his mother, following the guards down the hall.

"I can hear your heart racing," his mother commented. "Whatever happens, I love you, Vorkalth."

"I love you, too, Mother," Vorkalth said, squeezing her hand one last time.

The arena was filled with thousands of citizens who had traveled a long way to witness the Wondrous Trials. Vorkalth caught sight of the current rulers, the ones who governed Saint Salvusburg and Ackermere. There were six of them to be exact, all of whom had their eyes locked on him.

Suddenly, Vorkalth felt a tug from his left arm. He turned to see Anikstasha trying to get his attention.

"How are you?" she asked.

"Better now that I've seen you," Vorkalth answered, a flush creeping over his face.

"I haven't stopped thinking about you since we got separated during our arrival. I felt I would regret not seeing you one last time before we take part in the Wondrous Trials."

Vorkalth's mother gave him a knowing look and then left, giving them space to talk privately.

"Anikstasha," Vorkalth started. He debated whether to tell her about his feelings. But what good would that do now? It would only make matters harder for them. "I—"

"—I know," Anikstasha interrupted. "I do, too. But we cannot let our emotions cloud our judgment. This will only end one way. We can never be together."

"But what if there was a way?" Vorkalth suggested. "What if there was a chance for both of us to live?"

"Don't be so foolish, Vorkalth. You've heard the rules. Three die, one lives. There is no other way. We cannot cheat the Gods."

"I would cheat the Gods if it meant the two of us could be together. There is nothing more I want in this world. I'd give up my abilities for you."

Anikstasha pulled away, leaving Vorkalth feeling cold and hollow.

"Enough," Anikstasha begged him. "There is something I must tell you. If I am to survive, I am to marry Daymion Bellemore. I have accepted his proposal."

Vorkalth felt his heart drop.

"You… You did what?" Vorkalth said, breathless, like the air had been yanked from his lungs.

"There was no way you and I could be together, Vorkalth. I am sorry, but this is the reality we have to accept. The moment we realized I had the potential of being selected by the Gods, we should've stopped this affair between us."

"Do you love him?" Vorkalth said, his demeanor shifting into something heavier, darker, the hope from just moments ago lying dead at his feet.

"What?" Anikstasha said.

"Do. You. Love. Him."

"*Yes*. Very much so. More than you, I am afraid. Even if the Wondrous Trials didn't come between us, Daymion Bellemore surely would have. And he did. I love him, Vorkalth. I'm sorry."

Vorkalth shook his head in disbelief. She was not sorry. He could see it in her eyes; there was no remorse, only pity. Vorkalth hated pity.

"You will be sorry," Vorkalth said, words curling with anger.

Vorkalth dismissed himself, heading to his mother. She stood next to a white marbled oval pod filled with water and bath salt. Wires twisted along the bottom of the tank, trailing through the water and over to where the guards stood.

"Are you alright?" his mother asked.

"You already know, don't you?" Vorkalth asked, emotionless. "I tend to forget you have super hearing. I don't appreciate you eavesdropping."

"I'm sorry."

"Yes. I've been hearing that a little too often for my liking. I would like to get this Wondrous Trials over with."

Vorkalth's mother pulled him in, leaning close to his ear as she said, "Don't you dare do anything stupid. Remember what I said. If you get too caught up in your emotions, you will forfeit your life. That silly girl will mean nothing in the end when she perishes, and you are crowned victor."

Vorkalth did not care to hear what she had to say. It seemed her words went in one ear and out the other. There was only one thing on his mind right now: *Rage.*

The four Primes stood beside their pod, awaiting their next instructions.

One of the governors emerged from the shadows, heading for a microphone to speak to them. "Those who have traveled long and far," said the governor, Zukul, "we thank you for coming. We are all aware how difficult life has been in the past few years since the asteroid came down upon us. The Gods were gracious enough to give us a second chance at life, and for that, we are forever indebted to them.

"There are other worlds out there that chose not to help us, and for good reason. We destroyed our planet, used out all our resources, and endangered our neighbors. And for that, we must look to each other to ensure we keep this planet safe. We must restore it to what it once was. The Gods have created what is called 'The Wondrous Trials.' Four unique mortals have been selected to participate in this experiment. If successful, one of these Primes will become the ultimate elemental who will possess the elements of fire, water, ground, and air. They will be known as the Emperor or Empress of our nation, and we will look to them and their future bloodline for guidance. Today, we will usher in a new dawn and witness the first elemental being."

The audience roared with excitement as they prepared themselves to witness the dawning of a new age.

Anikstasha looked to her right shoulder and observed Vorkalth. Though Vorkalth did not turn to her, he could feel her eyes set on him.

Zukul continued, "After today, we will use the Wondrous Trials as a practice to determine the element for the new generation of children to come. Instructed by the Gods, the mortals will be tasked with finding one of the four elements in a dream-like state. They are in the form of colorful gems. The Gods refer to these gems as the 'Eternal Elements.' Once found in the dream-like state, it will unlock the mortal's element upon returning to the real world. However, in some cases, performing the ceremony will run the risk of never waking up if choosing the incorrect gem."

Zukul shifted his focus onto the four Primes as he went on to say, "As for our competitors, they will be tasked with finding all four of the Eternal Elements. Three of you will perish, and one will succeed."

Vorkalth clenched his fists. *I will be the one to win,* he thought, furious. *They will learn*—she *will learn.*

Vorkalth looked around the arena, feeling anger towards every single observer who cheered on their upcoming demise. He had never really questioned the idea of the trial, why it must be the way it is, until now, with thousands of leering faces leaning forward to be entertained.

Vorkalth finally turned to see Anikstasha. He wanted her to feel what he felt at that moment. *I was willing to look for a way for us to be together,* he thought, *and she chose the easy way out. Everyone is here to watch a show? Then I shall give them a show... They'll get what they're asking for. All of them.*

Zukul raised his arms, signaling the guards to proceed with the next step. The Primes entered the pods, then they were injected with the wires. Once Vorkalth lay still, his body began to float in the water. Closing his eyes and emptying his mind, he felt his body lift to heights unknown. He felt nothing while doing so. When he opened his eyes, there was only darkness that surrounded him. It was as if his soul was being pulled away into a void of emptiness—and it felt comforting.

Vorkalth's body floated in the void until he came across a small green electric ball. Its energy was immaculate, and every impulse in his body wanted to touch it.

"This is not the Wondrous Trials," he whispered, realizing with creeping certainty that things were not as they should be.

There were no gems.

There was no arena.

There was nobody but himself and this ball of energy.

"*The world you've been forced to live in has been cruel and misguided,*" the

238

energy spoke to him. "*I can grant you what your heart desires. I am the void that can fulfil what you are missing. Merge with me, and I can show you things beyond your wildest dreams.*"

Vorkalth was hesitant. Was this truly what he wanted? Would this void give him what he's been searching for?

"*Indeed, I can,*" the void responded.

Vorkalth was left in suspense. It would hear what he was thinking.

"*The supernatural beings were the cause of Mr. Kelf's death. They were the cause of a lot of things. Your Creator made a poor choice in creating them. They're parasites, bringing nothing but destruction. Together, you and I can avenge Mr. Kelf. You can even get the girl of your dreams. There is a way for you two to be together. Just one touch, and it'll all be yours…*"

Temptation was setting in. And with one tap, that green, sinister energy consumed every ounce of Vorkalth's body.

And so, the once loveable being on the planet found himself to be the most dangerous being alive. He did not let the void in—he was the void now.

\* \* \*

The void showed him the truth of his origins in the form of images. One of the four Gods, Pyrocian, flew down from the Heavens and fell in love with an immortal woman. He offered her a gift, and it would grant her the impossible: A baby. Vorkalth was that baby. He was a half-breed. Half God, and half immortal.

"*My son,*" an angelic voice echoed from beyond. "*You have dealt with so much pain, and yet you continue to put a smile on your face. Do not let one small incident ruin the potential of something great.*"

"Screw the pain I've endured, Father," Vorkalth hissed. "It is *my* turn to inflict pain on the world. To be given a father figure and then see him murdered in cold blood. To be used as a pawn in other people's games and be rewarded with nothing. To be shown love, only to have it taken away from me. I've been bullied, called a demon child at a young age, because of who my mother is. And in the end, I've always shown love. Where did that get me in the end?"

"*You mustn't think in such a negative light. The Planet of Zorall may have* been cleansed, but there is much work to be done to live in a world of peace and harmony. You are not the only one who has gone through something in these difficult times. What makes you different is that you have an advantage, unlike the others—a connection to angelic energy. By tapping into the void, you are putting the world in a great deal of danger that cannot be undone. If my angelic brothers and sisters were to learn of the law I have broken by having a child, I'll be damned for all eternity to the Underworld."

Vorkalth did not shed a single tear, feeling no sadness or remorse. Instead, he let the darkness overtake his heart.

"I can see why our Creator gave up on us. You're all a bunch of hypocrites. Every last one of you. I do not wish to be part of your world. Zorall had its chance to fix its wrongs. Now, I will do right and finish what our Creator started. I shall burn this world to the ground and let you live for all eternity with regret."

A burst of green light emerged around Vorkalth.

With a blink of an eye, he found himself back in the real world. Everyone in the arena looked at him, but they weren't looking down. They were looking *up*. Vorkalth was floating in midair, eyes dark as night. The void had officially consumed him. Green flames emerged from the palms of his hands.

Looking down at the pods where the other Primes resided, Vorkalth spotted Anikstasha as she awakened. *No*, he thought. *It cannot be.*

Anikstasha was the first elemental being.

Vorkalth quickly flew towards her; however, Anikstasha did not show signs of fear, but rather determination.

"What did you do to yourself?" she asked.

"What's the matter? You don't like me like this?"

"This isn't you. You cheated the Gods."

"So? We can be together now. You don't need to marry that imbecile. Take me as I am, and together we can rebuild a new world."

Vorkalth held out his hand, but Anikstasha did not take it. Instead, she tapped into her newfound abilities and flew up into midair as well, going up against her ex-lover.

"I am the first elemental being, not you," Anikstasha declared.

240

"You chose the void. You and I can never be together. I love Daymion Bellemore, and nothing will ever change from that, Vorkalth. You must be stopped."

"I can make you love me. I am a God. I can create elemental abilities of my own free will." Vorkalth closed his eyes and reached deep into the void, seeking dark energy across the universe to help aid him in his creations. A burst of green light shot out of his body. "If I cannot have you, then I shall vow my revenge on you and your bloodline to come. A curse."

"We'll see about that." Anikstasha aimed the palms of her hands toward Vorkalth. A swirl of fire, water, ground, and air came from all corners of the arena and targeted Vorkalth, attempting to take him down. "By the Gods, I call on thee in your support. Please!"

The arena ruptured, the ceiling exploding into pieces as four angelic beings came down from the sky. They were gigantic and did not have mortal bodies. They looked like monstrous, extraterrestrial creatures with wings. Each was different from the other. One had a circular shape with an enormous eye, another was made of six rings that secured a ball of fire, the third was square-shaped entity with vast water contained inside, and the fourth was a being made of rocks, yet had the structure closed to a mortal.

The four brothers were quick to transform their appearances into similar features as the mortals, however.

"*Vorkalth, you have failed in your task to choose peace and love over hate and envy,*" Aerislark declared. "*Due to your actions, you shall be sentenced to death by fire. Nobody who seeks dark energy from beyond shall roam this planet freely.*"

Vorkalth burst into laughter. "You cannot kill me. I am Pyrocian's son! A God cannot kill another God. There is nothing you can do to stop me, Aerislark. Your time to fix this planet has run its course. I will start anew. This time, with the planet lit up in flames."

"*Make no mistake, Vorkalth. You are no God. A half-breed will never be a full God. We may not be able to dispose of your unholy soul completely, but we can keep it contained for all eternity. You see, a prophecy foretold years ago by our Creator that an angelic being of His own would betray us when the time came. It seems that betrayal came from our very own, Pyrocian. Your father will be dealt with accordingly, but as for you…You will be sentenced to purgatory—a prison world where you will be accompanied by the void you've grown so fond of. Perhaps one day you may understand the mistakes you have made here today."*

"Fools! Nothing will keep me contained," Vorkalth roared, summoning his newfound powers to lash out at the angels.

A sword suddenly emerged through Vorkalth's chest. Floating behind him was Anikstasha, the one who impaled him with the weapon. Tears ran down her face as they both fell to the ground.

*"As long as you do not possess a physical body, you will always be weak, Vorkalth. I've gifted Anikstasha my Holy Blade, the Sword of Aerislark. It was an artifact created by our Creator with a drop of His light. Only a darkened soul will fall to death from such a blade. Now your soul shall remain trapped in what my sister, Eytrosus, likes to call: The Dark Dimension."*

Vorkalth's body dropped to the ground with a thud, blood oozing from the wound in his chest.

Another angelic being appeared; however, this one was different from the others. She was a Goddess who went by the name of Eytrosus, Goddess of Death. She slowly leaned over and set a kiss on Vorkalth's lips, resulting in his body turning into ashes.

Anikstasha dropped the sword and stood on her knees, watching as the Gods and Goddesses vanished.

* * *

Malakai gasped for air, eyes shooting open.

For some reason when he woke up, his throat was dry and in desperate need of oxygen. Once his lungs adjusted and he calmed down, Malakai realized that he was still standing in front of Narkissa as she resided on her throne. She was in the middle of filing her nails when she caught him returning to the present day.

"One minute," Narkissa said, impressed.

"W—What?" Malakai questioned, confused.

"It took you one minute to travel through those memories. I'm sure it might've felt like a lifetime while you were there." Narkissa sat up straight and crossed her legs. While she did so, Malakai realized that what she said was true. It did feel like an eternity wandering through those memories.

"So, did you get the answers you needed?" Narkissa asked.

"Yes and no," Malakai said, somewhat disappointed. "I have a better understanding of Vorkalth and his origin, but it does not answer how we can start to try and control it. Nor does it explain to me how I can kill Vorkalth and stop him from manipulating the Elder Guardians."

Narkissa raised an eyebrow. The way she looked at Malakai made him feel like he might have offended her by what he said, but he couldn't comprehend which part of his sentence made her feel that way.

"You want to know what will kill the Shadow Lord?" Narkissa questioned.

"Yes."

Narkissa snapped her fingers. Her servant passed over the holographic device. Once activated, illustrations appeared. It showed a crescent moon amulet, an anklet, a sword, and a chalice. *This looks like what Silianna and the Mirror of Gold were talking about*, Malakai thought.

"The four artifacts that house the Eternal Elements," said Narkissa. She switched to the next slide, where it showed the four objects merging. "Once you collect all four, you must perform a spell that will merge all of them. It will create a weapon strong enough to destroy the Shadow Lord forever."

Malakai squinted his eyes suspiciously. "And how would the Vampyre Queen know such a thing?"

"My dear boy… Was it not that obvious? I am his birth mother. I am the one who fell in love with Pyrocian, the God of Fire."

## 34
## Cosmic Love

**RAHAF**

The lingering taste of Eli's lips left a tingling sensation through her body as Rahaf waited behind the doors that led out to the garden, where the ceremony would commence. She could feel the shame twisting her stomach into knots as she counted down the seconds before the music would notify her that it was time to walk down the aisle. Rahaf couldn't stop thinking about Eli, and it made her sick to feel that way when she was about to marry Theodosis. This was everything she ever wanted, so why did it feel like it wasn't enough for her? More importantly, why did Eli feel the need to kiss her now, in all places? It was inappropriate, and yet somehow it felt...

*Stop.*

Queen Senso was standing behind Rahaf ensuring that the last detail on her hair was perfect. There was no sight of Nerumi, and Rahaf did not blame her if she was a no-show. *Thank the Gods*, she thought, relieved. One thing about Nerumi was that she had the uncanny ability to spot a dishonest person a mile away, and Rahaf reeked of it.

"You're trembling," said Queen Seona. "Are you nervous?"

Rahaf took a deep breath, trying to settle her nerves. "I'm okay. I just never thought that this day would come. It's all I fantasized about for years."

"It feels like a dream, doesn't it?"

Rahaf nodded her head. She refused to respond with words for the simple fact that she feared Queen Senso would notice she was lying.

One of the servants appeared and motioned for the queen to step aside so they could talk. In a hushed, frantic whisper, the servant informed the queen that Nerumi was nowhere to be found. The queen responded furiously, demanding as many guards as possible to be sent to locate her. The servant ran out of the room while Rahaf settled back into place, pretending like she hadn't been eavesdropping.

"Is everything alright?" asked Rahaf with an innocent tone.

"It's my niece," the queen replied, exhausted. "I expected more from her, especially since she would have to present herself in front of the entire kingdom tomorrow and claim her title. Either she's having second thoughts or something terrible has happened to her."

Rahaf swallowed harshly. More guilt ensued as she thought about the conversation she had with Nerumi earlier today. The discussion of their feelings surely convinced Nerumi to do something about it.

"Dear, why is the bottom of your dress dirty?" the queen asked, voice rising several octaves. "We have to get this fixed!"

*Crap.*

Rahaf started to panic. She regretted going out into the woods earlier. First, the kiss with Eli, then she was possibly the reason for Nerumi's disappearance, and now her dress was noticeably dirty. *What else could possibly go wrong?*

The music came on suddenly as the queen tittered over Rahaf's dress.

There was no going back now. Rahaf had no choice but to start walking down the aisle. She thanked the queen quickly, waving away her worries, and got into position. Her life was about to change, but she wasn't confident that it would be for the better or the worse.

The doors opened, and a breeze blew through.

Rahaf looked out to the beautiful garden and everyone who was in attendance. Theodosis stood at the altar where the statue of Aerislark resided. Next to him was King Keon and the man officiating the wedding.

Neon blue butterflies flew down the aisle, giving a whimsical experience as Rahaf slowly began her walk with Queen Seona by her side. Music chimed at the perfect time as it aligned with her steps.

Rahaf's heart raced like never before.

She wished to have Silianna by her side. She needed guidance on what to do, even at the last minute.

She examined the air prince in all his glory. Butterflies swirled all around her stomach as a smile slightly curved across her face, though she couldn't tell whether the smile was from nerves or happiness.

The man who stood across the aisle, her soon-to-be husband, had a smile that she could not resist. Smooth pale skin, black hair, dark gray-blue eyes, muscular body features. He looked just like when she first met him, minus the fact he now had a full black beard that made him more handsome than before.

*"When you were questioning your feelings for Theodosis, when did you finally realize it? When did it finally click for you?"* Rahaf heard Kelton's voice ask in her head. It was part of a memory from months ago when she escaped her arranged marriage. Kelton was conflicted with his feelings for Malakai, and he came to her for advice.

*"I knew the moment I laid eyes on him,"* she had replied. *"Though, I was in denial at first. And I think it was one of two of my greatest regrets."*

Rahaf felt her eyes watering, but she fought back the feeling. She felt like a horrible person for entertaining Eli's emotions when she was still in love with Theodosis. It was not okay for her to be acting the way she was.

Rahaf was sure that if Seraphina Blackworth were here, she would say something along the lines of, *"It's okay to love both of them."* There was no reason to hate Seraphina for what she did to Kelton and Demetri when she was heading down the same path as Theodosis and Eli.

This madness had to end after tonight.

*My name is Rahaf Soulryth. After tonight, I will be forever known as Rahaf*

*Steelhart. I love Theodosis, and I am to bond myself to his love forever—until death do us part.*

Rahaf arrived at the end of the altar and joined hands with Theodosis. Both their eyes locked.

"How are you feeling?" asked Theodosis, his voice gentle.

"I'm not going to lie, I'm freaking out," she admitted.

"Are you having second thoughts?"

Rahaf shook her head. "No. I've waited for a long time for this. I just never thought I would see the day."

"Well, Princess, your dreams are about to come true." Theodosis winked, almost leaning into her kiss, but then remembered where they were. A soft flush spread across his cheeks, and Rahaf could feel herself falling a little more in love with him.

The officiator began his speech. By the time he got to their vows, Theodosis went first. He pulled out a cream colored paper with his cursive handwriting as he read aloud, "Rahaf Soulryth, as I stand before you, knowing the elemental laws defy our union and seek to divide us, I lay my heart bare and true. Our paths crossed within the walls of Cressmoore Academy, and something between us flourished beyond those walls. It was an energy much grander than either of us could anticipate. I knew the moment our eyes locked that we were destined to be together. The flames you possess ignite a passionate hold on me that no storm could encompass." Theodosis was choked up, fixing himself before continuing. "I vow to stand by your side through thick and thin, because together, we are the tempest, storm, tranquility, and stillness that merge air and fire. I choose you, not just today, but for all eternity, as my heart remains true to you until the day I perish."

The energy between the two began to escalate as their emotions poured through the garden. Theodosis set the paper in his back pocket, and he reached over to lock hands with Rahaf. A swirl of fire and air could be seen circling both their arms, showcasing their elements flourishing.

Rahaf did not need a piece of paper, for she knew for years what her vows would entail. "In the time of our separation, I waited

247

patiently for the day that destiny would reunite us. Our paths did not cross by accident. In fact, I firmly believe it was written in the stars. The world may have forbidden our union, but our hearts have always known the truth—you and I belong together. Perhaps our cosmic love will be a prime example to the world that it is time for change."

Rahaf caught herself. For some sudden reason, the image of Eli kissing her came into frame. It was ruining her vows, the ones she had planned many moons ago, and she needed to compose herself quickly before anyone noticed something was off.

"You are the air I breathe, Theodosis Steelhart," she continued. "And you contain the fire I hold. I vow to honor our love, to cherish the bond we've forged, and to release any negative energy that may pull us apart. For you are my eternal air, and I am your eternal fire."

They were slowly intertwining as one now, and Rahaf could feel the magnetic pull. She was being drawn closer to Theodosis, ready to collide as one and kiss.

"If there is anyone who does not agree with this union, speak now or forever hold your peace," said the officiator.

Rahaf looked around the garden. There was no sight of Eli.

Rahaf felt a surge of relaxation.

The officiator continued. "Do you, Prince Theodosis Steelhart, take Princess Rahaf Soulryth to be your lawfully wedded wife?"

"I do," said Theodosis.

The officiator looked at Rahaf. "And do you, Princess Rahaf Soulryth, take Prince Theodosis Steelhart to be your lawfully wedded husband?"

Rahaf took a slow breath, steadying her mind. She knew there was no going back now. But in those moments before she said those two words, she oddly enough felt like the world would be okay. *I'm going to marry Theodosis—I'm going to be his wife. He is mine, and I am his.*

"I do," she replied.

"By the powers vested in me, I now pronounce you husband and wife. You may now kiss the bride."

Theodosis closed the gap between them, sealing their lips together.

The crowd stood from their chairs and began to clap. It was a beautiful feeling to know that there was a group of individuals who approved of their marriage. To have two different elementals marry was not common, and in most cases looked down upon. But at that moment, Rahaf felt loved and welcomed.

"Are you ready to go on our little honeymoon?" asked Theodosis.

"I thought you would never ask," said Rahaf, smiling.

Rahaf and Theodosis held hands as they strolled out of the wedding, the guests tossing cherry blossom petals as they passed them by. Rahaf was about to embark on her short-lived honeymoon. *Tonight, we celebrate. Tomorrow, we begin a new journey.*

At the corner of her eyes, Rahaf noticed a strange movement. Although she was reluctant to look, curiosity got the best of her. She had a hunch about who it was.

Standing by the corner of the garden, leaning against a pillar with his arms and legs crossed, was none other than Eli-zak Vakloon, looking like the world had been pulled out from under him.

Rahaf looked away, squeezing Theodosis' hand even tighter, swallowing down her shame and moving forward.

# 35
## Minor Inconvenience

**ELI**

Eli flew through the night skies, an endless sea of mountains beneath him as he flapped his wings. There was no telling where he was headed, but he knew flying would get his mind off the wedding. From the direction of the wind, Eli assumed he was heading East of Aeris.

While he was lost in thought, Eli was suddenly pulled down by an unexplained force. He tried to divert his attention from this magnetic pull, but it was too strong for him to escape. Eli was plummeting fast, and the only thing that came to mind was the trauma he endured the night Malakai's mother died. While they were running from the caedose soldiers, one of them shot a net and caught him, causing him to fall from the sky. Only this time, nothing was pulling him down but a magnetic force.

The view of the mountains grew, and trees came into his view. Eli's heart began beating heavily as he tried to figure out a solution to his situation before he crashed.

Out of the corner of his eyes, he saw Annalu standing by a pond surrounded by willow and cherry blossom trees. In her arms was a folded cloak.

The harsh force slowly simmered, allowing his tiny feet to touch the grass gently. Eli quickly transformed into his mortal body, hiding behind a bush so Annalu wouldn't see his unclothed features.

"You must be out of your mind to be wandering far from Ackermere Palace," Annalu said, furious. "You forget that Saint Salvusburg, Terrane, and Pyroc have the kingdom of Aeris cornered. If you went past the borders, who knows what authority would kill you?"

"I'm fine, Annalu. I just needed some space to clear my head," Eli replied.

Annalu frowned. "You're missing the point. It is my responsibility to make sure that nothing bad happens to you. You were not supposed to be here, and given the fact that you are the grandson of Lord Hussayn, this makes the situation ten times more serious if I have a royal member parading on my watch."

"You don't need to worry about me. I can take care of myself. I've gone through a great ordeal before you came into the picture, and I will deal with it long after we've gone our separate ways."

Annalu tossed the cloak in Eli's direction to cover himself up. Once he did so, Annalu flicked her wrist. Eli's body flew away from the bushes, his back crashing against a tree with an intensity.

"I've had just about enough of your disobedience, Eli-zak Vakloon," Annalu roared, her face turning red. "You are to return to Ackermere Palace and stay put until the witches and I conjure another portal."

Eli groaned. "Oh. We're on a full-name basis now, huh?"

"I can sense your sarcasm is a deflection. You don't want to speak of your emotions, but they are precisely what are causing you to act out." Annalu squinted her eyes and crossed her arms. "Does this have to do with the fire princess?"

Eli looked away, guilty. He knew if he lied that Annalu would figure it out in a heartbeat. Then again, it didn't matter because Annalu always seemed to find the truth in the end.

"How did you know?" he asked.

Annalu huffed. "Did you think I was going to let you, Prince Antonious, and the fire princess wander around Centuris without having my witches keep an eye on you? It was blatantly clear that was when you caught feelings for her. Had you stayed put and listened to instructions, you wouldn't be in the situation you are now."

*Yeah, yeah, yeah. I've heard this already from myself,* Eli thought. *I should've listened to the Lady of Glisten Lake and let fate do its thing. I learned my lesson… A little too much.*

"Word of advice," Annalu started, "Your emotions can be your greatest enemy. These feelings you have for her will only bring you more misery. She's in love with Prince Theodosis."

Eli's fingers fisted in his wrinkled cloak. "I'm not sure what you think you know about my affections, but you're wrong."

"Spare your nonsense. I need you to remain in Ackermere Palace. I cannot have my eyes on multiple places at once. Your safety is my top priority in a never-ending list of priorities. Please do not argue with me on this."

Before Eli could counter her statement, a gust of wind grabbed hold of him, latching itself on both of his arms, and flew him up into the air. Eli was still in his mortal form, unable to shift into an owl for some strange reason. Whatever grabbed hold of him was surely mortal due to the hands securing him as his body dangled. Eli's heart was racing as he tried to see above him. Unfortunately, his cloak was gripped tightly by whatever was carrying him.

"Let go of me!" Eli shouted.

"Eli! Hold on!" Annalu shouted from below.

Eli was able to look down and see Annalu using her flying abilities to try and reach him. As she got closer, the unknown entity decided to fly off, releasing Eli as he plunged down. Within seconds of being released, Eli shifted into his owl form without a care that the cloak was falling, never to be recovered again.

Angry, Eli decided to fly in the direction where the unknown entity went. Annalu was right behind him, tailgating as she too was concentrated on catching this thing.

"Don't let her get away!" Annalu demanded.

*Her?* Eli questioned. *Does Annalu know what this thing is? If so, why did it target me?*

Annalu managed to pass Eli, her flying far superior to his own. Eli's wings started to strain as he slowed his pace. Within a matter of seconds, he started to run short of breath.

Sure enough, Eli began to fall.

From above, he could see Annalu contemplating whether to rescue Eli or continue her pursuit of catching whatever the entity was. In the end, she chose to rescue Eli.

Annalu cupped her arms and caught Eli. She flew them down by a nearby stream and gently set him on a rock.

"You can shift back into your mortal form," Annalu said. "Don't worry. I'll turn around if you're embarrassed."

Annalu turned around, and Eli shifted. He went into the water to rinse himself from the dirt he managed to get on himself when Annalu set him down.

"What was that thing up there?" he asked, tossing water on his face.

Annalu sighed. "I think it was the Superior Witch. I've been trying to locate her for years with little success. Tonight was my only chance, and now she is gone forever…"

"The Superior Witch?" Eli repeated, confused.

"Yes," Annalu replied, nodding her head, staring deeply into the opposite side of the river stream. "She is the highest magical being of our era. The magic-folk rely on her to guide us. In simpler terms, she would be our queen. But no one has seen her in decades. There was a predecessor before the current one who was killed due to her mischievous behavior, tapping into dark magic. We magic-folk can feel when the spirits select a new witch, warlock, or wix to pick up the mantle. But it is up to them to determine whether they want to reveal themself."

"But why did she feel the need to grab me and fly me up into the sky?" Eli scratched his head, trying to have a better understanding of the situation.

"I'm not sure." Annalu shrugged. She looked to the West, and then smiled, pointing. "On second thought, I think she was trying to take you back."

"Take me back? Back where?"

"Look."

As Eli looked over Annalu's shoulder, he caught a glimpse of Ackermere Palace from a far-off distance. *The Superior Witch wanted me back there*, he thought.

Eli rolled his eyes and faced Annalu, unhappy with the fact that he was actually going to give her credit for being right.

"Okay," he groaned. "I'll head back to Ackermere Palace."

Once Eli finished giving himself a quick rinse, he shifted back into his owl form and flew off into the night sky, Annalu following him.

# 36
## Collison

**MALAKAI**

There was a storm brewing outside after Malakai's encounter with the Vampyre Queen. Everyone agreed that it wouldn't be safe to venture out at this time of night. So, Destiny graciously offered the boys and the guards a place to sleep in the West Quarters.

Malakai paced back and forth, chewing on his nails, in the large room he was given. He was anxious, trying to settle his endless thoughts. After a while of pacing, Malakai decided to dust off the bed sheets and puff his pillows, keeping himself busy.

There were no windows in the guest room. The only form of light came from the candles that were set all around him. Malakai didn't know a ton about vampyres, but he thought he heard a rumor that after a hundred years, they could walk in the sunlight without being harmed. Maybe the lack of windows was for the comfort of the new, fledgling vampyres. But who was he to assume?

The door opened behind him. When Malakai looked, he was pleased to see Kelton enter.

"Hello, my love," said Kelton, his voice soothing and calm.

*My love.* Malakai smiled, though he made it his mission not to let Kelton notice. It warmed his heart to hear him say it.

"Strolling through the castle?" Malakai asked.

"Unfortunately, no. I was making sure Demetri settled into his room. He wasn't pleased by my company, but I wanted to make sure he was safe."

"Demetri is a big boy. I'm sure he can take care of himself."

"I agree with you a hundred percent, but I'm concerned he'll pick a fight with one of the vamps and kill them." Kelton chuckled, then made his way over to the bed as he sat on the edge, kicking off his shoes. "So, how did it go with Narkissa?"

Malakai inhaled and exhaled. "There's something I have to tell you, but you have to promise not to get mad," he said nervously. Kelton was reluctant, then eventually nodded his head in agreement. Malakai proceeded to explain the situation about Seraphina, the device she had to conjure portals, and the exchange for the device for Narkissa's assassination. "And I don't know how to fake her death because I have no intention of killing her."

"Do you believe a thing that comes out of that woman's mouth? Seraphina, I mean…" Kelton asked, concerningly.

Malakai shrugged. "I don't have a choice. But that's why I am here, aside from getting answers about the Dark Dimension, I'm going to try to convince Narkissa to give me something to 'prove' I killed her, and also to have her lend her army for battle. I'm praying to the Gods that my honesty will be more than enough to have her army join us."

"You'll do great. I have faith in you. You've gotten this far." Kelton held out his arms, offering for Malakai to go over and hug him. A smile grew across his face. Malakai then gave in to temptation and walked over.

Kelton wrapped his arms around Malakai's lower waist and kissed him on the neck. The tingling sensation from Kelton's stubble caused Malakai to giggle.

"Are you going to shave your face at some point, or do you plan to grow a beard?" Malakai asked.

"*Hmm.* That depends. Do you think I would look sexy with a beard?" Kelton purred. He pulled Malakai closer to him, their bodies pressing against each other.

"Very much. I think I'd like you with a beard." Malakai brushed his hands through Kelton's dirty blond hair, enjoying how soft it was. "Your hair is starting to get long, too. You going to grow it out?"

"I'm not sure. There's already one Eckwood brother with long hair."

"I don't know… Think it might suit you better than it does Demetri."

Malakai used his hold on Kelton's hair to pull their faces together, sealing their lips. The kiss was gentle, and before Malakai could push in any further, his mind suddenly filled with visions. He pulled back quickly, a gasp torn from his lips, as the images overwhelmed him.

*"He's coming," Kelton said, though it wasn't his voice.*

*"W—What's happening?!" Malakai questioned, petrified.*

*"I will burn you and the Nine Lands to the ground. There is no rest for the dead."*

Kelton's black eyes haunted Malakai's mind. The encounter he had with him in the infirmary came back to him. *How could I forget that?* He questioned, mortified. *This isn't the first time I've seen it.*

"What's the matter? Are you okay?" Kelton asked, concerned, his hands holding firmly onto Malakai's shoulders.

Malakai struggled with what to do, whether or not he should tell Kelton about what he saw, but he didn't want to risk sending Kelton into another episode.

"Nothing," Malakai lied. He pulled away from Kelton and headed for the bathroom. As he was about to close the door, Kelton intervened and held the door from closing. "Kelton, let go."

"Not until you tell me what's wrong," he demanded.

"I don't want to talk about it right now."

"Is this about Demetri?"

Malakai was appalled by Kelton's question. Demetri had nothing to do with his distancing.

"No. This has nothing to do with Demetri. Why do you insist on bringing him up?" Malakai asked, annoyed.

"Well, what else am I supposed to think? You've been acting

weird with me ever since you started hanging out with him."

"*Right.* And here I thought we agreed we'd communicate when we have these thoughts."

"I *am* communicating. Right now. But you're standing there lying to me that nothing is bothering you. So, tell me."

Malakai shook his head. "You know that's not what I mean. And if you want the truth, I've been acting weird because I was reminded of the episode you had yesterday. You attacked me in the infirmary and said some awful stuff."

Kelton slowly separated his hand from the door. The anger he had simmered away, turning into concern. Malakai could tell that Kelton was settling into a dark place.

"I... I don't remember any of that," Kelton said, his voice shaking.

"You seriously don't remember? *Any* of it?"

"No. This isn't the first time, either. This has been happening since I was a kid, and I don't know how to control it. Malakai, if I hurt you, I swear I didn't mean to. There's something inside me that just takes control and I—"

"—It's Vorkalth," Malakai interrupted. "I had my suspicions, but it's more apparent than ever. I'm not sure how he's doing it, but I fear he might be the one controlling you just like the Elder Guardians."

Malakai thought back to the moment Vorkalth slithered his way into the Elder Guardians' mind. There was a piece of a mirror, the same mirror Emperor Stephanus and Empress Farrah Bellemore used to conjure him all those years ago, and somehow DeVault came into contact with it. *Could Kelton have come into contact with it at some point?*

"There's no way," Kelton said in disbelief. "I was *born* with this— the spiritual and ground element. There must be some sort of explanation. I just know it isn't Vorkalth."

"You're in denial. There is no other explanation. I didn't want to accept it myself, but we have to stop it. Silianna and I have, or had, access to the Dark Dimension too, but we've never been able to do what *you* could." Malakai cleared his throat. He didn't want to go into much detail about his conversation with Narkissa, but he felt he had no choice. "Narkissa showed me Vorkalth's memories. I saw when the Dark Dimension was created. I know what can kill him. We just need to collect—"

"—STOP." Kelton's voice suddenly roared, demonic and not his own. His green eyes slowly started to be overtaken by black, like spilling ink.

Malakai knew instantly what was about to take place.

Kelton raised the palm of his hand, and an invisible force struck Malakai, sending him flying across the room. He collided with the bedframe, banging his head against the wood. He groaned and raised a shaky hand to his forehead, pulling it back to see blood staining his fingers.

"Your knowledge will be the death of you," Kelton hissed.

"I know it's you, Vorkalth," Malakai said, panting. He was breathing hard, his chest feeling as though it was tightening. "I won't let you take control of him."

"My dear prince, you have no idea how long this has been in motion. If you had any intention of stopping me, you are far too late."

Malakai's vision started to blur as a ringing noise buzzed in his ears. The next thing he knew, Malakai saw Demetri and a couple of the guards barge into the room.

Through barely open eyes, Malakai saw Demetri rush towards Kelton, anger clear on his face. He tried to sit up, stop the fight before it happened, but he couldn't move. As Demetri collided with Kelton, everything went dark.

# 37
## Settlement

**DEMETRI**

The vampyres had escorted Malakai and Kelton into an unusual chamber made of grey bricks and stone slabs. The two boys had been placed on floating medical beds. The atmosphere going down the elevator left Demetri uncertain. He caught a whiff of what smelt like bloody metal once they reached the bottom, something he could only imagine was dried up blood of some sort. *I wonder how many innocent lives were taken down here to be tortured for the bloodsuckers' amusement*, he thought.

There was a thick metal door with a gold sign labeled "EXPERIMENTAL FACILITY." It was alarming to see *this* was where they were taking his brother and the Lost Prince to provide them medical attention.

The bruises on Demetri's knuckles were too fresh, burning as he clenched his hands into fists. When Demetri came into the room and saw Malakai lying on the floor with Kelton standing over him, anger consumed him, destroying his reason. He'd lunged forward, attacking Kelton with punch after punch. Sadly, he did not believe his attack was what caused Kelton to pass out. There was no blood, no bruises, no nothing. Kelton couldn't get hurt, and even if he managed to get cut, the wound would heal in the blink of an eye.

Something else must've caused him to go unconscious. The thought infuriated Demetri.

"Your heartbeat is racing at an incredibly alarming rate, Prince Demetri," said Destlyn, calmly. "And I can hear you clutching your fists. If you do it any harder, you'll reopen your wounds."

Demetri was in no mood to humor him. "You would feel the same if you saw two of the most important elementals fall unconscious," he replied, bitter words squeezing from between his teeth.

"Unfortunately, my heart does not beat, nor do I have anyone I care for to be so anxious and upset. But if you have concerns for them, I can assure you that our Healers will do everything in their power to help."

Demetri huffed. He was familiar with all sorts of supernatural beings having their own form of Healers, including elementals and mortals. But something about the thought of a vampyre healer made him feel tense. There was only one thing he could think of, and he did not agree with such a thing.

"*Your* Healers?" Demetri said mockingly. "What are they going to do? Give Malakai and Kelton a drop of their blood so they can heal quickly? I don't think so."

"Prince Demetri, I urge you to restrain yourself," Destlyn said patiently. "Our Healers have other ways of providing medical attention besides vampyre blood. We understand the risks for someone to transform into a vampyre accidentally had they died with blood in their system. We would *never* do such a thing without consent."

Demetri stood like a dangerous statue, hardly blinking. He never liked the bloodsuckers, and he still didn't. But he agreed with Destlyn on one thing—he needed to be careful with what he said. Malakai and Kelton's lives were in their hands, and Demetri needed to stay on their good sides until they were able to leave.

\* \* \*

It had been three hours, give or take. Demetri was slouched down on his chair in the waiting room he had been placed while he awaited some news. To keep himself occupied, he communicated with Celdric and Nehila through his glass communication device. Originally, he tried to reach Silianna, but her device seemed to be off after three attempts. Luckily, the Celdric picked up.

The kids were catching him up on their class assignments and asking when he and Malakai would be coming home. Of course, Demetri had to brush off the conversation and give as little information as possible so they wouldn't be too concerned about Malakai's well-being.

"Anyways, have you been working on your battle combat skills?" Demetri asked Celdric.

"I have, actually," Celdric answered gleefully. "Since Kai isn't breathing down my neck, I've been able to practice with some of the guards. They're cool, but they're not you."

Demetri smiled. "There's no teacher who's as good as me." Demetri switched his focus from Celdric to Nehila. "What about you? Are you having fun with Silianna?"

Nehila tilted her head, puzzled by his question. "What do you mean? I haven't seen the water princess in a while…"

Demetri nearly lost his sanity. "W—What do you mean you haven't seen the water princess? She was supposed to be watching over you two. If she isn't there, then who is keeping an eye on you guys?"

"Honestly, nobody," Celdric said, not bothered by the fact that he's unsupervised. "It's just been me and Nehila for the most part. I make sure she gets her class assignments done, take her for breakfast, lunch, and dinner, and then we just relax. The guards haven't even questioned why we're roaming the castle unsupervised."

Demetri placed his hand over his face, followed by a groan. *What is even happening around here?* He questioned. He had hoped contacting the kids would relieve some stress he was having for Malakai's well-being, but this was making everything worse. It all made sense now, why Silianna hadn't been answering her communication device. *Something must've happened to her.*

"Okay," Demetri began, "Celdric, I need you to request for the

Grand Empress Dowager and notify her that Silianna might be missing. She hasn't been answering any of my calls nor have either of you heard from her. I'm concerned something might've happened and we need to make sure she is okay. Do you understand my instructions?"

"Yes, Sir." Celdric nodded. "I'll go find her now and notify her."

"Good. Keep in touch with me if you get any updates. I'll talk to you later." Demetri turned off his device and placed it back in his pocket. He then got up from his chair and began pacing back and forth, digging his fingers into his palms as he juggled with what his next plan would be.

The door opened behind Demetri, and entering the waiting room was none other than the Vampyre Queen herself, Narkissa. She wore a short silk black dress with a pair of leather black heels, and her platinum blond hair was tied up into a casual bun.

"Hello, Prince Demetri," the queen said seductively. "You look so ravishing when you're angry. What seems to have worked you up?"

"Aside from the fact that my brother and Malakai are unconscious, I'm stuck on an island filled with vampyres, and my best friend is missing?" Demetri kept his distance from Narkissa as she took a few steps toward him. "What's the latest with Kelton and Malakai?"

"Destlyn informed me that they are almost done analyzing their conditions. They have ideas about what might be going on with them, but they do not wish for me to relay the information until it is confirmed."

"Are either of them dying? That's all I need to know."

Narkissa shrugged, signaling that she couldn't care less what happened to either of them. Demetri wasn't sure if this was just an act of hers, but he wasn't entertained by it for a second.

"You're telling me you have no idea whether Kelton and Malakai are going to live? Because I swear I will drive a wooden stake through your fucking heart right now. Queen or no Queen, I am in no mood for your silly games."

Narkissa smiled, her nose crinkling. "I like you. You remind me so much of myself. You love them both, and I have to respect that." Narkissa sighed, annoyed. "To answer your question, regardless of how bad their conditions are, we can ensure that they're well."

"You're not giving them vampyre blood."

"If you say so… There's only so much we can offer before we resort to our *gift*. But I digress. Whatever the circumstances are, we'll find a way. I need the Lost Prince just as much alive as the nation of Baskaria does."

Demetri squinted his eyes, suspicious as to why that was. "Why do you need Malakai alive? What do you have up your sleeves?"

Narkissa looked down at her sharp black nails, then reached down and pulled out a nail file from between her breasts.

"I showed Malakai a memory that pertained to the Shadow Lord. His origin story, if you will. Vorkalth should never have been born, and I am partially to blame for that. So long as he exists in some capacity, I bear the *Death of Affection*. I can't have intercourse, let alone a simple kiss, without someone instantly dying. It was a curse bestowed upon me by the Gods."

"I don't understand. What did you do to make the Gods curse you? Did you drain an entire village of their blood or something?" Demetri asked.

"That is such a stereotypical thing for you to say. I am not a monster. I simply fell for someone I shouldn't have had many moons ago." Narkissa examined Demetri's clueless facial expression. "Did the Lost Prince not inform you of any of this?"

Demetri shook his head. "No. He went straight to his guest room. I did not get to speak to him after you two had your private moment together."

Narkissa gasped, though it was for lack of surprise. Her hands reached his face as she cupped the bottom of his chin and pulled him close to her.

"You're so adorable. And yet, *so* cliche. I can sense you were bitter saying that out loud. '*Oh, how I wish the Lost Prince picked me instead of my brother!*' So tragic…" Narkissa burst into laughter.

"You're in love with him, aren't you? I can hear your blood pulse when I mention him. I'm curious to know if he feels the same way about you."

"I will kill you if you say another word," Demetri said, grinding his teeth. "Keep your distance."

"*Mmm*," Narkissa purred. "Looks like I hit a nerve. That's fine. Your reaction is so telling. I love getting a rise out of others. But anyway, I suppose we can get back to the original topic..." Narkissa walked off, dropping Demetri's face. "What the Lost Prince learned was that I am the Shadow Lord's biological mother. It is why I was able to showcase Vorkalth's memories to him earlier. I fell in love with the God of Fire, Pyrocian. It was not pretty when the first Wondrous Trials happened, trust me. My life has plummeted drastically ever since."

Demetri was not an expert when it came to the vampyres, but one thing he knew for certain was that vampyres could not procreate. Were the laws of physics different when it came to a God? Either way, Demetri did not want to know. Learning that Narkissa was the Shadow Lord's mother was enough for him to want to vomit.

"So let me get this straight," Demetri started. "You need Malakai alive so he can rid Vorkalth from existence, in which case the curse the Gods cast on you will be removed and allow you to sleep around once more?"

"Careful, Prince Demetri. I've been very generous to let you speak to me so disrespectfully, but my patience is wearing thin."

"Doesn't matter," Demetri said, crossing his arms and leaning against the brick wall. "All I care about is making sure Malakai makes it out of this island alive. You do whatever you feel is best to punish me, but I just want Malakai to be safe."

"It's funny. You didn't mention your brother. Why is that?" Narkissa questioned.

Demetri held his tongue. He wasn't sure why he didn't mention Kelton. A while ago, he was concerned about his safety. But if it came down to it, Demetri had much rather neither he nor Kelton survived if it meant Malakai living. Perhaps he felt that if he couldn't have Malakai, no one could.

"I've grown bored of this conversation," Demetri said with a frown. "Can you contact your little henchman and see if there are any updates?"

"You're in luck. Destlyn was on his way here. I heard his footsteps searching for us."

"About time," Demetri murmured.

Destlyn entered the waiting room. He had a holographic clipboard in his hand as he activated the device to showcase the charts and diagnosis for Malakai's records. Demetri disregarded whatever Destlyn was explaining at the start as he read from the charts what the vamps figured was going on with Malakai: Traumatic brain injury.

"It seems that when Prince Kelton pushed Prince Antonius to the wall, he did so aggressively that he caused severe head trauma. We discovered that the bleeding was coming from the back of Prince Antonius' skull. We were successful in stopping the bleeding from the outside; however, the inside of the skull took the most damage. He's suffering from internal bleeding."

Demetri, out of anger, managed to grab the holographic clipboard and smash it against the brick wall before yelling. "You bloodsuckers better do *everything* you can to ensure he gets better, or I'll burn this fucking place to the ground. We risked a lot coming here, and I will *not* have the Lost Prince die here after everything he's been through. Do you hear me?"

"Watch how you speak to Destlyn," Narkissa intervened. "Dare I remind you that it was your kind that inflicted this on the Lost Prince. Not us. You're lucky we're being generous enough to help him."

"How dare you. You may be of royalty, but you are no queen of mine. Dare I remind *you* that none of this would be happening if you had never fallen in love with the God of Fire. Everything that has occurred up to this point was because of *your* selfishness."

"My Queen?" Destlyn said, shocked by Demetri's outburst. "You told him your secret?"

Narkissa shook her head. "I spoke to you of that in confidence. Not many know of my affair with Pyrocian. You will do well to keep this secret if you wish for my people to continue giving the Lost Prince the care he needs."

Demetri knew the Vampyre Queen was deflecting and giving empty promises. There was technology that could fix fractured skulls and fix internal bleedings, but those machines would only be located back on the mainland. The vampyres did not need such devices, given their healing abilities.

"From the sounds of it," Demetri started, "there's not much any of you can do without giving him some vamp blood. His skull is fractured. Unless you have the technology to fix it, I'd say we're pretty much at a crossroads."

Narkissa and Destlyn exchanged looks. That only solidified to Demetri that they did not have the technology as expected.

"What do you propose we do for the Lost Prince?" Destlyn asked Demetri. "We'll hold his fate in your hands."

"Seems fitting, considering..." Narkissa bitterly commented.

"Well, we don't have much of a choice in the matter, I suppose," Demetri spat, already regretting the words that were about the come out of his mouth. "We'll have to give him some vamp blood."

"Very well," said Destlyn. "I shall notify the Healers to proceed with the injection."

"No," Narkissa interjected. She took a deep breath, not pleased with what she was about to say. "I shall be the one to give the Lost Prince my blood. It won't last as long in his system compared to regular vampyres, but it will remain within him for twenty-four hours. At which time, you, Prince Demetri, will have to ensure he is kept out of harm's way so he does not die with it in his system. Once the twenty-four hours are up, he will be perfectly fine."

"You mean to tell me you could've offered your blood after all this time and you stood there and let me ramble on?" Demetri said, annoyed.

"You were adamant that the Lost Prince should not have

vampyre blood in his system. Why would I waste my breath?" Narkissa smirked, enjoying the fact that she made Demetri eat his own words. "But I also just came up with a brilliant plan to trick your ex-lover into thinking the Lost Prince killed me. So long as he has my blood in his system, he can use a glamour mark to make Seraphina Blackworth believe I am dead."

"How is that possible?" Demetri questioned.

"I had an affair with a God. Things happened… There's a reason I was given the title of '*The Vampyre Queen.*' I'm one of a kind."

"Whatever. Let's just get this over with. We'll figure out the whole 'glamour' thing after Malakai has recovered." Demetri felt relief for a split second before he remembered Malakai wasn't the only one with the Healers. "What about my brother, Kelton?"

Destlyn frowned. He looked down at the damaged holographic clipboard and then back at Demetri.

"I wish I could show you, but alas," said Destlyn. "Nevertheless, it seems he just needs a rest. But we were wondering if we could keep the prince here a little bit longer so we could run some tests on him. For whatever reason, Prince Kelton shows traits of a vampyre when he heals. It is unusual for an elemental to have such unique abilities."

*Damn.* Demetri was so focused on Malakai, he had forgotten that Kelton had fallen under the radar for years without anyone speculating. It seemed his secret was slowly coming to an end.

"My mother and father have done their best to keep this hidden from the public, but Kelton has had this *thing* inside him since he was born. There's been speculation on what it is, whether it is an unknown spiritual element or perhaps something out of this realm. Either way, he is not your typical Terrane elemental. Kelton has tried to suppress these dark abilities, but I fear they may have gotten worse recently."

Narkissa's mouth fell wide open. Destlyn's reaction was not far off from hers. His eyes were wide open like he'd just seen something terrifying.

"You don't suppose he's referring to the Dark Dimension, do

you, My Queen?" Destlyn asked Narkissa after a hard swallow.

"It would make a lot of sense, but even more so a reason to keep him here and run some tests." Narkissa redirected her attention to Demetri. "I might have a way to help your brother. Anyone who is tapped into the Dark Dimension can run a great risk of falling under Vorkalth's control. If it isn't too late, we can start working on creating a block."

Demetri cocked his head. He was intrigued by the idea, but he was also concerned about leaving his brother here in Theuros. The Grand Empress Dowager gave everyone a return date, and if they did not return to Avala by tomorrow night, then she would wreak havoc on the vampyres.

Thinking strategically, Demetri reminded himself that Malakai's intention was to also convince Narkissa to lend her army to battle. If that were to happen, perhaps Demetri could make a deal.

"I'm willing to have you run tests on Kelton, but on one condition," said Demetri.

"There's always something with you elementals," Narkissa responded, unamused. "Name your price."

"A big reason we came here was to ask if you would be willing to lend us your army as we prepare our attack on the remaining Elder Guardians. I know it's a lot to ask, but we're desperately trying to outnumber them, so they have no choice but to surrender. It's the only way Malakai can claim the Baskarian throne without them getting in his way."

"Historically speaking, elementals have been known to treat vampyres like the runt of the litter. I would need reassurance from the Lost Prince that my people will be protected when he claims the Baskarian throne."

"Then I shall have him perform a Blood Oath to seal the deal if that is all you wish from him."

"Perfect," Narkissa said with a slow, unsettling smile. "Now, let us head to the boys and get them all situated before they worsen." Narkissa looked at Destlyn. "Prepare for the procedure."

"Yes, My Queen," said Destlyn.

Destlyn went on up ahead, leaving Demetri and Narkissa as they walked side-by-side down the hall. By the time they reached the door to the experimental facility, Demetri was quick to stop Narkissa and pull her to the side.

"Not so fast," said Demetri. He stared coldly at Narkissa. "I want to ensure that my brother will be safe while he's being tested on."

"What do you propose?" Narkissa purred.

"A Blood Oath of my own. Show me I can trust you. Prove us elementals wrong and that you vamps are more than we believe you to be."

Narkissa paused. It almost looked like she was pleased to see Demetri had decided to give her and her people a chance to see them in a different light. Nothing delighted her more, and Demetri knew when he saw a sincere smile crease across her face.

A settlement was made.

## 38
## Miracle Forest

**SILIANNA**

The sun rose in the sky, shining on Silianna and Nerumi as they flew through the morning sky in a Rem hovercraft. Both of them had managed to sneak one out early while it was still dark out. Luckily, no one caught them or tried to stop them from taking off. Time was ticking until her forty-eight hours were up. This would be her last chance to seek some help from the fae-folk regarding the Dark Dimension, or she'd end up just like her uncle.

Silianna had spent most of last night catching Nerumi up on everything she'd missed since Malakai came into her life. Nerumi was a bit taken aback by the whole thing, but she was quick to reassure Silianna that the fae-folk could help her with her issue. One of the biggest takeaways of last night was the fact that Silianna had a burn mark on her wrist. Nerumi was frightened of the idea that Silianna could get injured even in a world that wasn't physical. Though, there was very little she could do about it. Silianna accepted this fact.

Nerumi navigated the vehicle while Silianna sat in the passenger seat. She was adjusting her bag as she double-checked the extra clothes and health products she had packed. There was no telling how long they would be in Miracle Forest, but Silianna felt it would be best to bring the essentials.

"Are you nervous?" Nerumi asked, her eyes locked on the sky.

Silianna looked up. She tried to play it cool like nothing was bothering her, but it was clear she was anxious. "Nervous? Me? Why would I be nervous?"

Nerumi glanced at Silianna's facial expression. "I know that look. You were overthinking. You used to do it all the time at Cressmoore. You're thinking about the Dark Dimension, aren't you?"

Silianna sucked her teeth. "I mean, how could I not? After that encounter with Kelton, I'm more convinced Vorkalth has something up his sleeves." Silianna pulled out her glass communicator and scrolled through her contacts. Whenever she tried to contact Malakai or Demetri, the system refused to connect her to them. "I've tried reaching out to the boys, but for some reason, they don't have service. I'm worried about them. If there's a way to stop Vorkalth from attacking me or Kelton, then I'm going to do it. Even if it means putting my trust in the fae-folk."

Silianna swallowed down her worries. She knew it was risky, but what other choice did she have? Nerumi said it herself—Narkissa, the Vampyre Queen, was no help. And the magic-folk were occupied with the issues in Aeris.

Silianna rubbed the burnt mark on her wrist. "The Dark Dimension is all I think about. Vorkalth is terrorizing my friends and me. I feel helpless. I should've never helped those Lost Souls cross over to the afterlife. My uncle is mad at me, Vorkalth wants me dead, and the spirits no longer want me to have my spiritual element. It's a horrible feeling."

"I understand. That was your outlet for practicing being a Healer differently. That's where your passion lies, and it sucks to have to be punished for that." Nerumi shifted the navigation as the hovercraft slightly tilted. "Hold that thought. It looks like we've officially arrived at Miracle Forest."

Silianna looked out the window and saw the colorful sea of trees down below. They had glitter substances that allowed the leaves to shimmer even without the sun shining on them.

"There's some information I should relay to you before we land," said Nerumi.

"I'm all ears," Silianna said, her eyes still locked on the colorful trees.

"First, don't eat or drink anything that these folk give you. Everything is a drug there, and you'll be hallucinating for days."

Silianna nodded. "Got it. Next."

"Second, don't try to make a deal with them. The fae-folk typically bind their contracts through words. If it sounds like you're being offered a deal, most likely, it is. Just don't respond to them."

Silianna took a mental note of that warning and nodded her head again. "Alrighty. Anything else?"

"And thirdly, *never* tell them anything personal about you. They keep your memories and use them as leverage to blackmail you in the future if they need to. There's nothing worse than thinking you've gotten free with no problems, only to have one of those distrustful fae ruin your day in the snap of a finger."

Silianna took a deep breath. She knew she was getting herself into some crazy stuff, but she didn't realize just how serious it was. *All I want to do is get some answers and stop Vorkalth from hurting me and my friends*, she thought.

Nerumi landed the Rem hovercraft on the ground.

Silianna was the first to exit the vehicle. She took one step and saw all the flowers around her glow in bright, beautiful colors. There was an overwhelming scent of warmth, woody, with fresh hints of a fruity, sweet scent.

"This is a peculiar smell," Silianna commented, wrinkling her nose.

Nerumi exited the vehicle, wearing a pair of sunglasses and an umbrella to give herself some shade. Silianna wanted to ask why she was wearing all that when it was warm outside, but her thoughts were forgotten as Nerumi spoke.

"You'll have to get used to the smell. I've heard that's what the entire forest smells like," said Nerumi, unpleased. "After a while, it starts to give you a headache. Or maybe that's only me. I don't know."

"How come you know so much about this? I don't recall any of our professors teaching us this stuff at Cressmoore," Silianna questioned, feeling slightly suspicious.

Nerumi shrugged. "I wandered around Ackermere Palace and stumbled across my grandparents' belongings. They were locked away in a room, collecting dust. Books and technologies with stored information of our history were in there, and that's how I educated myself on the matter."

Silianna held her tongue. It seemed like Nerumi wasn't going to give up any more information, so prying would only agitate her. The two proceeded to a wooden gate with unique carvings of the fae-folk holding spears. The images looked to be of them guarding a circular object in the middle. Some swirls circled inside the object, giving off an illusion of water. Silianna gathered that perhaps the image was of them guarding the portal—a similar one that Annalu and the witches conjured.

"Why does their gate have that?" Silianna pointed at the portal imagery.

"That's a doorway to the spirit realm. I believe that's where we'll get our answers regarding Vorkalth." Nerumi reached into her small leather bag and pulled out the Disk of Wisdom. "Remember, if things get too hectic, I will activate the device, and we'll travel out of here."

"Should we have a safe word in case things get out of control?"

"A safe word? *Hmm*." Nerumi wandered in thought for a few seconds before randomly suggesting, "I got it. *Islane*."

"Islane?" Silianna snorted. It was a famous fruit back in the North; something she hadn't had since she arrived in Avala. An islane was a blue triangular fruit. It was one of many things created when the asteroid plummeted into Zorall over a millennium ago. "I suppose we can use it. But now I'm craving some islane…"

"We'll find you some," Nerumi promised.

As they approached the gate, the doors swung open to reveal over a dozen fae-folk guards standing guard, holding weapons. All of them had pointy ears with all sorts of colored eyes and skin that ranged from blue, pink, purple, green, orange, and red. One of them, a female guard with muscular features and braided pink hair, approached the two. She glared as her purple eyes locked on Silianna's. The guard had shimmering pink skin and wore metallic armor with sharp shoulder pads.

"Turn back around or face the consequences," demanded the guard.

"Please," Silianna started. "We've come to speak to Lord Liri. We come for his help on a difficult matter."

"You speak of the Shadow Lord and his Prison World, don't you, *Princess of Limus?*" the guard said.

Silianna was left in disbelief. "H—How did you know of—"

"—We're close with those who roam the spirit world. We know you and your little escapades there. You have infuriated the Shadow Lord." The guard pointed at the burn mark on Silianna's wrist. "He's marked you. We do not wish to have you bring such darkness upon us. Turn back around or face the consequences."

"Please! This is bigger than just me. Prince Antonius Bellemore and—"

"—Yes, we know of the Lost Prince and Prince Kelton Eckwood all too well. Those two will bring nothing but destruction upon the Nine Lands." The guard snapped her fingers. Sparkly dust emerged from her hands and floated in midair. The dust then formed into an image of a woman. "The Lady of Glisten Lake came to Lord Liri after the Lost Prince was announced alive to the South. We've heard her testimony, and we've collectively decided not to interfere with you elementals. This is your war, your mess. Deal with it."

*Deal with it.*

Those three words lingered on repeat as Silianna accepted their decision. The fae-folk were just as everyone said they were. *I can't believe we wasted our morning coming out here*, she thought.

As Silianna turned around, heading for the hovercraft, she heard Nerumi step forward. She argued with the guards, her voice roaring, as she said, "Listen here, you conniving-pointed ear freaks, we're here to speak to Lord Liri, and we're not leaving until we have. You're speaking to two Royal-Bloods, and we demand to be treated as such."

Silianna looked back and stared at Nerumi in disbelief. She was furious, and for some reason, Silianna felt her cheeks flush. The way she stood up straight, her chest puffed up, and her eyes dead set on the guards; it was like she was ready to tear them apart. Silianna was attracted by Nerumi's demeanor.

"You dare speak to us this way? You dare *challenge* us?" The guard pointed the tip of her spear in Nerumi's direction. "Make no mistake, you elementals are no match for our strength."

Nerumi pulled out an Insully blade and pointed it at the group of guards. "You have no idea just how capable I am of taking you all down."

"Nerumi, don't!" Silianna pleaded. She took hold of Nerumi's forearm, trying to pull the Insully blade down. "It's not worth adding another enemy to the list. You have to remember, what we do affects Prince Antonius. We cannot do anything that will cause more division."

Nerumi groaned. She put the Insully blade down and reached for her neck, pulling up the chain until her necklace slid from under her clothing. There, she showed the fae-folk her necklace. It was a black crystal wrapped in a silver chain.

"I'm sure you recognize this," said Nerumi. The necklace dangled from her hands, then she set it back on her neck. "It's a Rylrum artifact. I'm willing to give it to your people in exchange for a conversation with Lord Liri. If there's anything I've learned, it's that you fae-folk cherish magical objects crafted from the soils of this world. None of you can resist having it here in Miracle Forest."

All the guards exchanged looks, then they moved slightly closer to each other and started conversing in hushed tones with one another. Silianna was confused by what the whole fuss was about regarding the necklace. Looking at it herself, it seemed like a silly little crystal. *What could that necklace possibly mean to them?*

"Nerumi, I thought you said that we're not allowed to make a deal with the fae-folk?" Silianna questioned, whispering.

"Don't worry about it," Nerumi replied. "It's only if *they* offer the deal. You have to beat them to the punch first."

The guards finally finished consulting with one another. The pink guard nodded her head and reluctantly welcomed the two into Miracle Forest.

* * *

Silianna and Nerumi followed the guards deep into Miracle Forest. There were wooden huts that resided within the trees and bridges connecting to allow for easy travel between buildings. So many fae-folk were wandering around, staring at the princesses as they strolled by.

There were vine curtains that covered what was beyond the trail ahead of them. When Silianna walked through, she was pleased to see a ginormous tree in the middle of a pond. There, sitting on a wooden throne, was Lord Liri. His green legs dangled lazily as he used a wooden brush to comb his lushly long black hair.

"My Lord," the guard announced. "You have an audience from the outside."

Lord Liri fixed his posture and sat up straight. "Hello, young ladies. I am Lord Liri, son of Lady Jarabella Crinthe. To what do I owe the pleasure of your presence?"

"Good morning, Lord Liri. My name is Princess Silianna Beauchamp. And this is Princess Nerumi Steelhart. We've travelled from Avala in hopes of getting some answers regarding Vorkalth and the Dark Dimension."

Lord Liri examined the young ladies from head to toe. At first, he examined Silianna, but then he looked at Nerumi and tilted his head peculiarly. His eyes then locked on Nerumi's neck and observed the necklace she possessed.

"Princess Nerumi Steelhart, you say...?" Lord Liri murmured, not sounding convinced. "Are you certain of that?"

Silianna couldn't help but laugh. "I am certain of it. I've known her practically most of my teen years. We've been friends for a long time."

"*Hmmph*. If you say so…" Lord Liri continued, a suspicious glint in his eye.

Rising from his throne, Lord Liri revealed his half-naked body, only a white cloth covering his long legs. His green-like skin reflected the movement of the water as he stood in a sinuous movement.

"So, what is it that you want to know about Vorkalth and the Dark Dimension?" he asked, flipping his lush, long black curls over his shoulder.

"Well, it all started when I went to meet my uncle for his help. Reju had been meddling with the Dark Dimension his whole life. Long story short, he unlocked something within me that caused me to obtain a spiritual element." Silianna held her wrist up, showing her burn mark to Lord Liri. "Let's just say that I fear I may face the same fate as my uncle."

"*Tssk, tssk*. You foolish girl. It's pretty simple what you have to do if you wish not to meet the same demise as Reju Tufte."

Silianna sighed. "You're talking about giving up my Eytros element. Aren't you?"

Lord Liri nodded. "The spirits have told me that you've made up your mind. Time is ticking, princess. By tomorrow morning, your forty-eight hours are up. So, what's stopping you?"

"It's my friends. Kelton and Malakai. More specifically, Kelton, as I've come to speculate, Vorkalth may have done something awful to him. I cannot give up my Eytros element if there is a way to save him and stop Vorkalth."

"Your loyalty to your friends will be the death of you, my darling. Take it from me. Putting your trust in 'friends' will cost you. Look what happened to my mother—betrayed by the elementals who claimed to be hers." Lord Liri turned back to his throne and leaned back, evidently tired of the conversation. "There is nothing I can offer you but advice: Get rid of your spiritual element."

"No!" The word echoed across the forest, followed by the water in the pond vibrating and the ground shaking as Silianna stood there. *Did I cause that?* She wondered.

"Darling, you will die either by Vorkalth's hands or by your own body." Lord Liri held out both of his arms and looked left to right, highlighting the impact Silianna just had on the environment around them. "It is clear you cannot house two elements. The fact that you were able to cause this event is proof of how catastrophic that is."

"There must be something you can do!" Silianna cried out. "Or perhaps you have some sort of fae substance that can suppress it a little longer. I just can't accept the fact that I won't be able to help my friends."

Lord Liri took a moment to think. Then, he pointed at Nerumi's necklace. "In exchange for that Rylrum artifact, I will allow you to enter the portal. There, you will locate the Celestial Gates. You can plead your case to the Beyond and see if they will permit you to keep both your elements."

Silianna pulled Nerumi to the side, whispering quickly. "Nerumi, please. This is my one chance of getting answers. Are you willing to sacrifice the necklace so I may get to the Celestial Gates?"

Nerumi was hesitant to accept the exchange for her necklace. Silianna figured that Nerumi must've been bluffing when she first offered it at the entrance, but it was sadly time to pay up and hand over what was promised.

"Just remember what I told you about making deals with the fae-folk," Nerumi whispered. "Your actions will reflect poorly momentarily."

"Nerumi, I'm desperate," Silianna responded. "I'll deal with the consequences afterwards."

"I'm sure you will."

Lord Liri walked Silianna and Nerumi to where the portal was located. It was on a far walk on the left side from where the throne was located. When they arrived, three guards stood in front of the portal.

"Before you proceed," Lord Liri started, "you should know that your family curse started when your ancestor traveled through the Celestial Gates. You are about to embark on a dangerous journey, my darling."

"Wait a second! Do you know about the Beauchamp Curse?"

Silianna asked, intrigued.

Nerumi groaned. "Enough of this nonsense! Out of my way." Nerumi pushed Lord Liri to the side and grabbed Silianna's arm. "I'm done playing pretend. It's time to get rid of you once and for all. Tell Vorkalth I sent you. Bye-bye, sweetie!"

Nerumi shoved Silianna into the portal.

Silianna was falling backwards, her arms trying to reach for Nerumi, who stood behind. She was slowly getting smaller as she was slipping into oblivion. But as Silianna continued looking at Nerumi, her appearance shifted to someone else once Nerumi handed the necklace to Lord Liri—someone from her past.

Seraphina Blackworth.

# 39
## Honeymoon Detour

**RAHAF**

The guest house was high up in the mountains, overlooking the Ackermere Palace and the city below it. There was a calm silence that hovered in the air. The only thing Rahaf could hear was the birds chirping, Theodosis' snoring, and Aleek purring at the end of the bed when she woke up.

Rahaf took it upon herself to sneak out of bed, careful with her movements to avoid disturbing them. When she did, Rahaf took the time to make a cup of tea and stare out from the balcony. The clouds were so close to the guest house that she would have assumed the place was floating in midair.

She wasn't sure how long the honeymoon would last, but she reminded herself that she needed to get as much intel regarding the Eternal Element of Aeris for Malakai. Unbidden, an image of Eli came to the forefront of her mind, but she shook her head, banishing the thought. She was married now and needed to focus on helping Malakai. *There's no time for foolishness*, she thought.

After stepping quietly out of the room, Rahaf took time to explore the guest house. She stumbled upon a glass bookshelf, tall and packed full of different tomes. She suddenly felt a vibrating sensation on her ankle and glanced down to see that her anklet was trembling. She felt an inexplicable tug in her gut, driving her to look closer at the bookshelf. Rahaf dragged her hands along the spines, hoping for a sign of what she was meant to be looking for, and as her fingers brushed one of the big leather-bound books, her ankle finally stopped vibrating.

"This one?" she muttered, unsure. She pulled the book out of the shelf and held it close to her chest with both her arms. Rahaf sat down at the dining table and began flipping through the pages. "Okay. Let's see what I'm supposed to be looking for."

The anklet started to vibrate again. The more pages she flipped through, the less it moved. Once she reached around three-fourths of the way through the book, the anklet stopped altogether.

Rahaf read through the pages and noticed that it was talking about all four of the Eternal Elements. There were gems of different colors, attached to four objects. A crescent moon amulet, an anklet, a sword, and a chalice. The amulet and anklet were the exact ones Rahaf and Malakai had. *If these are the Eternal Elements, then that sword must be the Sword of Aerislark*, she thought. If that wasn't a clear indicator, the wings on the hilt of the sword sure was. She remembered exactly what Silianna told her, and it was for her to find the sword with wings.

A part of Rahaf knew that she wanted to help Malakai for the simple fact that her mother would've done the same thing. Roslynda Soulryth sacrificed her life to help Prince Antonius escape that night at Blackstaer Palace years ago. Rahaf knew it would've been her responsibility to finish what her mom started, regardless of the outcome.

As she continued reading through the book, trying to get some answers about the Sword of Aerislark, Rahaf gathered the same information she had received from Queen Seona. The sword was located in the Temple of Retribution, and anyone who wanted to retrieve it would have to face three deadly tasks. Even if one retrieves the sword, they wouldn't inherit its Eternal Element without facing Aerislark's judgment. The true wielder of the sword, one with a warrior's heart, would be able to conjure Angelic Fire from the steel blade, impaling any of its enemies with a single slice. Nobody has been successful in retrieving it. So much so that the King and Queen took it upon themselves to close it off to prevent any more casualties. Unfortunately for Rahaf, the book did not specify what the tasks entailed.

*"Find the sword."*

Rahaf's ears perked up. The voice sounded similar to that of her mother. That small moment left her questioning whether or not her mother was trying to tell her something from the Other Side. With Malakai and Silianna's connection to the Dark Dimension, she had quickly learned that anything was possible.

*"You must go now."*

"Okay, Mother," Rahaf whispered. "I promise."

"What are you doing up so early?"

Rahaf jumped out of the chair, spinning around to see Theodosis leaning casually in the doorway with a loose smile on his face.

"Hey!" Rahaf replied cheerfully, trying to calm herself down. "How did you sleep last night?"

"Amazing. I got to sleep with my lovely wife." Theodosis leaned over and kissed her. When their lips parted, he pulled out a chair and sat down next to her. "What're you reading?"

"Oh, just some stuff about the Sword of Aerislark. I'm very curious about it." Rahaf closed the book.

"How come you're so invested in that sword?"

Rahaf frowned. "I know it's annoying for me to talk about, but I owe it to Malakai and my mother to find it. You may think I'm crazy, but I have a weird feeling it is what my mother would want me to do."

Theodosis did not respond to her with words, but rather by affection. He held her hand to his face and kissed it. Theodosis then smiled and said, "I married you knowing that you were going to come with baggage. Whatever you want to do, just know I will be by your side every step of the way, okay?"

Rahaf felt warmth spread through her veins. A part of her expected Theodosis to argue with her about not searching for the sword, but she was pleasantly surprised to learn that was not the case.

"Do you love me enough to want to travel to the Temple of Retribution and risk our lives to get that sword?" Rahaf asked.

Theodosis was hesitant to speak at first, but he must have seen the determination in her eyes because he simply sighed and then nodded his head. "We'll have to sneak our way through those guards if we do. My mother and father have that place heavily secured."

"I'm sure we can get past them," Rahaf said, squeezing his hands. "It's you and me against the world, baby!"

Theodosis dragged the book from Rahaf's side to his side and stared at it. Rahaf wanted to know what he was thinking.

"You said you owe it to Malakai and your mother," said Theodosis, confused when he repeated Rahaf's earlier statement. "What did you mean by that?"

"The night of the Bellemore assassination, my mother saved Prince Antonius from getting killed by the Elder Guardians. She was found out years later and held prisoner at Sorrow Tower until they killed her in the end. I have to fulfill her wishes and see to it that Malakai claims the Baskarian throne. And if I plan to make it happen, I first need to get my hands on that sword. Once Malakai collects all four of the Eternal Elements, he'll be the most powerful elemental across the Nine Lands."

Theodosis nodded his head. "Okay. I will help you. No matter what becomes of our fate. At least I can say that I got to marry you, Rahaf *Steelhart*."

Rahaf jumped from her chair and gave Theodosis multiple kisses around his face. She was thrilled to know he was on her side, no matter what the circumstances were.

"There's only one more thing," said Rahaf.

"There's more?" Theodosis said, concerned.

"Yes. We have to bring the shapeshifter with us. He's Malakai's best friend, and he will do anything to help Malakai claim the throne."

## 40
## Shadow Blood

**KELTON**

Kelton was unsure where he was, but the last thing he recalled was being in the guest room with Malakai before everything went dark. A screeching sound echoed from above, causing him to look up quickly. The sky was black with gray clouds looming over. Lightning bolts struck, followed by a roar. As Kelton observed more carefully, he saw an enormous creature with wings and a long, sharp tail flying through the sky. His heart began to beat quickly as terror seized him. He scrambled to his feet and started running forward, unsure of where he was going.

As he ran, Kelton looked around, trying to figure out where he had woken open. He quickly realized he was back in the Dark Dimension, and a dread settled over him like a heavy blanket.

A little ways ahead of him, Kelton spotted a dark, towering castle. It was dark and foreboding, but Kelton ran toward it anyway, desperate to find some shelter as the roaring behind him got louder. When he got closer, Kelton saw that the gates were already open, and no one was standing guard.

The screeching continued. Kelton turned to see that the creature was following him. Besides the horrifying large wings and sharp tail, the creature also possessed a sharp black beak—one that was aiming for him. The monster was dripping some sort of black substance from its body, falling like rain onto the ground below. *Come on, Kelton encouraged himself, you can make it to the castle.*

Dead trees lined the path Kelton ran down. As he passed, the trees began to shift in place, like they were coming alive. Then, the branches from the trees grew, lowering themselves and spreading across the ground. The branches then latched themselves onto Kelton's wrist and ankles, holding him in place.

Tugging on his restraints, Kelton was not surprised to see Vorkalth rise from beneath the ground. He floated in midair, looking just as he had appeared the last time they had met.

"What do you want from me?" Kelton barked; his teeth clenched together in fury.

"*I am so close to achieving one of my greatest tricks*," said Vorkalth ominously. "*And you are the product of that achievement.*"

"I don't understand."

"*That's the idea, my dear boy.*" Vorkalth raised his hand, his claws pointing to the sky where a bolt of lightning touched the tip of his sharp fingernails. A tiny metallic box then appeared in his hand. "*You have no idea how hard it was to create you. I may have failed with Prince Antonius, but you are proof that the impossible is possible.*"

"You don't scare me," Kelton responded.

"*I may not, but do you scare yourself?*"

The Shadow Lord tossed the box into midair. It started to rotate counterclockwise before projecting images into the air. It revealed the incident that occurred with Kelton and Malakai in the guest bedroom. Kelton was horrified to see he had hurt Malakai. *Why did I do that?*

Kelton felt his heart sink as he was forced to view the scene, watching Malakai's head bounce off the wall and suddenly go still. This wasn't the first occurrence, and as more images appeared, Kelton became enraged with himself. No matter how hard he tried to contain it, he still managed to hurt Malakai. All Kelton wanted to do was fix the damage, hug Malakai, and tell him that everything would get better. But he knew the reality. There was no chance things would get better. It only seemed to be getting worse.

The Shadow Lord flicked his wrist and snapped his fingers. The images vanished, and Kelton was left floating there, the vines still securing him from escaping. Tears ran down Kelton's cheeks as he accepted defeat.

"*You've lost, my dear boy,*" said Vorkalth.

"Why? Why are you doing this to me?" Kelton asked, quivering.

"*Because power comes from rage. And you have so much of it, as I do. Once you've tapped into your darkest potential, I can wield it to my liking. So, lose yourself to it... Use all your rage on me for what I've done to you—for what I made you do.*"

No.

Kelton did not tap into his darkest potential. Instead, he believed in himself. More importantly, he believed that his love for Malakai was true and real. The Dark Dimension always seemed to be connected to dreams, and Kelton questioned at that moment whether the Dark Dimension could be altered the same way he could alter his dreams. The love he had for Malakai was strong, and he knew instantly that the creativity that drew his dreams was inspired by Malakai. Tapping into that source of energy within him, Kelton was capable of conjuring a bright light to build around his body, like an aura visible to the naked eye. Once he was able to contain that energy, Kelton used the light to blast the branches that secured him in place. He was free.

"*W—What?*" Vorkalth gasped.

"You don't hold the power over me that you think you do," Kelton said, taking a taunting step forward.

"*It's impossible!*"

Kelton tilted his head, playfully confused. "But didn't you say that the impossible was possible? I believe I've just proved your point. And now, it's my turn to be your worst nightmare."

Rather than reach for his Terrane ability, Kelton tapped into the light power surrounding his hands. He did not know what it was, but it had the power to hurt Vorkalth, and that was all that mattered.

Vorkalth aimed the palms of his hands in Kelton's direction. A ball of black light emerged, hurling towards Kelton's chest. Acting fast, Kelton faced the ball of light and shot a beam of it as well. Both the light and dark collided, causing the ground below them to shake immensely.

"*You cannot beat me, fool!*" Vorkalth shouted. "*I am the product of angels—Gods. You are nothing against me.*"

"The love I have is what gives me the upper hand, Vorkalth, and you have none of that." Kelton's beam of light grew, eclipsing Vorkalth's dark power. With a sudden *boom*, Vorkalth fell to the ground, panting harshly. "You may be the product of the Gods, but that doesn't make you better than anyone else."

Flowers miraculously began to grow beneath Kelton's feet. Every step he took toward Vorkalth, a new flower grew, causing a trail in his wake. Kelton didn't understand how he managed to do it, but he knew one thing for certain: He could craft the Dark Dimension to his image just like Vorkalth had done before.

"*You've done it,*" Vorkalth said, amused.

"Indeed. I can do exactly what you can do. Which also means I can do this." Kelton flicked his wrist. A square jail cell made of bright light appeared, locking Vorkalth inside. "You are never going to escape this prison of yours. Not as long as I live."

Vorkalth burst into laughter. "*You're more foolish than Prince Antonius. Do you think this will stop me? I have plans in motion that you could not even begin to comprehend. Who do you think has been orchestrating everything in Windsor Keep? I have eyes and ears everywhere. You may have suppressed my control in the Dark Dimension, but my control outside of this prison world is unstoppable.*"

"DeVault and Aldothfex will be easy to handle. You're already down two Elder Guardians."

"*Who said the Elder Guardians were the only ones I have under my control?*"

Kelton raised an eyebrow. "What are you talking about?"

"*Look around you, my boy. You have the ability to see the Dark Dimension in all its glory now. Take a look and tell me what you see...*"

Kelton looked at the darkness that surrounded him. In the blink of an eye, what seemed to have been a shield of glamor had suddenly vanished. The veil that separated him from what the Dark Dimension truly was had finally been revealed. So many souls stood all around him, watching. They were on their knees, looking up at Kelton as if he were their savior.

"Please, release us!" one begged.

"We've served our time!" another shouted.

"Peace. Bring us peace."

They were all speaking at the same time, yet Kelton couldn't comprehend half of what was being said to him. The only thing he understood was that all of them were trapped and in so much pain. They wanted to move on from this nightmare.

"You... You've kept these Lost Souls here to torment them for your amusement after all this time?" Kelton asked Vorkalth.

*"So long as they enter my domain after death, they shall bring me the strength I need."*

"But you have no strength against me."

*"You mistake intelligence with strength, my boy. Do you think this cage you have me in somehow grants you victory? If anything, you've done exactly what I needed you to. I told you to look around, but it wasn't the Lost Souls I was referring to. Take a closer look."*

Kelton did so. He observed the crowd. Within it, he caught sight of not one, but three large cryogenic glass tubes. The tubes were filled with green liquid, but that wasn't the only thing inside. Three individuals were asleep, floating inside the green liquid with small wires attached to their noses and mouths to allow for oxygen.

"It cannot be," Kelton said under his breath, disbelief setting in.

*"As I've told you, the Elder Guardians weren't the only ones I have under my control. Bliss Steelhart was so kind enough to involve her grandchildren in the scheme. Why bother with the King and Queen of Aeris when I can use these two to target Princess Rahaf and Princess Silianna? It was a brilliant plan, and I was sad to see Bliss meet her demise."*

If that was the case, then Kelton knew that Malakai, Demetri, Rahaf, Silianna, and Eli were in serious trouble. Because the three people Vorkalth managed to have under his control were Kelton,

Nerumi, and Theodosis.

*"You may have achieved your ability to control the Dark Dimension, but you have failed to escape back into the real world,"* said Vorkalth, gloating. *"You will be stuck here with me forever. And I will continue to control your mind just as I've had since you were a child. The only difference this time? I have full access to your body now."*

"It's impossible!" Kelton cried out.

*"Is it?"* Vorkalth chuckled. *"But the impossible is possible... Right?"*

"You were able to control me for most of my life. How?"

*"You have the blood of the Gods within you. But not only that, you have the blood of the oldest vampyre and the most powerful sorceress across the Nine Lands. Since you want to know so terribly, I shall tell you: I am your father. You are the product of my creation."*

"Bullshit! You've tried that line before on Malakai. The Lady of Glisten Lake told him that you weren't his father."

*"It is the truth, my boy. I may have lied to Prince Antinous, but not to you. I had hoped it would be enough to distract him—to cloud his judgment. If it weren't for Damaris Caerlight, I would have succeeded. Prince Antonious would have resorted to the darkness, and I would have had full control of him. But I realized quickly it wouldn't work. No. What better way to get to the Lost Prince than to have the love of his life destroy his heart? It is perfect. Fate wanted you two to be together, and if your love is real, then my presence shall surely put that to the test."*

Kelton had no time to adjust to what he learned. With one blink, he found himself in the cryogenic tube, floating in the green liquid alongside Nerumi and Theodosis. He was trapped there, helpless, screaming into nothingness.

# 41
## Temple of Retribution

**RAHAF**

Rahaf wasn't sure if Theodosis was going to pull it off, but she waited patiently until he arrived downstairs with Eli. She knew that there would be some resentment if she went to his door and asked to join them in searching for the Sword of Aerislark. So, naturally, she put Theodosis to the task. She did feel bad about the whole thing, especially since Theodosis knew nothing of their kiss—*kisses*. Rahaf's biggest fear was whether or not Eli would tell Theodosis what happened and ruin everything, though she also hoped that he'd think of the bigger picture and realize that if he ruined their marriage, it might risk Aeris joining the Resistance.

Right on time, Theodosis arrived with Eli. The two of them walked down the steps while Rahaf and Aleek remained below, waiting.

Rahaf was pleased to see that Eli had decided to join them. *Let's just hope he hasn't said anything stupid*, she thought, concerned.

Aleek rubbed himself against Rahaf's leg, comforting her. She patted him on the head, communicating her thanks.

"So, what's the plan?" Eli asked. He avoided looking at Rahaf.

"We're going to fly out to the Temple of Retribution and sneak in without getting caught," Theodosis explained. He pulled out three green gummies from his pocket and held them in the palm of his hand. "These are invisible edibles from the magic-folk. They should last us roughly ten to fifteen minutes. It's enough to get us through the gates without the guards noticing."

Rahaf was getting some serious déjà vu when she saw the green gummies. If memory served her justice, these were the exact ones Demetri's two goons gave them so they could sneak into the City of Terrane.

"And how did *you* get those?" asked Rahaf.

"I may or may not know some people who smuggle drugs," Theodosis said ominously, a hint of a smile tugging at his lips.

"*Hmmph*. We'll talk about that later. In the meantime, we should get a move on before anybody notices us."

They proceeded down the halls and into the warehouse, where most of the flying vehicles were located. There were three hovercrafts to choose from: A Rem, Glax, and Defender. However, Rahaf argued that they shouldn't use any of the hovercrafts given how big they are and instead they should use a regular flying vehicle. The boys did not argue with her and did as she said.

Once they got in and started the engines, they were off into the sky as they headed East of Ackermere Palace.

* * *

They parked the vehicle somewhere far from the entrance of the mountain. Rahaf was getting herself situated while Theodosis filled Eli in on what to expect. Rahaf listened in, cautious about any words exchanged between the two.

Aleek was sniffing around the bushes while Rahaf finished fixing her belt and shoelaces. Once she did, she grabbed one of the green gummies from Theodosis' pockets and split it in half.

"Why are you splitting it?" Theodosis asked.

"Because you forgot to include Aleek. He's my Eni, and I will not leave him behind. I will share my gummy so he can pass through as well."

"But if you eat half a gummy, you will have a shorter amount of time to sneak past the guards."

"Then I guess Aleek and I will have to move quickly and get in before the effects wear off. Now, are we done chit-chatting, or can we go? The fate of the world is in our hands, and we need to ensure Malakai gets that sword."

Theodosis and Eli exchanged looks, surprised at the fact that Rahaf was getting down to business and not playing around.

Feeling empowered, Rahaf flipped her hair and led the group up the trail to the entrance. Aleek followed, and the boys trailed behind her.

Once they were close enough to where the caedose soldiers could see them, Rahaf hid behind one of the boulders and was preparing herself to consume the edible. Aleek was next to her while they waited for Theodosis and Eli to get themselves situated.

On the count of three, all four of them would eat the gummies. And so, they did. Within a matter of seconds, their entire bodies disappeared from their view. Rahaf started speed-walking her way towards the entrance, hoping that the caedose wouldn't hear the sounds of her steps in the process. There was no telling whether the boys made it safely through or not, but she could only hope that they did.

As Rahaf maneuvered her way past the caedose soldiers, she started running into the temple without looking back. Her vision was darkening the further she went, realizing that the inside of the temple was a cave as she headed in an unknown direction. The sounds of footsteps behind her were alarming as she finally turned around.

"Theo?" she whispered.

"Nope," someone responded.

Rahaf was taken aback. She used her Pyroc element to create a fire from the tip of her fingers. It provided light, which revealed Eli standing in front of her. Soon after, Aleek appeared.

"Has it already been more than ten minutes?" she asked.

Eli shrugged. "I guess so. From my understanding, time works differently when you enter this place. But what do I know? I'm just a stupid shapeshifter."

Rahaf looked puzzled. "What's *that* supposed to mean?"

"Nothing. Nothing at all."

"Eli, now is not the time for dramatics. If we make it out alive, you can be upset with me for however long it takes. But right now, we need to stay focused!"

"Whatever. I'm only doing this for Malakai. That's it."

Finally, Theodosis appeared from the darkness. Rahaf was relieved and reached over to hug him.

"Now that we're all here, let's stick together and prepare ourselves for whatever awaits us," she said.

They all proceeded through the path as Rahaf held the flame in her hand to light the way.

## 42

## Compromise

**MALAKAI**

Malakai blearily opened his eyes, feeling like there were several sandbags placed on his chest. He glanced to the side, hoping to see Kelton, but spotted Demetri in a chair next to his bed. The second Demetri saw Malakai's eyes open, a smile grew on his face, and he quickly stood up from his chair and moved close to him, giving him a once-over.

"What're you doing?" Malakai asked.

"I'm just making sure you're okay," Demetri said, placing a hand on Malakai's forehead. "You are okay, aren't you?"

Malakai did not answer right away. He was enjoying Demetri's touch, his warmth as his hand caressed his forehead.

"I've never been better," Malakai said, feeling still unmoored from reality.

"Good. We should really be heading back to Avala. You've been asleep for an entire day. It's nightfall already."

"By the Gods. My grandmother is going to be furious. Where's Kelton?"

Demetri seemed hesitant to answer the question. When he finally did, Malakai felt a headache emerging. From what he understood, Kelton had blacked out and knocked Malakai unconscious. Then

Demetri intervened and punched Kelton, which resulted in him falling unconscious, too. Demetri was then giving everyone a hard time until they were successful in keeping Malakai and Kelton alive. In the end, Demetri and Narkissa made a deal to inject her blood into Malakai's system so he could heal after suffering internal bleeding in the head. As for Kelton, he was to remain with the vampyres so they could conduct who knew what sort of experiments on him.

Needless to say, Malakai was very unhappy.

"You sold off your brother?!" Malakai yelled.

"I—I did it so you could heal," Demetri justified.

"I don't care. How am I to trust that they will keep him alive? What if they do something horrible to him and we won't be here to stop it?"

Demetri reached over and held Malakai's hand. He slowly guided it to his chest and placed Malakai's hand where his heart was located.

"Feel my heartbeat," Demetri said softly. "You feel how steady it is? That's because I'm not lying when I tell you that nothing bad will come of Kelton. I performed a Blood Oath with Narkissa to ensure everything will be okay. As much as he gets on my nerves, I would never let my brother fend for himself in this forsaken domain."

Malakai slowly pulled away, nodding his head in understanding. "I believe you," he said. "But I still have to speak to Narkissa. I cannot leave here without convincing her to lend her army."

"That won't be a problem. I've consulted with her on that matter as well. She is willing to offer her army in exchange for the vampyres safety when you claim the Baskarian throne. To make sure the deal won't fall through, she wants you to perform a Blood Oath of your own."

Malakai swallowed harshly. Performing a Blood Oath was not something he was too keen on, especially since it was one of the things his father forbade him to ever practice when he was in his pre-teen years. Well, his adoptive father, Thaddeus Thorns, to be exact. Thaddeus had done a Blood Oath with Eli's family long ago to make sure that the Thorns family would survive.

"What's the matter?" Demetri asked.

"I don't—It's just a little overwhelming. I'm expected to put my life on the line for a Blood Oath to ensure that the vampyres are protected when I claim the Baskarian throne?"

"Think of it this way: You are protecting an entire nation from being ruled by a sadistic maniac lurking in the Dark Dimension. Without the vamps, we may not be able to take over the Elder Guardians. We know for a fact that Pyroc, Limus, and Saint Salvusburg will be the hardest to take on. I have no fear of Terrane, but those three are a concern. With Avala, Theuros, Centuris, and Veilios on our side, we can take them down. But it all starts with you, Malakai."

Malakai took a deep breath. "Okay. I'll do it. But before we do anything, I want to see Kelton. No matter what state he's in, I want to see him one last time before we fly back to Avala."

"Then we'll make it happen, Your Imperial Highness."

* * *

Kelton was lying on a bed, still asleep, with small medical wires trailing into his arms and legs. When Malakai asked the reasoning for the experiments, Destlyn explained that they were looking for ways to control his unexplainable abilities. Destlyn expressed great concern that the scent of the Dark Dimension was all over him. Malakai was also given a digital file of all the tests so far and what slim results they had found. The open honesty was unexpected, but Malakai still felt unsettled by the whole thing.

Destlyn gave Malakai and Demetri privacy to talk amongst themselves while they kept Kelton company.

Malakai kept his eyes locked on Kelton. There was so much he wanted to say, but nothing sounded right. He pulled up a chair and set it alongside the bed. Malakai put his chin on Kelton's arm, turning his face into the warmth he felt there.

"A big reason I was scared to tell him that I love him is that I feared I'd lose him forever. It happens to everyone that I love or care about," Malakai finally said. "Both my biological and adoptive parents. Then Eli's father, followed by his mother and brother. Now here we are, where I am being proven right again. Kelton is suffering, and I don't know what to do. What if he dies and it's all because I told him that I love him?"

"That's ridiculous, Malakai. We all lose the people we love eventually. But Kelton is strong. He'll pull through."

"Well, how am I supposed to react? Vorkalth obviously has a hold on him. I can feel it. I *know* it. I feel helpless… I no longer have access to the Dark Dimension to stop him from getting hurt. It's only a matter of time before Vorkalth does the worst thing imaginable to get back at me."

Demetri took both of Malakai's wrists and pulled him in close, looking down at him with a determined gaze. "Malakai, I won't let anything happen to him. The whole point of this experiment is to help *prevent* Vorkalth from hurting Kelton. You need to be strong and have faith in them. Narkissa knows a lot about the Dark Dimension. She confided in me about what the two of you discussed. If there's anyone who is going to help Kelton, it'll be her. Okay?"

"Okay," Malakai said, feeling the weight of Demetri's certainty. There were a lot of aspects of Demetri's personality that were difficult, but whenever he firmly believed in something, it was obvious in the steady strength of his voice. "But if anything happens to him, I will never forgive any of you."

"I'm willing to take the chance," Demetri replied.

Malakai turned back around to Kelton and placed his hand on his hair. He then bent down and kissed him on the forehead. For a split second, Malakai hoped that the kiss would somehow wake Kelton up. Unfortunately, he did not.

"I love you, Kelton Eckwood," Malakai whispered in Kelton's ear.

"*I love you, too,*" Kelton murmured in his sleep.

Malakai felt lighter, and he wanted nothing more than to hug Kelton, but he was mindful of disrupting the tests. *Kelton can hear me,* he thought, hopeful. *He's still in there.*

"Kelton, if you're in the Dark Dimension, I promise everything will be okay. You need to fight whatever it is Vorkalth is making you face. You are stronger than you think. Please. Fight it."

* * *

Afterwards, Malakai walked out of the room and made his way into the hall. He told himself to leave at the moment, or he would've never left. It was hard to have to leave Kelton behind while he went back to Avala. But he knew that once everything was situated, he'd be making his first stop at Theuros. He would wreak havoc if anything got in his way.

Destlyn guided Malakai and Demetri to the entrance of the castle. The guards that arrived with them were waiting in a single-file line.

The further away Malakai was from Kelton, the harder it was to accept he'd have to leave him on the island. *There has to be another way*, he thought.

Narkissa arrived at the nick of time as Malakai and Demetri were about to depart. She waved her index finger back and forth tauntingly.

"We're not done yet, Lost Prince," said Narkissa, teasing. "We have to perform a specific 'bond' and secure a deal. My army in exchange for their protection once you claim the Baskarian throne."

Malakai slightly groaned. "I don't like the idea of tying my life to the vampyres, but as long as you hold your end of the bargain, then I shall comply."

"Splendid."

Destlyn positioned Malakai and Narkissa in front of each other. They straightened their postures and held hands. Destlyn then pulled out a small dagger and pricked Malakai's shoulder. Blood slowly started to ooze out, maneuvering its way down to where his hands were. Destlyn did the same to Narkissa, which Malakai was fascinated to see. Narkissa did not heal as quickly as she should've when the blood came slithering down to her hands. Both of their blood then formed an infinity shape around their arms, colliding as one.

"The two of you will be able to hear each other's thoughts for a split moment as you agree to your terms for the Blood Oath," Destlyn explained. "Once it is finalized, the blood will evaporate into thin air." Malakai nodded his head.

"*You worry for Prince Kelton?*" Narkissa asked, speaking through Malakai's mind.

"*Yes, I do,*" Malakai admitted.

"*I can promise you that we will do everything in our power to take care of him.*"

"*For all your sakes, I hope you do.*"

At the same time, both Malakai and Narkissa agreed to the terms: Malakai Thorns shall ensure the protection of the vampyres so long as he reigns the Baskarian throne. In return, Narkissa shall lend her army to fight alongside him and the Resistance so they may take down the remaining Elder Guardians.

The blood evaporated. A whoosh of wind separated Malakai and Narkissa. The Blood Oath was finalized.

Malakai wasn't entirely sure how he felt about signing his life away, but he knew there would be consequences in the far-off distance.

"Before you go, Lost Prince," Narkissa started, "I should inform you that my blood flows through your bloodstream. You will need to come into contact with Seraphina Blackworth as quickly as possible before it wears off. My blood will allow you to influence her beliefs and convince her that you killed me. Do I make myself clear?"

"Crystal clear. I'll be sure to find her after I meet with my grandmother."

"Wonderful. I'm hoping she has the guts to travel back to this island under the impression that I'm dead. She'll be in for a rude awakening."

"Make sure she suffers tremendously," Demetri commented, disgusted. "A woman like her shouldn't roam this world so freely."

The guards that arrived with Malakai, Kelton, and Demetri yesterday came running into the hall in what seemed to be panic. One of them took the initiative and approached Malakai and Demetri, panting before he spoke.

"Your Imperial Highness, we have a serious problem," the guard said, shakingly.

"What is it?" Malakai asked.

"It's the hovercraft... The engine is jammed. We fear someone is trying to prevent you from leaving."

# 43
## Slow Dancing in the Light

**DEMETRI**

Demetri suspected the vampyres were behind the sabotage of the hovercraft; the agreement had gone far too easily, so he wasn't even necessarily surprised. He couldn't put his finger on it, but Demetri feared something sinister was at play. Either Narkissa was involved, or she had no idea that someone might be plotting some sort of attack. One thing was clear: Demetri was going to keep his eye on Malakai's whereabouts at any cost.

Although Narkissa seemed somewhat concerned about the interference, she quickly jumped at the opportunity to invite them to the event happening later that night: The Gilded Moonlit Ball. Demetri half suspected she was actually happy with the delay, since she now had the chance to parade them around at her little ball. He didn't want to attend, but given they were currently stuck until their hovercraft was fixed, he also did not want to risk Narkissa's ire.

Malakai was surprisingly keen to attend, but Demetri felt that was only so he had an excuse to spend more time by Kelton's side.

While Malakai went off with two of the guards, Demetri took it upon himself to get in contact with the Grand Empress Dowager before she started raising havoc over her grandson being missing.

The service continuously gave him a hard time, but once he got a connection, he waited for a response.

"By the Gods, I was beginning to worry," the Grand Empress Dowager said, answering the call. "Where have you all been?"

"We've run into some complications with the hovercraft," Demetri answered. "But not to fear, they're working on getting it fixed. As for the mission, we've succeeded in having the vampyres join us in the Resistance. The Vampyre Queen seems to show trust in Malakai."

The Grand Empress Dowager released the pressure from her chest. "That's wonderful to hear. The vampyres are very unpredictable. I'm glad my grandson was successful. When do you think all of you will be able to return to Avala?"

"We're hoping within the next few hours. Perhaps even less."

"Wonderful. I will notify the guards to keep watch for your arrival." The Grand Empress Dowager was interrupted by the presence of her robotic advisor, Celsa. "Oh. Celsa wanted me to inform you that they found the Thorns children unsupervised. Did you not assign anyone to keep watch before you departed?"

"I'm glad you brought that up. Princess Silianna was supposed to keep watch, but the kids told me that she was nowhere to be found. Have you any idea where she might've gone?"

The Grand Empress Dowager looked somewhat shocked. "I think I might have. She was last seen heading upstairs with an unknown female. The surveillance was blurred out after that, but we believe they may have taken one of our hovercrafts. We do not know where they went. Celsa is doing his best to track them down."

Demetri's mind wandered. He considered that perhaps Seraphina found a way to get into Windsor Keep and somehow blackmailed Silianna into doing something against her will.

"Did the female have long, auburn curly hair by any chance?" he asked.

The Grand Empress Dowager shook her head. "From what we gathered, the female had colorful hair. Perhaps she had purplish-pink hair. It was hard to tell due to how static the video was."

*Purplish-pink hair?* The one person Demetri would think of with that description was Nerumi Steelhart. But there was no way it was her. How could she make her way to Avala from Aeris? It was impossible. *It must have been someone part of the fae-folk,* Demetri speculated. *I'll have to look into it when I get back.*

As Demetri was finishing up his conversation with the Grand Empress Dowager, one of the female vampyres caught him in the middle of the hall and pulled him away as she insisted that he get ready for the event tonight. Demetri was reluctant at first, but conceded he needed a distraction from his runaway thoughts.

* * *

The Gilded Moonlit Ball was extravagant.

Demetri walked out into the field where the night stars and the two moons shimmered over everyone as they danced to the music being played. Demetri's vision went from a clear view to everything being sparkly and blurry, kind of like he was partying with the fae-folk. The champagne glasses were sparkling, along with the tablecloths, the water, and even the trees glinted with gold leaves.

There was a gilded cage at the center, where a vampyre pianist was playing a song. The moonlights were fixed on the gilded cage, allowing it to reveal a beautiful aura around it.

Narkissa was nowhere to be found, which Demetri was not surprised about. But it wasn't Narkissa's absence that alarmed him. It was Malakai's. *Where was he?* Demetri wondered if he was still down below where Kelton was being held. If that was the case, Demetri was ready to ditch this strange party and find him. He promised himself that he would keep an eye on Malakai and of course he was already screwing it up.

As he turned around to leave, Demetri was pleasantly surprised to bump into Malakai.

Malakai wore a red suit with black accents that had hints of glitter in them. To go with the outfit, he also had a black feather cape that dragged two inches from where his feet were. Compared to Demetri, who wore a simple black button-down long-sleeved shirt and black dress pants, Malakai was the main star of this event tonight. He looked stunning, and Demetri almost couldn't tear his eyes away. Something about Malakai so easily drew him in, made him want in a way he had never wanted before. He cursed the Fates who had placed Malakai in Kelton's path first, when there was no doubt in Demetri's mind that the prince belonged with him.

"There you are," Demetri said, trying to hide how affected he was by Malakai's presence. "How was your evening?"

"It was alright. I spent most of the time with Destlyn. I wanted to see if there were any changes with Kelton. So far, nothing. But Destlyn thinks in an hour or two, they'll be able to pick up on some new information." Malakai examined Demetri from head to toe. Demetri liked to imagine Malakai was also attracted to him and was simply holding himself back out of loyalty to Kelton. "Sometimes I forget that you have a dragon tattoo on your arm. It always intrigues me."

Demetri gave Malakai one of his signature devilish smirks. "If you wanted me to unbutton my shirt and see my tattoo, all you had to do was ask."

Malakai didn't seem pleased by the flirtatious comment. Instead, he replied, "I think I'll pass for tonight. Do these vamps have any food, or is it just blood?"

The way Malakai was playing hard to get had Demetri going crazy with endless thoughts. Demetri was certain he was aroused for a split second just seeing Malakai get close to him. Those lips were begging to be kissed, and Demetri wasn't sure how much more he could resist.

"Are you going to stand there, or are you going to offer me a dance?" Malakai asked.

"Y—You want to dance?" Demetri repeated, not daring to hope he had heard Malakai correctly.

"I'm bored, and if I'm not going to eat, I might as well get a dance out of it." Malakai wrapped his arm around Demetri's. The two then headed down to the dancefloor.

The music ended, promoting a new song to play at the perfect time. Demetri adjusted his posture and held Malakai's hands. He took the initiative to lead the dance. Malakai's eyes widened, and Demetri knew instantly that he had him hooked as he made the first move. Malakai followed his lead, and they both matched the beat of the melody.

"Do you mind my asking where you got the outfit?" Demetri asked, breaking the ice.

"Oh." Malakai looked down at his outfit and back up at Demetri. "I wasn't planning on coming, but Destlyn insisted. He offered me one of his designs that he was working on. He said it would go well with my hair color, so I figured, why not?"

"You look extravagant." Demetri's tone was serious, but cautious, unsure how far Malakai would let him push.

"Thank you. I was feeling a little insecure wearing it. I'm still getting used to wearing all these fancy clothes. I'm not sure if you gathered this already, but I'm typically the guy who wears a loose t-shirt, baggy pants, and hunter boots."

"Believe me, I've gathered. That's how you were raised most of your life. You've learned what is most comforting to you. That's what makes you so unique—being yourself."

"So, you think I look better without this suit?" Malakai questioned.

"I did not say that."

"*Hmmph.* But you implied it. You think I'm unique when I'm being myself. So, you prefer me with my poor clothes."

"I don't think I've ever seen you with 'poor' clothes." Demetri stared into his eyes, contemplating whether to make an inappropriate comment. The way Malakai looked, it was like he was begging Demetri to say something. Demetri's pulse was racing, and he could feel his body heating, like the temperature of the room had increased. "But to answer your question… Yes, I think you would look better without that suit. Wearing nothing, to be exact."

Malakai let out a breath. He was shaking, Demetri felt it as he tightened his hands on Malakai's. But he was pleased when Malakai didn't try to pull away.

"Demetri, don't…" Malakai whispered.

"Don't what?" Demetri asked, his voice smooth and quiet. "I'm just complimenting how beautiful you are."

"That's fine, but friends don't say those sorts of things to each other."

"So, we're officially friends?"

"I'd say we are now. I feel our little bonding these past few days has solidified that."

Demetri chuckled. "I'm glad. If I recall, just a few days ago you were ready to rip my head off for encouraging Celdric to join the Resistance, and now we are close friends." Malakai did not respond. Demetri was curious to know what he was thinking, but he knew Malakai wouldn't be fully honest. Not as long as he was with Kelton. "What? Are we not close friends?"

Malakai smiled, though he also looked a little sad. "It's not that. I hear 'close friend,' and I'm reminded of Eli. I'm worried about him. I have so many obstacles to go through, and all I want is to make sure Eli and Kelton are safe."

*Make sure Eli and Kelton were safe.* Demetri repeated that sentence over and over in his head until a lightbulb went off in his head. He, too, was reminded of a close friend: Silianna. When Demetri spoke with Celdric and Nehila, they informed him that Silianna had not been watching them.

"Why do you look so worried?" asked Malakai.

"Huh? Oh... I, uh," Demetri paused. He collected himself before speaking. "There was so much that happened while you were unconscious, I feel like I keep giving you new information that I should've mentioned earlier."

"Okay."

"Right. Well, I contacted Celdric and Nehila. They seemed fine, and I made sure the Grand Empress Dowager took care of them while we were on the island."

"Why would you make sure she takes care of them? Didn't Kelton say that Silianna was going to watch them?"

Demetri sighed. "The kids said Silianna never was watching them. When I spoke to the Grand Empress Dowager after your

307

Blood Oath, I explained the situation. She informed me that they learned of it and got a handle on it. But they have no idea where Silianna has gone. According to Celsa, one of the hovercrafts is missing. They believe Silianna took one and flew off."

"Flew off where?" Malakai said, voice rising in pitch.

"They're not sure. Celsa advised me to keep my communicator close by so she can notify me where she has gone. But it's been quiet since I last spoke to them. As for Celdric and Nehila, they're doing just fine."

"I'm glad they're okay, but now I have to worry about Silianna, too. She's already going through so much as it is."

The song ended, and a new one began. The crowd of dancers that surrounded them exited the dance floor and allowed Demetri and Malakai to be the center of attention. The pianist interrupted the two and guided them inside the gilded cage where the piano was. The pianist instructed them to dance when the music started.

Vampyres from all directions formed a circle around the gilded cage and started chanting an unusual language. The moons above glowed a golden light, which shone specifically on Demetri and Malakai. The two held onto each other, worried about what the vampyres were up to. *Something isn't right*, he thought.

The music got louder, and an unknown force of energy took control of them as they started to dance. Demetri was trying his best to pull away, but he couldn't.

"Why can't we stop?" Malakai asked, glancing around worriedly.

"I don't know," Demetri replied. "I think the vamps are doing something to us."

"Really? What gave it away?" Malakai frowned.

"Now is not the time for your snarky remarks, Your Imperial Highness."

The vampyres stopped chanting. The gold light simmered away, and the music came to a halt. The boys finally stopped dancing and stood in the middle.

"What'd you bloodsuckers do?" Demetri demanded the crowd.

"We performed a protection spell," said a familiar voice. Pushing her way through the crowd, Narkissa had revealed herself. "We couldn't let you leave until we ensured the Lost Prince was bestowed a protection. The rare moonlights give us vampyres the ability to perform a sacred ceremony. Whenever the Lost Prince is around you, Prince Demetri, he shall remain safe from harm's way."

Demetri and Malakai exchanged looks. He wasn't certain how he felt about the idea. Regardless, he did feel a surge of pride knowing that whenever Demetri was near, Malakai would be safe. Kelton certainly couldn't make that promise. He'd need to do some more research on it, though, but for now, he had other priorities on his mind.

"So, you're the one who sabotaged the hovercraft?" Demetri asked Narkissa.

"Indeed. I feared that both of you might not comply with the ceremony, so we had to keep it hidden from you. We did not trust that Prince Kelton could be the Lost Prince's protector. We have more faith in you, Prince Demetri. I apologize for not informing you sooner, but my people rely on the safety of Prince Antonius Bellemore claiming his right to the Baskarian throne." Narkissa turned her attention to Malakai. "For far too long, we've been treated like disposable waste while other supernatural beings were treated like normal civilians. We're counting on you to change that."

"You have my word," Malakai said, making it clear to all the vamps that surrounded them. "But I won't allow dishonesty. After all, we cannot expect to live in a world of peace if we cannot learn from our history. We will be doomed to continue the same cycle until we break."

"You are correct," Narkissa said, nodding in acceptance. "We must break the cycle. You shall never worry about me or my people having malicious intent moving forward."

All the vamps bent the knee and bowed their head, letting Malakai know that they were at his service. Demetri had had enough of the little show, however. He grabbed Malakai's hand and the two left the dancefloor, heading back into the castle where they would gather their guards and head to their hovercraft.

## 44
## Loss of Identity

**RAHAF**

They must've travelled for what felt like hours when light finally appeared from afar. As they continued, Rahaf saw two beautiful, marbled pillars and an archway leading into a rectangular-shaped room. The flooring was also made of black and white marble in a diamond shape.

At the center of the room, there was a bronze oval mirror that floated in midair with nothing hanging onto it.

Eli went ahead of them first, walking toward the mirror and examining its essence. There was no telling what would happen, but the fact that no one has ever made it out of the Temple of Retribution alive alarmed Rahaf.

"Just because it looks like a mirror doesn't mean it is one," Rahaf warned him. "Be careful."

"I see something in the mirror," Eli said. He struggled to read whatever it was. "There's wording on it. Come take a look."

Theodosis went ahead first, then Rahaf and Aleek followed behind. Rahaf was holding Theodosis's hand as she felt a sense of worry crawl through her body. When they arrived in front of the mirror, Theodosis could not pick out what the words said either. It seemed Rahaf was the only one who could, considering her vision was as clear as day, staring at it.

"Neither of you can seriously read what it says?" Rahaf asked, worried.

"No," they both replied.

Rahaf sighed. "Well, the mirror says, 'There is nothing more noble than sacrificing what identifies an individual. When identity is taken, it comes anew. One who is true in sacrificing their identity may survive this task, but one who is deceitful to themself will surely inherit the ultimate fate.'"

"Sacrificing their identity?" Eli repeated. "What does that mean?"

Rahaf tried to comprehend the message. It could be interpreted in many ways, and yet none of them would know for certain until somebody made a move. But of all the questions they could think of, the most important one was on the table: Who was true and willing to sacrifice their identity?

There was an understanding between Rahaf and Eli as they looked each other up and down, knowing that neither of them would be true enough to participate in this task. Even a slight attempt at it would sentence them to death, and they knew it. As long as Theodosis was with them, it was a no-brainer that Rahaf would refuse to be as true as possible.

Suddenly, a forcefield appeared in front of the entrance. A timer appeared in the mirror, counting down for five minutes.

"We're trapped!" Eli exclaimed. "Somebody has to interact with the mirror."

"Why don't *you* do it?" Rahaf suggested to Eli.

"Are you crazy? You and I both know that would be the dumbest idea ever."

"Well, you agreed to come on this adventure. You knew what the stakes were."

"You're unbelievable, you know that? I can't believe you're seriously standing there and suggesting I offer—"

"—Enough!" Theodosis scolded. "None of this arguing will get us anywhere. I'm not sure what it is about you two, but I will *not* have it! If neither of you are going to do it, then I shall gladly offer myself.

I am truest to myself, and I can sleep at night knowing such."

Theodosis walked forward to the mirror, but before Rahaf could interfere and stop him, Theodosis placed his hand on the mirror. There was a force of wind that pushed Rahaf, Eli, and Aleek away from Theodosis. A circle of smoke emerged and surrounded Theodosis and the mirror.

As Theodosis' hand remained on the mirror, the mirror began to move in a wave-like motion. There was a humming sound that sang from within the glass.

"*A Prince of Nobility and Love,*" the mirror said. "*Such bravery and devotion for the one he loves. But you question whether she loves you as much as you love her. Nevertheless, you remain indebted to her. A man true of heart shall survive this task, but not without losing something in return. Your identity is what I seek. Within every elemental's identity, it is not the name or the memories they hold. It is their element that holds them true to who they are. Do you wish to sacrifice your element to move on to the second task?*"

"No!" Rahaf pleaded. "Theo, it's not worth it. Don't you dare give up your element. Please."

Theodosis looked down at the ground. He was lost in thought, contemplating. Rahaf knew what his decision would be in the end, but all she could think about was how miserable he would be if he gave up his air element. For that, he might as well give away his soul.

"You'll be miserable the rest of your life," Rahaf said. "Let's just go back around."

"We can't, Rahaf!" Theodosis argued. "It's too late to turn back now. We're trapped, and the Temple of Retribution won't let us out. I have to do this."

Rahaf was torn. Seeing Theodosis stand there, his hand still touching the mirror, made her feel terrible. All Rahaf wanted to do was break that smoke circle and run towards him. But there was no telling what the consequences would be if she interrupted the process.

Looking at the time, Theodosis had less than a minute left to make his final decision.

"I'm going to do it, Rahaf," Theodosis said. "I'm doing it for us.

It'll be perfect! No one will frown upon us for being married. I'll be a regular mortal, and we can be together without disdain from anyone else. You can reign the kingdom because we've broken no laws now."

"You're insane, Theodosis... Not at the expense of your happiness."

"You *are* my happiness, Rahaf. Forever and always."

A beam of light emerged, and for a split second Rahaf was blinded by it. When the light simmered down, she was able to see Theodosis lying on the floor, and the mirror remained still. The circle of smoke vanished, which prompted Rahaf to run over to him.

"Are you okay?" she asked.

"I—I'm fine. Just have a horrible headache," Theodosis responded. He picked himself up and looked at his hands. "It's gone. My element... I can't feel it pulsing through my veins anymore. I feel ten times heavier than before."

Rahaf held Theodosis while he tried to maintain his composure.

While they did so, the door on the other side opened, prompting the group to head out.

"Looks like we passed the first task," Rahaf said.

"Great," Eli said sarcastically. "I wonder what the next one will have in store for us."

"Whatever it is, it won't be good," Theodosis commented.

Abruptly, the cave shook, causing tiny rocks to plummet onto the ground. Rahaf held Theodosis tightly as they endured the drastic shaking. Then, the sounds of explosions in the distance rang out.

"What's going on?" Rahaf asked.

"I'm not sure," said Theodosis, "But I have a feeling our kingdom might be under attack."

# 45
## The Celestial Gates

**SILIANNA**

Seraphina Blackworth.

Silianna couldn't believe that Nerumi was Seraphina the entire time. It took a second for her to process how it was possible, but then she thought back to the necklace around her neck. She remembered from her time at Cressmoore learning about channeling magic into objects, especially for disguise magic. The necklace somehow gave her the ability to look like Nerumi. In the grand scheme of things, Silianna had to give that woman credit for her dedication. There was no way Nerumi could've retrieved an artifact that allowed her to teleport. *I should've seen it a mile away*, she thought. *I feel so stupid.*

Silianna's body floated through a sea of stars. She could not move nor blink, or smell. Everything was frozen in time, except her body continued to float, heading towards something.

Ethereal music echoed from behind her. The harmonies were soothing, which helped Silianna to relax as panic was beginning to set in. Then, amid her travels, a voice emerged from beyond and spoke from all directions:

*"Zorall was the first planet created across this galaxy. The*

*gift of knowledge was bestowed upon the Creator. The mortals used this knowledge to flourish and become the most advanced civilization across the galaxy. However, the mortals slowly started to become greedy with power. They used up all their resources on their planet, which caused them to tap into energy beyond their control. Portals were created, allowing them to travel between worlds. They influenced these other words and took back what they've learned and their resources. Because of this, it allowed Zorallians to create the 'perfect' world. Nothing could stand in their way. It was not the Creator's intention to have these Zorallians obtain such power. Because they took advantage of the Creator's gift, the planet of Zorall was sentenced to annihilation. However, four brothers flew down from the Heavens to help those who survived the asteroid sent for them. They were hence more known to civilians as their Gods. These four brothers gifted a piece of themselves to the mortals in hopes that they would restore balance to what Zorall once was—peace and harmony."*

The voice stopped.

Silianna's body landed on a flat surface. When she looked underneath her, she saw she was standing on glass flooring. Before her, there was a path to a golden archway. *The Celestial Gates*, she thought.

Running towards it, Silianna was stopped by the appearance of her uncle, Reju Tufte. He stood in the front of the gates, preventing Silianna from going further.

"*Stop*," he warned her.

"Uncle Reju!" Silianna said. "Please, I'm running out of time."

"You can't go through that gate. It's what started our family's curse. You don't want to add more to the bloodline."

"Oh, *now* you want to talk about that. I think you're a little late."

"Silianna, don't do anything you will regret. Just look at what happened to me. Do you want to end up stuck here for all eternity?

It's not worth it."

Silianna became frustrated. She had no time to waste. Either she was going to get some answers, or she was going to go through those gates.

"Tell me about the Beauchamp Curse," she demanded. "I have a right to know about it, especially if my life is at stake. If you don't tell me, then I'm going through those Celestial Gates." Silianna started for the gates, however, Reju swooped in and stopped her from doing so.

"They will not permit you to keep both your elements. Your great-great-grandmother, Laryse, tried doing that a long time ago. She wanted to see her husband after he passed away. She was convinced that he was trying to reach out to her on the Other Side. Laryse was so desperate that she tapped into energy far beyond this world, just like Vorkalth did. Only, it wasn't rage she sought out like Vorkalth. It was desperation and heartbreak—far deadlier than rage when uncontrolled. Laryse stumbled upon this gate many years ago and begged permission for the Celestial Ones to give her the ability to travel through realms. She wanted to see her lover, and instead she got something far worse."

"What could be worse than never seeing the love of your life again?" asked Silianna.

"She was turned to stardust, and that stardust has since flowed through the bloodstreams of those that share our bloodline. It's what allows us to travel through the Dark Dimension. Sometimes it skips a generation, sometimes it doesn't. I was picked, and now you. But unlike those before you, you have a way to be rid of your spiritual element. Do what we wish we could do. Don't fight to keep it."

"But my friends… I can't leave them to fend for themselves."

"Prince Kelton is too far gone, I'm afraid. There is no saving him."

"No. I won't accept that. When there is a will, there is a way. And I will fight until my last breath for those I care about the most."

Silianna pushed past Reju and started for the Celestial Gates.

Suddenly, Silianna felt herself sucked into darkness. The stars were gone, and so were the Celestial Gates.

"No!" she screamed.

There were spirits all around Silianna and Reju as she looked around her. They were speaking in an unknown language, though Silianna could not gather what it was they were trying to do while speaking.

"What's going on?" she asked Reju.

"I'm sorry," said Reju. "But we can't let you do this."

# 46
## Space Song

**MALAKAI**

Malakai and Demetri waited on the rooftop until Destlyn notified them of the hovercraft's repair. The tension between the two was awkward, especially since Malakai was still grappling with his feelings towards Demetri as of late. There wasn't telling how their friendship would fare if they were to keep this up. Malakai was still thinking of their dance during the Gilded Moonlit Ball. That rush of excitement filled his body with energy he'd never felt before, and yet it was quickly overshadowed by guilt.

Since their little adventure in the city, Demetri had shown just how much he cared for Malakai. Although Demetri made questionable choices and said some strange things, Malakai found himself looking past that and focusing on Demetri's loyalty, his strength, and his steady presence. Malakai cared about Kelton, of course, he did. But Kelton had been acting so strange lately, so different from the man Malakai had developed feelings for. Between his secrets and his isolation, and his anger, Malakai felt further away from Kelton than ever, even when they were in the same room.

"You're a bit quiet over there," Demetri said. It sounded like he was battling with himself to comment. "Something on your mind?"

*Yes... You.*

Malakai shook his head. "I'm just wondering how long it's taking the vampyres to fix the engines. What about you?"

"I'm thinking."

Malakai contemplated whether or not to continue talking. It seemed like a dead-end conversation. But what was the point in standing in silence? Demetri was the first to start the conversation, so it was only fitting that Malakai kept it going. It seemed they'd be waiting for a bit for Destlyn to notify them anyway.

"What are you thinking about?" asked Malakai.

"You," Demetri answered, coldly. "Your safety. My brother's safety. Just a lot of stuff on my mind."

"Well, you can worry less about me. I'm doing fine, thanks to Narkissa's blood."

"Correct. You are fine... for right now. But what happens if someone endangers you? As long as you have Narkissa's blood running through your system, you are at risk of transitioning into a vampyre in the event you die. The Grand Empress Dowager would have my head if that were to happen."

"I'll be careful. I won't disobey anyone's demands, and I will remain in Windsor Keep until the blood passes my system."

Demetri huffed. "You are the *King* of Stubbornness, Malakai Thorns. I have very little faith that you will do as you're told. I've grown to accept that a long time ago. That's why I vowed to keep an eye on you at any cost."

Down below, Malakai listened to the musical, ethereal waves and neo-psychedelia beats rung in his ears, somehow creating an emotional hold between Malakai and Demetri as they redirected their attention back on each other.

"The vampyres really know how to make beautiful music," said Malakai, his eyes still locked on Demetri's. "It gives off a sort of space song sound effect—like I'm floating throughout the stars in a far-off galaxy."

"They've lived longer than we ever will. I can only imagine how sad and miserable they must feel to create such depressing, yet beautiful, sounds." Demetri's voice cracked. He cleared his throat and sniffled. "Sorry. The music is bringing me back to a specific time in my life. It's hard reliving it…"

"Don't be sorry. We got nothing but time." Malakai reached over and held Demetri's hands. "You can tell me anything. I promise I won't judge."

Demetri pulled his hands away.

Though it didn't happen, Malakai felt like Demetri had slapped him across the face. His emotions were heightened, and he wanted nothing more than to walk away as embarrassment flooded his face with red.

"Why do you do that?" asked Malakai.

"Do what?" Demetri questioned.

Malakai frowned. "You shut me out. You become cold-hearted and pretend as if you don't have a shred of emotion in you. Why don't you at least *try* to open up to me? I thought these past few days have helped us grow our friendship. Or was I the only one thinking that?"

"I have my reasons, Malakai. I do not mean to be the way I am. I guess I've gone through so much disappointment and betrayal in my life. It's caused me to give up on trying to be a better person. No matter what I do, it amounts to nothing. My biggest fear is that I will open up to you and you will never want to talk to me again. I cannot bear the thought of you distancing yourself from me again."

Demetri took a second to collect himself before he continued. "The truth is: I've enjoyed spending time with you these past few days. Probably the most fun I've had in a very long time. I'm… I'm just worried it won't last forever."

"Demetri."

"Don't. I don't want to hear it." Demetri's eyes began to water. He walked quickly over to a nearby bench and set himself down, clearing his face.

Malakai followed soon after and sat down. Their shoulders bumped against each other as he settled. There was a tingling sensation that vibrated through Malakai's arms. He straightened his posture and tried to control his thoughts. *Why do I feel like this around him?* He questioned. *Can nothing ever be straightforward with Demetri?*

"I would love nothing more than to open to you," Demetri admitted, staring off into the night sky. He refused to look down at Malakai. "But as I've said, I don't want you to stop talking to me if I do. I want to have your word. I *need* to have your word. Otherwise, there is no point in continuing this conversation."

Malakai sighed. The beating in his chest roared, his body started to heat, and his hearing became hard. He had a feeling about what Demetri was going to say, or at least he had hoped Demetri would say it. *Is he the boy with black hair and blue eyes that saved me that night at Blackstaer Imperial Palace? Please, I need him to finally put that missing piece of my memory to rest. I need to know.*

"You have my word," Malakai finally said.

Demetri inhaled and exhaled. "For years, I've found it hard to find those I can trust. The ones I did trust have proven to me that good people are hard to come by. It is why I only consult with Theodosis, and recently, Silianna. But other than that, it's quiet." Demetri adjusted his focus so that he was facing Malakai. "I doubt you have memories of me, but you and I were once close friends. I was thirteen and you were ten the last time I saw you. For so long, I prayed to the Gods that you were still alive. I refused to believe that DeVault killed you.

"When you arrived in the Throne room four months ago, I was in disbelief. Everyone may have believed you were a regular smulder living in the poor area of Terrane, but I knew... I knew that the Lost Prince was standing before me after all those years. It is why I suggested the Wondrous Trials. I had to be sure, but more so to buy you time in the event my father was going to execute you."

"I knew you were hiding something from me when I first met you," Malakai responded. "I just wasn't sure what it was. But if that's the case, and you had a feeling I was Prince Antonius, why did you resort to being so terrible at the Masquerade Ball?"

"I was interested in getting to know you. But once I gathered that Kelton was growing a similar interest to you, the same way he did for Seraphina, I held myself back. I was enraged with the idea that Kelton beat me to the punch at another chance at happiness. So, I chose to let my anger mask my insecurities. There is no excuse for my actions, and perhaps things would have been different between us if I had taken a different approach with you. No amount of apologies will ever be good enough, Your Imperial Majesty. All I can hope is that you may forgive me for how I treated you."

Malakai smiled, feeling a little overwhelmed by Demetri's words. He wanted nothing more than to see Demetri in a different light— one that showed a sense of remorse, beauty, and love.

"You are forgiven," Malakai said softly.

"I never thought I would hear those words out of your mouth," Demetri admitted. He reached over and cradled Malakai's face in one of his hands. "But there's something else I have to ask you. It is a long shot given what Annalu said, but I have to know. Do you remember me from your childhood?"

"I won't lie, there's a lot I still don't remember. But I do recall playing hide-n-seek with Rahaf and Yal. For some reason, that day Yal passed away from the juxure flowers, it stuck with me as Malakai Thorns, even before I started to have dreams of Kelton." Malakai looked at the palm of his hand and noticed that his scar had disappeared. "My scar... It's gone! I remember you healing me that day in the barn."

Demetri held Malakai's hand and observed it. "Narkissa's blood must've healed your scar. I never thought that vampyre blood could heal old wounds."

Malakai recalled that moment at the Masquerade Ball where Demetri interrogated him. That moment finally made sense now that he heard his point-of-view.

"*I knew it,*" *Demetri said ominously.* "*You have the same scar on your palm. I can't believe you're alive. Where have you been all this time? I've spent countless nights praying that the Gods would bring you back to me.*"

"You knew for certain it was me when you saw the scar on my palm, didn't you?" Malakai asked. Demetri nodded without hesitation. "That could have been your moment. I wish you had handled the situation differently."

The music down below got louder, and the stars above shimmered brighter. There was a gush of wind that passed the boys, causing Malakai to shiver. Demetri took off his black leather jacket and wrapped it around Malakai for warmth. Malakai tugged on it and enjoyed the sweet scent of woody notes like cedar and sandalwood.

"I have a story for you," Demetri said. "A few years after the invasion, things happened to me. It was a big reason I assisted Silianna in killing Quill Dorell. I had convinced myself for a while that killing him was simply to help Rahaf and Theodosis be together, but in all reality, it was for my own revenge. You see, he took the one thing I had going in life since I lost Prince Antonius. The one thing I cherished the most... My innocence."

Malakai tried to follow what Demetri was implying. There were a couple of ideas that came to mind, but he'd hoped that neither were what he was going to say.

Demetri continued. "The truth is, I developed feelings for you when I was young—feelings for Prince Antonius. Before I was friends with Theodosis, my inner circle was Dallec Beauchamp and Quill Dorell. I always saw myself as one of the 'cool kids' because I hung out with the older crowd. Unfortunately, during the holidays, I decided to stay at Cressmoore Academy instead of flying home with Kelton. The boys and I drank and partied a little too much. I somehow slipped to Quill that I used to have a crush on Antonius and openly admitted that I still held out hope that you survived. To beat me down, Quill said some horrific things. He implanted the idea that you and I would never work and that it was a good thing you were dead. Quill hated the Bellemores, and his family never shied away from expressing that hatred. I'm not sure why I opened up to him about it.

"Then the worst came to light. Quill blackmailed me into doing some of his bidding to keep from telling anyone about my childhood crush for you. I felt embarrassed and was desperate to keep it quiet. So, Quill forced me to smuggle some drugs throughout Cressmoore Academy. I wasn't sure how he was getting his hands on the substances, but if I dared question it, he would knock me down and beat me to a pulp. To cover it up, Quill would then heal me from those injuries so nobody would notice or prevent me from reporting it.

"After a few weeks of dealing, Quill found a better opportunity to gain some aspar. He flew me out to a parade held in Pyroc. I was told Dallec and Silianna would be there, so I felt a little better knowing that Quill had no intent on having me do anything illegal. Of course, I was naive to believe such a thing. While we attended the parade, Quill pulled me to the side and said he needed me to kill some addicts who owed him aspar. They refused to pay him, and Quill didn't want to be traced for their murder. At first, I fought not to participate in such foul acts. But my argument was very little to the blackmail he had over me. It was no longer just about my feelings for Prince Antonius—Kelton was now a topic of interest. Somehow, Quill discovered Kelton's unexplainable ability. My family and I thought we were discreet about Kelton's conditions, but it seems we were blinded by Quill's conniving capability to gather intel. Essentially, I was his little pawn.

"But I just kept reminding myself of the importance: I needed to protect Kelton. I understood what resulted in those who possessed elements outside the four mains, and I refused to have Quill be the reason my brother was executed because of it. I never told my parents, more so because I knew they would find a way to blame me for everything. I am the older brother, and it was my duty to ensure that everything was operating smoothly."

There were a lot of things Malakai would assume as to why Demetri was the way he was, but hearing his story was not one of them. Malakai felt a heavy weight on his shoulders, and his heart broke for the man who sat next to him. *He went through all that because of me and to protect Kelton*, he thought, remorseful.

For the first time, Malakai saw Demetri in his most vulnerable state, and he wasn't sure how to react. There was so much information to process, and he wasn't sure anything he could say would really help.

Demetri cleared his throat and cleaned his face. He sighed as he said, "Before Thaddeus Thorns passed away, Dallec and Quill were competing for leadership as Thaddeus was getting ready to retire from his role. Everyone knew Thaddeus favored Dallec over Quill. When I heard there was a chance Quill could pick up the mantle, I knew I had to intervene. I got in contact with Dallec, and we talked for hours. Eventually, I gave in and told him what happened to me. I told him about you. I told him about Kelton. Dallec was heartbroken and furious. He looked at me as a brother figure, so I could imagine what was going through his mind."

"D—Demetri," Malakai said, hesitantly. "Silianna and I had conversations about her brother's passing. It happened the same day that my father passed away during the battle with the rebellion. Was…was Dallec killed because—"

"—Because of me?" Demetri interrupted. "Yes. I could not leave Terrane while the battle was taking place. So, I had Dallec promise to kill the bastard when the time came, to make it look like one of the supernatural beings was responsible for his death. When I heard of Dallec's passing, I knew what had happened. I could not bear to tell Silianna that he died because of me. The poor girl was stripped of everything. She wanted to be a Healer, but since Dallec was gone, she was now next in line for the Limus throne. I vowed at that moment that I would get my revenge. For you, for Kelton, for Dallec, and my innocence." Demetri stood up from the bench. He shifted his body to stand in front of Malakai, and then he bent a knee. Demetri held Malakai's hand as the two locked eyes on each other.

"You don't need to tell me how fucked up I am. Everyone around me ends up getting killed because of me. I told myself I would never tell you about this because I fear what happened to Dallec and Seraphina would result in you dying, too. I would rather die than see anything ever happen to you. I shut myself off and resorted to being a jerk because it was the only way I could keep my distance."

Malakai wrapped his arms around Demetri tightly and buried his face in Demetri's shoulder.

"What happened to them was not your fault," Malakai whispered. "This is all because my family and their need to give birth to me. My existence has quite literally ruined the lives of so many across the Nine Lands. I am the reason you had to go through all that, and I will forever be sorry for that. I understand why you acted the way you did toward me, and I forgive you. You don't need to ever shut me out. I'll always be here to listen. And I promise nothing bad will happen to me because of it."

"Don't blame yourself. Your existence did not cause all this madness. I believe this world has waited for a beacon of light to guide them through the darkness, and I believe you are that beacon. You are golden, Malakai Thorns. Stubborn and annoying, but still golden." Demetri chuckled, his quick side joke lifting the tension between the two. "And you want to know something? I'm glad you found Kelton in the forest four months ago. He's the better brother—the good brother. I just give him shit because he's never known real pain aside from Seraphina."

There was a strange urge for Malakai to lean in and kiss Demetri. His entire body ached for that connection, and yet he pulled himself together as he reminded himself that he was with Kelton. That fiery sensation boiled intensely as he continued to look at those ocean blue eyes.

"You don't know how badly I want to say three dangerous words to you right now," said Demetri. His voice deepened, and the weight of his want was clear. "I've been wanting to say it to you since the moment you stood before me at the Masquerade Ball."

"Demetri," Malakai said, breathless. "Don't. Don't say it."

"I know. I promised myself that I would never cross that line again. I'd rather keep myself in check than have a repeat of Seraphina." Demetri stood up and adjusted his clothing. "Right now, this little moment between us is the least of our concerns. We need to focus on heading back to Avala and informing the Grand Empress Dowager of your success in convincing Narkissa to lend her army."

Right on que, Destlyn appeared. He notified the boys that the hovercraft repairs were complete and that they were ready for their departure. The boys wasted no time as they collected themselves and started for the hovercraft, uncertain of their feelings and what lay ahead.

# *Act Three*

# 47

## Invasion

**DAMARIS**

A storm was brewing, and it was only a matter of time before the Fates turned the wheel and created a new path. The Prophecy of Old and New was written in the stars centuries ago, and it was Damaris Caerlight's mission to ensure that everything aligned perfectly. A slight change in the plan could cause a catastrophic event, and Damaris needed to prevent that at all costs. The whispers in her head warned her of something going off track in the kingdom of Aeris, and she'd been flying around since to figure out what may be the root of that concern.

Damaris guessed that perhaps it was the shapeshifter best friend belonging to the Prince of Dust and Shadows, but that had not been the truth.

Damaris figured that informing the shapeshifter of his mother and brother's whereabouts would prevent him from acting out irrational ideas, but she feared she may have only heightened them. Hearing the mess the shapeshifter, the prince, and the fire princess caused in Centuris was alarming at best, but she'd hoped that after the shapeshifter learned his lesson, he would restrain himself from looking for more trouble. Obviously, that hope simmered away when she saw him in the mountains arguing with a witch, far from where he was supposed to be.

*How did he end up in Aeris? What is his motive for coming here? Is he trying to sneak into Saint Salvusburg and rescue his family?*

So many questions ran through Damaris's head, and she could only hope it was her overthinking.

But, alas, she finally received her answer. Something was indeed off track, and it all had to do with the infamous Shadow Lord, Vorkalth.

Somehow, the venomous bastard had maneuvered his way into the Ackermere Palace. She's not sure how he accomplished it, but it was her job to cut him off at the source, and she intended to be successful.

With the storm coming in full force, Damaris felt as though there was something following her from the sky. She was currently hovering over the city, surrounded by mountains, and Ackermere Palace was not that far from the city. There was an army of caedose soldiers marching to the gates of the city's entranceway. Curious to know what was going on, Damaris decided to keep her focus on whoever was gaining on her. When she turned around, she was stunned to find it was one of the witches.

"Not again," she mumbled.

Quickly, Damaris used her force to rise even higher through the clouds, planning to lose the witch tracking her. She felt she had succeeded, given that after a few minutes, there was no one in sight. *Perhaps it was the same one who was with the shapeshifter*, she thought. Damaris was still in awe of how the witch had nearly caught her last time. It was impossible, especially since the title Damaris was given many moons ago after the passing of her sister—The Superior Witch.

*BOOM!*

An explosion shook the air around her very suddenly. Damaris dodged to the left, narrowly avoiding a large ball of fire. The ball wasn't aimed at her, however. She just so happened to be in the way of the actual target: Ackermere Palace.

Damaris' heart started to race. She knew this was a possible outcome based on her visions while in Glisten Lake. However, she never thought she'd be there to see it unfold.

Pyroc had declared war on Aeris.

"I've been searching for you for years," said a voice.

Damaris turned around, still floating high up in the sky. Behind her was the witch she was worried about.

"How did you find me?" Damaris demanded.

"Time and dedication," the witch answered. "So, you're the one who's been selected to be the next Superior Witch. Why have you forsaken your coven? The magic-folk have waited for what has felt like a lifetime for you to show yourself. All along, you were here in the North."

Damaris observed the witch who dared speak to her with such disgust. She had unique purple eyes, fair skin, short dark red hair, and a very slim build. The witch also wore a green leaf-like dress that reached down to her mid-thighs and had a smattering of freckles across her shoulders. Damaris knew by the intensity in the witch's eyes that she was going to be a problem unless Damaris made a stand.

"That is *not* what I've been doing," Damaris testified, her voice a low growl.

"Really?" The witch crossed her arms. "Because that's what it looks like to me. We magic-folk are close to *extinction*. Our only hope of survival is to have our ruler—*our heir*. That would be you, Madam."

"You know nothing... This is bigger than the magic-folk. We're talking about the end of the world. I may be the Superior Witch, but I have a duty to the Gods. The Prophecy of Old and New is at the cusp of happening, and I need to ensure the planet of Zorall survives the outcome. It won't matter if the magic-folk survive if the entire world doesn't. Don't you get that?"

The witch held her tongue and remained silent, staring at Damaris.

"I'm sorry," Damaris apologized, making an attempt at peace. She held out her hand, an offering for understanding. "I should introduce myself. I am Madam Damaris Caerlight, more famously known as '*The Lady of Glisten Lake*.' I was trapped there for years until Prince Antonius Bellemore stumbled upon my domain. He freed me, and ever since, I've been ensuring everything aligns the way it should. Fate is a tricky business, and sometimes, they are beyond the Gods' control. Since the death of my sister and my imprisonment, I was given abilities no other Superior Witch has ever had—a connection to the Gods. I hear them speak out to me once in a blue moon."

The witch shook Damaris' hand. "My name is Annalu. I am the leader of my coven. We serve the Grand Empress Dowager, Maelena Bellemore. My apologies for assuming you did not care for our people. It's been a nightmare ever since the Elder Guardians reigned over the North. I tend to forget that we're not the only ones suffering. It is an honor to meet you, Madam Damaris."

*BOOM!*

Another explosion shook the air around them. Both Damaris and Annalu's hands separated, and they looked at the war below them.

"I fear I must ask," Annalu started, "but is this war written in the stars? Was it meant to happen?"

Damaris nodded. "I'm afraid so. Lives will be lost, but better days will be ahead once we pick up the pieces."

"If you don't mind me asking, why did you snatch the shapeshifter from me? Is he part of the prophecy?" Annalu asked.

"Yes," Damaris answered coldly. "I thought that his being in the North would cause him to go off track from his destiny. But now, I know that he is right where he needs to be. He and the fire princess must find the Sword of Aerislark. As much of a headache he may cause you, it is all part of a greater plan. You are to protect him just as much as Prince Antonious Bellemore. Those two are close friends for a reason."

Annalu sighed. "I wish you didn't tell me that. Both of them together are nothing but pure chaos."

"Well, let us hope you can contain that chaos until Prince Antonious Bellemore claims the Baskarian throne. There is much to be done, but first, you must return to your coven and protect the

King and Queen of Aeris. I sense the Shadow Lord's presence has tainted the Ackermere Palace. I can't explain it, and the Gods refuse to confirm my suspicions. All I know is that something sinister is at play, and I must find the root of it before the future is shifted."

*The South.*

*Avala.*

*He needs you.*

*Vorkalth is near.*

*Go.*

*Now!*

The voices rang in Damaris' ears like a struck bell, repeating each other over and over until she found herself back in the present.

"Madam Damaris?" Annalu said, concerned. "Your eyes. They suddenly turned white. Is everything okay?"

Damaris collected her thoughts. She knew the voices in her head were the Gods. They wanted her to fly out to the South. Damaris wasted no time as she vanished into the clouds, leaving Annalu to handle the invasion. *I have to find the Prince of Dust and Shadows immediately.*

# 48
## The Mind of Weakness

**MALAKAI**

Malakai entered the garden where Nehila and Celdric were located. Nehila was in the middle of building a snowman when she caught sight of her older brother. She left her unfinished project as she dashed toward him, jumping into his arms and hugging him. Malakai felt a surge of relief to see that both of them were safe.

"It's good to see you two are alright," said Malakai.

"I missed you!" Nehila said. "I wish I had gone with you guys."

Malakai laughed. "Trust me, you did not want to go where we went."

"Did you get us a gift from the island?" Neihla asked innocently.

Malakai opened his mouth, but he realized there was no point in lying to her. "I'm sorry, Nehila. I completely forgot. There were a lot of grown-up businesses that got in the way. I promise I will make it up to you." Nehila pouted, but she did not make a scene about it.

Malakai shifted his attention to Celdric, who stood by the unfinished snowman. "Well? Are you going to give me a hug or what?"

Celdric reluctantly walked over with his arms spread out. Malakai figured he was still a little upset that he didn't want his little brother fighting in the war. But given the fact that Celdric hugged him,

Malakai felt things would get better between the two in time.

"How did it go with the vampyres?" asked Celdric.

"Horrible. But we accomplished what we went there to do. It is just a matter of time before we gather our army."

Celdric raised an eyebrow. He stared at someone from behind Malakai, then looked back at Malakai. "Where's your boyfriend?"

Malakai stiffened in surprise. He didn't think anybody would notice Kelton's absence, at least not immediately. But it seemed he may have underestimated Celdric's intelligence as he stood there waiting for an answer.

"I, um..." Malakai cleared his throat. "He went upstairs to rest. He hurt himself earlier, but I'm sure he'll come down later."

Celdric squinted his eyes, as if he was making it known that he had caught onto Malakai's lie. Luckily, Celdric did not bother to question it further. Instead, he grabbed Nehila's hand and tugged her back towards the snowman.

Demetri hovered from behind Malakai's shoulder and said, "We should find the Grand Empress Dowager and relay all the information we have. I'm sure she is eager to learn everything there is to know."

"Wait! Can we go with you?" Nehila asked.

"You cannot, Nehila. I'm sorry. But I promise I will come and find you afterwards. Deal?"

Nehila groaned. "You're always making promises. I guess..."

Malakai frowned, feeling bad for her. Demetri intervened once more and grabbed Malakai's arm gently, guiding him into the halls of Windsor Keep. He waved his goodbyes to Celdric and Nehila while Demetri pulled him away. Once inside, Celsa welcomed the two of them back.

"Ah! Your Imperial Highness," Celsa said, his robotic voice thrilled. "I've wondered when I would see you again. Come along then. I shall guide you to the Grand Empress Dowager."

\* \* \*

Celsa guided them to the elevator and brought them up to the conference room. There, Malakai saw his grandmother across the large glass table, nervously rapping her fingers against the table while she looked out the window, staring at the glass city of Avala. She wore a peculiar black dress and gloves, almost like she was in mourning.

Celsa closed the door behind them.

Malakai went up ahead of Demetri. The Grand Empress Dowager turned away from the window to acknowledge his grandson's return.

"By the Gods, I was beginning to worry," she said, her voice sounding thankful.

"Hello, Grandmamma," Malakai said, smiling. "I'm sure you will be pleased to hear that I convinced the Vampyre Queen to lend us her army."

"So, I've heard. I'm proud of you. Truly." Maelena Bellemore walked over to Malakai and hugged him, holding him tight in her arms. "The moment you left here, I felt a great sense of regret in my bones. I worried about your well-being every day you did not return. I'm just so thankful you are unharmed."

"I'll always come back to you, Grandmamma. I'm a tough nut to crack—so I've been told," Malakai said, mind drifting back to when Kelton said those words to him the first time they met in the woods.

Demetri chuckled in the background. Malakai assumed he agreed with Malakai on that statement. Malakai rolled his eyes and brushed Demetri's laugh to the side.

"Where is Prince Kelton?" Maelena asked. "Last I saw, three of you went to Theuros. And yet, only two of you have come back to me. Did I miss something?"

Malakai was juggling to find an excuse, but he was having difficulty coming up with something. *Whatever I say, it needs to be convincing.* Malakai swallowed and was about to open his mouth, but it seemed the Fates had other plans for him. A beeping sound started from the ceiling, cutting off his response. Malakai looked up as a flash of red lights followed. There was an emergency, and he instantly feared for his siblings' lives.

"Celdric and Nehila," Malakai said, turning quickly towards

Demetri.

"It's okay. The alarm isn't for a breach in the castle," Demetri said, attempting to calm Malakai down. "Celdric and Nehila will be okay."

"Then what's this alarm for?"

Demetri pointed behind Malakai. When he turned around, he saw his grandmother standing in front of a holographic projector—the images depicted over a dozen hovercrafts flying towards Ackermere Palace. Bombs were falling out of the vehicles, slamming into the ground below. The symbols on the hovercrafts belonged to Pyroc. *No*, Malakai thought, fearing the worst.

Maelena reached for her glass communicator and attempted to connect but was unsuccessful. She then pressed a button on a nearby control panel, summoning her guards. In a matter of seconds, they came rushing into the conference room and lined up in a single-file line.

"Pyroc has declared war on Aeris," Maelena announced. "We'll need to send some of our forces over there."

"It will take hours until we can arrive," one of the guards said.

"As long as the King and Queen remain alive, that's all that matters. Now, do as I say and get everyone ready for battle. I want to see all our hovercrafts in the sky immediately."

"Very well, Your Imperial Highness," the guard complied.

Once the guards rushed out of the room, the doors closed, and the room fell into a tense silence.

Demetri took a few steps forward. "Grand Empress Dowager, if you will let me, I want to fight alongside the Resistance. Rahaf and Theodosis could be in grave danger, and so will the shapeshifter. If you allow me, I will make sure I retrieve them and bring them back here."

"What?" Malakai shouted, striding up to Demetri. "I forbid you! You're going to get yourself killed." Malakai looked to his grandmother, feeling hopeless. "Please, Grandmamma. There must be a way for you to contact Annalu and get her to conjure a portal."

"I'm sorry, my dear," his grandmother replied. "It is out of my hands. Annalu has not contacted me in a while. I can only assume the worst. If Demetri is willing to offer himself up for the task, then I cannot stop him. He's stronger than you may think."

Malakai shook his head. "I can't lose you, too, Demetri. Everyone and everything feels like it's slipping through my fingers."

Demetri reached out, clasping a hand on Malakai's forearm. "You won't lose me, Malakai. I will be back, and I'll rescue our friends."

"After everything we've been through... After you opened up to me about your past. You're just going to leave me here by myself?"

Demetri's lips quivered. He was struggling to say something, and Malakai could see it. He desperately wanted Demetri to say anything, but the other man remained silent.

"You suck," Malakai said, wiping a hand across his eyes. "If you're going, then I'm going with you."

"No," Demetri and Maelena simultaneously.

"Screw what either of you think! I'm going to Aeris whether you like it or not. I'm not going to sit by and wait to hear news that anyone I love is dead. We could get more done if I'm there."

Maelena Bellemore slammed her hand on the glass table. The sound echoed around the room. "If you think about stepping one toe out of this castle, I will have you locked away until further notice. Do I make myself clear?" she said coldly.

Malakai felt fury burn through him. He was tired of being constantly babied and tucked away when he could be out there, doing something to help people. He gathered that neither of them would let him leave, and it would be foolish of him to try sneaking on one of the hovercrafts. There would be guards all over the place. There was only one option. *I need to find Jaeyse Caerlight and get more information on that portal*, he thought.

Once he made up his mind, Malakai looked at Demetri. He was observing Malakai while he was thinking. Demetri must have seen something in the grim set of Malakai's mouth and the determination in his eyes as he stepped forward with a hand extended in preparation.

"Malakai, do not do it!" Demetri said.

Malakai chanted *"Pyro"* as a beam of fire came soaring from his palms. Demetri countered his attack by using his Terrane element. A rock emerged from the floor and was crafted into a flat, circular shield.

*"Malakai!"* Demetri yelled, a desperate waver to his voice.

Malakai did not dare look back as he escaped into the halls, aiming for the elevator door. Adrenaline was taking over him, not caring for the chaos he had left in his wake. However, Malakai's escape plan was quickly compromised when Celsa appeared before him. The robotic being managed to hold tightly on Malakai's wrist and handcuff him with the electric handcuffs—the same device that would restrain him from using his elemental abilities.

"My apologies, Prince Antonius," said Celsa. "This is for your own good."

# 49
## Guidance

**MALAKAI**

Malakai hugged his legs and buried his face in his knees as he sat on the cold cement floor, trying to keep calm and not scream from frustration. The electric handcuffs prevented him from using his elemental abilities to escape, leaving him helpless and locked in this tower. The memories were threatening to overwhelm him—being reminded of the time he was locked away in the East Tower of Castle Caestshire. The only good thing he could say about Castle Caestshire was that he was treated like a guest. The tower here had no bed, no blankets—nothing. Just a cold, hard surface.

What made the situation worse was the fact that his grandmother was the cause of his imprisonment. And Demetri...he stood there and let it happen. How could Demetri have been so open and honest with him, then turn around and betray him? There was no coming back from this. Malakai would never forgive Demetri.

Higher up on the wall was a small window, barred from the outside. The moonlights shone through, giving Malakai the only light possible to see his surroundings.

Malakai looked out the small window from where he sat and admired the two moons that glowed. It had been hours since he had last seen Demetri or his grandmother. Malakai speculated that

Demetri was long gone with the others, flying off to Aeris. It infuriated him to think about it. All he wanted at this moment was Kelton. *If I could travel through the Dark Dimension to talk to him, I would,* he thought.

"I feel so stupid," Malakai mumbled.

The little bit of light from the moons was dimmed as a shadow was cast over the window. Malakai jumped up, startled. He squinted, trying to make out the shadowy shape, and was surprised to see the mystical Lady of Glisten Lake hovering outside. *Damaris Caerlight.* She looked the same from the last time he saw her. Pale skin, long black hair, and the same shimmering light blue dress.

"You are not stupid, Prince Antonius," said Damaris.

"But I am," Malakai said, annoyed. "I was trying to escape, and I got caught."

"Why were you trying to escape?" Damaris flicked her wrist. The metal bars melted off, sloughing off onto the floor, allowing her to float through the window.

"I was actually on my way to find your father." Malakai raised an eyebrow, hoping to get a reaction out of her. "His name is Jaysese Caerlight. He told me about you a few days ago."

"Oh?" Damaris said, testing Malakai. "And what did he say?"

"My best friend, Eli, somehow got mixed up with Princess Rahaf. She accidentally dragged him into a portal with her and a coven of witches. I resorted to your father for help since he had resources on a location for a portal. He told me about your sister—how she passed away. And then you went missing not long after. Jaysese offered his portal in exchange for your return. I thought it was impossible, but seeing as you're right in front of me, perhaps that is not the case."

"Anything is possible as long as you believe," Damaris said, gleefully. "I'm sure he's been waiting to see me again. But now is not the time. Not yet."

"But why not? What's stopping you from reuniting with him?" Malakai asked.

"It's much too complicated to explain. I have a duty. I must ensure that everything aligns so the Prophecy of Old and New may come to pass. Until then, I cannot put my personal needs before fate."

Malakai huffed. "It's not fate if you're interfering."

"As I've said, it's much too complicated to explain. My duty, and my abilities, are connected to the Gods and the Fates. I serve them, and they in return serve me. It is the title I was bestowed when I became the Superior Witch."

"Superior Witch?" Malakai questioned. "Why does that sound familiar?"

"Perhaps that is a story for another time. But I did not come here to discuss my father. And you shouldn't be meddling with portals either. I've come here to offer you some guidance."

Malakai squinted his eyes suspiciously. "What kind of guidance? Please don't offer me any riddles. My brain cannot take any more confusion for one night."

The Lady of Glisten Lake formed a fist and held it out in front of Malakai. She blew on it and then opened it up. In her hands was a piece of folded paper. Malakai reached over and took it. He then unfolded it and saw that it was a documentation of someone named Jarabella Crinthe, the Lady of the Miracle Forest. The documents explained that she was sent to the Sorrow Tower for suspicious activities. Reading more into it, Malakai learned that the "suspicious activities" were an orchestrated terrorist attack against the Bellemore family at the request of the spirits on the Other Side—or so she claimed. When Malakai looked at the dates, it seemed to have occurred one year before he was born.

"Why are you showing me this? What guidance could this possibly give me?" Malakai asked.

"Your father, King Stephanus Bellemore II, made a terrible mistake sending Lady Jarabella Crinthe to the Sorrow Tower. The 'suspicious activities' were not of her doing. She was framed. By whom? I do not have an answer." Damaris flew closer to Malakai, her feet never touching the ground. "You have armies from Avala, Centuris, Theuros, and the West of Veilios. All you need is the fae-

344

folk, and the remaining Elder Guardians won't stand a chance."

"And how do you expect me to convince them?"

"Lord Liri holds a grudge against the elementals. If you wish for his people to fight alongside you, you must assure him that you will release his mother from Sorrow Tower when you claim the Baskarian throne. There is a lot at risk, Prince of Dust and Shadows. You will lose this battle without them at your disposal, I fear."

Malakai took a second to process the information relayed to him, thinking of how much he already had on his plate. His list of errands seemed to be never ending.

"I know it is a lot to process," said Madam Damaris, "but you must undo the damage your father has inflicted on the fae-folk. Show them that you will not betray them. Show them how different you are from the rest of the world. If you succeed, then you've already won the battle before it's even begun."

"That's easier said than done. Can't you use your magic to help me escape from this place? I can get more done if I weren't locked up." Malakai held out his wrists, waiting for the Lady of Glisten Lake to break his electric handcuffs.

Damaris held her index finger and waved it. "No. I'm not going to help you that easily. If you want out of here, you must reach within yourself and resort to your gift. There's a little fiery friend of yours who has yet to transform into your spirit animal. She will guide and protect you. Call out to her."

"But I can't use my elements with these handcuffs!" Malakai cried out.

"Exactly. Call out to her. She'll get you out. And once she has, you will be able to do extraordinary things. You both have a part to play in that battle with Aeris and Pyroc. Tilt the wheel—change destiny."

Damaris flew away, leaving Malakai alone.

Malakai recalled what he was taught about Enis in the past: Lustrisqull, the Goddess of Guidance, her ultimate goal was to allow a mortal and an Eni to bind each other for guidance and protection. Those tiny creatures would be the ones to choose their owner. Once they were attached, the Eni would transform into the embodiment of one's true soul—a spirit animal. And with that, they provided guidance and protection. The first step was to name them. After that, the two would join together as the transformation would be completed.

"Okay." Malakai took a breath. He closed his eyes and emptied his thoughts. All he could focus on was Bluu. *She must be near*, he told himself. "Come to me, Bluu. I know you can hear me out there. You can't be far."

Opening his eyes, Malakai was pleased to see Bluu floating through the window and heading towards him. She cooed and spun herself around three times, showing Malakai her excitement to see him back in Avala.

"Bluu!" Malakai exclaimed.

Bluu looked at the electric handcuffs and made a cute, yet sad, noise. Malakai felt her emotions—she did not like the fact that he was restrained. Bluu took it upon herself to use her fiery hands to melt the restraints off. It was slow going, but after a few minutes, the cuffs fell apart around his wrists.

"Yes! Good girl," Malakai said. He held out his hands. Bluu then sat in the middle of his palm. "I wish we could have taken more time with this, but it seems we don't have any. I need you to become your spirit animal so I can get out of here. Show me what you got."

Bluu's bright, fiery light started to glow brighter than usual. Malakai's eyes widened, intrigued to see what she would become.

The door to the tower burst open abruptly.

Malakai, startled, stood up straight and pressed his back against the wall. Bluu jumped from his hands and floated in front of him, her bright light shimmering back to her normal blue shade.

At the entrance, Malakai saw Demetri standing there dressed in the gold and black armor he had purchased from Jaysese Caerlight. The spikes on his shoulder pads made him look twice as dangerous—and somehow attractive. However, he quickly stopped himself from thinking so fondly of the older Eckwood brother and remembered what he had done not too long ago.

"You coward!" Malakai cried out.

"Keep your voice down before I have to fight more of the guards," Demetri said. Malakai glanced down to see a body lying at Demetri's feet, the unconscious form of one of the guards. "Did you really think I was going to Aeris without you? I knew what your grandmother would think about you traveling there. I had to pretend I was on her side so she wouldn't throw me in here with you."

Malakai felt like an idiot. "Y—You were pretending?"

"Yes. Now, are you going to just stand there, or are we going to get you dressed for battle?"

Demetri was right. Malakai looked at Bluu as they both nodded their heads at the same time. He quickly ran out of the tower, Bluu following right behind him as they prepared to fight.

# 50
## Take My Hand

**RAHAF**

The passageways were pitch black as they wandered endlessly through the caves. Rahaf guided the boys and Aleek with the tips of her fingers on fire. Her mind was still reeling after seeing Theodosis give up his Aeris element. *I wonder what must be going through his head*, she thought. Rahaf felt the only thing she could do was hold his hand with her free one. She'd hoped it would give him a sense of comfort, a sign to know that she would be with him every step of the way, regardless of what came next after they got out of the Temple of Retribution.

Eli was shockingly being a good sport about the situation. Rahaf expected him to ruin what she and Theodosis had, but he didn't. *Maybe I was wrong about Eli*. Still, it didn't matter. After she got her hands on the sword and handed it over to Malakai, Rahaf intended never to see Eli again. It didn't matter how she felt for him. Theodosis sacrificed so much for her in the end. He gave up his title, his element, and was willing to marry her, knowing that a war would break out.

*War…*

Goosebumps crawled across Rahaf's arms. She was also thinking about what Theodosis had said a while back. *"I have a weird feeling our kingdom might be under attack.*" If it was true, Rahaf was glad to be in the Temple of Retribution.

Walking through an archway, Rahaf was the first to stumble upon a crystal-like room. At the center, there was a chromatic box floating in midair. Small shimmering particles surrounded the box, giving it a shiny illusion. Then, a vibrating sound came from within the box, making the hair on the back of Rahaf's neck stand up. *Theodosis had already lost his element*, she thought, *so what could be next?*

"Do you see any writing?" asked Eli.

Rahaf leaned forward, though the writing presented on the box was unreadable. "Nothing," she responded. "I can't read what it says."

"May I?" Eli said politely. Rahaf stepped back and allowed him to read the text. "Nope. I can't read it either."

"Allow me to take a look," Theodosis offered. He went ahead and leaned forward. "*Hmmph.* I think I can make it out."

"Well? Don't keep us guessing, Theo. Read it out loud!" Rahaf said impatiently.

"Right." Theodosis cleared his throat. "It says, 'Tell me your secrets and I shall tell you no lies. Answer me truthfully, and you will receive your prize. Deceit will send you down a spiral, for consequences are not desirable. A soul with a heart of bravery may pass this test, but either from truth or bloodshed will you uncover the rest.'"

Rahaf gulped. Being a soul with a heart of bravery was something she could identify with, but sharing her secrets would prove she would fail this test. If this weird box were to put her to the test, it would surely make her come clean about whatever it was she felt for Eli.

Rahaf looked at Eli and Theodosis. She refused to let Theodosis take part in another task. He'd already given up his element, and it would hurt her to see him lose something else. There were only two options: Her or Eli.

"So," Rahaf started, staring at Eli, "between the two of us, who do you think is the best person to face this thing?"

"I'm not afraid to share my secrets," Eli responded coldly. "I'm not sure the same can be said for *you*."

Rahaf felt that comment rip into her heart. She knew Eli was upset with her. He had every right to be. There was no greater regret she endured than entertaining Eli for as long as she did. The truth always had a way of coming out in the end.

"Then you've made up your mind?" Rahaf asked Eli.

"Whatever it takes to get the sword." Eli rolled up his sleeves and walked forward to the box. "For Malakai. For my mother. For Orian. For the nation of Baskaria. I will risk the consequences. *A soul with a heart of bravery.*"

Rahaf and Theodosis stood back as Eli took center stage.

Theodosis pulled Rahaf closer to him as he whispered, "What's with all this secrecy? I'm starting to gather that you may not be telling me something. Is everything okay, Rahaf?"

Rahaf panicked. She wasn't sure how to respond, but she knew she had to think strategically.

"It's my sister," Rahaf lied. "I'm feeling guilty. I told Eli about her, and I expressed how I feel her imprisonment at the Sorrow Tower was my fault."

"Don't be ridiculous. That was your father's fault. Not yours. Once this is all over, we will rescue her from that cruel place. I swear on my life." Theodosis kissed Rahaf on the side of her face.

Rahaf was feeling guilty for lying, but it was safer than telling the truth. Besides, it wasn't a complete lie—she did feel bad about her sister still trapped in that cruel place. Whenever the world settled down from the chaos, Rahaf swore she would go and rescue Jacquiline.

"What are you thinking about?" Theodosis asked her.

"Nothing," Rahaf said. "I'm just anxious that something bad is about to happen."

"Trust me, it'll come soon enough." The tone in Theodosis' voice was off-putting, mostly because Rahaf could've sworn it was somebody else who said it; however, she brushed it off, considering she was already in her head about all these other issues.

Theodosis reached into his bag and pulled out a flask filled with water, but Rahaf refused to drink it. Instead, she redirected her attention to Eli as he was about to put his hand inside the box.

"Here goes nothing," Eli said, taking a deep breath. "If anything happens to me, tell Malakai I love him. That stubborn idiot is like a brother to me, and I would do anything for him."

Rahaf's body felt numb. To hear Eli sound so emotional, knowing that if anything were to happen to him, in the end the person he most cared for was his best friend.

"Don't talk like that, Eli," Rahaf said, her voice shaking. "You said it yourself. Your heart is brave. Be true to you."

"Do you really want me to be true?" Eli asked, his voice softening. "I don't think I can if you don't wish me to…"

"Do what you must. If the questions come up, then so be it. But I cannot look Malakai in the eyes when he asks the reasoning behind his best friend dying."

"You'd risk the alliance for a shapeshifter?" Eli asked her, his hand secured inside the box with no way of pulling it back out.

"I—" Rahaf was choked up. She could sense Theodosis was lost in thought, but he did not look at her for one second. Maybe he figured it out, or maybe he didn't. Regardless, the secrecy was starting to become unbearable. "I would risk it. For Malakai. For your family. For the nation of Baskaria. With or without their help, we'll figure it out together."

"Okay." It was the last word that slipped out of Eli's mouth. A bright light emerged, causing Rahaf's vision to blur. She could feel Theodosis' presence disappear beside her.

When the lights simmered, Rahaf looked around. Eli was facing a creature floating above the box. It had a round face with black horns and claws so sharp they seemed like small knives. The creature also had a long tongue sticking out, sharp teeth visible from the insidious smile it had across its face.

"Eli-zak Vakloon," hissed the creature. "Grandson to Lord Hussayn. You offered yourself for the next task. Do you have a heart of bravery, or will you face the consequences of your deceit?"

"Bring it on," Eli challenged.

Rahaf looked at her side and noticed that Theodosis was standing in the corner, his hands in his pockets, avoiding eye contact with her. He looked upset, and rightfully so. There was no doubt in Rahaf's mind that he put the pieces together. But she knew him too well. He would hold off in addressing her until they retrieved the sword. Rahaf then turned her focus back to Eli and the creature.

"Where does your loyalty lie in this world?" asked the creature.

"Easy. My loyalty lies with the Thorns family," Eli answered.

The room lit up a bright light, followed by a loud thumping sound. Rahaf assumed it meant he had passed the first question.

"What is your goal in life?" asked the creature.

"To rescue my mother and brother. To protect the Thorns family. To find love and happiness…"

"You do not wish for the royalty you have recently discovered? To be part of a bloodline where your grandfather rules?"

Eli shook his head. "It means nothing to me. I have chosen my family. Granted, it is nice to know where I come from, but it will never be the same as those I have built a bond with. They will never understand the hardship I have gone through with my friends in the North."

The lights burned brighter, and the thumping sound chimed again. Eli had passed another interrogation. Rahaf felt a little bit relieved.

"Now, do you believe you will find love and happiness?" asked the creature.

Rahaf's feeling of relief vanished. She knew where the creature was heading with that question. *Here we go*, she thought.

"I—I think in time I will find happiness. But as for love, I believe I have already found it. Sadly, it doesn't mean I will get it."

"And do you believe love and happiness are one and the same?" asked the creature.

Eli nodded his head. "With love comes all sorts of emotional baggage. Happiness is temporary in love, but it is still love. You must put in the hardship and dedication if you want to see that happiness flourish. I surely have a lot of it to give."

The lights went off once more, followed by the thumping sound. Rahaf figured that was the last question. It had to be. What else would the creature want to know?

"Lastly, who do you most desire?" the creature asked.

The question echoed across the room. The air was thick with tension. All Rahaf could do was stand there and wait for the answer to slip from his mouth. *Just say it already*, she thought. *End this whole thing, and we can move on to the next task.*

"No one," Eli answered.

Rahaf's eyes widened. He chose to be deceitful. She couldn't believe what he had just done. *Did he really just sacrifice himself to keep the secret?* Rahaf was furious with him, but she was also concerned for what was about to happen. She was about to intervene, but Theodosis appeared next to her and held her back.

The creature's eyes glowed red like rubies. It stared deep into Eli's eyes as a small tornado formed in the room.

"Deceit was your choice, and so bloodshed shall follow," said the creature. "Though you have chosen this path, your heart remains brave. As punishment, the hand in your box will no longer be yours."

Rahaf shrieked. "STOP!"

The chromatic box closed shut, slicing Eli's hand.

Eli's scream was so loud it hurt to hear. It was the scream of a panicked animal, dying in the hunter's grasp.

The creature slunk back into the darkness, and Eli was left falling to the ground. The floor was slick with the blood pouring from Eli's arm. Rahaf wasted no time running over to him. Aleek jumped in, ripping a piece of Eli's shirt from his lower area. Rahaf then pulled the fabric from Aleek's mouth and started to chant "*Pyroc.*" Fire appeared, and she pressed the heat on Eli's wound. He was crying in agony, but Rahaf did not stop. She had to stop the bleeding, and once she did, she quickly wrapped it up with the fabric.

When she looked back up, Eli was unconscious, head lolled to the side. Rahaf couldn't help herself and held his head close to her chest.

"I won't let you go," she whispered. "I promise."

At the corner of her eyes, she saw Theodosis walking off. He was heading to the next task when the door opened. But Rahaf did not care to follow him. She'd stay as long as it took until Eli woke up.

# 51
## Memory Lane

**DEMETRI**

While Malakai was getting himself dressed, Demetri headed to Silianna's bedroom, hoping to find some sort of answer as to where she'd gone. With everything that happened, Demetri refused to forget that she took off without a trace. The Grand Empress Dowager told him that she would find Silianna, but he feared it wouldn't be her top priority. *It's up to me to figure it out*, he thought.

Entering the bedroom, Demetri started going through all her belongings. Clothes were everywhere, shoes tossed to the corner, her blankets undone, and books were scattered all over her bed.

Nothing.

As he was about to leave, Demetri stepped on a small piece of paper. Curious, he pulled it from underneath his foot and read:

- *Fae-folk have a portal to the Dark Dimension. Do they have answers to Vorkalth's weakness?*
- *Twenty-four hours to release my spiritual element before Vorkalth comes after me.*
- *Contact Demetri and Malakai to warn them that Kelton might be possessed by Vorkalth.*

355

Demetri's hands were shaking as he read the last bullet point. There was no way Silianna was stupid enough to fly out to Miracle Forest. Demetri refused to believe it. *I have to find Malakai.*

Running down the hall, Demetri suddenly felt himself tugged by an invisible force. His body came crashing down into one of the guest rooms, and the door closed shut behind him. A cold breeze followed, along with a scent that was all too familiar: *Peppermint.* There was no denying who was behind his paranormal encounter.

"Seraphina," Demetri said, grinding his teeth.

Picking himself up, Demetri was not surprised to find her standing by a fireplace. Next to her was a demonic entity, dripping some sort of black substance onto the floor. Demetri figured it was the same one that must've attacked everyone the day Annalu conjured a portal to Aeris.

"What's the matter, my love? I thought you would be happy to see me." Seraphina fake-pouted, then smiled sinisterly.

"I knew it. You were behind those demon attacks. You also were the one who gave me that box, too. But why? What do you gain from this? Are you jealous of Malakai or something?"

"*Pfft.* The last thing I care about is whether Malakai has you and Kelton wrapped around his finger. I can easily persuade you both to take me back in a heartbeat."

"You don't even have a heart to beat," Demetri said, challenging her.

"Precisely. Which means I don't want either of you. In fact, I'm just doing what I'm ordered to do. This is bigger than either of us, and I was offered a pretty sweet deal in exchange for my meddling around the castle."

"How are you able to wander around the castle? Aren't you supposed to be invited in?" asked Demetri, confused.

Seraphina shrugged and played with her long, curly hair. "I have my ways. Since I've turned into a vampyre, I've learned a couple of things. For instance, I can compel anyone to do what I want without realizing they're under my influence. Another thing, too, I can hear your heart beating. It's the same one that beat when we last spoke. I don't think we were finished with that conversation."

Seraphina was talking about Demetri's feelings for Malakai. He wouldn't give her the reaction she was looking for. Not this time. Instead, Demetri decided to head for the door, leaving Seraphina to talk her nonsense.

"Oh no," said Seraphina. She snapped her fingers, and the demonic entity slithered its way to the door, guarding it. "You're not going anywhere."

Demetri exhaled loudly—just like a growl. "What do you want from me? Whatever it is you've got planned, save it for another time. Malakai and I have more important things to do than deal with your delusional vendettas."

Seraphina walked over to Demetri, the sound of her heels clicking rung in his ears. With every click, his body got more irritated.

Seraphina placed her hands on Demetri's chest plate, lowering her eyelashes. None of it was appealing to Demetri, though. If anything, he wanted to grab her by the throat and jab a wooden stake through her heart. But given that the demonic entity was behind him, there was no choice he'd make it out of here alive if he killed Seraphina.

"I know you miss me," said Seraphina. "I can hear it in your heart. The blood rushing through your veins says it all. Maybe I was wrong after all. Maybe you are still in love with me."

"Seraphina, there are a few things I've learned myself since I've been in the South. One, I spent so much time hating Kelton because of your selfishness and greed. I was foolish to let someone as pathetic as you come between us. Second, I've lost any shred of attraction I had towards you a long time ago. The heartbeat you hear isn't from affection, but rather hate. I want nothing more than to kill you where you stand." Demetri pushed Seraphina away from him. "Now, do me the biggest favor and go somewhere far away from me."

Seraphina hissed at Demetri, her sharp fangs showing just how lethal they were. None of it phased Demetri.

"Are you done?" Demetri asked.

"I could rip your throat out right now," said Seraphina, spiteful.

"No, you won't. If you wanted to, you would've done it by now. Besides, I'd rather be dead than waste another second talking to you. As your heart no longer beats, neither does mine for you."

Demetri turned around, facing the demonic entity still guarding the door.

"Move before I send you back to wherever you came from," he demanded.

The entity roared, the stench of decay coming from his mouth causing Demetri to gag.

"I wonder," Demetri said, turning back around to face Seraphina, "before you became a vampyre, you said you were going to leave Kelton for me. Were you really going to follow through on that plan? Or were you always going to stay with him?"

"My love for you was true and genuine," said Seraphina, mouth flicking down into a frown.

"I can't help but think you were only keeping me around for your entertainment. Tell me the truth. You don't love me. You only love the fact that we were fond of you and gave you attention."

Seraphina shook her head. "I was in love with you, but the truth is that darkness will always attract darkness. You are no darkness, my darling. The only thing dark about you is the personality you chose to possess. But the darkness I'm talking about is from the one who was born with it—*Kelton*. I know your truth, Demetri. You fell for me because I remind you of the Lost Prince. And the sad reality is that Kelton only fell for Malakai because he reminded him of me. Yet here you and I are. Both without the one we truly want to be with. Isn't life full of surprises?"

"You don't know what you're talking about, Seraphina."

"Oh, please. We've had this talk before. Nothing changed. I've lurked around Windsor Keep enough times to see the way you drool for Malakai. It's time you stop living in a world of denial and embrace it."

"Enough," Demetri warned her.

"Does he know that you were the boy who saved him the night the Elder Guardians invaded Blackstaer Palace?" Seraphina said, voice tinged with delight. "I heard you when you spoke to the Grand Empress Dowager when you came to the South. I know more than you think I do."

Demetri plunged forward, throwing himself on top of Seraphina. He grabbed hold of her neck and started choking her. The demonic entity then lunged onto Demetri's back. He tried to tackle both of them at the same time, but before he could make a move, the door swung open, revealing Malakai standing in the entryway.

## 52
## Wandering Stars

**MALAKAI**

Malakai took in the scene before him with his mouth agape. Of all the things he expected to see when he followed raised voices into the room, Demetri strangling Seraphina Blackworth on the ground while a Dravkyn Demon attacked Demetri's back was not one of them. Even Bluu seemed shocked, hovering over his shoulder. Malakai had so many questions running through his head, but he wasn't sure which one to ask first.

"Malakai, this isn't what it—" Before Demetri could finish his sentence, Malakai held his hand and stopped him.

"—*Don't*. I'm really not in the mood to know how or why." Malakai took a deep breath. "I came to find Silianna, but it seemed you beat me to the punch. And, of course, you found Seraphina and…a Dravkyn Demon?"

Demetri shoved the slim creature off of him and stood, wiping his hands against his legs. Seraphina used her vampyre speed to fix herself up as well, then stood by the window with the demon.

"Hello, Prince Antonius," said Seraphina. By the sound of her tone, she wasn't too pleased to speak properly to him.

"I'd say it's nice to see you, Seraphina, but I've gone through enough drama this week. To keep things simple, I believe there's something that you owe me." Malakai held out his hand.

"You killed Narkissa?" Seraphina sounded shocked. "I don't believe it."

Malakai thought back to what Narkissa had told him to do to convince Seraphina of her demise.

*"Before you go, Lost Prince," Narkissa started, "I should inform you that my blood flows through your bloodstream. You will need to come into contact with Seraphina Blackworth as quickly as possible before it wears off. My blood will allow you to influence her beliefs and convince her that you killed me. Do I make myself clear?"*

Influence her beliefs.

Malakai wasn't sure how he could accomplish that. He was a little upset at himself for not asking Narkissa how to do it, but it was too late now. He'd have to improvise or lose his chances of getting the portal device.

"Do you have proof?" asked Seraphina.

"I—Uh, yes." Malakai cleared his throat. He walked forward in her direction and focused on trying to manipulate her mind. He hoped whatever he was doing would work. "Just listen to my pulse carefully. Listen when I say: Narkissa is dead. I killed her and escaped before the vampyres could catch me."

Seraphina stood still. She looked somewhat hypnotized by what he said.

"I killed Narkissa," Malakai repeated. "You can do whatever you want now. All I ask is that you respect our deal and give me the Disk of Wisdom."

Seraphina reached into her red cloak pocket. She pulled out the circular object and held it in her hands.

Malakai broke his focus on Seraphina and exchanged a look with Demetri. Demetri seemed nervous. He kept looking back and forth between Malakai and the Disk of Wisdom. All Malakai could do was hope the compulsion lasted long enough for him to grab it from Seraphina's hands.

"You killed Narkissa?" Seraphina asked.

"Yes," Malakai answered.

Looking dazed, Seraphina held out the device in Malakai's direction.

From the corner of Malakai's eyes, he caught Demetri reaching for the metal fire poker that resided by the fireplace. In the blink of an eye, Malakai then saw Demetri shove it into the Dravkyn Demon's head. Black liquid splashed all over the room.

"Demetri!" Malakai cried out.

Seraphina roared, using her vampyre speed to attack Demetri. Malakai intervened and used his Pyroc element to conjure a ball of fire in her direction. Seraphina's red cloak lit up in flames. She pulled it off before it could spread anywhere else on her body.

"That's enough," Malakai demanded. "No more fighting."

"He killed my demon," Seraphina complained, her fangs poking out.

"I don't care. We've done everything you asked. I don't want to see you wandering around Avala anymore. You can go back to Theuros and do whatever it is you intend to do. Narkissa will not be a problem for you anymore."

Seraphina let go of Demetri and reluctantly accepted defeat. She opened the bedroom window, and snow twirled into the room. Seraphina was getting ready to jump out and leave the castle, but Malakai was quick to stop her.

"Wait," he said, observing the Disk of Wisdom in his hands. "How do you activate this thing?"

"You activate the button that's on the edge. Once you press it, a portal will appear. I'm sure you can figure out the rest," Seraphina explained, looking annoyed.

Malakai pressed the button. The device popped out of his hand and dropped to the floor. A blue circular portal appeared in front of him. It smelled vaguely of salt water, like the breeze from the ocean.

"Do we just jump in?" Malakai asked Seraphina.

"All you have to do is think about where you want to go," Seraphina said. "Once you have an idea, then you'll just jump through. You'll be there in the snap of a finger."

Demetri ran to Malakai's side. "Are you sure you want to do this?

What if it's a trap?"

"Well, unless you have a better idea, I'd say our options are pretty limited. I can't risk anything bad happening to Eli, Rahaf, or even Theodosis. We need to rescue them and get them back here."

Seraphina appeared behind Malakai and Demetri suddenly, laughing. She looked them both up and down, a curious glint to her eyes.

"What's so funny?" Malakai asked.

"Oh, nothing," Seraphina teased. "I just enjoy watching you two. The chemistry is astounding."

"Chemistry?" Malakai was puzzled. "I'm not sure I follow…"

"Seraphina, stop," Demetri warned her.

Malakai looked at Demetri. He was taken aback by the way he spoke to her. Was there something that Seraphina knew about? If so, why couldn't Malakai know about it, too?

"Demetri, we're running out of time," Malakai said, impatient.

"When are you going to tell him the story about the boy who saved a prince?" Seraphina asked.

Before Demetri could say anything, all three of them jumped back as a hand reached out of the portal. The hand was quickly followed by a head and the rest of the body. The intruder then pulled himself completely through. And adjusted his posture. It had been a while since Malakai last saw this person, and he couldn't help feeling a little freaked out to see him. The burnt mark across his face was still there, indicating that the Healers never got to heal him in time. It was the same burnt mark Malakai gave him when the two fought by Glisten Lake.

"DeVault…" The name slipped through Malakai's mouth, heavy as a stone.

"Hello, Prince Antonius," DeVault said. "We meet again."

*Holy shit*, Malakai thought, *I just let one of the rebel's greatest enemies into the South of Baskaria.*

"How did you get here?" Demetri asked.

DeVault faced Seraphina. "My precious little spy, Seraphina, has been in cahoots with the Shadow Lord and me for quite some time.

It was pretty clever of us to locate her after you all escaped to the South. She was on the run, traveling through portals to stay under the radar from Narkissa. When she accidentally stumbled upon the Tower of the Guardians, I knew the Gods were working in our favor. So, we hired her. I even gave her a necklace that once belonged to Roslynda Soulryth. It allowed her to shapeshift into anyone who was still alive. For all you know, you've probably spoken to her without even realizing."

"That's enough, DeVault," Seraphina said, cutting him off. "I think they've heard plenty. Now, let's throw them to the wolves. We hope you enjoy fighting in the middle of the war."

Seraphina shoved both Malakai and Demetri into the portal. Darkness swallowed them whole, visions of stars blurring them, and the portal closed shut.

# 53
## Insidious

**SILIANNA**

In one moment, she stood before the Celestial Gates, and in the next, there was nothing.

When Silianna finally opened her eyes, a pounding sensation in her head prompted her to sit up straight. Her vision was blurry, but after a few blinks, she started to regain her sight. Gold bars surrounded her, and she couldn't figure out whether this was real or if she was in the Dark Dimension. Either way, she was trapped.

Silianna picked herself up and looked around. It appeared she was locked in a gilded cage, which dangled in the center of a circular room.

Silianna recollected the last few things she remembered to better her understanding of the situation. First, she traveled to Miracle Forest. Nerumi somehow turned out to be Seraphina Blackworth in disguise, and she pushed her into a portal. Then, Silianna found herself running toward the Celestial Gates when her uncle stopped her.

"The Beauchamp Curse," Silianna murmured.

Those three words circled in her head. It was still mind-boggling to uncover what her great-great-great-grandmother did to curse her family's bloodline. Yet, there were more questions she wanted answered. She intended to interrogate Reju the next time she saw him.

Below the gilded cage, there were five glass cryogenic tubes, and three of them were filled with an unusual green liquid. The other two were emptied, glass shattered. Silianna could tell that there were bodies inside the three still intact, though she couldn't figure out *who* they were.

"Hello?" she shouted. "Is anyone there?" Silianna felt stupid for asking. She had hoped that maybe the people in the glass tubes would respond in some form, but they remained eerily silent.

In the distance, she could hear a muffled roaring sound. Her skin felt like tiny bugs were crawling around her, though there was nothing in sight. She needed to find a way out of here, but she wasn't sure how to go about it—she didn't want to stick around to find out what was making that noise.

The gilded cage started to rock back and forth as Silianna paced around, trying to find a loose bar she could push out, but the cage stayed stubbornly closed.

The creaking sound of a door opening caught her attention. When Silianna looked down, she saw a man in a black cloak floating down the hall, heading for the glass tubes. Silianna felt her body go cold—it was Vorkalth. The Shadow Lord was going to kill her. There was no other reason for her to be trapped in the gilded cage. *Time does work differently here*, she reminded herself. *Maybe my forty-eight hours are up.*

Silianna felt as if ice was spreading through her veins—dread threatened to overwhelm her. There was nowhere else for her to go. She regretted not giving up her spiritual element sooner. But at least she would die knowing that she helped some of those Lost Souls cross over to the afterlife, finding peace. *I only wish to had seen Nerumi one last time. The* real *Nerumi. Was any of it real? Did Nerumi get to see and feel the things Seraphina did when she pretended to be her? I wish I could know for sure...* That feeling of uncertainty hurt Silianna the most. If she were to die, she'd at the very least have liked to know whether it was all true. Whether Nerumi did love her or not.

Vorkalth was humming a melody that echoed across the enlarged room. Silianna took it upon herself to sit down, cross-legged, and wait for whatever may come next.

The chains that hung the gilded cage started to rattle, and the entirety of the cage slowly came down. *Here goes nothing*, she thought. *Fight as much as you can.*

Once landing, Silianna was face-to-face with the cloaked figure. She wished she could see what he looked like, but his face was masked by the black hood over his head.

"If you're going to kill me, you'll have to put up a fight," she spat.

"*No need for the dramatics,*" said Vorkalth.

Behind him, Silianna took a closer look at the glass tubes. Inside, it was Aldothfex Soulryth, Rahaf's grandfather, and DeVault Beauchamp, Silianna's grandfather. The third person to the far right was an older man with a long white beard wearing a blue velvet robe.

"So, this is how you control them?" Silianna asked.

"*Indeed,*" Vorkalth replied. "*Their souls will never be whole as long as they remain here. I can control them when I need to.*"

"Who's the old man over there?" Silianna pointed to the unidentified man.

"*Nobody you should concern yourself with.*" Vorkalth opened the gilded cage, but he didn't go inside to pull Silianna out. Instead, he held out his arm, gesturing for her to come out with her own free will. "*Don't keep me waiting, child. Seeing as how I have no intention of letting you out of the Dark Dimension, you might as well get a glimpse behind the scenes.*"

Silianna was reluctant, but she did as she was told. Getting up off the floor, she walked out of the gilded cage and toward the cryogenic tubes. Her guard remained up, keeping her eyes darting back in case Vorkalth tried anything. Once she stood in front of her grandfather's tub, she stared in sorrow. Silianna couldn't remember what it was like before DeVault was taken over by Vorkalth. *Would he have been any different? Was he nicer? More caring?*

Silianna walked to Aldothfex's tub next. Both he and DeVault were in an endless slumber, but she couldn't tell whether they were in pain or not. They just seemed to be peacefully sleeping. Silianna assumed the worst, wondering if this would be her fate now. It had to be the only explanation as to why Vorkalth was showing her any of this. He did not intend for her to escape the Dark Dimension. Whatever it was he was after, she knew he'd use her as a pawn like the others.

Moving to the last glass tube, Silianna saw there was a button next to the handle of the glass. She assumed that perhaps this button would be able to release the old man; however, the tubes her grandfather and Aldothfex resided in did not have one, oddly enough.

Something in her gut told her that she needed to find a way to release this stranger. He may be able to help her, and she planned to act on it.

She turned to Vorkalth, but she kept her hands behind her back where the button was located. "So, what now? You got me here. What do you have planned next?"

"*I've been watching you for quite some time. I couldn't find you here in the Dark Dimension for a while, but I did manage to study you through Kelton's eyes,*" the Shadow Lord explained. "*It wasn't hard to understand where your love for Nerumi Steelhart started. That's why I offered Seraphina Blackworth a deal she couldn't refuse. She was able to get Nerumi in contact with the mirror that Emperor Stephanus and Empress Farrah Bellemore conjured for me eighteen years ago. To my surprise, Prince Theodosis was there. Not only did I get to play with your head, but to trick the fire princess as well. It was so easy to manipulate the prince into marrying her. It didn't take long for me to inform Aldothfex Soulryth about the marriage. Oh, King Bastille was furious. But I was pleased…Because I helped cause the war between Pyroc and Aeris. Such a beautiful sight.*"

"You…" Silianna was in disbelief. Everything he revealed to her was unfathomable. "What have you done to Rahaf? Where is she right now?"

*CLICK!*

Silianna quietly pressed the button, hoping that it would release the stranger from his captivity. She then moved around to where

Vorkalth wouldn't be able to focus on the green liquid vanishing.

*"She's about to partake in the final task at the Temple of Retribution. Once Princess Rahaf gets the Sword of Aerislark, I'll take control of Prince Theodosis and retrieve the Eternal Element of Aeris."*

"No!" Silianna gasped.

Vorkalth chuckled. *"I'm afraid you cannot stop my insidious plan. Malakai, or rather, Prince Antonius, won't stand a chance once I get my hands on that sword. And as for the Eternal Element of Limus, well, don't worry. You're going to help me in due time."*

"Screw you! I will never help you in a million years."

*"Are you so sure about that, princess? Because, from the looks of it, I seem to have all the cards in my hands. And you? You have nothing."* The Shadow Lord raised his hands, and a green ball of energy formed in the middle of his palms.

Silianna took a few steps back, moving a little further away from the tubes in hopes of Vorkalth following her. The green liquid inside the tub was nearly emptied, which meant this stranger would awaken soon. In a shocking turn of events, Vorkalth did as Silianna hoped— he started to follow her. His back was still turned from where the tubes were, unaware of what was taking place.

The old man regained consciousness, his fragile legs shaking as he took his first step outside the tube.

Vorkalth continued to elaborate. *"The only reason I'm not killing you now is because you have something in that pretty little head of yours—a map. It will guide me to the Chalice of Limus. Once I learned you were connected to the Beauchamp Curse, I knew you'd serve me well. My Dravkyn Demons saw you consulting with Reju Tufte at the Celestial Gates. I killed him because he refused to tell me where it was. But you? Oh, you will do just fine."*

Amid Vorkalth's monologue, Silianna caught a glimpse of the old man conjuring an electrical current between the palms of his hands. She ducked in that moment as the energy zapped Vorkalth, causing him to fly across the room and crash against the wall, leaving a crack.

"W—Who are you?" Silianna asked, her voice shaking.

"I've gone by many names," the old man said, "but my most famous one is 'Wulissek Noire, The Great Warlock of Baskaria.'"

The name rang a bell in the back of Silianna's mind. She wasn't too familiar with the stories told regarding the night of Prince Antonius' birth, but what she did know was that there was a warlock who helped Emperor Stephanus and Empress Farrah to send the Shadow Lord back into the Dark Dimension when he broke free. *Could this be the same warlock?*

"How did he trap you here?" she asked.

"I was helping Prince Kelton when the Shadow Lord ambushed me. Because I tried assisting him, he took it upon himself to punish me in endless torment like the Elder Guardians."

Vorkalth was slowly regaining his strength, and Silianna could see her time was surely limited to escape.

"Thank you for releasing me, Princess Silianna, but you must go now," Wulissek encouraged her. "My energy source won't hold him off for long, but it'll be enough to get you out of here. Stop Vorkalth from achieving his goal and save your friends before it's too late!"

Silianna thanked the warlock, taking off in the opposite direction, hoping she could find a way out.

## 54
## Experiment 716

**KELTON**

*"I love you, Kelton Eckwood," Malakai whispered in Kelton's ear.*

*"I love you, too," Kelton murmured in his sleep.*

*"Kelton, if you're in the Dark Dimension, I promise everything will be okay. You need to fight whatever it is Vorkalth is making you face. You are stronger than you think. Please. Fight it."*

The conversation he overheard Malakai say still lingered in his mind as Kelton remained trapped in the Dark Dimension. Vorkalth had locked him away in a glass tube where his soul could not return to his physical body. It killed him that he couldn't be with Malakai now. Hearing his voice, knowing he was still alive, was the only thing keeping him going. No matter what Vorkalth would put him through, Kelton knew he could take it.

*Malakai.*

He was Kelton's anchor. It was all he needed to develop the strength and courage to fight this hold over him. Kelton vowed to get out of this place and reunite with Malakai no matter how long it took.

When his eyes opened, Kelton's vision was a sickly green, distorted by the liquid surrounding his body.

Vorkalth was pacing back and forth, lost in thought. He had no clue that Kelton was awake, and Kelton planned on using that to his advantage.

Focusing on the structure of the glass, Kelton lifted his hand and tapped on it. One tap. Two taps. Three taps.

*CRACK!*

Kelton's heart started to race. He wasn't sure how he did it, but he caused the glass to crack. The lines spread across the tube, nearly ready to shatter. With one forceful shove, Kelton came plummeting to the ground, green liquid sloshing all around him.

Winged demonic creatures screeched in fury from the sky, circling angrily.

Vorkalth turned and faced Kelton as he stood up.

"H—*How did you do that?*" Vorkalth asked.

"At this point, you really shouldn't be surprised," Kelton focused, trying to control the energy the way he had before he was trapped. He pictured an Insully blade in his mind, and slowly, one formed in his hand.

Kelton charged Vorkalth with a yell, lifting the blade over his head. However, Vorkalth managed to fly up into the air and over Kelton's head, landing behind him in the blink of an eye.

"*You're a fool if you think you can beat me,*" said Vorkalth. "*I have been around for over a millennium. You've only existed for nineteen years.*"

"*Hmmph.* I'll be twenty soon enough," Kelton said, spinning around quickly. He knew now wasn't the time to get smart with Vorkalth, but he loved to know that it would get under his skin. "Now, stop being a coward and fight me."

"*You wish to fight me? You'd be wasting your time. You're weak.*"

"If you know anything about me, then you should know I say what I mean. Let's go, old man."

An Insully blade appeared in Vorkalth's wrinkled, grey hands. He pointed the tip in Kelton's direction.

"*Go ahead, boy. Make your move.*"

Kelton charged after him, and Vorkalth followed soon after. Both their blades were about to clash when a bright light beamed in their direction, blinding Kelton.

"What is that?" Kelton asked.

"*My exit*," Vorkalth replied.

Before Kelton could fight Vorkalth, he was pushed to the ground. Vorkalth was aiming for the exit, which was a circular light that would've allowed Kelton to return to the real world. It was the Dark Dimension's version of a portal; one Kelton had used many times in the past.

With little time to waste, Kelton tapped into his creative mindset, where he envisioned roots growing from beneath the ground and capturing Vorkalth. To his surprise, that's exactly what happened. Whatever it was he was continuously doing, it was working.

"You're not going anywhere, Vorkalth!" Kelton shouted.

As Kelton went running for the light, he could hear the voices of Malakai and Demetri getting louder. This must be his way back into the real world. He wasn't far off. Kelton had one chance not to screw this up. *I'm coming back, Malakai!* He'd wish Malakai could hear his thoughts. He felt it in his heart that Malakai wanted him to wake up.

In the middle of his run, Kelton found himself trapped in a metal cell. It happened in a matter of seconds, and there was no way to expect it either. The cell was far from reach from the light. Whatever had happened, Vorkalth somehow teleported Kelton into the cell.

"No!" Kelton screamed.

"*You can't out-master the master, my boy,*" said Vorkalth, who was a few steps away from the light.

Kelton accepted defeat at that moment. There was no way he'd escape the cell and reach the gate in time. Vorkalth jumped in the light and vanished without an inkling of a trace.

\* \* \*

Opening his eyes, Kelton was pleased to find himself breathing fresh air in the real world again. It had been ages since he had last taken a proper breath. Sadly, the fresh air was tainted with the smell of blood and metal, and the cloying scent of the undead. There were wires attached to his body, and Kelton did not hesitate to pull them out. The puncture wounds from the wires healed in seconds, allowing Kelton to sit up straight and look at the bloodsuckers that surrounded him.

"Prince Kelton?" one of them asked.

Although the name sounded familiar, Kelton knew that wasn't his name. No. His name was Vorkalth—son of Pyrocian and Narkissa. He'd successfully managed to take control of Kelton's body.

Before he could properly enjoy the physical form, there was a sudden pull in his brain. Vorkalth hissed, grabbing onto his head. The pain was excruciating, like a needle stabbed between his eyes.

Vorkalth growled, digging his fingers into his scalp as the pain reached a fever pitch. "Make it stop! Now!"

"It appears Experiment 716 is having a strange reaction," another vampyre said, turning to another vampyre behind him.

"The pain, you incompetent parasite!" Vorkalth ground out, breathing through his teeth.

The vampyres exchanged looks. It was evident they were catching on to Vorkalth's scheme. If he didn't do something about it now, they would surely report back to Narkissa. No. Vorkalth couldn't have that.

Vorkalth tapped into the dark energy he obtained a millennium ago—the same one that resulted in his demise during the Wondrous Trials. Only this time, that darkness allowed him to push past the hold Kelton had over him. Now, the pain in his head was no more. Vorkalth had full access to Kelton's body.

The vampyres got close to him, making the attacks much easier for Vorkalth to handle. There was a thought that crossed his mind on how he should handle each of them. First, he experimented with the strength Kelton's body possessed. He shoved his entire arm through one of the vampyre's chests, holding out its dead heart and squeezing it in his hands until it exploded like confetti. The hollow body collapsed to the ground; blood spread across the floor in the process. Vorkalth thrived with feral thoughts as his hunch came to fruition. There is no match for these vampyres, he thought maliciously. Kelton's body had super strength, something Vorkalth intended when impregnating that sweet, innocent witch nearly two decades ago. I may have failed in making Prince Antonious my offspring, but Kelton will surely satisfy in my plans.

The other vampyres started to panic, rushing for the doors. However, they weren't fast enough for Vorkalth as he took them one by one. He swiftly ripped two of their heads off with his hands, disembodied one of their arms, and ripped the heart out of another. Blood was all over the walls, doors, and floor. There was no mercy for anyone who got in his way.

Vorkalth looked at his son's reflection in the puddle of blood. He looked so similar to how Vorkalth once looked, minus the fact Kelton had dirty blond hair, and Vorkalth used to have platinum blond.

Vorkalth broke the doors open, walked down the hollow hall, while blood dripped from his fists.

Entering the hallway was the henchman Vorkalth once knew from his childhood, Destlyn. Behind the pale, bald man was the Vampyre Queen, Narkissa. After centuries roaming this planet, she remained the same in all her elegant beauty.

"What on Zorall have you done?" Destlyn asked, petrified.

"Prince Kelton, this isn't you," Narkissa said, mortified that her lifeless vampyre creations were scattered around. "W—What happened to them?! My children!"

Vorkalth tilted his head, a sickening grin stretching his face. "What's the matter, Mother?" Vorkalth asked, taking a taunting step forward. "I thought you would've loved to reunite with your son— your *real* child."

Narkissa's eyes widened. "This can't be possible."

"Why not? After all, Kelton has so much resemblance to you and I. Did it not cross your mind when you saw him?" Vorkalth knew his mother was too focused on the fact that her son was standing before her. He changed the topic quickly as he said, "It doesn't matter. I've waited a millennium to see your face when I escaped the Dark Dimension. There were multiple ways it could've gone, but I guess impregnating a witch worked out to my advantage. I want you to watch as I burn this world to the ground, Mother. Everything the

Gods worked so hard to rebuild will perish."

"Vorkalth, you must stop this now! There's no way any of this ends well for you."

"I know… and I'm okay with that. So long as you all go down with me."

Kelton's body floated in midair. Destlyn and Narkissa were getting ready to charge after him, but they were no match for Vorkalth's speed. He flew and smashed through the ceiling, leaving a gigantic hole in the castle as he flew off into the night sky.

## 55
## Anchor

**KELTON**

Kelton fought to take control of his body again. He almost had it, but just as he was reaching forward to regain it, sudden movement broke his focus. When he looked across from his cell, Kelton saw Theodosis jolt awake from his slumber. He was still floating in the cryogenic tube when he awakened, drowning.

Kelton tried to figure out a way for him to break free of his cell. He wanted to help Theodosis—he *needed* to help him. Kelton thought back on what he did when he confronted Vorkalth earlier. He was somehow capable of creating a path of flowers when he walked. *It's all in the mind*, he thought. *Maybe I can play with my mind and alter the illusion.*

With Vorkalth out there in the real world, Kelton figured he could try to alter the Dark Dimension without his interference. He tested the theory by changing the lock in his cell into a bubble—and he succeeded. Kelton was thrilled as he pushed the gate open and ran out.

"Don't worry, Theo!" he shouted. "I'm coming."

Rushing to Theodosis's tube, Kelton was quick to use his imagination to shrink the green liquid, allowing Theodosis to stand; his legs wobbling. Theodosis was gasping for air as he nearly drowned to death. Kelton then focused on turning the glass door into dust. Suddenly, dust was scattered around Kelton's feet.

"H—How did you do that?" Theodosis asked, catching his breath.

"It's too much to explain," Kelton responded. "Just know we're getting out of this place, and we're going to get you control of your body again."

Next to Theodosis was a glass tube where Nerumi resided. She was still unconscious, but Kelton was hoping that once he released her from captivity, he'd be able to wake her up.

"How did we end up here?" Theodosis asked. "Last thing I remember, I snuck in with Rahaf to the Temple of Retribution, then everything went *dark*. I can't remember anything after that."

"I'm not sure what happened, but I think somebody has been roaming Ackermere Palace and managed to get you and Nerumi under Vorkalth's compulsion. Otherwise, neither of you would be here."

"Vorkalth?"

"He's the Shadow Lord—the one who rules the Dark Dimension. It's a place for the Lost Souls who have unfinished business and roam in purgatory looking for closure. Vorkalth has been torturing them for a millennium. You two aren't the only ones under his compulsion. It turns out the Elder Guardians had fallen victim as well. That's why they assassinated Emperor Stephanus and Empress Farrah. As long as you two are here, your lives are in grave danger."

Theodosis' breath started to quicken. "W—Wait a second! If we're all under his compulsion, then we should be able to release DeVault and Aldothfex from his control as well."

"That's a great idea, Theo, but I don't see those two anywhere. They must be stored somewhere else. Our priority is to get out of here as soon as possible. We don't have time to go searching for them and risk Vorkalth returning."

Suddenly, a flock of Dravkyn Demons appeared, this time evolving into entities with wings. One of them grabbed Theodosis and tossed him to the other side, where Kelton stood. His body clashed with the wall, then he fell unconscious onto the floor.

One of the demons saw the collision and lunged for Kelton, ready to attack. Kelton used his imagination to create a wall, shielding himself as quickly as he could. He was seconds away from the creature's claws sinking into him.

With the Dravkyn Demon injured, Kelton turned to Nerumi's tube and started pressing any buttons he could find until finally the green liquid started going down. Nerumi's eyes began twitching before finally opening, and she gasped for air. Kelton opened the tube and grabbed hold of her.

"W—Where am I? Why is it so cold?" Nerumi said, teeth chattering.

"Don't worry." Kelton grabbed the jacket he was wearing and put it over Nerumi's back. "Keep your arms around my shoulder. I'm going to get you and Theo out of here."

"Theodosis is here?" Nerumi said. "How did we get here?"

"Nerumi, I *really* need you to stop talking. We're up against some vicious entities, and I can't—" Before Kelton could finish talking, one of the Dravkyn Demons leaped over the wall Kelton created and attempted to attack Nerumi; however, Kelton was quick to push her to the side.

Two more of the entities emerged from over the wall. They went on all fours and charged after him.

Before their attacks could land, a beam of light shone in the creatures' faces.

By the exit doors, Kelton saw an old, wrinkled man with a long white beard, purple eyes, and a blue velvet robe covering his fragile body. In the old man's hand was a wooden staff with a crystal ball at the top.

"I've been searching for you since I learned of your existence," the man's hoarse voice rattled.

"I'm sorry, but do I know you?" asked Kelton.

"We met by the green river, Prince Kelton. I was trying to warn you of the Shadow Lord before he held me prisoner." The man walked closer to him, and with every step, Kelton's chest felt tighter. "My name is Wulissek Noire—The Great Warlock across the Nine Lands."

Kelton was stunned. *The Great Warlock*. He remembered now. Kelton also remembered when he told Malakai about this warlock when he took Malakai on a tour around the City of Terrane. From what Kelton understood, Wulissek was the one to return Vorkalth to the Dark Dimension. Because Emperor Stephanus and Empress Farrah made a deal with him long ago to have a child, it allowed Vorkalth the ability to wander the real world once more. The warlock had sacrificed himself to ensure the safety of the entire world. Unfortunately, Vorkalth managed to curse Malakai when he was just an infant, which caused Malakai to have the spiritual elemental.

Before Kelton continued his conversation with the warlock, he looked back to find Nerumi helping Theodosis from the floor. *Good*, Kelton thought, *they're doing fine*.

"You must be careful with those Dravkyn Demons," the warlock warned him. "Vorkalth has been transforming the Lost Souls into those sinister things for ages. He's building an army, and if he gets his way, you may have to face those things in the real world. You must prevent that from happening."

"But how is he able to get them out into the real world?" asked Kelton.

"Simply put: *You*." The warlock pointed at Kelton's chest. "You are the key. As long as he has control of you, the portal between here and the real world will remain open. You have to resist him. Find your anchor and hold onto it."

*Find your anchor and hold onto it.* Kelton knew what his anchor was, or rather, who. It was Malakai. His love for Malakai was what allowed him to wake up in the first place. If it hadn't been for Theodosis waking up, Kelton probably would've succeeded in getting his body back.

"I know what to do," Kelton said.

"I know you do. Please, protect Prince Antonius. I sacrificed my life for him. Your love for each other might be the answer to defeating him. So long as it is true, you can either restore or destroy the Nine Lands."

Kelton swallowed. The pressure settling onto his shoulders felt immense, but it was a burden he would have to bear. He nodded his head in understanding.

"My friends, I have to help them," said Kelton, looking back at Nerumi and Theodosis. The two of them stood idly by, listening to the conversation.

"I helped Princess Silianna return to the real world, and I can help them too," Wulissek assured Kelton, his hand pointing at Theodosis and Nerumi. "Don't worry about them. Return to your body before he has full control. Go!"

Kelton did not hesitate for a second longer. He cleared his thoughts and focused solely on Malakai. All the memories he had of him, whether good or bad, overpowered him. Then, when he felt the surge of power crawling through his body, a light emerged from afar.

He ran for that light.

* * *

There was a power struggle that took every ounce of his body. Vorkalth was fighting for control, but a sudden force managed to push the Shadow Lord's control out, allowing Kelton to return to the real world. At first, his legs and arms were numb, but after a couple of attempts to wiggle his fingers and toes, Kelton felt them once more. *Finally, I have my body back*, he thought. However, Kelton was surprised to see that he was standing in the middle of the entranceway of Windsor Keep. Last he knew, he was in Theuros. *How long have I been under Vorkalth's control? How did he manage to get me back here?*

"Kelton," said a voice.

Turning around, Kelton saw Celdric and Nehila behind a chipped pillar. "Celdric? Why are you guys hiding back there?" he asked, confused.

"Why are *we* hiding? Kelton, you were *flying* in the middle of the room," Celdric said, voice shaky. "Your eyes were pitch black. We thought you were going to kill us."

"I'd never hurt either of you." Kelton held out his hands, grateful neither of the kids was hurt. He would never be able to live with himself if harm came to either one of them. "Come. I promise, everything is okay."

Both of them reluctantly, and Kelton didn't understand why that was until he noticed his entire arm was filled with blood. He looked at his clothes and noticed they were bloody as well. *By the Gods, what did Vorkalth do?*

"It's okay," Kelton reassured them. "This wasn't me. I swear, I can explain…"

Nehila made the first move and grabbed Kelton's hand. Kelton smiled and hugged her.

"I know it wasn't you." Neihla smiled and pointed at his eyes innocently. "I could tell by your eyes. They're green and pretty!"

"I—" Kelton's lips quivered, feeling emotional that a young girl like Neihla could notice when he wasn't himself. "Thank you, Neihla. It really means a lot."

Celdric then walked towards them, still hesitant and alert. "You better be telling the truth, dude. I'm not trained to fight someone as powerful as you…"

Kelton chuckled, knowing Celdric was trying to break the tension in the room. "I have no ill intent. Let's go find your brother."

## 56
## Beautiful Creature

**MALAKAI**

Demetri landed first, slamming against the ground with a jarring *thud*. The armor seemed to help with the impact, preventing him from getting seriously injured. Malakai landed on top of Demetri right after, groaning as he hit metal hard. Bluu quickly followed, hovering anxiously above them. When Malakai looked up, the portal above them had shrunk until it disappeared. Demetri was cursing under his breath when Malakai picked himself up.

Looking around, Malakai saw that they were surrounded by rocky mountains and thick clouds. It was cold, but thankfully, Malakai dressed warmly. He wore a blue velvet coat stretched down to his ankles, long black pants, dark navy leather boots with matching gloves, and a gold dragon necklace. It was the same necklace he had worn the day he woke up from his coma after arriving in the South. His grandmother had given it to him, and he wore it when introducing himself to the citizens of Avala.

While Demetri was adjusting his armor, Malakai and Bluu walked around the rocky pathway to get an idea of where they should head.

"It's so beautiful here in the mountains," said Malakai. "We made it to Aeris."

Eli had mentioned how his family grew up in the mountains prior to the Elder Guardians taking over. There was a whole town run by the shapeshifters. Malakai would love to come back here one day after the madness was over to have Eli show him around properly.

"If I'm not mistaken, we're on the outskirts of the city," Demetri responded, joining Malakai. "We'll need to sneak in from the entrance gates, which I doubt will be operational while there's a war going on. Most likely, we're going to have to climb."

The sounds of explosions could be heard from a far-off distance. Malakai was beginning to feel nervous knowing that he got what he wanted—and there would be consequences for it.

"Is there no other way to get into Ackermere Palace without being in the middle of the war?" Malakai asked.

"I'm afraid not. But remember, we're back in the North. I'm sure DeVault has already notified the caedose soldier of our location. We'll need to get a move on before anyone finds us and stay aware of our surroundings."

Malakai sucked his teeth. He knew Demetri was right, and there would be no point in arguing. Demetri made the first move, walking forward to begin their hike. Malakai followed behind, willing to leave the navigation to Demetri.

After a while of silent walking, they reached a wooden red bridge. Bluu took it upon herself to fly ahead and take a look.

"Where is that thing going?" Demetri asked.

"*She* is looking to see what's up ahead," Malakai corrected him. "And her name is Bluu."

"You named it?"

"Yes. And stop referring to her as an 'it.'"

Bluu flew back to them, seemingly petrified. She was making an unusual sound. Malakai attempted to understand what she could be trying to say.

"What's she doing?" Demetri asked.

"Not sure," Malakai answered. "I think she might be warning us of something."

*BOOM!*

The very mountains seemed to vibrate under the deafening

impact. Demetri held Malakai in his arms and used his Terrane element to secure their feet with the rocks, locking them into place. Smoke emerged, and Malakai's vision became blurry. He could still feel Demetri's weight on him, but his concern was more towards Bluu's well-being.

"Bluu!" Malakai cried out.

A blue light appeared within the smoke. Bluu revealed herself and circled Malakai's head. She managed to form a wind that blew the smoke away, allowing Malakai and Demetri to see clearly.

"Are you okay?" Demetri examined Malakai's head and arms. "Are you bleeding anywhere?"

"I'm fine." Malakai used his Terrane element to release his and Demetri's feet from the rocks. He then turned to Demetri and said, "I think we might be in trouble."

"What gave it away?" Demetri asked sarcastically.

A group of caedose soldiers made their presence known in the distance, marching over one of the bridges. Malakai's heart sank into his stomach. He hadn't seen one in so long since he escaped the North. The white suits and neon blue lights were a familiar, yet terrifying, sight.

"I don't suppose that Eni could provide us with some sort of protection?" Demetri suggested.

*Protection.* The word rang in Malakai's head as he thought back to the events at Theuros and the ceremony the vampyres had performed under the moons. Narkissa had said something about Malakai's protection whenever he was around Demetri.

"I'm not sure what Bluu can do, but I remember what Narkissa said." Malakai pointed up to the night sky. "Remember what the vampyres did? They enacted a protection around us. As long as I'm with you, I'll be fine."

"Malakai, now is *not* the time to test that theory. I don't trust anything those bloodsuckers tell us. We don't have any weapons to fight other than our elements. I had no time to prepare for Seraphina, and DeVault hijacked our plans."

An extensive amount of weight plunged onto Malakai's body as he collapsed to the hard surface. He struggled to push whatever was on top of him off. When Malakai looked to his left, he saw that Demetri was fighting two caedose soldiers. Somehow, the caedose soldiers snuck up on them. *How did we not notice?!*

Bluu was flying toward Malakai's aid when she used an invisible force shield to push whatever the weight was off Malakai.

"Keep your filthy hands off him!" demanded Demetri, eyes burning with fury.

"Demetri Mykael Eckwood," one of the caedose announced. "We're hereby sentencing you under arrest at the request of the King and Queen, Alistair and Viktoria Eckwood. You will be sent to Terrane where you will be tried for treason."

*No.*

Malakai struggled to pick himself up. The pain he ignored from the caedose soldier jumping on him was rapidly evolving. His lower back was the source of that pain, along with minor sores from his shoulders. He focused his energy on the fire within him and used it to create a wave of flames to hurtle towards the soldiers. Some managed to avoid it, but a few fell into the flames.

While they were distracted by their fallen troops, Demetri punched the caedose soldier closest to him in the mouth and elbowed the other on the neck. Both of the soldiers fell to the floor, unconscious.

"Demetri," Malakai said, out of breath.

Demetri ran to Malakai and grabbed onto his forearms, holding him upright. "I got you. You're alright. Can you stand up straight?" Malakai nodded his head. "Good. Okay. Here, wrap your arm around my shoulder, and I'll carry you. Can you walk?"

"Y—Yes," Malakai said, unsure. "I just need a second."

"Malakai. We don't have a second. I'm sure there will be more coming here if we don't get a move on it now."

"We're never going to make it to Ackermere Palace…"

"I thought I was supposed to be the negative one," Demetri said, trying to make Malakai laugh. "Here. Hold onto me. We're going to move."

As they started walking, Malakai and Demetri were suddenly stopped by Bluu. She was waving her tiny fiery arms in front of her face. Both of the boys exchanged looks and wondered what she could've been trying to do. Malakai focused on her and realized that her blue fire was burning bright, just like she was when she was about to transform into his spirit animal. *She wants to merge*, he thought.

Malakai reached his hand toward her. When his fingers touched her, Bluu turned into a ball of bright light. He couldn't explain it, but Malakai felt his spirit leave his body, transcending upwards. A beautiful melody surrounded him, echoing in his ears, drawing him onward.

Voices were whispering in all directions in Malakai's head. He couldn't hear what they were saying, but they were there. Perhaps it was the spirits trying to communicate with him, or maybe it was something beyond that.

Suddenly, Malakai was back on the ground, still standing next to Demetri. The bright light was high up on the ground, and the two watched as it transformed.

"It's happening," Malakai whispered in awe.

A burst of wind caused Malakai and Demetri to go flying. Their bodies landed next to each other on the ground. When Malakai looked up, he was speechless. Bluu made a loud screeching sound, and he was sure that the scream was loud enough for the entire kingdom of Aeris to hear.

Bluu had a serpentine body structure—similar to a snake—with four legs and three toes on each of them. Gold antlers like the deer Malakai hunted countless times in the forest protruded from her head, with a horse-like head, too. There was white hair with blue tips that shimmered from the crest of her head straight down to the base of her tail. Bluu also possessed the talons of an eagle, the feet of a fierce tiger, and the cycloid pearl-colored scales that reflected the shimmering starlight in the night sky. Her eyes even radiate a fiery blue, shining like a rare gem.

"By the Gods," Demetri said, mesmerized by Bluu's appearance. "What did you transform your Eni into?"

"I—I think she's a dragon?" Malakai said, still in shock. "I don't know, but that's what my spirit animal is."

"Malakai, that's one of the legendary Rlyrum dragons." Demetri pointed at his arm, though it was covered by the gold armor he wore. "It's the same tattoo I have here. This is insane! Could you be part of the Rlyrum bloodline?"

Malakai shrugged. "Nobody tells me anything about my heritage, really. I guess we'll have to ask my grandmother when we get back to Avala. She has some serious explaining to do. I mean, where am I supposed to keep her? She's massive!"

Bluu landed on the ground with a loud *thump*, scattering dirt around her. She bent her head and closed her eyes, allowing Malakai to place a hand on her face. He could feel her breathing and then an electric tingling sensation formed between the two.

"Woah," he said under his breath. Malakai then adjusted his clothes and climbed on top of her. "Come on, Demetri! We can fly to Ackermere Palace and stop the war."

"Do you even know how to ride this thing?" Demetri asked, concerned.

"Of course not! But we're going to learn today." Malakai grabbed onto Bluu's gold antlers once Demetri set himself behind him. He wrapped his arms around Malakai's waist. "Alright. Let's get this show on the road."

Bluu surged off into the sky, and they headed for the war.

# 57
## A Sword of Reign and Steel

**RAHAF**

Rahaf had Eli's arms around her shoulders while she assisted him with walking. Aleek was behind Eli, doing what he could to help Eli remain standing. Eli was shivering most of the time, and the only thing Rahaf could think of was the fact that he was in shock. She was terrified of what the final task might entail. Theodosis sacrificed his element, and Eli sacrificed his hand. There was no point in denying that Rahaf was next to partake in the final task.

With the amount of walking they did through the caves, it surely felt as though hours had gone by. She was warned that time ran differently inside, but it was still extremely disorienting to experience.

Suddenly, Aleek growled from behind. When Rahaf looked back, she saw her bobcat making a peculiar face. The tip of his nose pointed ahead of them. When she turned back to the front, she caught a lovely scent of lavender. As they continued walking, a bright light slowly appeared, signaling to the three of them that they were about to enter the final room.

Rahaf's heart was beating fast, and her hands felt sweaty. Whatever was to come her way, she hoped all these sacrifices would be worth it. *For my mother, for Malakai, and for the nation of Baskaria.*

Those were the three things she kept repeating in her head to keep her feet moving forward.

Aleek circled Rahaf and Eli, heading for the entranceway to scope the area. He didn't seem worried, which was a relief for Rahaf.

"Rahaf," Eli said, breathless.

"Try not to talk," Rahaf said. "You need to save your strength."

"I just need to say it this once, please."

"Don't. Not right now. Whatever you have to say, you can say it when we get that damn sword and make it out of here alive. But as of right now, we need to stay focused."

Eli didn't respond.

Entering the last room, Rahaf was surprised to see that the room was not a room at all but rather an enormous cave with sharp rocks at every corner, and a bridge that led to the Sword of Aerislark. It's an angelic steel sword with a white handle, wings spreading out on both sides. There was a white gem that was set between the wings on the handle as well. Unfortunately for the group, the bridge that led to the sword was broken off in the middle. No matter how far they jumped, they wouldn't make it. They'd fall into the abyss.

Rahaf picked up a tiny rock and tossed it down below them. She stood there, waiting for a sound. Nothing. However far down this cave was, she knew for certain that it was far enough to have them killed if they were to fall.

Theodosis was standing at the edge of the bridge, his eyes locked on the sword. Rahaf went to approach him but stopped when she realized he was muttering under his breath. She couldn't quite make out the words, but the distant look in his eyes alarmed her.

"Theo?" Rahaf questioned. "Are you okay?"

"His prize is near," Theodosis replied, just above a whisper.

"You mean Malakai?"

Theodosis shook his head. "No. Not him. He does not deserve the Eternal Element of Aeris. Nobody connected to the Bellemore bloodline does. Anikstasha's family tree will cease to exist, and I will ensure it."

Rahaf was alarmed. She let go of Eli and reached for her anklet, fear crawling up her spine. Theodosis would never say something like that, which meant... This wasn't Theodosis.

Aleek moved in front of Rahaf, teeth bared as he hissed in Theodosis' direction.

"Theo, don't do this," Rahaf begged.

"Surely you've gathered by now that your precious husband isn't here. Come now, princess, I thought you were smarter than that?" he asked.

"Rahaf, stay back!" Eli exclaimed.

Aleek leaped forward and locked his sharp teeth on Theodosis' arm. Theodosis screamed in agony, trying to pry Aleek off his arm, but Aleek's teeth were firmly lodged.

Rahaf turned to Eli in horror. "What is happening? What is wrong with him?"

"I'm not sure. I—I think he might be under Vorkalth's control. It's like what Malakai had told me about the Elder Guardians. He must've been in contact with an object that gave the Shadow Lord access. No doubt it was his grandmother, Bliss."

Rahaf thought back to that day at Glisten Lake. Malakai went up against DeVault Beauchamp and burned his face. It was also the same day that he killed Bliss Steelhart, the other Elder Guardian. She knew they had somehow been influenced to do the Shadow Lord's bidding. And now Theodosis may have fallen victim as well.

"Vorkalth?" Rahaf questioned, staring into Theodosis's eyes. She prayed to the Gods that it wasn't true. "What have you done to Theodosis?"

Theodosis grinned, a sinister smile unnaturally cruel on his usually kind face. Rahaf knew instantly that Eli's theory was correct.

Rahaf took a horrified step back, and Theodosis took that moment to swing Aleek away from him, freeing himself.

"Aleek!" Rahaf went to his aid, but Theodosis was quick to step in front of her, causing her to step away. "How long have you been messing with his head?"

"I've been plotting this for quite some time. Your little friends have been giving me nothing but trouble in the South. Princess

Silianna and Prince Kelton. But no worries, I shall surely accomplish one goal—and that's getting the Sword of Aerislark."

"Theodosis no longer has an element, and you don't seem to have a weapon on hand. It looks to me like you're not getting that sword." Rahaf transformed her anklet into a whip and swirled it around her body. "Release Theodosis, *now*."

Theodosis, or rather, Vorkalth, burst into laughter. "You're a fool. If you hurt me, then you hurt your precious husband. There's nothing you can do to stop me."

Suddenly, Theodosis fell to his knees and screamed in pain. He held his hands to his head, continuing to scream. Rahaf was torn between her instinct to help and her fear that it was all a trick intended to lure her closer. She swayed on her feet, unsure of what to do.

"Rahaf!" Theodosis cried out in a different tone than before, more scared than taunting. More like the Theodosis she knew and loved.

"Theo?" Rahaf said, taking a cautious step forward.

"Finish the last task!" he begged her, fingers digging into his head. "I—I can hold him off." Theodosis took a deep breath. "Please…"

"Rahaf, do it," Eli encouraged her. "Do the last task *now*. Before it's too late."

Rahaf tore her eyes away from Theodosis and looked around, desperately trying to find a clue. She wasn't sure where the last task was located in this vast cave. Her eyes scanned around until she finally caught a glimpse of a metallic black box with unique gold carvings on all sides. The box was blended in with piles of rocks. Rahaf rushed over and dusted off the dirt to get a better look.

"Okay, now what?" she asked Eli.

"One of us has to read the instructions. You read for Theodosis, he read mine, and I guess now I read yours."

"You're confident in that theory?" Rahaf sounded concerned in her question.

Eli frowned. "My theories haven't failed so far. Activate the box and let's find out. Your husband doesn't have a lot of time." The way Eli said 'husband' sounded more like an insult than it did a compliment.

Rahaf brushed his little comment to the side and pushed down on the button located on the bottom of the box. Once she did, a puff of smoke emerged and twirled in a spiral formation. She kept her guard up and focused her attention on whatever was about to occur.

Slowly, a blue light appeared and formed nothing but scribbles.

"What is this supposed to mean?" she asked Eli. "Are the lines supposed to represent something?"

"No," Eli replied. "Those aren't lines. You just can't see it. It's instructions that say, 'Regret is the ultimate killer, filling our heads with endless thoughts of darkness. You must face your greatest regret in life and let that part of you go forever. If you cannot succeed, that darkness shall swallow you whole for all eternity.'"

Rahaf took a deep breath. "Well, looks like I'm not making it out alive with this one. Tell everyone it was nice knowing them."

"Don't tell yourself that. You can do anything. You're Rahaf Soulryth, the strongest warrior princess I have ever met. You let no one walk over you. Why let this stop you now?"

Rahaf smiled. "Thank you, Eli."

"Now, hurry up and do what you need to do before the Shadow Lord gets control again."

Rahaf turned and faced the tornado in front of her, ready to accept whatever might happen next. Then, the smoke slowed down. It started to flow toward her, causing her vision to be clouded.

Eli, Theodosis, and Aleek were nowhere to be found.

Rahaf's heart pounded intensely as she awaited her 'greatest regret' in life. There were many things she regretted, and she wasn't sure which one the box would select. There was the situation with Theodosis and Eli. There was also the regret of not doing anything for her mother or her sister. Maybe there was even some regret about having hurt her grandmother the day she escaped her arranged marriage. Or perhaps it was the fact that she wasn't there for Silianna when she was at her worst. Silianna had gone through so much heartbreak when it came to Nerumi and the death of her older brother. She felt awful for being a terrible friend. And yet, here she was getting married and putting another lifelong goal before her best friend. Silianna was obviously in need of rescuing, especially when everything that had gone with her attachment to the spirit realm. She'd only hoped that Silianna was smart enough to let that part of her go before it was too late. Considering the circumstances Theodosis was under, it worried her thinking about the possibility that Silianna was still dealing with all that.

"Hello, Rahaf," said a voice. It echoed in Rahaf's head, and it took her a second to process who it could've been. When the person revealed themselves, it nearly caught Rahaf by surprise. The voice was different and older. To be fair, Rahaf had vivid memories of what her older sister once sounded like.

"Jacqueline...?" Rahaf said, puzzled. "Is it truly you?"

"You left me to rot in that tower," Jacqueline said. She appeared from the smoke, revealing her features. She was pale, the complete opposite of Rahaf's olive skin complexion. Jacqueline was skinny and frail, like she had been starved to death. Rahaf swore that she saw Jacqueline's bones sticking out, too. Her jet black hair was short, and her eyes were sunken in. There was no visible soul left in her body.

"By the Gods," Rahaf cried. "What did they do to you?"

"I begged for you night and day, hoping that you'd come to my rescue," Jacqueline said, voice thin and frail as the rest of her body. "And yet, you never came. I lost hope in you—in the world. You failed me. You failed Mother. I can't believe that while I was being tortured, you were running around with your friends and falling in love with not one, but *two* men. Everyone and everything were more important than myself. What did I ever do to you to deserve this treatment? Was I not a priority to you after all these years?"

"There was no way for me to get to you! Sorrow Tower was far from Pyroc. Our father would've caught me and punished me as well."

"*Excuses*," her sister snapped. "You were in Terrane long enough to journey and save me. You chose to assist the Lost Prince instead. You've proven time and time again that I am no priority to you."

"That is a lie! You have to let me explain."

"No! I've had enough of your lies. You deserve worse than what Mother and I had gone through. You're selfish. You can't even be married without being loyal. Nothing will ever satisfy you for as long as you live. Is it not exhausting to live daily, always making mistakes that you will regret later? Face it, Rahaf, you are not cut out for this world."

Jacqueline pulled a knife from her pocket and handed it to Rahaf. It felt shockingly real in her hands.

"Go ahead," Jacqueline offered. "Do what you should've done a long time ago. Join Mother in the afterlife. She is waiting for you. Everyone is waiting for you."

Tears ran down Rahaf's face. Nothing her sister said was a lie. She was selfish, no matter how many times she tried not to be. She always put her own needs before anyone else's.

Rahaf grabbed the knife and pointed the tip at her wrist. She knew what her sister wanted her to do, and if it brought her happiness, then she would do it. She would end her life for her sister's happiness.

"Stop," said a gentle voice.

Rahaf looked up and saw her mother, Roslynda Soulryth, pulling the knife away from her.

"M—Mother?" Rahaf was in awe.

"It is not your time," Roslynda said. "That is not your sister speaking to you. It is merely an illusion of your darker self. Focus on the opposite of what she says."

"But there are no lies," Rahaf testified. "Everything she said was true. I'm selfish. I put myself before others."

"No. You didn't. You had no way of reaching Sorrow Tower without your father knowing. You helped reunite Prince Antonius with his grandmother. You rekindled your friendship with Silianna and stood by her side when she needed it. Even if it wasn't at the right time, you made up for it. You guided Kelton to the best of your ability to do the right thing when he knew of Prince Antonius's sibling's whereabouts. You've tried to help Demetri be the better version of himself. You must stop dwelling on the negative aspects of your life and look to the positives. Otherwise, you will never succeed."

Rahaf cleaned the tears from her face and took a deep breath. She understood what her mother was trying to say. She was right. Maybe she wasn't perfect, but nobody was. The only thing that counts was trying to fix the mistakes she has made in the end.

"Thank you, Mother," Rahaf said, looking her mother up and down. "Is this real? You standing in front of me."

"The smoke you've entered originated from the afterlife. Similar to how your friends wander the Dark Dimension, this allows you to visit the dead, too. That thing standing over there is not your sister. Don't be fooled."

Roslynda vanished in thin air.

Rahaf was left standing there facing a form of her sister. When Rahaf looked at her hand, she noticed the knife was still there. The tip was close to impaling her skin. However, she was quick to pull it away and have it face her sister instead.

"You have no power over me," Rahaf declared. "I no longer have regrets for what has been done. I have tried the best I can to fix my wrongs, and I accept now that I am not perfect. No one is. My sister will be rescued in time. And you are nothing more than a sadistic entity who will not harm another living soul again."

Rahaf jabbed the knife into her sister's stomach. A bright light burst through, causing the smoke to return into the box.

Rahaf fell to the floor and tried to comprehend everything she had done. Her heart felt warm, and her body felt lightweight.

"I did it," Rahaf said, hardly able to believe her success.

"I knew you could do it," Eli said.

Rahaf looked down at Eli's missing hand, unable to feel a bit of guilt at getting off so easily with her own trial. "How are you feeling?"

"I'm not sure. I think I'm still in shock, but I can deal with it once this is all over. Once the shock wears off, I'll start to feel just how painful this really is."

"It's okay. We'll get your hand fixed in no time. But first, I should grab that sword before—" Rahaf caught her tongue. When she looked over, she noticed the bridge was now fully intact. And, of course, Theodosis was running straight toward it. "No! Vorkalth, stop!"

"Don't bother wasting your breath, my precious daughter." The mysterious voice behind Rahaf caused the lightness in her body to return to a heavy feeling. The hairs on the back of her neck stood, and goosebumps rose across her body.

At the entranceway, there stood her father, Bastille Soulryth, and her grandfather, Aldothfex Soulryth. Both of them had flames bursting from their hands, ready to intervene and steal the sword.

## 58
## Unfortunate Demise

**RAHAF**

Aleek made the first move, jumping out of the way just in time to dodge the flames soaring towards him. He sprinted towards Aldothfex and lunged forward, sinking his teeth into the man's neck. Rahaf joined her bobcat in attacking her father next. She used her enchanted whip to slash his arm, but the armor he wore deflected the blow.

Rahaf figured the best course of action was to fight fire with fire—literally. She chanted *"Pyroc"* as flames surged through her hands and formed waves. Bastille managed to dodge them, but not without singing at the top of his head.

Rahaf looked down at her hands and then at her whip. She had an idea, and if it worked, she'd question for the rest of her life why she never thought about it until that very second. Her father started running towards her, both his arms forging a wave of flames to help boost his speed. Rahaf nervously closed her eyes and focused on her connection with the God of Fire, Pyrocian. She searched deep within her soul as she prayed. Then, opening her eyes, Rahaf managed to light her whip up in flames. She jumped high up in the air and twirled her body, her fiery whip creating a circle of fire that collided with her father and knocked him back to the entranceway. He landed on the ground next to Aldothfex, who was still fighting Aleek.

Eli, still standing behind her, was completely impressed by what she had accomplished. "That was the hottest thing you've ever done. And, yes, the pun was intended."

Rahaf laughed, but the humor of the moment was cut short as she looked over her shoulder. Theodosis was close to grabbing the Sword of Aerislark.

"Vorkalth, stop!" Rahaf shouted. She was running faster than ever before. However, she remembered that Theodosis no longer had his element. She'd feel bad about what she was going to do, but the pain would only be temporary. *"PYROC!"* Flames burst through her hands. It caught onto Theodosis, causing his back to burn. He fell to the ground and started rolling around in the dirt, trying to stop the fire.

Rahaf was able to hold him off just long enough for her to reach the Sword of Aerislark. The weapon was floating in midair, suspended in a beam of light. The origins of the light were unknown, but she could hear a lullaby playing the closer she got to it.

From behind, Rahaf could hear some sort of commotion. She worried what it might've been, but she forced herself to keep her eyes on the sword.

"For my mother, for my sister, for Malakai, and the nation," she said out loud.

Rahaf's hand touched the sword. A burst of wind flew through her long, brunette hair and knocked everyone else to the floor.

"I did it," she said in disbelief. "I have the Sword of Aerislark!"

A roar of pain caused the cave to shake.

When Rahaf looked, she saw Aleek had been stabbed in his lower stomach by her father. King Bastille then helped Aldothfex up, and the two got hold of Eli.

"Don't make this any harder than it has to be, Rahaf!" said King Bastille. He conjured a ball of fire and held it close to Eli's face. "I will burn your little friend to ashes. All we want is the sword, and we will leave you alone."

"Father, why are you doing this?" Rahaf asked. "Can't you see that Grandfather is under the Shadow Lord's control? Grandfather never had such horrific views when I was younger."

"Enough with your ridiculous nonsense. The only one I see trying to ruin our family dynasty is *you*. I should've seen it a mile away. Your sister may have been different, but I fear she might've been a better fit to keep the dynasty afloat. You? You were a mistake."

From the corner of her eyes, Rahaf saw Theodosis standing straight. He looked up at Rahaf, grimacing in pain, but his eyes were soft and familiar—the eyes of the man Rahaf loved.

"Theo? Is that you?" Rahaf said, hardly daring to hope.

"Yes, my love. It's me." Theodosis smiled. However, it was short-lived when he saw both King Bastille and Aldothfex standing across the bridge. "How did they get here?"

"Long story, but I think they've been following us this entire time. And you were under the Shadow Lord's control. I'm not sure how he's done it, but I'm glad to see you're back."

"It wasn't easy. He had Nerumi, Kelton, and supposedly Silianna as well. But we escaped, and now all we need to do is give Prince Antonius the sword before it falls into the wrong hands."

"I fear that won't be happening," King Bastille interfered. "Hand over the sword or your friend dies. This is your final warning."

Behind King Bastille, Aleek appeared and attacked, using what little strength he had left, biting into his leg. As the king screamed out in pain, Eli managed to pull away and run towards the bridge. Rahaf could tell from the way Aleek was handling the attack, he was weak from his stab wound. Blood dripped from the cut in his side.

Aldothfex raised a dagger over his head, fury in his eyes, and went to attack Aleek. However, Rahaf was quick to use her whip and lock it onto one of the long, pointy rocks that hung in the cave. She lunged her body forward and swung across the bridge.

Rahaf's legs were facing forward, ready to kick her grandfather away. As she crossed to the other side, she landed the hit, but instead of falling to the ground, her grandfather stumbled towards the edge of the abyss. For one terrifying second, he struggled to get his bearings, but his feet gave out from under him. He locked eyes with Rahaf as he tumbled over the edge, face twisted in pure terror, and then he was gone forever.

Rahaf sprinted towards the edge, horrified, trying to see if she could still see him, but there was only inky blackness.

Rahaf stumbled back, guilt gripping her heart. She didn't have long to mourn before she heard movement behind her. King Bastille was making a move, trying to take advantage of her distraction. Rahaf spun on her heel and swung her fiery whip in his direction. The hit caught him around the stomach, and she used her momentum to slam him into the nearest wall, where he crumpled to the ground.

Rahaf dragged a hand across her face, wiping away sweat and the few tears that managed to escape, and moved over to where Aleek was lying.

"It's okay, Aleek. We're going to fix you up, I promise," Rahaf said. She hugged Aleek tightly, fearing letting him go.

Eli and Theodosis came back from the bridge and rushed to Rahaf and Aleek's aid.

"You are nothing but a disgrace to the fire kingdom," King Bastille spat. "You should never have been born."

"That's enough, Bastille," Theodosis barked, gritting his teeth. "Your reign of terror is over."

"How dare you speak to me in such a vulgar tone? You are to address me as *King* Bastille, you arrogant fool!"

"I do not serve dictators. And since Rahaf and I are married, we will overthrow you as Pyroc's ruler and start anew together—no matter what the laws state."

Eli took over tending to Aleek and told Rahaf to go finish handling her father. Rahaf was reluctant at first, considering she might be losing Aleek forever. Eli reassured her that nothing bad would happen to him as he explained, "You forget that I am a shapeshifter. All types of supernatural beings have some form of healing. Even elementals. I, myself, can take away some of the pain that Aleek is experiencing. Perhaps I can take away enough where the wounds will heal on their own."

"Are you sure you can do it?" Rahaf asked, shaking.

"Yes. Now, go. Do Aleek some justice." Eli winked at Rahaf, and it was all the confidence she needed to do as he said.

Rahaf dug the tip of the Sword of Aerislark into the dirt and intervened between her father and Theodosis.

"This ends now, Father," Rahaf said, her voice deepening. "Call off the war and send your soldiers back to Pyroc. Or else, they will have to answer to their new King and Queen."

King Bastille shook his head. "You don't have the guts to kill me. You're weak. You're just like your mother. I was so pleased to know that they had finished her off at Sorrow Tower. She brought dishonor to our family, and you have followed in her footsteps."

Rahaf felt her throat tighten. She'd always suspected her father had something to do with her mother's death, but hearing it so plainly said was certainly a shock.

Rahaf held her enchanted whip tightly in her hand and started hitting her father repeatedly. He quickly raised a shield of fire, blocking her blows. She then raised her hand, summoning forth a large ball of fire in the hopes of breaking through the shield. As she threw it forward, King Bastille countered with his own, and the two clashed in midair, spreading white hot flames out in all directions.

"Give up, Father!" Rahaf shouted.

King Bastille growled and then swung his hands to the side, throwing their conjoined fire into the nearest wall, blackening it. He then rolled quickly, swiping the dagger her grandfather had dropped from the ground. Before Rahaf could swing her whip again, he threw it forward. Rahaf just managed to move to the side, laughing at her father's pathetic attempts.

"Is that all you have?" she challenged.

Rahaf lifted her whip, ready to strike, when she heard a choking noise. She looked over her shoulder, and her blood turned to ice. The dagger King Bastille had thrown was lodged in Theodosis' chest. Theodosis was clutching it with two hands, staring at Rahaf in shock.

"Theo…" His name slipped from her mouth as she stumbled

forward, reaching out towards him.

"I—I'm sorry," he said, right before falling to the ground.

"N—*No! No. No. No.* This can't be happening!" Rahaf fell to her knees and desperately clutched at Theodosis's hand. "Eli! Please. You have to do something. Use your healing powers or something to help him. Please. I can't lose him. I can't!"

Eli knelt down by her side and placed a hand on her shoulder. "Rahaf, I can't. No amount of healing can help someone with a fatal wound. Aleek's wasn't too fatal, but that dagger is in Theodosis' *heart.* I'm sorry…"

"You're sorry? Please! There has to be *something* we can do. Anything!"

Theodosis coughed, sending a spray of blood across his face. He opened his mouth, looking up at Rahaf with a desperate plea. "T— Tell Demetri. Tell him I… I'm sorry. I should've avenged him. Kill Quill Dorell…" Tears leaked from his eyes as he struggled with the words. "My best friend… My brother… I'm sorry, Dem—" Theodosis didn't finish saying his name before his eyes rolled back in his head and he went limp.

## 59
## Enter DeVault

**SILIANNA**

Gasping for air, Silianna awakened from her sleeping captivity. She found herself peacefully lying on her bed back in Windsor Keep. There was no recollection of her being in her room, considering the last thing she remembered was traveling to Miracle Forest before getting pushed into a portal by Seraphina. Or was it all just in her head? *Did I ever even step foot in Miracle Forest?*

Outside her bedroom it was suspiciously quiet. Suspicion circled her mind, wondering if this was another attempt at Vorkalth to mess with her. She couldn't tell what was real and what wasn't anymore with all these mind tricks. It was driving her mad.

Silianna stood up and walked around the room, dragging her fingers along the top of the dresser, the wall, the heavy curtains parted on either side of the window, trying to see if it was all real. She couldn't explain it, but the feeling of being in the Dark Dimension was vastly different, and everything she touched right now was real. *I actually managed to escape.* With that confirmation, there was no time to waste. Silianna needed to warn everyone of the dangers ahead.

Strolling through the castle, Silianna tried to think of the best place to go where she would be most likely to find some help. The library was the nearest option, so she headed in that direction with a determined stride.

As she approached the stairs, Silianna was shocked to find that the walls and ceilings were destroyed in the entranceway. It looked as though someone had fallen from the sky and crashed into Windsor Keep. Whether that was the case or not, she started to question how long she'd been asleep. Time worked differently in the Dark Dimension, or so she'd been told in the past.

The sound of glass shattering drew Silianna's attention. It came from behind the doors to the library. When she opened the doors, Silianna found Nerumi searching for a book.

"Nerumi?" Silianna said, tilting her head.

"Sil! Where have you been? I was so worried..." Nerumi said, tone off enough to raise alarm bells in Silianna's mind.

"You're not Nerumi, are you?"

"Of course I am! What are you talking about? Remember what we talked about last night? I found a device to teleport me from place to place."

Silianna wasn't going to be fooled again. She chanted "*Limus*," and water burst out from the pipes within the walls and lifted Nerumi, surrounding her in a sphere-shaped water ball.

"Enough with your sick games, *Seraphina*. I know it's you. I can't believe you are so evil as to impersonate the one person I fell in love with. I knew you were insane, but this is twisted even for you."

Nerumi shook her head, and then landed on the floor, coughing up water as Silianna let go of her control. Nerumi then pulled her necklace off, revealing herself to be Seraphina.

"I was hoping you forgot about my little push," Seraphina said, clearly making a joke about a very serious situation she had caused.

"Spare me with your tasteless humor. Was any of it real? Did we go to Miracle Forest?"

"Yes. To be fair, I was hoping the Shadow Lord would've killed you while you were there. I'm starting to question whether he's as powerful as he claims. If you were able to beat him so easily, how *did* you get back to the real world?"

Silianna frowned. "Doesn't matter. The fact is that I am back, and I'm going to make sure you pay for what you've done." Silianna redirected her attention to the necklace Seraphina wore. "I thought you handed that over to the fae-folk?"

"What? This?" Seraphina held the crystal necklace and shrugged. "I may or may not have killed some fae-folk. It's a good thing I had the Disk of Wisdom to escape. Which, speaking of…" Seraphina pulled out the portal device from her cloak pocket. She activated it, and a portal appeared.

Silianna figured Seraphina was about to make her grand escape, but she wouldn't allow that. Seraphina needed to face the consequences of her actions.

"You're not going anywhere," Silianna demanded.

"Who said I was going anywhere?" Seraphina smirked. She straightened her posture, still drenched in water, and headed towards the portal. "I figured you should have a little family reunion since you think you can try taking me down."

Silianna's mouth opened, ready to say something. However, she held her tongue as she saw someone walk out of the portal. It was none other than her grandfather, DeVault Beauchamp.

"You've got to be kidding me…" Silianna said.

"On the contrary, I am *very* serious," Seraphina replied.

"Why are you doing this? What did I ever do to you?"

"You want a reason? *Pfft!* That's easy. You're guilty by association. Those idiotic Eckwood brothers caused me to be the way I am. There was an organization attempting to assassinate Kelton after they discovered who his biological father was. Those juxure flowers were meant for him, and yet I ended up getting hurt. I get turned into a vampyre, and what did those guys do instead of mourning me? They go fighting for Prince Antonius' love and affection! Pathetic."

"You're the idiot if you think they didn't mourn you. Those two boys fought endlessly because of your death. The only villain in this story is *you*. Instead of blaming everyone around you, why don't you take some responsibility for your actions?"

Seraphina used her vampyre speed and ran to Silianna. She then grabbed her by the neck and threw her across the library. Silianna's body hit one of the bookshelves, causing the shelves in the other aisle to go tumbling down. She lifted her arms over her head to block the books from hitting her.

"That is enough, Seraphina!" DeVault shouted. "I've seen quite enough of this melodrama. I will handle my granddaughter from here."

Seraphina walked back to where DeVault and the portal remained. She leaned in close to his face with a dangerous smirk. "I'd say it was nice seeing you, Mr. Beauchamp, but that would be a lie. Now, if you'll excuse me, I'm leaving. The portal will remain open until you cross through."

"Thank you for the note, Ms. Blackworth," said DeVault, disdain clear in his voice.

Seraphina did not hesitate to throw herself into the portal, leaving Silianna to face her grandfather.

"Well?" Silianna said, challenging DeVault. "Are you here to kill me or what?"

DeVault shook his head. "My dear granddaughter, one thing you should learn in this cruel world is that there are far worse fates than death."

Silianna clenched her fist. She feared that whatever happened next, one of them would end up dead by the end of the night. And she intended to come out on top no matter the cost.

"I'm done playing this back and forth with you, Grandfather. The games end *now*."

Both of them used their Limus element at the same time. Water was coming from all sorts of directions. From the window to the ceiling, the walls, and the floors. Had they gone long enough, they would've flooded the entire library.

Silianna used the water below her to float. She aimed her fist at DeVault, and she was able to knock out one of his teeth with a clean shot. Blood dripped from his mouth, and while he was busy looking at his missing tooth floating in the water, Silianna came back and knocked him on the head.

*Kneel for no man*, she thought. It was all she could remind herself of, and she kept hearing Nerumi's voice while doing so.

Silianna manipulated the water into returning to where it originated. DeVault lay there on the floor, panting.

"Your body is starting to weaken, Grandfather," Silianna stated.

She observed the fragile man. The side of his face was burnt, twisted, and disfigured. She could tell by the look on him that the Shadow Lord was draining what little energy he had left. She felt bad, considering a part of her knew that he must've fought endlessly to get control of his mind. But he was weak. There wasn't much she could do for him now.

"I'm sorry for what has happened to you," she said. "But as long as you live, I would be doing the nation of Baskaria a great disservice. I will always love you—the man you could've been. Unfortunately, all hope is lost for you."

"*Coward!*" DeVault roared, the veins in his neck bulging under the strain. "We are Beauchamps. We always find a way. You are choosing the easy way out. Don't you want to save your grandfather? Come back to the Dark Dimension and save him."

Silianna's eyes widened. Vorkalth was speaking to her through DeVault.

"Sorry, Vorkalth. You don't scare me anymore. Not even pretending to be my grandfather would convince me to fall for your tricks again."

"You better not show your face in the Dark Dimension again. I will *destroy* your very soul."

Silianna smirked. For once, she felt empowered. Vorkalth's reaction was exactly what she needed because his threats only meant that he was afraid of her.

"I'm counting on it," Silianna said. "Goodbye, Vorkalth. And Grandfather, I'm sorry. I have to do this."

As Silianna prepared to deal the final blow, she felt the muscles in her hand spasm, and the water she was forming splashed to the floor.

*No.*

Her element was rejecting her again.

DeVault chuckled. "Limusic is unhappy with you. You still have both elements. So many have warned you, and now you have forfeited your chance of killing one of my connections." DeVault picked himself up from the floor and stumbled back into the portal, disappearing from sight.

## 60
## The Rise and Fall

**MALAKAI**

Malakai embraced the wind as he admired the view from the sky. There was something about riding on a dragon that made him feel alive. The adrenaline rush was intense, leaving him reeling. The sensations were so strong, he could almost forget about all the problems back on the ground, if only for a second.

He caught the scent of burnt wood in the air as they continued flying. When Malakai looked ahead, he saw flames spreading all around the mountains. The caedose soldiers from Pyroc were destroying everything in their path, and it hurt Malakai to see so much culture being erased by hatred. He wanted to go down there and stop them, and as the thought crossed his mind, Bluu veered down and flew towards the warriors. Malakai realized that Bluu could read his mind and responded to his thoughts without him even needing to speak.

Arriving down below, Bluu aimed for the caedose soldiers and knocked them down with her large, pearl-white tail.

Quickly after, Bluu inhaled all the fire into her mouth, swallowing down the flames. There was smoke residue left behind, but the fires were out. Malakai was curious to know how Bluu could inhale all that fire. *There's a lot I'll have to learn when this is all over.*

"That was incredible," Demetri commented.

"I'm glad to contribute to you living out your fantasies," Malakai said, teasing. "But let's focus. We need to go."

* * *

The Ackermere Palace could be seen not far from where they were. Malakai was excited and nervous to arrive there and see the place for himself. It was a little upsetting that his first time going there would be in the middle of a war, however.

Bluu shifted her navigation lower to the mountains. Malakai could hear the fighting and explosions getting louder the closer they were.

"We can't just do nothing about it," Malakai told Demetri. "We should help them fight. Bluu can do a lot of damage."

"It's too reckless, Malakai," Demetri responded. "Bluu can hit our enemies, but she can also hit innocent people in the process. There's only so much we can do. Our main focus is to head to Ackermere Palace and find the King and Queen. It should be our only goal right now."

Malakai sighed. It felt wrong, but he understood what Demetri was saying.

Suddenly, Bluu cried out in agony, and she started falling from the sky. Malakai felt a terrible pain in his stomach at the same moment and gasped out. His heart was racing; he was unsure what he was about to expect when they crash-landed.

Demetri held on tightly to Malakai, and Malakai was gripping onto Bluu's gold antlers as their lives depended on it.

*SPLASH!*

They landed in the water. Malakai was deep in, but once he gathered his strength, he started swimming to the top.

The fresh air rushed into his lungs. Malakai looked to see if Bluu was okay, but she did not resurface. He was panicking because Demetri had yet to come out of the water as well. *Are both of them dead?* He wondered. His thoughts surely did not help him stay calm.

Miraculously, Demetri surged out of the water, lungs filling with air rapidly. The two then started swimming to the shore.

"Did you see what shot the dragon?" Demetri asked, panting.

"No," Malakai responded. "But I did feel something hit her."

Reaching land, Malakai conjured a ball of fire to warm the two of them up. They stood there for a few minutes, hoping that somehow, Bluu would emerge from the water. Unfortunately, she did not.

* * *

"It looks like we're behind Ackermere Palace." Demetri pointed in the direction of the building beyond the sea of trees ahead of them. "By the Gods. We were heading in the wrong direction. I should've known. Luckily, we can still make it there in time."

"But what about Bluu? We can't just leave her here!" Malakai said, eyes darting desperately over the surface of the water.

"Malakai, what would you have us do? *Carry* her out of the water? It would drown us both."

"I—I can't leave her, Demetri. I just got her."

"By the Gods, Malakai. You have to focus. I am sorry that she is gone, but if we don't complete our mission, she won't be the only one to fall tonight. We have to keep going."

"*No.* I'm so tired of losing everyone. My parents, my friends, and now my Eni?! I must be cursed! No matter who is around me, they always end up dead."

"Hey! You are *not* cursed. You are an extraordinary gift from the Gods, and you were sent here for a reason," Demetri said, forcing Malakai to look him in the eyes. "Do you understand me? I may not be the best person in this whole world, but I'll be damned if I don't remind you how special you truly are. Everything happens for a reason, and none of it is your doing. You need to remind yourself of your worth because every time I'm around you, that's *all* I ever see."

Malakai bit his lip, trying to hold back the tears threatening to well up in his eyes. He appreciated Demetri's honesty and knew he was right, but the loss of Bluu still stung like an open wound. He took a deep breath, collecting himself, and nodded. Words wouldn't quite come yet, but Demetri seemed to understand.

* * *

After some time, the two stumbled upon a gate that led to the gardens belonging to Ackermere Palace. Malakai was so relieved he was finally going to be able to reunite with Eli. However, that excitement was short-lived as he overheard a group conversing with each other. Malakai looked over to see that it was a group of caedose soldiers with Insully blades ready in hand.

Malakai unconsciously took a step back, putting distance between himself and the soldiers.

*CRACK!*

Malakai jumped at the noise and looked down to see a broken branch underneath his foot. The soldiers went quiet for a second and then moved forward towards where Malakai and Demetri were hiding.

"Real smooth," Demetri said, annoyed.

"I'm sorry!" Malakai said.

"Forget it. Get ready to fight."

One of the caedose moved towards Demetri, swinging his crystal blade. Demetri was quick to dodge out of the way, then he used his Terrane element to lift rocks from the ground and aim in the caedose's direction. The soldier was knocked down, the Insully blade in his hand falling to the ground.

Malakai ran for the blade and picked it up. One of the soldiers charged after him, and Malakai was successful in knocking the enemy onto the ground with one slash across the stomach. He spun quickly to block an attack from another soldier, grunting with the effort to block the blade. Malakai raised his free hand up and sent out a ball of fire that struck the soldier in the chest. But instead of growing, the flames simmered out on impact with the armor, and the soldier looked unfazed.

"Duck!" Demetri warned Malakai.

Malakai threw himself onto the ground as Demetri grabbed the soldier by the throat and started choking him. Demetri pulled off the soldier's helmet and started hitting him repeatedly in the face. The gold armor was a devastating weapon, making each punch harder and more dangerous.

Once Demetri had tossed the soldier's body away from him, he came to Malakai's aid.

"Are you hurt?" Demetri asked, hovering over Malakai. He examined his face, neck, arms, and legs for any injuries. "I don't see any damage."

"No, I'm okay. Thank you."

"We need to get you on some more training sessions. Remind me to schedule some time when we get back to Avala. Fire may not be so effective anymore if they made the suits heat-resistant."

"Yeah, I'll need your help practicing my ground element, I freaking suck."

"Your wish is my command, Your Imperial Highness."

Demetri picked Malakai off the dirt and cleaned up his blue velvet outfit. The two then journeyed up steps to Ackermere Palace. When they reached the top, they were welcomed by destroyed structures, dead bodies, and no one alive to talk to. Pillars were broken in half, pieces of the roof were scattered, and windows were smashed into pieces. It seemed the caedose soldiers had invaded the area and left their mark on the air kingdom. Malakai wasn't sure where they were supposed to go, but he hoped that wherever Eli and Rahaf were, they were alive and well.

"Stand close to me," Demetri ordered, his arms securing Malakai behind.

They didn't get far from where they started. An undulating, throbbing movement caused Malakai to hold onto Demetri. The floors beneath them were shaking, their bodies wobbling back and forth while they struggled to keep their feet latched onto the floor. When the palace stopped moving, Malakai wondered whether the soldiers had dropped a massive bomb nearby.

"Bomb?" The only word that came out of Malakai's mouth was in the form of a question.

"Perhaps," Demetri answered.

Malakai's body started fluctuating at an unusual pace, though nothing else around him was moving like before. Even Demetri remained still, concerned for Malakai's well-being. The buildup was intensifying, and he felt a lightweight in his head. He felt there was a tug and pull in his soul, unsure which direction to turn. Images of Bluu in her dragon form were spiraling in his head. *What is my body trying to tell me?* Malakai envisioned Bluu surging from the water from which she sank. She was soaring to the night sky and flying her way to Ackermere Palace.

After his body settled down, excitement registered in his mind first. Whatever the shaking was earlier, it wasn't a bomb—it was Bluu. She was alive.

Bluu appeared as a dragon. She hovered over the opening of the damaged roof above Malakai and Demetri. She roared to the city, warning any threat nearby that she would obliterate them in a heartbeat.

Malakai held out his hands, reaching out for her touch.

"Bluu!" Malakai shouted.

"S—She's alive?!" Demetri was beside himself. "I'll be damned."

Bluu transformed into her fiery blue form and flew straight for Malakai. He held out his hand, and she sat on it like it was her personal throne. Malakai pulled her in and gave her a gentle hug, letting her know just how much he'd grown to love her.

"I thought I'd never see you again!" he cried out.

Bluu cooed and purred in his hands, letting Malakai know that she loved him just as much as he grew to. Malakai then set Bluu on his shoulder and patted some missed dirt off his blue velvet suit.

"Looks like we found ourselves the Lost Prince," said a familiar voice.

When Malakai turned around, he expected to face a caedose soldier. However, he was in complete shock to see it was his best friend, Eli-zak Vakloon, standing before him. Eli was applying pressure to his hand, which was covered in a dried, bloody cloth. *Is Eli hurt?*

"Eli!" Malakai exclaimed. He brushed Demetri to the side and ran to hug Eli. "I am so glad you are here. What happened to your hand?"

"It's a long story, but just know we sacrificed a lot to get the damned sword." Eli looked at Rahaf, who was walking toward them

415

with Aleek by her side. She looked distraught, but in her hand was the infamous Sword of Aerislark. "We got you the Eternal Element of Aeris."

"H—How?" Malakai wasn't sure what to say. "What did you guys have to sacrifice?" Malakai's eyes went from the sword back to Eli's missing hand. "Eli... You did not. You couldn't have. Not for me."

"Dude, it's okay. I'd do anything for you. You're my best friend, my brother."

"I promise we'll get it fixed. Maybe we can get you one of those super fancy robotic hands. I don't know. My grandmother must have something up her sleeves."

Malakai looked back at Rahaf. There was something off about her. If Eli sacrificed his hand, then what was it that she had to sacrifice? Aleek seemed to be in pretty good condition. The sword was in her hand. What could've... Malakai saw a wedding ring on Rahaf's finger. There was a moment of pure silence. There was no sign of Prince Theodosis, the same man Rahaf had been speaking about nonstop for months. Where was he if not by her side?

Demetri walked past Malakai and Eli. He reached over to hug Rahaf. Malakai knew instantly: Theodosis Steelhart was dead.

"How did it happen?" Demetri asked softly.

"We got married, and our honeymoon was short-lived," Rahaf said, her voice shaking. "We went to the Temple of Retribution to get the sword. I knew that Malakai was depending on getting the Eternal Element of Aeris. I couldn't sit idly by and not do anything about it. Needless to say, we all had to make sacrifices. Theodosis sacrificed himself to save me. My father murdered him in cold blood."

Demetri mourned the loss of his best friend. It was evident that he was struggling to speak. All he did was look down at the ground, lost in thought. Then, his eyes fixed on Rahaf's hand. The wedding ring she had on broke his heart the most. Malakai read his facial expression so easily.

"You know, I was hoping to see him at least one more time before you two got married," Demetri said, voice thick with emotion. "He was my best friend. I should've been by his side."

"No," Rahaf countered, steady even as tears slid down her face. "You were where you needed to be. Malakai's safety is Baskaria's number one priority. I'm sure Theo would've understood. He loved you so much. In his final words, he told me to tell you that he was sorry. He should've been the one to avenge you for what Quill Dorell did. Whatever that means. Even in the end, you were the last person he thought of."

Hovercrafts flew over the group, heading South from Ackermere Palace. It broke the moment of mourning between the two.

There were civilians from Aeris who appeared from hiding. They began cheering, celebrating the fact that the remainder of the Pyroc caedose soldiers were returning to their kingdom. It looked as though they had won the war... For now, anyway.

When Malakai observed his surroundings, he felt a sick twist in his gut. Bodies were scattered everywhere still. All this horrible violence, all these lives lost in the name of petty arguments. He felt the weight of every life lost on his shoulders.

As Malakai tried not to throw up, they were approached by the young woman with unique colored hair. She had hints of purple, pink, and grey in her hair. It complemented the silver armor she wore.

"Hello, Demetri," said the young lady. "It's good to see you again."

"It's good to see you, too, Nerumi." Demetri shook her hand. "I trust you've heard about your cousin?"

Nerumi nodded. "I just informed King Keon and Queen Seona. They are in mourning."

Shortly behind Nerumi was the leader of the coven, Annalu. She had battle wounds on her face and arm, but they didn't look like they bothered her much. She was marching her way to Malakai with a serious look on her face.

"I'm not sure how you got here, but I will be gathering my witches so we can conjure a portal. I can imagine the Grand Empress Dowager will be infuriated to learn that her precious grandson made it all the way to Avala and risked his safety."

"Actually, that's not entirely true," Malakai testified.

"Oh? I can imagine you have quite the story to tell me. Let's hear it." Annalu crossed her arms.

"Well, Demetri and I were ambushed by his deranged vampyre ex-girlfriend, Seraphina Blackworth. She somehow has a device that can create portals, and she threw us in. Demetri and I have been trying to find you guys since. Also, not to mention that my Eni, Bluu, managed to transform into a dragon."

"Hold up. That was your dragon on the roof?!" Eli exclaimed. "Dude, we *have* to ride her when we get back to Avala."

"Absolutely not!" Annali demanded, fed up. "You and your little friends have been nothing but a constant headache since the moment you all arrived. I will *not* have you flying around with a *dragon* and risk hurting someone."

"I'm sorry," Rahaf interrupted. "But it's confirmed that Seraphina is truly alive? Because if I find out she was behind all those demonic attacks at Windsor Keep, she is going to wish she was dead.

"Well, it seems you all have a mess to clean up in Avala," said Nerumi. She straightened her posture. "I will notify the King and Queen of your departures. You can count us in as your allies for the war. The Elder Guardians won't see us coming when the time is right."

"Thank you," Malakai said. He shook Nerumi's hand. "I look forward to seeing you in the future."

"Likewise. I believe we have much to discuss about this so-called 'Dark Dimension.' I have a feeling you may be able to assist me with your knowledge."

Malakai was speechless. "Don't tell me you have the spiritual element too…"

"Worse. I was somehow under the Shadow Lord's control. He also held my cousin captive, and Prince Kelton came to our rescue. If it weren't for the help of that warlock, too, I may as well be dead."

Malakai and Demetri exchanged looks. That was a lot of information to process all at once. Clearly, there was a lot that

Malakai would need to catch up on when they returned to Theuros and retrieved Kelton.

Nerumi was getting ready to dismiss herself after the bombshell when Demetri stopped her in her tracks. "You don't want to come and see Silianna? I know she'd love to see you. Surely we can get you back to Aeris in time."

Nerumi shook her head. "I cannot. I must put my people first. Maybe she and I will cross paths once the dust is settled. Until then, I have a mess of my own I need to clean up."

Demetri shook his head. Malakai was intrigued to learn what the whole fuss was about, but he figured he'd learn about it soon enough when they got back home.

By the time the group was caught up in their crazy adventure, Annalu returned with her coven. They gathered in a circle and performed a spell that would conjure the portal.

Malakai, Bluu, Eli, Demetri, Rahaf, and Aleek were in a single-file line as they awaited their instructions. Once the portal was opened, Annalu had them each venture in one by one. However, as the group was departing, there was a sound that was too similar to what a KT7 Foxsull laser beam made. Malakai was left in despair, worrying that someone may have been shot amid their departure.

## 61
## Birds of a Feather

**MALAKAI**

Snowflakes landed on Malakai's auburn hair, and the icy floor he lay on caused his body to shiver. Malakai was certain that he was back in Avala, but the question remained: *Where* did he end up in Avala? Even though his vision was a bit blurry, he could tell he wasn't in Windsor Keep as originally intended. There were shimmering tall structures that surrounded Malakai, which prompted him to believe he was somewhere in the city.

Crunching sounds echoed around him as he lifted his head slightly, trying to get his bearings. It came from Malakai's front side, but he was still unsure of what was approaching him. First, it was just a black shadow, and then it transformed into a bright light. When Malakai's vision slowly returned, he was facing Demetri, who was holding out his hand to help him up. Demetri's gold armor was still intact. He held the Sword of Aerislark in his other hand.

At the sword's handle, Malakai caught sight of the white gem that resided there, glowing with a bright light. It was the exact one he'd come across from the crescent moon amulet and Rahaf's enchanted gold anklet, only this one was white compared to the others that were green and red.

If Malakai hadn't known any better, he'd say that the Sword of

Aerislark was *meant* for Demetri to hold. It may have been an object created by the God of Air, but it complemented Demetri's sharp gold armor. *A Terrane elemental holding a sword from Aeris*, Malakai thought. *What a funny world we live in.*

Malakai grabbed Demetri's free hand. Once he stood up, he looked around to figure out where they landed. It was only the two of them there—the rest of the group must have been split up.

"What do you think happened?" Malakai asked.

"I'm not sure, but I have a bad feeling we might've been sabotaged. I heard someone get shot right before we crossed over. You're not hurt, are you?" Demetri asked, examining Malakai's body.

"No. I'm fine. But I did hear that shot, too. Sounded like a KT7 Foxsull."

"That's what I was afraid of. We need to get one thing out of the way." Demetri held the sword out for Malakai. "You need to absorb the Eternal Element of Aeris before it ends up in the wrong hands."

Holding the sword in his hands, Malakai tried to remember how he obtained the last two Eternal Elements. It sort of happened on its own, so he relaxed his body and tried to allow the magic to flow through him.

Malakai had the sudden urge to look up towards the sky. When he did, he saw a bird circling high above. It was no ordinary bird. The creature was white with hints of red and pink. The wings spread out for at least a foot and a half. When the bird's wings flapped, it left a trail of gold shimmer behind it in the air. The bird cried out, flying in a dizzying circular pattern.

"What is that thing?" Malakai asked.

"I might be way off here, but I think it is a form of Aerislark," Demetri said, mouth slightly gaping open. "He must be aware that you have his sword."

Malakai looked at the sword, and then at the bird. The weapon began glowing the more the bird remained in the sky. Then, within the blink of an eye, the bird exploded into gold dust. One of the feathers was left behind, slowly rocking back and forth in the sky until it landed on Malakai's free hand. As it touched his skin, a gust of wind swirled around Malakai's body. The energy inside the white gem transferred over to his body, and the feather disappeared into the snow.

*I did it. I have the Eternal Element of Aeris.*

"How do you feel?" Demetri asked.

"I—I feel like my body is vibrating. Like I want to…" Malakai chanted "*Aeris*," and his body jumped high off the ground, then landed back on his feet. "Woah! Demetri, I did it! Did you see me?"

"I did," Demetri said, grinning. "But you might want to practice a little bit when we get back to Windsor Keep. You almost landed on your ass for a second there."

Malakai examined the Sword of Aerislark in his hand and frowned. It didn't seem right to him to have such a beautiful weapon. If anything, it belonged to Demetri. Plus, Malakai had an Insully blade latched onto his sword belt; he didn't need the extra weapon.

"Here. Take it." Malakai held the sword out. "I think it'll serve you better with that armor."

"Malakai, I'm not accepting that. The God of Air came to *you*. It was intended for you to have, not me."

"You're wrong. He circled both of us. I was intended to have the Eternal Element of Aeris, but not the sword. I have my crescent moon, Rahaf has her anklet, and now you should have the sword. I'd rather we each hold onto one of the angelic items than have me be in charge of all of them."

Demetri shook his head. He pointed at the gold dragon necklace around Malakai's neck and said, "I don't see you wearing the crescent moon."

Malakai smirked and accepted Demetri's challenge. He reached into his pocket and pulled out the amulet.

"I may not wear it often, but I always have it with me," he said, the amulet dangling from his hands. "Not only because it is an angelic item, but because it reminds me of my mother and father. They kept it hidden from me until I was old enough. I'm pretty sure my mom said it was intended for me on my twenty-first birthday, right before she died."

"If that day never happened, we'd probably never have met each other again." Demetri's voice thickened, lost in his memories. "Malakai, I am truly sorry for how I treated you at Castle Caestshire. I should've never sunk so low. You mean everything to me, whether you know it or not. I can only hope the time we've spent together has made up for my behavior."

Malakai didn't respond right away. A part of him worried about where Demetri was going with this speech, and he feared that he had much more to say. But one thing that struck Malakai was that first sentence. *If that day never happened, we'd probably never have met each other again.* Malakai had been so focused on the fact that Demetri had feelings for him that he never questioned what the last moment they'd had together was *before* Malakai lost his memories. He had a hunch about what it was, but Demetri had to say it out loud.

"Demetri," he started, "when was the last time you saw me? Before I took the identity of Malakai Thorns."

"Don't do that. I vowed never to speak of it." Demetri took a few steps back, but Malakai followed. He was going to get the answers he wanted, no matter what. "I begged the Grand Empress Dowager not to say anything."

"What is there to hide?" Malakai asked. "I can take an educated guest, you know? You were the boy I played hide-n-seek with the day Yal died. You were also the boy who saved me when the Bellemore assassination took place. There's no point in denying it. Let's get everything out in the open."

Demetri sighed. "Yes. It was the night of the assassination. I overheard my parents speaking of the Elder Guardians' plot to ambush Blackstaer Palace. I knew I'd have to intervene, and considering you and I were close, we had discovered so many hidden places. So, when the attacks happened, I rescued you."

The boy with black hair and blue eyes. All this time, the memory pressed against his mind, and he was by Malakai's side. He'd just gotten older now, but he was still the same person deep inside.

"W—Who else knows?" Malakai asked, words sticking together

in his throat. "Besides my grandmother. Who else knows, Demetri?"

"Silianna found out. She's clever—*too* clever, in my opinion. We promised never to speak of it in exchange for holding her secret."

"What secret?"

"She's in love with somebody that she cannot be with. Very similar to what Rahaf was going through, only Rahaf had it much easier with Theodosis."

"But you two agreed because it was also similar to what *you* were going through, too, isn't it?" Malakai questioned. He got closer to Demetri, his heart racing. "You, too, are in love with somebody you cannot be with. History has repeated itself, not once, but twice. Because you're…"

Demetri stood, shoulders stiff and hands clenching at his sides, clearly trying to hold his emotions back. His eyes said it all, however, screaming with want.

"I was scared that if I intervened, you would've ended up like Seraphina," Demetri said. "It was before I knew she was alive. I begged the Grand Empress Dowager not to say anything. I feared you would've ended up dead. I had already lost you once, and if you being with Kelton secured your safety, then I would accept being alone forever. The sad truth is, I'd rather you stay alive and us not be together, than have you dead and I be the cause of it. I am… I'm in love with you, Malakai. I have been for a long time. Perhaps for too long. I fear there will never be anyone else for me, in this life, or the next."

*I'm in love with you.*

The secret was finally out.

Unfortunately, Malakai did not have time to address it. Standing opposite the boys was Seraphina Blackworth. *Leave it to her to kill the moment,* he thought.

"*Awww.* You two are like birds of a feather," Seraphina said, teasingly. "That was quite a show! I'm sorry to ruin the mood, but I think if I stuck around for another second, I'd probably vomit all over my expensive boots."

"Seraphina," Malakai barked. "You threw us into a portal! I

should kill you for what you've done."

Seraphina rolled her eyes. "Enough with the theatrics. 'An eye for an eye' and all that good stuff. After I got rid of you two idiots, I did a quick investigation. So, imagine my surprise when my little spy informed me that Narkissa was still alive. I'm not sure how you tricked me into believing you did it."

Malakai couldn't reveal to her that he had Narkissa's blood running through his system. She'd use it to her advantage and try turning him into a vampyre. Instead, he chose to play dumb.

"Trust me, it wasn't that hard to convince you," he lied.

"Well, either way, I warned you that there would be consequences. If you thought getting shoved into a portal was bad, imagine what I can have coming out of one." Seraphina held the Disk of Wisdom in her hands and activated the device. A portal was conjured, and within seconds, it formed a black cloud of smoke. "I'm sure by now you've heard that Vorkalth was creating these new creatures called Dravkyn Demons.' Those poor Lost Souls didn't stand a chance when he forced them to transform into these vicious creatures. But, they sure know how to obey a command."

As she spoke, around a dozen Dravkyn Demons crawled out of the portal, screeching in horror.

"Oh, and if you hadn't figured it out, this was how I got them to wander Windsor Keep." Seraphina blew a kiss in the boys' direction, then winked. "You two deserve each other. I suppose I'll see you in the Underworld when all is said and done. Ta-da!"

Seraphina moved too fast for them to follow. She was gone, the portal along with her.

The Dravkyn Demons moved forward eagerly, roaring, growing louder. Malakai gathered that they were getting ready to attack, and he had no choice but to grab his Insully blade and hold it close to his chest, preparing himself for battle. Demetri did the same with the Sword of Aerislark, and he stood in front of Malakai, offering to make the first move.

"Get ready to fight," Demetri said.

"I don't think I have a choice," Malakai said, shaking.

Suddenly, the Sword of Aerislark burst into white hot flames. Both of the boys jumped, startled. Malakai's jaw dropped at the view, whereas Demetri was frozen and embracing its potential. There was a translucent aura that appeared before Malakai, blinding him from anything else around him. An angelic voice spoke in his mind, "*Only the true wielder with a warrior's heart can conjure Angelic Fire from the Sword of Reign and Steel.*" The aura then submerged, and Malakai was back to facing Demetri.

"D—Did you see that?" asked Malakai.

"See what?" Demetri's eyes were still mesmerized by its heavenly beauty

"Demetri, that's Angelic Fire," Malakai emphasized. "You might think I'm crazy, or maybe not, but I think Aerislark *spoke* to me just now. Only a true wielder with a warrior's heart could conjure Angelic Fire. I think he wanted you to be its owner."

"Is that so?" Demetri raised an eyebrow, impressed. "That certainly boosts my confidence by a couple of thousand."

The Dravkyn Demons hissed at the fire, stopping their forward momentum to cower back. *Fire has to be their weakness*, he thought. *Aerislark must like Demetri if he's willing to lend him this level of power.*

Bluu was hovering over Malakai's shoulder and then moved to the ground, transforming into her dragon state.

"Oh, sure... she couldn't have turned into a dragon earlier?" Demetri asked.

"Shut up," Malakai responded. He looked up at Bluu. "Try to find that vampyre and give her a taste of her own medicine. If you can't, come back here to help us with these demonic creatures."

Bluu nodded her dragon head and flew off, searching for Seraphina.

Malakai refocused his attention back to the Dravkyn Demons up ahead; although they still seemed afraid of the flames, they were moving again, ready to attack.

Demetri ran first, and Malakai followed behind him.

The Angelic flames flared as Demetri slashed the sword in all directions. A small portion of it managed to touch the side of

Demetri's face—miraculously healing the scar well hidden by his grown beard. It was the small scar Quill Dorrel bestowed upon him for rebelling against his orders. Malakai wasn't sure whether Demetri was aware of it or not, but he didn't dare bother him as Demetri impaled another Dravkyn Demon, turning it into dust instantly.

Taking advantage of Malakai's distraction, one of the creatures threw itself at him. Malakai used his strength to keep the creature's sharp claws from scratching him.

After stabbing the Dravkyn Demon in the stomach with the Insully blade, which did very little damage, Malakai chanted "*Pyroé*" and caused the flames to creep up the length of the blade and burn the creature from the inside out. Malakai then chanted "*Aeris*," moving his arms in a circular motion to form a ball of wind to push another creature far away.

Demetri had massacred three of them in one go, and Bluu returned in the nick of time to swallow one of the Dravkyn Demons attacking Malakai.

There were six of them left, and Malakai was already losing his strength. Two lunged forward, and Malakai channeled the energy within him, shooting an enormous blast of fire out of his hands, burning the demons to ash. Malakai fell to his knees and tried to breathe, feeling completely drained.

"Malakai!" Demetri yelled, spinning on his heel to avoid the bite of a demon.

Malakai wanted to respond, but he didn't have it in him to speak.

Bluu was flying back around, rushing to Malakai's aid at the same time Demetri was. However, Malakai wasn't fast enough to warn Demetri of a Dravkyn Demon sneaking up behind him. It managed to grab Demetri around the ankle and knock him to the ground. The Sword of Aerislark fell out of his hand, and the Angelic Fire disappeared.

Bluu transformed back into her smaller form to check Malakai's breathing, and then she flew to his eyes, examining his condition. Bluu then blew air his way, and somehow it allowed him to regain his strength.

"I didn't know you had healing powers," he whispered.

Malakai noticed that Bluu weakened herself in exchange for him. He grabbed her and gently set her on top of his shoulder.

"Sit there and rest up," Malakai ordered Bluu. "I can take it from here."

After Bluu adjusted herself, Malakai ran to the Sword of Aerislark and kicked it in Demetri's direction. Demetri caught it, and the Angelic Fire surged once more. He impaled the demonic entity, leaving three left to go. *But where are the remaining three?* Malakai wasn't sure where they'd gone. There was a dozen at the start, and now there were none. It was impossible.

Abruptly, Malakai was knocked off his feet. He landed on his back and groaned from the blow. Three of the Dravkyn Demons hovered over his body, snarling down at him. Malakai managed to raise his Insully blade just enough to block one set of teeth as they tried to bite him, but he couldn't attack or use any of his elements.

One of the other demons lunged forward, grabbing Bluu in its jaws. Her body hung almost lifeless in its mouth, and after giving strength back to Malakai, she had no energy left to fight back.

Just as his arms almost gave out under the strain, Malakai had black blood splashed over him. Bluu's tiny fiery body landed on top of his chest, lying still. Malakai wasn't sure what had happened, but the three Dravkyn Demons that hovered over him were all decapitated. Their heads were missing, and then their bodies turned to dust.

Looking up, Malakai was stunned to see it wasn't Demetri who saved him. It was Kelton.

"Sorry, I was late, my love," said Kelton. He helped Malakai up and cleaned the blood off his face with the sleeve of his shirt. "There you are. Much better."

"Kelton? H—How are you here right now? I thought you were in Theuros!" Malakai exclaimed.

"It is a *very* long story," Kelton responded. He grinned, and Malakai watched in shock as his feet rose off the ground and hovered in the air. "Take my hand. We have a lot to catch up on."

Malakai turned to Demetri, who was standing there quietly. He nodded his head, signaling that it was okay for Malakai to go with Kelton. Regardless, Malakai didn't need Demetri's approval, but it felt reassuring knowing that it wouldn't bother him either.

Malakai grabbed Kelton's hand, secured Bluu in the other, and then Kelton carried him in his arms as they soared off into the starlit sky.

\* \* \*

The view of the glass city from the clock tower was always breathtaking. Kelton had landed there after a bit of flying, grinning at Malakai, just like he had on their first date in the very same building.

"How are you here right now? How can you *fly*?" Malakai asked eagerly.

"There's a lot to catch you up on, but first and foremost, I just wanted to tell you how much I love you. If it wasn't for you, I don't think I would've made it out of the Dark Dimension. I discovered that Vorkalth has had access to my mind for years, which explains why I'd have these dark episodes. But more importantly, a big reason I have access to that dark part of me is because..." Kelton hesitated, his grin falling as he fought to find the right words. "Vorkalth is my father."

Malakai's heart sank to his stomach.

"H—How is that possible? Are you sure he's telling the truth? Vorkalth said the same thing to me once, and the Lady of Glisten Lake said that he was lying. What makes you think he isn't lying now?"

Kelton shook his head. "He's not. I know he's telling the truth. I may not have had control of my body at the time, but I could hear everything that was being said while I was unconscious. The vampyres speculated I might've been related to Narkissa in some capacity, they just didn't know what until Vorkalth possessed me." Kelton grabbed Malakai's hand in comfort, and he refused to let go. "And I heard what you said, too, before you left. You gave me the strength to keep fighting. You are my anchor."

"We anchor each other," Malakai corrected him. "If Vorkalth is your father, that changes nothing about who you are or how I feel for you. I love you, and I will stand by your side every step of the way to ensure we get rid of him forever."

"I'm so glad to hear you say that."

Kelton leaned forward, both their lips locked as they shared a kiss.

# 62
## Balance

**SILIANNA**

Silianna felt like the world was out to get her. No matter what she did, there were always repercussions for her actions.

1) *The Gods and Goddesses were upset with her.*
2) *Her elements were rejecting her.*
3) *Her grandfather managed to escape.*
4) *Kelton was being controlled by Vorkalth.*
5) *Seraphina tricked her into thinking Nerumi was with her all this time.*
6) *And finally, she was ambushed while traveling to Miracle Forest.*

Silianna could list so much more, and yet all she wanted at that moment was to cry in her best friend's arms. Rahaf was in Aeris, and there was no telling when she'd be able to see her again. Everything around her was falling apart. It must've started when her great-great-great-grandmother came across the Celestial Gates. *The Beauchamp Curse.* It must surely be the root of all her problems.

The library had been quiet for a little over half an hour. Everything in there was water-damaged, and Silianna was partly to blame for that. She'd spent four months in this magnificent room, and within seconds, she was the cause of its demise.

Gathering her strength, Silianna snapped out of her spiraling thoughts and came back to reality. There was work that needed to be done. She may have lost today, but that won't stop her from moving forward.

Silianna walked through the halls until she saw a group of guards huddled around each other, talking in low voices about the damage to the building.

"Is the Grand Empress Dowager around?" Silianna asked.

"Her Imperial Highness is busy at the moment, I'm afraid," one of the guards informed.

"I'm sorry, but I have some very important information. Windsor Keep's security has been breached, and I fear for the safety of Prince Antonius Bellemore. I must speak to her immediately."

"With all due respect, Princess Silianna, Her Imperial Highness cannot see anyone right now. I urge you to wait until she is finished consulting with Lord Hussayn and the queens of Centuris."

Growing impatient, Silianna turned on her heel and walked quickly down the hall. If the Grand Empress Dowager wouldn't make time to see her, Silianna would come anyway.

As she was approaching the elevator that would take her to the conference room, Silianna heard a startled scream. She stopped dead in her tracks and turned just in time to see a strange sight.

There was a portal and stumbling through were none other than Eli, Rahaf, Aleek, Annalu, and the other witches.

Rahaf managed to make a tight smile at Silianna before pitching forward and dropping to the ground, blood spreading around her fallen form.

"What happened to her?" Silianna asked frantically, running to Rahaf's side.

Eli quickly hoisted Rahaf back up, slinging her limp arm around his shoulder. "One of the caedose soldiers shot her with a KT7 Foxsull. We need to get her to a Healer quickly; she's losing a lot of blood!"

"No need, I can help her," Silianna said. If there was one thing she could do, it was use her Limus element to heal. She'd only hope that Limusic did not prevent her from using her element for some good. "Stand back and let me concentrate."

There was a puddle of water on the floor nearby. Silianna used it to her advantage and maneuvered the water in Rahaf's direction. The water swirled, covering the large wound in Rahaf's side. Channeling her powers, Silianna encouraged the wound to close and the bleeding to stop.

An electric shock from her fingers had Silianna losing her concentration. Her body was rejecting her element once again, but luckily, this time, she did what she intended to do with her Limus element before the interference. The water wobbled and then splashed to the ground.

Suddenly, Silianna felt her consciousness be yanked forward, yanking her away from reality.

The force pulled her back into a realm where stars surrounded her.

The Celestial Gates were not that far off, burning as bright as the sun. When her body was set on the bridge that led to the gates, Silianna noticed that there were three unknown individuals marching towards her.

*Is this what my great-great-great-grandmother did all those years ago?* Silianna wondered.

As the three individuals approached her, Silianna was able to get a better look at them. They had bodies of mortals, but the faces of animals. One was a fox, the other a bear, and the last one was a goat with glasses. They wore white robes and gold necklaces with pendants housing engraved symbols of the constellations. They were the Celestial Ones.

"Silianna Beauchamp, you have been summoned to the Celestial Gates on grounds of insubordination," said the fox.

"You have been warned on numerous occasions by Limusic and Eytrosus. You can only obtain *one* element," added the bear.

"And as a result, we have sent you here to bring order back," finished the goat.

"Our roles in the celestial sea of stars are to track those who may pose a threat to various planets," the fox explained. "We were tasked with closing portals due to Zorall influencing other worlds of knowledge not intended for them. Our Creator plotted to rid your world, but then the Angels came and defied their orders."

"We are no fans of your 'Gods' and 'Goddesses,'" the bear chimed in, "but we respond to our Creator. Like so, we must keep the balance with the Travelers."

"Essentially, you are a Traveler who is tipping that balance at every turn," the goat finished.

Silianna was appalled by these accusations. With everything going on in Zorall, they were seriously blaming her for tipping the balance? Portals were being conjured at every turn. Evil entities were corrupting her world. Innocent lives were being lost. But *she* was tipping the balance?

"No." Silianna knew saying it would infuriate the Celestial Ones, and the fact that she was standing in front of celestial beings was terrifying—she had finally reached her limit.

"*No?* This is not up for discussion, I'm afraid," said the fox. "You will do well to learn what happened to your family before you."

"Do I have to repeat myself? *No*," Silianna fiercely responded. "I'm not going to comply with any of these rules. You three stand there and pretend to care about balance when there is so much wrong going on around you. I don't know what it is that possessed you all to grant my great-great-great-grandmother this family curse, but whatever it is you throw at me cannot be worse than what I have already gone through."

Silianna straightened her shoulders and clenched her fists. She made her choice clear, and though it may cost her in the end, at least she knew she was standing for something.

"My name is Silianna Beauchamp, and I will *not* give my elements away. If you want me to obey your request, you're just going to have to kill me."

Silianna stomped her foot on the bridge, and multiple cracks formed beneath her feet. The fox, the bear, and the goat all exchanged fearful looks. Silianna wasn't sure what she did, but she knew that it had surprised them. *Kneel for no man—not even the Celestial Ones.*

Another stomp and the bridge shattered. Silianna plummeted down until the darkness consumed her whole.

\* \* \*

The darkness that engulfed her was nothing but emptiness. It did not last forever, for the Shadow Lord made his presence known and pulled her out of that void.

"Y—You saved me?" Silianna was confused. "Why?"

*"You should've listened to them when you had the chance,"* Vorkalth said.

"Please. They don't scare me. Neither do you," Silianna snapped. "I have reached my limit with everyone walking over me."

*"Oh, darling. You have no idea just how unlimited you truly are. I may not be able to leave this prison world for the time being, but you sure can."* Vorkalth flicked his wrist, and a portal was crafted. *"Did they tell you what really happened with the Beauchamp Curse?"*

"No," Silianna said, shaking her head. "What do you mean by that? Did my uncle lie to me about the curse?"

Vorkalth laughed. *"Are you surprised that he did? You are too easy, princess. Have a safe trip back to the real world. I'm going to have so much fun with you."*

Between one blink and the next, Silianna was yanked out of a portal, the world spinning around her.

When she opened her eyes, she found herself in a cell. But this one was vastly different from the one she'd been held captive in the Dark Dimension. This cell was real, and it was one she knew all too well. It was the one located underneath Stormgrave Castle—her home kingdom in Limus. The smell of mildew was a dead giveaway, along with some of the sea creatures that were imprisoned across from her. What crimes were they charged with? Silianna worried she'd find out soon enough. Somehow, Vorkalth was able to send her back to the water kingdom.

Looking at who appeared from the other side of the bars, Silianna knew instantly there would be no escape for her. DeVault and her parents stood in front of the cell, staring at her with disgust clear on their faces.

"Looks like you're not so powerful after all," said DeVault maliciously. Though, Silianna assumed that it was Vorkalth who was speaking.

# 63
## Lover's Grip

**MALAKAI**

Malakai and Kelton held hands as they headed for the front gates. Malakai was preparing himself for the chaos that awaited him at Windsor Keep, but he wasn't too worried, either. He had Kelton by his side, and just knowing that was enough to keep him moving forward.

When they got past the gates, Malakai was welcomed by Demetri, Eli, Celdric, Nehila, and the Grand Empress Dowager. Noticeably missing were Rahaf and Silianna, though Malakai figured they were having a catch-up on everything they'd gone through since their short separation.

Demetri's face was carefully blank, almost too expressionless, as his eyes darted to Kelton and Malakai's conjoined hands. Malakai felt a swirl of guilt, but there was nothing he could do. He still wasn't sure how to act in the face of Demetri's confession.

"Good to see you two enjoying each other's company again," said Eli, his arms crossed.

"And it's good to see you're all perfectly fine," Malakai replied.

Eli raised his hand, showcasing his new robotic hand. "Better than fine. Celsa graciously gave me a super cool robotic hand! What do you think?"

Malakai gaped at Eli, unable to comprehend what he was seeing. The guilt he already felt tripled, enough to make him feel nauseous. While Eli seemed fine, Malakai couldn't believe the sacrifice his friend had made in order to help him out. Malakai never wanted his friends to get hurt, to get *maimed*, all for his sake. He knew Eli didn't want his pity, however, so Malakai swallowed down the words he wanted to say and shoved them to the back of his mind for later. He had a much more pressing issue, anyway - his grandmother's eyes drilling into the side of his head.

"Grandmamma," Malakai started, though she didn't let him speak further.

"I don't want to hear it," she insisted, tired. "We were notified of your whereabouts in the city. And I'm a little wary to learn how Prince Kelton can *fly* on his own. You all have some explaining to do, but it is late, and you all have been through a lot. Get some rest. There will be plenty of time to scold you in the morning."

Malakai's grandmother led the way as the group walked into Windsor Keep. There was so much destruction in the castle, and all it did was make Malakai more exhausted than he already was.

Everyone gathered outside in the courtyard, where the guards were working together to clean up. The Grand Empress Dowager caught everyone's attention and asked them to stop what they were doing as she had an announcement to make.

"Prince Antonious Bellemore has returned to Windsor Keep," she began, "and with his return, we can now officially say that we have allied with Aeris!"

The crowd celebrated, cheering and throwing their arms up into the air. Malakai was happy to see everyone was in a celebratory mood. A group of centaurs emerged from the halls and blew their horns, creating a sound that would be loud enough for the entire castle to hear.

Demetri clapped briefly, then made a quiet exit. As much as Malakai wanted to go after him, he didn't. His hand was clenched on Kelton's grip.

"In addition to this news," the Grand Empress Dowager added, "my grandson has also convinced the Vampyre Queen, Narkissa, to lend her army. We have now unified all the kingdoms in the South and Aeris, minus the fae-folk. They've made it abundantly clear that they do not want any part of this war, and let it be known that there will be a price to pay for standing on the sidelines. Nevertheless, we shall relish in accomplishing new alliances!"

The crowd cheered once more. But this time, they were chanting Malakai's name.

Kelton leaned close to Malakai's ear as he said, "How about we go upstairs and have a celebration of our own?"

Malakai smirked. "I think we need to make up for lost time."

Malakai collected Celdric and Nehila, taking them to bed. He then walked Eli to his own room, wanting to say something, but Eli's hard look discouraged him from asking any questions. He bid his friend good night and headed back to his rooms to join Kelton, excited to reunite.

* * *

The last time Malakai was in his room, he was getting ready to meet Demetri and travel to Aeris. He still wore the blue velvet outfit, which was damaged and covered with dried blood. Malakai was observing himself in the mirror when Kelton walked behind him and helped him get undressed. Kelton started unbuttoning his clothes soon after to change into his sleep clothes.

While Kelton got himself undressed, Malakai chanted *"Pyroc,"* and a fire was lit for the fireplace. It kept the two of them warm as they sat next to each other on the couch, enjoying the company.

Kelton brought out two glasses and filled them with a liquid from a bottle called "Fyst." Malakai wasn't familiar with the drink, but he clinked their glasses together in cheers and took a large sip, feeling a calm settle over him for the first time in many days.

"It feels so good to be 'normal' again," said Kelton.

"*Pfft.* What even is 'normal' these days?" Malakai took a sip of his drink. "But I know what you mean. Ever since I lost my connection to the Dark Dimension, life seems so much better. Well, if you ignore everything else about my life."

"Hey, at least neither of us have to deal with Vorkalth. For once, I can finally sleep without the worry of him getting into my head."

Malakai frowned. It hurt him knowing that Kelton hadn't had a decent sleep in months. He'd hoped that things would get better, although Malakai was still a little confused by the whole situation regarding Kelton's encounter with Vorkalth.

"Tell me the story," Malakai requested. "Tell me how you managed to beat his control—how you found your way back to me. You said I was your anchor."

Kelton chuckled. "You just want me to say that you're my anchor again, don't you?"

Malakai fleshed. "Maybe a little."

Kelton pressed a kiss on the side of Malakai's face, leaning against his body. "You are so cute when you're embarrassed. I'll tell you everything, and then we will no longer have any more secrets between us. Okay?"

*We will no longer have any more secrets between us.* It was an easy agreement, but Malakai knew that it came at a price. He had to tell Kelton everything that happened between him and Demetri when Kelton wasn't around. Otherwise, agreeing to such a thing would be a festering wound in their relationship.

"Okay," Malakai said, nervous. "But after you speak, there's something I have to confess to you."

Kelton looked surprised, but nodded. "Oh. No worries. Whatever it is, I'm sure we can work through it together."

Malakai nodded. "I would like that very much."

And so, Kelton began. "I've been traveling through the Dark Dimension since I was a kid. I didn't know what it was at first, of course. I spoke to spirits, thinking they were real living beings. Sometimes, when I black out, my eyes would turn black, and I'll start floating, or so I've been told. I think Vorkalth would take the rage I had built up and consume that energy. It caused me to act out and have these insane episodes. When I told you about my suspicions back at Castle Caestshire of the Shadow Lord, I only knew of that lore because of what the spirits would tell me. I kept it to myself for years because I feared what my parents would do to me in retaliation. They'd beat me, thinking that it would help get rid of this forbidden element I had. But over time, the rage I had built up, and I think I'm the cause of Vorkalth's strength growing. He impregnated someone, and I'm determined to know who that was. If he's my father, then someone out there is my mother. I don't think that it is Queen Viktoria, the woman I was led to believe was my mother."

Kelton took a moment to breathe. Malakai could see that it was taking everything in him to finally say what he'd been holding back for so long.

"While I was traveling through the Dark Dimension this time around, Vorkalth was finally bold enough to challenge me. I discovered he'd been controlling Prince Theodosis and Princess Nerumi Steelhart. Luckily, they managed to escape. But for a while, Vorkalth had me trapped. It felt like years had gone by. The warlock who helped you as an infant came to my rescue—Wulissek. He was responsible for sending the Shadow Lord back into his prison world, but he sacrificed himself in the process. But what brought me back, what gave me control of my body again, was you. I focused on my love for you. You are my anchor. And if you ever doubted whether or not I love you more than Seraphina, I hope this shatters those thoughts once and for all."

Malakai felt relieved. It haunted him to think Kelton loved Seraphina more than him, no matter how many times he had said it in the past. It was reassuring to know it was something he didn't have to worry about anymore, but it did nothing to alleviate his guilt about Demetri.

"Thank you for opening up to me," said Malakai.

"You're not mad at me?" Kelton asked, eyes shining with worry. "It's something I should've told you a while ago, especially since you are my boyfriend. I was only worried about how you'd react."

"No. I understand. You've had to keep that part of yourself hidden for such a long time. I know what that's like—to keep a part of you a secret from the world." There was a tense moment when Malakai tried to find the words. "Kelton, Demetri and I learned a lot about each other—more than I ever thought was possible for someone as cold as him. In those short adventures we had, I believe there was a connection that formed—one that may have been a little too inappropriate if entertained further. But I swear, when it came down to it, I wanted to be with *you*.

"I know this is a lot for you to take in, and I know you might be flooded with anger. But I beg you not to fight with him. I've heard what's happened when it came to you, Demetri, and Seraphina. I do not wish for history to repeat itself. I don't want either of you getting hurt. I am not a prize to be won. I love *you*, Kelton, and Demetri's words can't change that."

Kelton broke eye contact with Malakai and focused his attention on the fireplace straight ahead. He was lost in thought, and Malakai couldn't blame him for it.

"Do you love him?" Kelton asked coldly.

"I—What?" Malakai replied, confused.

"Do you love him? It's a simple question."

Malakai took a deep breath. He couldn't ignore the feelings he had, especially when he thought back to the memory of that night so many years ago, the black haired boy who had saved his life. These last few days, Demetri had revealed a side of himself Malakai could hardly believe existed, a softer, more honest version of the man he'd thought he knew. The kind of man Malakai could see growing more attached to, could see himself falling for.

"I do believe I may have loved him at some point," Malakai finally said, fighting to keep his voice steady. "I discovered that he was the one who rescued me the night of the Bellemore invasion. My memory may be foggy, but I remember that boy with black hair and blue eyes. It was Demetri. And I fear that those memories I had as Prince Antonius will only reveal more about my friendship with him in due time. Annalu said it would take years until I get them back, and I don't know what memories I will discover concerning my feelings for him."

Kelton took a breath, hands trembling where they rested on his lap. Malakai knew the words were hurting Kelton, but he needed to continue on and get everything off of his chest. Only with no more secrets could they hope to continue forward.

"But Prince Antonius is gone," Malakai continued, determined, "I am Malakai, and I love *you*, Kelton Eckwood. You came to me when my life was shattering before my eyes. You showed me what it is to live again. You fought the Shadow Lord to get back to me. You defied your parents' orders to come rescue me when I took the Wondrous Trials. You've made so many sacrifices for me. And do you know what makes you different from Demetri? What made me realize that it was always you?"

Malakai placed his hands under Kelton's chin and slowly moved his face until their eyes were locked on each other's.

"You were never cruel to me when we first met. You offered me, my siblings, and Eli shelter, despite the fact that *I* was certainly not kind to you. As for Demetri? My first experience as *Malakai Thorns* was awful. He figured out who I was before I knew who I was, and still he chose to treat me poorly." Malakai ran a thumb along Kelton's cheek, wiping away a tear that managed to escape.

"Demetri may have a past with me as Prince Antonius, but I am far from who I used to be. My loyalty will always be with you, Kelton. You have always chosen me, Malakai, time and time again, even when you didn't have to. My past is still a mystery, intangible and out of my grasp. But you are here, with me, in this life, solid and real underneath my hands. You are my anchor, and I love you with everything I have."

"For so long I was terrified at the thought that Demetri would take you away from me," Kelton finally spoke, voice wet with unshed tears. "I knew you two were close in the past, and I'd hoped that wouldn't mean anything. I never got a chance to meet you when I was younger, and I wish I had. My mother and father kept me hidden because of my spiritual abilities. I missed out on a lot of experiences…" Kelton cleared his throat. "I love you so much, Malakai. You will never fully understand how much. I can't fault you for your past or who you were before. But I want to be a part of who you are now. Forever."

Kelton took Malakai's hands, pulling him close. He leaned forward, sealing their lips together, and Malakai closed his eyes, feeling his heart swell with love for Kelton. There were many things about his life he didn't understand, didn't know, didn't want—but Kelton was the one thing he would always choose for himself, over and over again.

# 64
## Parasite

**MALAKAI**

The following morning, Malakai and Kelton joined everyone for the celebration. When they arrived outside in the courtyard, everyone was dancing to the loud music while they ate and drank a breakfast feast.

Eli was dancing with Nehila, who was dressed in an adorable pink dress with flowers pinned on her short brown hair. Malakai's little sister was having the time of her life, and he was glad to see so after everything she'd experienced last night.

As for Celdric, he was making conversation with some of the centaurs. Malakai was intrigued to learn what it was his brother was talking about, fearing the centaurs were influencing him to join the Resistance, but Malakai decided to hold off on that argument for another time.

Looking around the courtyard, Malakai noticed that Rahaf, Silianna, and Demetri were not in attendance. The Grand Empress Dowager and Celsa were there, however. They were speaking with Lord Hussayn and… the two queens from Centuris? *Why are they here?* He questioned.

Malakai walked across the courtyard and joined the group. "Good morning, everyone. I trust we all had a good night's rest."

"My boy, there is no time for rest when a war is brewing," said Lord Hussayn.

"That is very true." Malakai smiled, then changed the topic. "So, what are we discussing?"

"We're discussing when we should prepare our attack on Terrane," Malakai's grandmother said bluntly. "It seems to be the most ideal kingdom to invade. With both of the Eckwood brothers at our disposal, it should be simple to dethrone King Alistair and Queen Viktoria. One of the brothers will step in line for the throne and then offer their army for battle."

"Not to mention, King Alistair has been in talks with the extraterrestrials in X-Zun," Lord Hussayn added. "We still have no idea how he managed to bring peace with them, but they may lend their army and blindside us."

"I forgot about that," Malakai admitted. "I crashed their Masquerade Ball when they arrived on our planet. Unfortunately, I did not get any sort of information on what they were plotting."

"Regardless, we must prepare ourselves for whatever they may throw our way," said Lord Hussayn.

"I agree. We'll need to send some spies to Terrane and gather as much information as possible," Maelena suggested.

"I'm already one step ahead of you, Your Imperial Highness. Now, if you'll excuse me, I'd like to spend some time with my grandson." Lord Hussayn looked at Maelena. "I'm sure the same could be said for you."

After mingling with some important faces and hanging with his grandmother, Malakai took it upon himself to wander the castle and take some alone time. He'd hardly seen a moment of peace in so long, and itched to have a simple walk. He came across a balcony and took a moment to breathe in the cold air, clearing his head. The music down below was loud, and he felt at ease knowing that nobody would come looking to bother him.

Sadly, that feeling of isolation did not last long. Princess Rahaf appeared, her pet bobcat following right behind her.

"You've gotten out of bed?" Malakai asked.

"I couldn't sleep." Rahaf rubbed her arms in comfort. "How come you're up here?"

"I needed to breathe. How are you holding up?"

Rahaf looked conflicted. "Terrible, for the most part. I had everything I ever wanted in the palm of my hand. And then... *poof.* Gone. Like, I never even had it to begin with."

"I'm sorry, Rahaf," Malakai said, turning towards her. "But don't think like that. What Theodosis did for you was heroic and noble. He did it out of love. You can't blame yourself for any of this."

"It's so much more complicated than that. You wouldn't understand."

"Try me." Malakai sat down on the cement bench and patted the empty seat next to him. Rahaf sat, remaining quiet. "It's okay to let it all out. You've gone through something traumatic. You're allowed to feel all sorts of emotions when you're grieving."

"I—I can't do this," said Rahaf. She picked herself up and stormed back into the castle.

Malakai ran after her, but she was already gone.

Malakai sighed, feeling completely out of his depth. He turned around, ready to continue his moment of solitude, but was met with a floating ball of green light.

Everything in Malakai's body told him to go in the opposite direction, but he couldn't. He was drawn to the light and felt his feet move without his consent to follow after it as it headed down the hall. It was the same experience he had when he first came into contact with Seraphina. There was no control of his arms or legs.

The light guided him through a few hallways and down a couple of stairs. He then arrived at the entrance of Windsor Keep, which was oddly not being guarded like he'd expected. The double doors swung open, revealing the bridge that connected the castle to the city of Avala. At the entranceway were two guards, their bodies hanging on a noose above. Malakai looked up in horror, but his body kept moving outside of his control, piloting him forward.

Waiting at the bridge, Malakai saw Kelton. He had his hands in his pockets while he stared at Malakai, an uncharacteristically cruel expression on his face. The green eyes Malakai had grown so fond of were gone. They were pure black.

Kelton tilted his head, examining Malakai's struggle to regain control of himself.

"*Vorkalth*," Malakai gasped.

"I knew you'd put the pieces together," said Vorkalth through Kelton's voice. "It's been a while since the last time I spoke to you. I trust you've had a splendid time in the winter kingdom?"

"Let me go!" Malakai demanded.

"Did you think I would give up control of Kelton's body so easily? He's a fool to believe you were his little 'anchor' as he says. I had other matters to attend to, which prompted me to let go of his control for the time being. Kelton is my flesh and blood—*my son*. I can control him no matter what, and there is nothing you can do about it."

Malakai's anger consumed him. He felt the Eternal Elements coursing through his veins as he broke his compulsion from the green light. The elemental energy in his body swirled forward, pushing away the dark magic. Vorkalth took a step back, eyes narrowed, as Malakai clenched his hands at his sides.

"I've had just about enough of you messing with my life," Malakai said, furious.

"I'm going to enjoy killing you and ending the Bellemore bloodline once and for all," Vorkalth said.

A gold whip appeared from behind Malakai. It managed to hit Kelton in the face, causing a slight cut to appear. However, the wound quickly healed in seconds.

"You're going to have to go through me before you lay a hand on him," Rahaf said, stepping in front of Malakai protectively. Aleek appeared next to her, growling in Kelton's direction.

"Rahaf!" Malakai exclaimed.

"Not right now," Rahaf responded. She redirected her attention to Vorkalth. "*You*. You manipulated my friends, my family, and the love of my life. You're the reason they're dead or suffering. I will destroy you for having my father kill Theodosis."

Vorkalth chuckled. "Fascinating. You truly believe I have control over King Bastille Soulryth? You are just as foolish as Prince Antonious over there. King Bastille didn't *need* any sort of manipulation. He's always been this cruel. Honestly, it worked to my advantage."

Malakai and Rahaf exchanged looks. Malakai could imagine that she was shocked to hear that revelation. If Vorkalth was not controlling King Bastille, then that means he killed Theodosis of his own free will.

"Y—You're lying!" Rahaf barked, words unsure.

"No, I'm not," said Vorkalth, shaking his head. "I was too busy dealing with a warlock—the bane of my existence. If it weren't for him and my son, I would've used Prince Theodosis to retrieve the Sword of Aerislark by now."

Malakai was trying to think strategically about what his next move should be while the two went back and forth. Although it may be reckless of him, he really had no other choice.

"Rahaf, we need to knock him unconscious," Malakai warned her. "We can send him back to the Dark Dimension and give Kelton some time to have control of his body."

"But that won't stop him from taking control in the future," Rahaf argued. "There has to be something we can do."

"There is. And it sounds crazy, but I should've done it the moment I got hold of the Eternal Element of Aeris."

"Malakai, what are you—" Rahaf held her tongue. She was trying to figure out what Malakai meant, and then understanding dawned in her eyes. "No. You can't!"

Malakai smiled. He was going to offer his Eternal Element to Kelton in hopes that it would protect him from Vorkalth. He saw no other way.

"I appreciate everything you've done for me, Rahaf. Theodosis's death will not be in vain. I promise you."

"But you need all four elements to claim the Baskarian throne!" Rahaf pleaded.

Malakai shrugged. "I would do anything to save Kelton, even if it means giving up my birthright. You should know more than anyone what that feeling is like. I love him, and I cannot allow Vorkalth to torture his mind another second."

Malakai chanted "*Aeris*," his body lunging into the air, and aiming for Kelton as he remained on the bridge.

Kelton's arms rose, and the bridge began to move in a wave-like motion. A black fog emerged from his feet, circling counterclockwise. The sounds of screeching horror roared from the fog, and suddenly, a slimy black arm with lethal claws popped up, crawling its way out of the fog and making its presence known. It was a Dravkyn Demon.

"Vanquish my enemies," Vorkalth ordered the demonic entity.

Malakai landed on the floor, kicking the demon's sharp jaw. It coughed up black liquid and collapsed to the floor.

"I don't think so," said Malakai.

"You'll need to do a lot more than that," Vorkalth gloated.

"*Pyroc!*" A powerful beam of fire surged from Malakai's palms. It scorched the Dravkyn Demon in seconds, turning it to ashes.

Three more of the vicious creatures crawled their way out from the black fog. Rahaf was quick to use her enchanted whip to slash one of them. Somehow, she caused the whip to light up in flames as she hit the creature a couple of times.

Malakai was knocked off his feet by a demon charging at him and landed on his back. The creature's claws wrapped around his ankle and dragged him until he was lifted off the ground. Malakai was dangling upside down, his head feeling the pressure growing.

Aleek lunged forward, locking his teeth around the demon's leg. The creature screeched in agony and released its hold on Malakai.

Malakai was let go, falling back onto the floor. When he picked himself up, he was stunned to see Demetri and Eli running towards them.

Eli wasted no time shapeshifting into a wolf, one of his paws transformed into metal, just like his mortal hand. Malakai took a mental note of how insanely cool that was.

Next to Eli, Demetri activated the Angelic Fire from the Sword of Aerislark and the two ran together, making their way to the Dravkyn Demons, bringing them to their gruesome end.

Kelton lowered his arms and made the fog disappear. He then floated in midair and caused the bridge to break up into pieces, causing the group to go flying in the air from where they stood.

Eli, still in his wolf form, hopped from one piece of the bridge to the other until he finally reached Malakai.

"Eli!" Malakai said, pleased to see his best friend come to his rescue. "We need to knock Kelton unconscious. I know how I can stop this."

Eli nodded his wolf head, then aimed for Kelton.

Malakai watched as Rahaf and Demetri joined one of the pieces of the floating bridge.

"Malakai!" Demetri shouted. "Hold on!"

"I'm trying!" Malakai assured him.

As Eli was about to jump and latch his wolf teeth onto Kelton's leg, everyone plummeted back to the ground. However, before they could fall too far, an enormous creature entered the fight. Everyone managed to land on the creature's backs as it flew, minus Eli, who was quick to shift into an owl and fly right behind them.

"Is this a dragon?" Rahaf asked in disbelief.

"It's my Eni!" Malakai clarified. "Bluu."

Malakai wondered where Bluu tended to run off to when he needed her, but he also had to give her credit for coming at the perfect time, too.

Everyone held onto Bluu as she circled her way back to Kelton, who was still floating in midair.

"Get him, Bluu," Malakai ordered.

Bluu flew forward, aiming for Kelton. Bluu successfully knocked Kelton to the entrance of Windsor Keep, banging his head against the stone wall. Malakai's heart was racing, knowing they only had so much time before he woke up. He needed to act fast.

"Bluu, take us to Kelton," Malakai said.

Bluu circled and aimed for Kelton once more. As she got close, everyone jumped off. Malakai immediately ran towards Kelton and fell down at his side.

Demetri and Rahaf were yelling at Malakai to stop whatever he was doing, but none of it registered in Malakai's mind. He needed to do this, or there would be no end to Vorkalth's torture.

*Okay*, he thought, *how do I do this? I want to offer my Eternal Element to him. Aerislark, God of Air, if you can hear me, please... I offer my Eternal Element to Kelton. Please.*

Nothing.

"No," Malakai said under his breath. "This can't be."

Kelton slowly regained consciousness. However, Malakai knew that it was Kelton and not Vorkalth. His eyes were back to their normal green shade.

"Malakai?" Kelton asked.

"Yes. It's me," said Malakai.

"What's wrong? Where am I?"

"It was Vorkalth. He got into your—" Malakai felt a sharp pain in his lower stomach area. When he looked down, he saw that three claws stuck out of his stomach.

Kelton's mouth gaped open as Malakai's blood splattered across his body.

"NO!" Kelton screamed.

"Kelton..." Malakai said, breathless.

The claws were pulled out, and an extensive amount of blood dripped out of Malakai's body. Kelton caught Malakai as he fell forward, revealing the form of a demon.

Demetri ran forward with a scream, stabbing the creature with the Sword of Aerislark and turning it to ash.

Kelton redirected his focus onto Malakai as he held him in his arms, feeling his warm blood leech through Kelton's clothes. Malakai felt his breath come out in heavy gasps.

"Don't," Kelton begged. "Don't die on me."

"I—I'm sorry," Malakai said, feeling darkness creep into his vision. "I—I love y—you."

"Don't talk like that. You're not saying goodbye. *We're* not saying goodbye. I can't lose you, too. I can't. I can't. I can't."

Malakai's vision was fading. It was clear that he was dying. He needed to act fast and give Kelton all three of his Eternal Elements. *Better Kelton have them than I*, he thought. *Terranequrk, Pyrocian, and Aerislark... Please. I offer my Eternal Elements to Kelton Eckwood. I offer them all. Please. Do not forsake me.*

A light emerged, connecting Malakai and Kelton as one.

There was an Angelic voice that spoke within Malakai's mind as it asked, *"You would hand your Eternal Elements to a boy tainted by the darkness?"*

"He is my world," Malakai answered.

*"Very well. Your love for him will be your ultimate downfall."*

The light simmered away, and Malakai felt his body shutting down. He took one last breath before fading to black.

Prince Antonious Bellemore was dead.

# 65
## Beaming Sunlight

**MALAKAI**

Malakai didn't want to wake up. He knew once he did, he'd have to accept the fact that he was now a vampyre. Narkissa had warned him and Demetri about what might happen, and the worst had come to pass.

Malakai opened his eyes reluctantly, taking in his surroundings.

Demetri and Kelton were seated on both sides of the infirmary bed. Demetri was asleep, his arms crossed and leaning against his head.

Kelton, on the other hand, was staring at him, concern etched into every line on his face.

"What's going on?" Malakai asked, his voice shaking. "Please tell me I'm not a vampyre."

Kelton laughed. "No, my love. You're perfectly normal." He leaned over and kissed Malakai on the forehead. "We were so worried about you. The Healers rushed to get you into the infirmary. Luckily, they were able to do a blood transfusion. You lost a lot of blood, but you made it out just fine. Narkissa's blood stabilized you long enough to get you help."

"Thank the Gods." Malakai tried adjusting his body, though the wires attached to his arms were bothering him while he struggled.

"So, just for clarity, I'm *not* a vampyre?"

Kelton shook his head. "Nope. You're still you—well, *mostly*."

"What are you talking about? Is it because I no longer have my Eternal Elements?"

Kelton held Malakai's hand. When he did, there was an electrifying intensity that sparked between the two, followed by a vibrating sensation.

"You didn't transfer *all* of it," said Kelton. "In fact, you somehow split them in half. No one knew such a thing could be done, but you mastered the impossible. We are each equal in strength. Together, we are unstoppable."

Malakai leaned forward and kissed Kelton on the lips. The connection they shared lit up, and the two of them glowed. A bright yellow light emerged around them, a powerful energy that swirled around their bodies. The light caused Demetri to awaken, and he groaned at the sight of them.

Malakai then pulled himself back and cleared his throat.

"Sorry," Malakai said to Demetri. "We didn't know that would happen."

"It's fine," Demetri responded. "I'm glad to see you're alright. And now that you are, I will give you two some privacy. I have other matters to attend to. Get some rest, Your Imperial Highness."

Demetri stood from his chair and walked off.

Malakai wanted nothing more than to rush after him, but he didn't know what he'd say. Clearly, Demetri was hurting, and it broke Malakai's heart to know his deepest secrets after everything they'd been through.

"Hey," Kelton said, "can I ask you something? When I was holding you in my arms, there was this bright light that circled us. I saw you talking to something, but I couldn't hear what you were saying or who you were speaking to."

Malakai exhaled. "One of the God's asked me if I would give my Eternal Elements to a boy tainted by darkness."

"Ah." Kelton sounded a little hurt. "And how did you respond?"

"I told them that you are my world. What did you think I'd say?"

Kelton was colored impressed. "Leave it to you to step out of line. I love you so much." Kelton stood up from his chair and fixed the blanket over Malakai, tucking it between his legs. "I should probably let you get some rest. There is a lot of work ahead of us, and now that Vorkalth can't hurt either of us, we will end him and the Elder Guardians once and for all."

Malakai nodded his head, then lay his head down on the pillow. *Everything will be okay*, he thought.

## 66
## Revenge

**ELI**

One week had flown by since Malakai was almost killed. Eli was still reeling from the fact that his best friend almost became a vampyre. Although he had to admit that it would've been pretty incredible to have a vampyre and shapeshifter dynamic duo taking on the Nine Lands' greatest enemies. Thankfully, Eli had a much easier time checking up on Malakai than he had with Rahaf, considering she was taking Theodosis' passing much harder. He'd only wished she'd allow him to offer some sort of comfort, or anyone, for that matter. Rahaf had been locked in her room most days, and it wasn't any better to learn that Silianna had vanished from the face of the world. She was all Rahaf wanted, and of course, her best friend couldn't be there.

Malakai and Kelton made it a priority to locate Silianna, but there had been little success. From the looks of the surveillance, after Silianna helped heal Rahaf, she wandered off to her bedroom and vanished without a trace. The only conclusion they could come up with was that she was taken somewhere to the North.

The Grand Empress Dowager ordered Annalu and her coven to rest because she would be sending them to scout for Silianna within the next couple of days in the North. They knew the risks of traveling there, but they were willing to do so for the cause.

While Eli was doing his daily check-up on Malakai earlier this morning, Demetri was quick to pull him to the side and inform him that Rahaf had snuck out of Windsor Keep at dusk. Supposedly, she ordered one of the guards to take her to Centuris and paid him an awfully large amount of aspar to do so. At that moment, Eli knew exactly where she would be headed, given their previous adventure together.

Eli was in his owl form, soaring through the morning skies in search of the fire princess. The endless snowy trees slowly turned green, signaling to Eli that he was entering the kingdom of Centuris. It was a beautiful tropical land filled with all sorts of beings. The environment was what he imagined paradise to look like, and he wouldn't mind living there when all this chaos was finished.

There was a section in Centuris that was off limits to the public, an area more commonly known as "Fell's Burial." A major reason for it being closed off was that it housed a magical object—the Orb of Fell's Burial.

Granted, Eli was aware now how stupid it was to go there to retrieve the object, but he didn't regret it for the simple fact that he got to do it with Rahaf. It was when Eli first realized he had feelings for her. It was safe to say that that was where Rahaf must've gone as he flew over the tropical city.

Eli remembered what she had said about the place once before.

*"This feels like home," she said, admiring the ocean view. "I love how there are cement stairs that lead out into the ocean. The smell of sea salt and the seagulls crying in the sky. For some reason, it brings me back to my childhood, before everything... If I could, I'd build a house here and never leave."*

*"So, what's stopping you? You're a princess, you can do anything you want," said Eli.*

*"Unfortunately, none of that will happen in this lifetime. You'd best use that orb now to locate your mother and brother before the queens learn we've trespassed."*

*Eli examined the orb in his hand, and at that moment he questioned whether it was worth using it.*

Yes. It was evident that Rahaf was at Fell's Burial.

After an hour or so in the sky since he arrived at Centuris, Eli had caught sight of the two stone gates that resided in Fell's Burial. Eli went further past it to where the stairs were. Sure enough, he caught the princess in the same wedding dress she wore when she married Theodosis. He figured this was her way of mourning him.

The bobcat, Aleek, wasn't far off. He was rolling around in the grass, content in a way Rahaf was not.

Eli flew down and shifted back into his mortal form, quickly redressing before he approached her. He took a seat on the steps beside her without saying a word, waiting for her to speak.

"Wow," Rahaf said, voice flat as she stared off into the ocean. "You got here faster than I expected."

"You expected me to come after you?" asked Eli.

"Yes. Only you would know where I'd go. There's nowhere else I'd want to be in the South. I've never been fond of Veilios, Avala is where I've been for four months, and Theuros is filled with a bunch of vampyres."

"I came here because I remember what you said about it. How you would build a house here if you could, and stay forever?"

Rahaf stared at the ocean view. "*Hmmph*. Are you sure it's not because this is where we shared our first kiss?"

"Okay… You caught me. Maybe because of that as well."

They both laughed, though Rahaf's laugh was short and weighed down by grief Eli couldn't even begin to imagine. She then placed her head on Eli's shoulder as they both stared off into the ocean. It was so rare for them to have a quiet moment these days with everything going on.

"So, what's next for the elusive Princess Rahaf Soulryth?" asked Eli. "If there's one thing I've learned about you, it's that you always have a goal in mind."

"Revenge." Eli couldn't see Rahaf's face, but he felt the heat of the word against his skin. "My mother was sent to Sorrow Tower by my own father. She was tortured for years for helping Malakai escape. And then he had her killed. My sister, Jacqueline, was also

459

sent to Sorrow Tower because she was different from the others. She, too, was tortured, and remains so to this day, while I roam freely on this planet. And then he murdered my husband in cold blood. I've now accepted that there is no other goal I have but to kill my father for what he has done."

"Y—You want to *kill* your father? Rahaf, that's insane! You'll get yourself killed."

"I'd rather die fighting to avenge those I've loved than live and do nothing about it. His reign of terror has gone on for far too long. My father deserves to pay for everything he's done."

"But if he dies, wouldn't you be next in line to rule the Pyroc throne? You'd be setting yourself up for failure."

Rahaf shook her head. "I will pass the title onto my cousin, Aidonese. Just like Theodosis did for Nerumi, I shall do the same. Ruling a kingdom that will forever see me as a traitor is not a kingdom worth ruling. But if I can convince Aidonese to help, then it will also be useful for Malakai. We can have the soldiers from Pyroc join the alliance. Saint Salvusburg, Terrane, and Limus will be outnumbered."

"I don't think Terrane has much to worry about," Eli admitted. "I heard Demetri speaking of plans to invade the ground kingdom. Reclaiming both territories will outnumber Saint Salvusburg and Limus. We'd most definitely win the battle."

"Then it's all the more reason to want to execute my father," said Rahaf, pleased by Eli's response. "And don't bother stopping me. I will burn everyone and everything that gets in my way."

Rahaf's fierce response only made Eli love her more than he already did. He understood where she was coming from, and if there was no way of stopping her from getting herself killed, then he'd make it his mission to protect her and fight alongside her.

"Then I'm coming with you," Eli responded.

Rahaf pulled her head away from his shoulder to look up at him. "You would seriously join me?"

Eli nodded his head. "I'd do anything for you. I'm sure Malakai won't mind me tagging along."

"You're insane. Malakai went through so much to go through a portal and bring you back to Avala."

"Well, Malakai needs to understand that if he wants Pyroc to join us, he'll have to let his best friend go and join the fire princess on a suicide mission."

Rahaf smiled. The two of them remained in Fell's Burial for a little while longer before they headed back to Avala, keeping each other company in silence.

Today, they would mourn.

Tomorrow, they would embark on a journey of revenge.

# 67
## Glimpse of Us

**MALAKAI**

Standing at the top of the clock tower, Malakai looked down at the glass city. For the first time, the world did not seem so gloomy, even if it was just for a short while. The sun was beaming bright, giving some warmth to the kingdom known for its winter wonderland. There was a spot by the frozen lake where Malakai had his eyes locked on longer than any other area of the city. It was the same place where he fought alongside Demetri.

That particular moment swirled his mind endlessly, knowing that Demetri laid out his entire heart and soul to him. Malakai knew it couldn't have been easy for him to say it, and yet it still had Malakai feeling heartbroken. He knew he loved Kelton, but he couldn't deny that somewhere deep down, he also had feelings for Demetri. At least, some part of him did… A part long lost to time.

Bluu flew around the clock tower in her dragon form. She was embracing the morning sky, roaring loudly. It was thanks to her that Malakai was able to be so high up in the clock tower. He needed a second to get away from all his problems back at Windsor Keep. Although he was successful in blocking Vorkalth from his and Kelton's minds, it did not change the fact that Rahaf was still in mourning, and Silianna was missing.

Malakai took a deep breath. There were surely better days ahead, but nothing would come of it if he didn't stay focused.

There was nothing left for Malakai to do but come forward and be the ruler everyone was counting on him to be. His grandmother, Maelena, was still hesitant to give him full reign, given her controlling nature, but after a few talks about his concerns of never progressing and being the ruler she expected him to be, Maelena was willing to work with him.

Malakai wanted the main focus to be set on retrieving Silianna from wherever she was. His grandmother obeyed his demands, ordering Annalu to gather her coven and head North in search of the water princess.

Armies across the South were training for battle, which was Maelena's main focus. Malakai was somehow able to meet her in the middle as they focused on *both* Silianna and the armies.

There were war plans that Malakai consulted with his grandmother about, and thankfully, Demetri was there to help keep things in order as well. Demetri had some ideas, and he was adamant that Malakai take the credit for them so Her Imperial Highness would see her grandson was worthy of the Baskarian throne. Malakai wasn't sure why, but the only conclusion he could come up with was that Demetri wanted Malakai to look like a serious ruler.

"There you are," said a voice.

Malakai turned to see Kelton. He wore a fancy black suit and had some flowers in his hands. "What are you doing here? And why do you have those?"

Kelton shrugged. "Am I not allowed to come visit the love of my life?"

"Of course, you're allowed to. But what are the flowers for?"

"I don't know. The last time I tried to give my lover some flowers, it didn't go so well. But in the interest of working on some past trauma, I wanted to try again. Hopefully, these won't melt your face off," Kelton teased.

Malakai walked over to him and pulled the flowers away. "How thoughtful." Malakai laughed, examining the flowers. He spotted a small card inside. "You even included a note. You're very dashing, Mr. Eckwood."

Kelton chuckled. He held Malakai's hand back from reading the note. "Don't read it yet. I had this whole speech prepared for you before you did. I want to make this right, and I can only do it if you work with me for a second."

Malakai held the flowers tight to his chest and allowed Kelton to speak. He could tell that the man was nervous, and Malakai couldn't help how his face flushed at how adorably awkward Kelton was.

"Malakai Thorns," Kelton started, "or rather, Prince Antonius Bellemore. When we first met, I knew you were going to be the bane of my existence. You were difficult, sarcastic, and downright stubborn. But all that did was make me more drawn to you because I knew I wanted to be with no one else but you. There was a spark between us, and we both knew it. I hoped that you would allow me to help you that day we met in the forest, and by some miracle, you did. I never thought I'd fall for a guy like you, or any guy for that matter. You opened my eyes to endless possibilities, and I am forever grateful that the Gods brought you to me. I know in my heart that we were destined for the stars, and if there is another life out there for us, I'd hope we cross paths again. But for now, we'll settle on this life as I ask for your hand in marriage."

Kelton kneeled on one knee and held his arms up as he bestowed a gold ring to Malakai.

Malakai was speechless, but when he looked into Kelton's emerald green eyes, all he could see was a glimpse of them in the near future. The two would be older, married, and with kids. They would be somewhere in a field of flowers, enjoying their company, without the weight of a war on their shoulders. A picnic by their side, and the kids running around in the field, gleefully. That feeling of love he had for Kelton would flow beyond their world, through the galaxy, and be surrounded by the stars that were written of their love story many centuries ago.

Plenty of thoughts were running through Malakai's mind, but all he could think of was one simple word. He had decided, and there was no care for what consequences may result from their union.

"Yes."

Kelton stood up and gently placed the ring on Malakai's finger. He was shaking while doing so, and all it did was warm Malakai's heart, knowing how nervous he was. Once the ring fit perfectly, Kelton picked Malakai up off the floor and gave him a twirl. Kelton kissed Malakai multiple times all around his face, and Malakai giggled from how much Kelton's now-grown beard tickled him.

"You've made me the happiest man alive," Kelton said.

"I'm glad because nothing would make me happier than to be with you the rest of my life. I love you, Kelton Eckwood. From the moment I laid eyes on you in my dreams and then in real life. I knew you were something special."

"Look who's cliche now!" Kelton joked. "That's what I said to *you* last week."

"Well, I never said I was original. But I meant every word I repeated." Kelton set Malakai back on the ground, and Malakai went to pull the little note out of the flowers. "Now, let's read what you had to say on this tiny paper."

*Dear Malakai,*

*You've made me the happiest man alive for accepting my proposal. There's only one other question I wish to ask you: Can we take a ride on your dragon to celebrate? I've never ridden a dragon before, and it seems only fair since Eli, Demetri, and Rahaf got to… Even the bobcat got a quick ride!*

*Sincerely,*
*Your Now Fiancé*

Malakai rolled his eyes and handed the flowers back to Kelton.

"You suck!" Malakai exclaimed, laughing at how silly Kelton was for writing that note. "Way to kill the mood. If I recall, *you* can fly by yourself. Probably the only one in the world that can do such a thing besides the magic-folk and the shapeshifters. How about I fly Bluu, and you race me back to Windsor Keep?" Malakai raised an eyebrow, awaiting Kelton's response to the challenge.

Kelton sighed. "It's not the same, my love. Yes, I can fly. But I can imagine the experience is vastly different on a dragon!"

"Fine. But you owe me a kiss before we go." Malakai leaned forward, kissed Kelton on the cheek, and then pushed Kelton onto the floor. He went running for the balcony, laughing loudly.

With a blink of an eye, Malakai jumped off the highest point of the clock tower, knowing that Bluu would be there to catch him.

Sure enough, she did.

Malakai and Bluu flew off into the sky, and Kelton was left behind at the clock tower, hollering at him for being a horrible fiancé. Malakai didn't care, though. He continued to fly, feeling the breeze brush through his wavy auburn hair.

# 68
## Golden Hour

**MALAKAI**

Later that afternoon, Malakai was requested to meet with the guards regarding any updates on Silianna's whereabouts. He sat in the conference room alongside his grandmother, taking in her serious expression.

Three guards sat across from them. The one who sat in the middle held a holographic device to showcase what had been retrieved from their research.

"With the help of Prince Kelton Eckwood's knowledge of the Dark Dimension, the books with notes left behind from Princess Silianna's bedroom, and Eli-zak Vakloon's encounters with Princess Nerumi Steelhart, we were able to come up with some theories." The guard activated the hologram, which showed images of Seraphina Blackworth, DeVault Beauchamp, and Silianna. "Given what Her Imperial Highness had conveyed to us prior to our search, Seraphina Blackworth was somehow in the possession of a peculiar necklace that allowed her to transform into another living being. This necklace was last known to belong to Queen Roslynda Soulryth. She used it to disguise herself as Her Imperial Highness in order to help the prince escape the night of the Bellemore invasion.

"Seraphina was using the necklace to disguise herself as Princess

467

Nerumi Steelhart. By doing so, she was able to manipulate Princess Silianna into following her. It ultimately led her closer to DeVault Beauchamp and the Shadow Lord. From Eli-zak Vakloon's encounters with Nerumi, he felt there were some differences when they first met, to his last encounter in the city before the Temple of Retribution. He encouraged her to find Princess Silianna, but now he speculates that perhaps he was speaking with Seraphina, and he gave her an idea on how to convince the water princess."

Malakai's eyes widened. There was so much information to take in. Some of it he knew ahead of time, such as the conversation Eli had with Nerumi. When Eli went into detail about everything that happened in Aeris, he did not leave out any details. He even admitted to the fact that he had kissed Rahaf before she went to marry Theodosis, which was shocking enough, but it paled in comparison to the information about how Theodosis was possessed by Vorkalth and then subsequently killed by King Bastille Soulryth's hands.

The guard continued. "Prince Kelton Eckwood was able to shed some light on his encounters with Princess Silianna before her disappearance. He ran into her while she traveled through the Dark Dimension. She battled the Shadow Lord and helped release a warlock from captivity. That warlock then helped him escape, along with Prince Theodosis and Princess Nerumi. It looks like the Shadow Lord was taking control of both of them, which would explain Princess Nerumi's absence, given Seraphina needed her hidden so she could continue pretending to be her."

Malakai shook his head. "You're wrong. Kelton didn't encounter Silianna. She'd already escaped by the time Kelton gained consciousness. But I will say, it's obvious what happened to her. When she was healing Rahaf, Silianna was sucked back into the Dark Dimension. Vorkalth was behind this. He's planning something, and whatever it is, it's because Silianna uncovered something massive. All you've done is tell me what I've already known, or at the very least speculated. What I want to know now is where she is. Is she in Limus, Saint Salvusburg, or anywhere in the North?"

The guards remained silent.

Malakai sighed, frustration creeping into his brain. The guards were useless. Like most things, he would inevitably need to take matters into his own hands. He glanced over to his grandmother, who was uncharacteristically silent. She had expressed before the meeting that she wished for him to lead the way this time, and he was silently grateful for the trust.

"Very well," Malakai said, breaking the silence, unable to keep the annoyance completely out of his voice. "I understand you have done what you could. See yourselves out. I will be meeting with the witches and Eli to discuss further action. Hopefully, they can actually tell me something useful."

The guards nodded and filed out.

Malakai was left alone in the conference room with his grandmother, who looked at him with a raised eyebrow.

"You have a lot of rage flowing within you, Antonious. Perhaps you should get some rest," Maelena said, voice a steady constant to the fire raging inside of Malakai.

"I cannot, Grandmamma. Without Silianna, we are doomed. She knows something. I can feel it. Perhaps it can help us in winning this war."

"We will win this war. We have the numbers, don't forget. Together, they will not be able to defeat us."

"Numbers mean nothing if there is an element of surprise waiting out there. I feel guilty for not checking on her before I left for Theuros. I should've known something was off with Kelton—I should've gone back inside and checked on her."

"You couldn't have known," Maelena said firmly, placing a hand on Malakai's shoulder. "Although, if you all had been more honest with us from the start, I would've done a better job at keeping an eye on her. I'm still furious to learn about their endeavors in the Dark Dimension. Not to mention the fact that Kelton is the son of the Shadow Lord. I'm not sure how much I approve of your relationship with him."

Malakai moved away from her and started walking towards the door, unwilling to listen to his grandmother's disapproval.

"Well, I suppose I will disappoint you further in informing you that Kelton and I are engaged." Malakai held his hand up, revealing the gold ring around his finger. "One cannot claim a throne without marriage, correct? Seems like a perfect time to tie the knot before I claim the Baskarian throne."

Malakai heard Maelena's stuttered rage from behind him as he exited the room, not bothering to look back. He would have to face her at some point, but he planned to delay the scolding for as long as possible.

\* \* \*

As he walked through the halls aimlessly, Malakai saw Demetri a little way from him, dressed in his golden armor. He was standing by the elevator, alone, with no guards in sight. Demetri had been distant from Malakai for quite some time since he recovered from his injuries, aside from meetings pertaining to war.

Malakai had yet to tell him that he was engaged, and it scared him to know what Demetri's reaction would be. Malakai slid his hands in his pockets in hopes that Demetri didn't notice.

"It's okay. I won't bite," Malakai said, approaching cautiously. "What brings you here?"

Demetri turned toward Malakai slowly, tense and unsure. It seemed as though he was scared to talk to Malakai, which didn't make any sense.

"We'll get her back," said Demetri, his voice dark and brooding. "Silianna is the strongest woman I know. Wherever she is, she can handle herself. I've already informed Nerumi about her disappearance, and she's making it her mission to find her."

"That's good to hear. Her soldiers can join Annalu and her coven to locate and rescue her. I appreciate you getting a handle on it compared to these guards. They've been nothing but a disappointment in getting things done."

"Wow," Demetri said, voice cold. "You've spoken like a true Bellemore."

"And what's that supposed to mean?" Malakai questioned, squinting at Demetri.

Demetri shrugged. "Just seems to me that you're turning into what Emperor Stephanus and Empress Farrah acted like. They were all about equality and peace, but spoke so poorly of those around them. The guards are doing the best they can. In all fairness, you kept a lot from your grandmother and the guards until the last minute. All these connections to the Dark Dimension are new to them. You need to cut them some slack."

Malakai huffed. "You're one to talk. The way you spoke of the vampyres is the same way I am expressing my frustration. It's a bit hypocritical of you to be making those sorts of comments about me and my biological parents."

"The difference is that it is who I am. That is not who you are. I spoke the way I did because I am overprotective of you. Anyone and anything that is a threat to you, I will speak poorly of. Those guards, on the other hand? They're not a threat to you. They're here to serve you for the greater good. You are the heir to the Baskarian throne, and you must act like so. Don't repeat the same patterns as those before you."

Malakai held his tongue, taking a few grounding breaths. Demetri was right. Malakai was letting his anger get the best of him. The stress of everything he had been through was stacking up and up in his head, with the slightest breeze threatening to topple it all over. The anger was simply a shield, futilely trying to stop the wind.

"You're right," Malakai admitted. "And I'm sorry. With everything that has happened... I hoped we had finally made some progress, but with Silianna missing, it is just another wall in our way. I feel so stuck."

Demetri got closer to Malakai, close enough that their bodies were nearly touching. Malakai worried where this was going, so he made it a point to step back and keep his distance.

"What's the matter?" Demetri asked.

"I—It's Kelton," Malakai responded.

"I see. You truly do love him more than me. Don't you?"

Malakai nodded his head. "I'm sorry, Demetri. Maybe if things were different, and you were the one I ran into that day in the forest, perhaps it would've been you I fell for. But it's like you said, I have to break the cycle and be true to myself. I love Kelton, and it'll always be Kelton." Malakai pulled his other hand out of his pocket and revealed the ring on his finger. "He proposed to me this morning."

The look on Demetri's face said it all—utter devastation. Malakai wanted nothing more than to hug him, but he knew it wasn't right. He had to remain where he stood and allow Demetri to process his thoughts.

"I know. I overheard what you said to the Grand Empress Dowager. I was just hoping I misheard you…" It was all Demetri said, but his eyes screamed his true feelings.

Malakai's eyes darted to where the scar once resided on the side of Demetri's face. It was the scar he received from Quill Dorrel when he defied his commands—when he was being blackmailed. Malakai felt for Demetri, knowing that he was tormented to protect his brother's secret and his feelings for Malakai. *He's been through so much*, Malakai thought, *and he gets nothing in the end for it.*

Malakai decided to do the opposite of what he told himself not to do. He walked to Demetri and gently reached over to brush his thumb on the area where Demetri's scar used to be.

"Do you regret it?" asked Malakai. "When the Angelic Fire accidentally healed your scar?"

Demetri shook his head. "No. My scar was placed there because of my love for you, and it was healed because of my love for you. All the Angelic Fire did was solidify that."

"Demetri, don't…" Malakai gasped.

"Don't worry. I will respect your wishes. Kelton may be your first love, but I will make it my life's mission to be your last, Malakai Thorns." Demetri's eyes locked onto Malakai's. "I understand now where I screwed up between us. If I hadn't been such a drunken fool to you at the Masquerade Ball, perhaps I could have persuaded you to fall in love with me. I knew who you were before anyone else, but I chose to be a jerk."

"We all make mistakes, but we can learn from them, too."

"Please, tell me. I only need to hear it once, and I will let you marry Kelton peacefully. Do you love me?"

Malakai struggled to answer it. He knew in the back of his mind what the answer would be, but he was scared of letting it out into the world. It was like pulling teeth to lie to Demetri, but in the end, the truth came out. "I may have feelings for you, and I'm sure our past may have played a part in why I feel that way. One day, I will get my memories back from when I was Prince Antonius and understand the connection we have, but as it stands, I am faithful to Kelton. I love him, too. I'm sorry, Demetri."

"I understand." Demetri cleared his throat. "I hope he makes you happy."

"I know he will," Malakai replied.

As if on queue, Celsa exited the elevator and entered the hall. The robot was dressed in fancy attire, though Malakai wasn't sure what the special occasion was for.

"Your Imperial Highness," Celsa addressed Malakai formally, "You've been summoned to the Great Hall. Some visitors demand that they speak to you and the Grand Empress Dowager. They say it is urgent."

Malakai and Demetri exchanged looks. *What could be urgent?* He thought. *Did someone finally figure out Silianna's location?* He put his anger for his grandmother behind him, collected her from the conference room, and they rushed down to the Great Hall.

* * *

When they arrived at the Great Hall, Malakai was overwhelmed to see so many people circling the entranceway. They all had smiles on their face, and it prompted Malakai's confusion even more. Who were the visitors?

Malakai looked over to see that Celdric and Nehila were consulting with a mysterious man. Kelton was by their side, seemingly keeping supervision of them. Nothing from Kelton's demeanor showed concern for their well-being, however. Nehila looked more pleased to speak to the man than anyone else in the room.

Malakai then turned his attention to Eli, who was running

473

through the crowd and giving two other visitors an embracing hug. Malakai was beyond himself because the two visitors Eli hugged looked almost identical to Stella Vakloon and Orian Vakloon—Eli's mother and brother.

"There's no way," Malakai said under his breath.

When he took a few steps down the stairs, he came to the realization that it was, in fact, Stella and Orian. They somehow escaped Saint Salvusburg and made it to the South in one piece.

At the corner of his eye, Malakai saw a woman in a shimmering baby blue dress and long black hair. When he gave her his full attention, he saw that it was none other than Madam Damaris Caerlight in the flesh. She smiled in Malakai's direction, winked, and then flew away. *She rescued them*, he thought, mesmerized by her generosity.

Malakai focused his attention back onto Celdric and Neihla. He didn't recognize the man right away that they were speaking to. His hair was long and shaggy, kind of like Celdric's. The man's beard was also long, with a mixture of brown and grey. His face and arms were dirty, along with his filthy clothes. It was clear to Malakai that he was much older, either in his late forties or early fifties.

The crowd formed a line, allowing Malakai and the Grand Empress Dowager to walk through and meet with the stranger. When the man looked at Malakai, he knew instantly who it was: Thaddeus Thorns.

The smile on Kelton's face as he stood behind Thaddeus solidified to Malakai that his speculations were right.

"D—Dad?" Malakai questioned.

Thaddeus smiled and held his arms wide open. Malakai no longer hesitated as he ran into his open arms. He couldn't believe that his father was alive. After all this time, he had survived the battle with the rebellion. But how?

It didn't matter now. All Malakai knew was that his father was alive.

"You have no idea how much I need you," Malakai said through the tears in his eyes, still hugging him and never wanting to let go.

"It's okay, son. I'm here now. I'll never leave you again."

*Son.* Thaddeus Thorns still saw Malakai as his son, even after Malakai discovered that he belonged to Emperor Stephanus and Empress Farrah Bellemore. It was all Malakai needed to hear at that moment. Although there were dark days ahead, he could relax knowing today would be a good one, surrounded by family, friends, and his fiancé.

*Epilogue*

**As the families reunited, Damaris felt a flicker of pride at her** decision to help Stella and Orian Vakloon escape their imprisonment at Blackstaer Palace.

The Elder Guardians had been holding them in a rotten cell underneath the old structures, starving them for months. It sickened her to know that it was happening, and Damaris wanted nothing more than to rescue them earlier on. But the Gods did not want her to interfere. Not until it was time.

It was the same thing she had told the shapeshifter, Eli-zak Vakloon. He had to be patient. When the time was right, they would be rescued. And now, they were finally reunited.

When Damaris helped them escape their imprisonment, she gave them a powder that would help guide them through Saint Salvusburg and Terrane. It would be the same method Reju Tufte provided Prince Antonius with when they journeyed to the South.

While Prince Antonius and his friends were running amok these past few days, the prisoners were on foot, traveling to the barrier. Damaris would fly by from time to time, ensuring that they were doing well while she continued doing her bidding for the Gods.

With that task now complete, all she needed to do was confiscate a very important object—one that would upset the Celestial Ones if they discovered that its existence was still around. The Gods made it abundantly clear that she needed to destroy it before the end of this night. They'd already been in enough trouble by their Creator, and to have the Celestial Ones budding in would only make matters worse for everyone in Zorall.

Damaris left the celebrations, flying above the trees to pursue her target. A woman in a red cloak was running through the forests of Terrane. She was heading North-West, presumably for the water kingdom, Limus.

The woman wasn't running like any ordinary elemental. No. She was speeding, like a vampyre, darting between the trees as quickly as the wind.

"Seraphina Blackworth," said Damaris, voice booming above the treetops.

She aimed her body at the ground. She landed with a loud thump, scattering dirt every which way.

Seraphina gasped. "H—How…"

Damaris raised her hand. "Save your words. You've been meddling with things far beyond your understanding, Ms. Blackworth. The Gods are furious with your involvement, and it is only a matter of time before the Celestial Ones find out about that artifact in your hand."

Damaris observed the artifact. The Disk of Wisdom. She could sense that its energy was regenerating, which would explain why Seraphina was not using it to travel to Limus easily.

"I'm not giving anything to you," Seraphina hissed. "I've killed witches like you before. Stay back, or I will do it again."

Damaris chuckled. "I am no ordinary witch. Have you heard of the Superior Witch? Do not trifle with me, or you won't live long enough to regret it."

Seraphina bolted, running fast through the trees in an attempt to escape.

Damaris flicked her wrist. An invisible force knocked Seraphina off her feet and sent her tumbling to the ground. Damaris then floated towards her. She grabbed the Disk of Wisdom and secured it tightly in her hands.

"You have no idea who you're messing with!" Seraphina shouted, fingers digging angrily into the dirt.

"Believe me, I do. And I am not intimidated by you." Damaris used her energy to trigger the Disk of Wisdom and summon a portal.

"What are you going to do with it?"

"Why don't you take a look for yourself?"

Both of them looked into the portal and saw a Throne room. Inside was a queen, standing on her bare feet and walking towards Damaris and Seraphina. The queen had platinum blond hair braided on her left side. She wore a long black dress with swirling ruby red designs, highlighting her deathly pale skin complexion. Narkissa, Damaris thought.

Seraphina was struggling to get herself up, but Damaris's force secured her on the ground until she levitated her into the portal. Damaris watched her fall onto the cement floor, her face next to the vampyre queen's bare, pale feet. Damaris then locked eyes with Narkissa through the portal and said, "I believe you've been looking for her. Consider this a gift from Prince Antonius Bellemore. Make sure she doesn't escape and cause any more trouble moving forward."

"Believe me, she won't be a problem much longer." The Vampyre Queen picked Seraphina up from her neck and held her up. "It was a pleasure seeing you again, Damaris Caerlight."

Damaris smiled. "Likewise."

Seraphina screeched before the portal closed.

In her hand, Damaris looked at the Disk of Wisdom. She chanted the spell the spirits had given her, and the artifact turned to dust. There would be no more portals in this world that could connect to others across the universe. More importantly, the Celestial Ones will never learn of what has happened here. Hopefully.

Damaris took to the sky again, flying to her next destination.

All that was left was for the Eternal War to begin, and the Prophecy of Old and New would come to pass. Just as the Gods intended.

## ACKNOWLEDGMENTS

**A SWORD OF REIGN AND STEEL is the second book in the** Baskaria Chronicles, and it is easily the most headache-inducing work I've done thus far. I knew heading into this one that it would be longer and darker. I wanted my six main characters to have a fleshed-out story, given that some characters were limited for the first book. Each character has a piece of me within them, so you can imagine the challenge I had to face when it came to putting words on paper for six separate storylines.

The stories I write usually have some sort of message. For book two's message, it is letting go of what no longer serves you, learning from your past mistakes, and building a better version of yourself in your darkest hour. There are always going to be obstacles that get in your way, but you can't let them knock you down.

*A SWORD OF REIGN AND STEEL* was my form of healing, and I'm grateful to finally write this portion through the eyes of Malakai and his friends. At the end of the day, books are meant to be interpreted in various ways. Perhaps you viewed this story as something completely different, and that's okay! I just hope you, the reader, enjoyed this book as much as I did writing it.

\* \* \*

To kick things off, I know that I said book one would be the longest acknowledgment I would ever write… I lied. *Sorry!* I've met so many incredible people between 2022—2025 and met some extraordinary friends that stood by my side while I busted my ass writing this book. I just can't forgive myself if I didn't give a proper acknowledgment.

I would like to give a shout-out to my closest friends who had an exclusive behind-the-scenes to the headache I went through with this book: Damaris Garcia, Pamela Garcia, Elijah Paige, Crystal Turpin, Elaine Soto-Romero, Yafreisy Rivera, Kiara Alfonzo, Grant Alfonzo, Jodi Falcone, Sydney Dickson, William Carrasquilla, David Carmo, Nicole Perez, and Mateus Ribeiro.

Thank you for being my rock when writing got stressful! Whether we played Fortnite, Dead by Daylight, explored new towns, new states, bookstores, restaurants, beaches, countries, etc. Looking back at this book, I will always cherish those memories forever.

\* \* \*

A little backstory, I returned to my writing journey in 2022 when my best friend, Yafreisy Rivera, got me a job working alongside an amazing group of people. I was at the lowest point in my life, jobless, and had no idea how to pick myself up. Yafreisy came to me after years of losing contact, and she embraced me with new opportunities I will never forget. We may argue like brother and sister, but we love each other like brother and sister, too.

Starting a new chapter of my life in 2022, Yafreisy introduced me to so many people who encouraged me to reach my goals. A lot of moments from both books, one and two, were written during my time with them. I'll always cherish those moments.

Without further ado, I would like to acknowledge my team, the ones I'd talk the most to anyways, in alphabetical order: Nina Afonso, Brandon Agront, Ja'Nita Akins, Joseph Alcala, Rachele Altenor, Madelyn Demetrio, Vanine Augustin, Celia Maria Azevedo, Rosa Bacian, Maria Bartolomei Rodriguez, Angie Bastidas, Kamla Boodoo, Janice Borden, Sasha Bowie, James Braxton, Pat Bryant,

Becky Campbell, Brittany Carrasquillo, Dee Centeno, Lisa Chojnowski, Barbara Clark, Ruth Colon, Liberty Craft, Kris Currier, Josh Danque, Robin DeMalignon, Mike Dowling, Carlos Feliciano, Kelly Figueroa, Dawn Ford, Cherry Fudge, Marcus Gardner, Jay Goldberg, Samuel Gonzalez Santiago, Aaron Gonzalez, Barbara Henderson, Oscar Hernandez Febles, Cristy Izmirlian, Boomer Johnson, Myrguedaelle Joseph, Zachary Klein, Sandra Kucia, Kelly Lanzo, Laura Lopez, June McClymont, Rafael Messen Reyes, Izzy Miller, Grace Minyard, Steven Morales, Aimee Nilsson, Pedro O'Farrill, Marilou Olegario, Mohamed Omar, Sam Onken, Axel Otero Falero, Emerald Parker, Sylvia Parker, Kate Paswaters, Panda Peltier, Paulina Pfaeffle, Jeff Phipps, Efrain Ralat Flores, Jalina Ramirez, Yvette Reyes, Franklin Rivas Dubon, Paul Robateau, Nicola Rowe, Frankie Sanchez, Lisa Sheikewitz, Emily Shentu, Katinka Silguero, Sunieta Singh, Roberto Stevens-Vega, Nora Sullivan, Faviola Valdez, Vicky Vega-Mora, Akane Wade, Amanda Wahrenberger, Nicole Weller Kijewski, Shirley Williams, Valma Williams, and Annette Wright.

Wait! I'm not done…

There's also my amazing leadership team, who took a chance on me and saw my potential for success: Angelica Aguilar, Mason Crabtree, Fran DeGrado, Ken DePaul, Richard Dookhdeen, Frankie Garcia, Hannah Hallenbeck, Shay Harleston, Colby Hart, Karina Hernandez, Bryan Holderby, Kayla James, Luke Lunsford, Sarai Menendez, Valeria Mendoza Fonfrias, Johan Milus, Ezequiel Muriel, Patrick Reagan, Aurora Rentas, Steven Sakakieda, and Lionel Toro.

\* \* \*

Alright.

Hold on.

You didn't think I was ending this without mentioning my book besties, did you? *Pfft!* This is a *book series,* after all, where the topic is *books*. Duhhhh! \*eye roll emoji\*

When I first started talking about my book on #Bookstagram and #BookTok, I met some really amazing people from all over the world. I have to give them a shout-out, more so because they've been amazing supporters and pushed me to keep going! Without them, I wouldn't be as delulu as I am now to publish these books!

Christina Arisa @kissysensei
Quan Williams @suchabibliophile
Rebel Carter @rebelwrites
Darcy Dahlia @darcywritesdark
Jupiter Belle @jupiterbelle
Morgan Vela @morganvelaauthor
Sandra Janet @sandrajanetreads

**Note**: At the time of writing this, these are what their social media handles were.

\* \* \*

As I've done for my previous book, I want to take the time to thank my wonderful editor, Rose Direnzo, for continuing this journey with me. You work effortlessly, and I appreciate all that you do. I cannot wait to see where the future takes us. She is an extraordinary woman with a great talent for storytelling, and I am so grateful the universe brought us together. I will continue to encourage her to write a book of her own until the day that I die because I know there is a story ready to burst out of her soul. Someone out there needs your story, girl! Let's put pen to paper and get cracking. Much love.

Qamber Designs, the team behind these *extravagant* book covers, deserves applause for their hard work and dedication. I don't know what I would do without them! I am *very* picky with the vision that I have, and they never fail me. Thank you for bringing these covers to life.

\* \* \*

The Baskaria Chronicles is a series I am going to have so much fun writing for the next few years. My only wish is that you all continue to join me on this journey, and hopefully, we gain new readers along the way!

Until next time. . . .

— *Castiel A. Steele*

**Castiel A. Steele is a Puerto Rican-American author and** screenwriter, born in New Jersey and raised in Florida. As an LGBTQ+ writer, Castiel lives with his Russian blue cat, Blue, and attends the University of Central Florida with an associate degree in General Studies. Castiel spends his free time reviewing films/TV shows, and books, or writing his next project. He began writing in seventh grade when he was introduced to a writing competition, famously known as NaNoWriMo. Since 2012, Castiel has found a passion for the writing/filmmaking world and plans to continue pursuing his dreams.

Visit – www.castielsteelebooks.com

Dive into the immersive world of The Baskaria Chronicles!

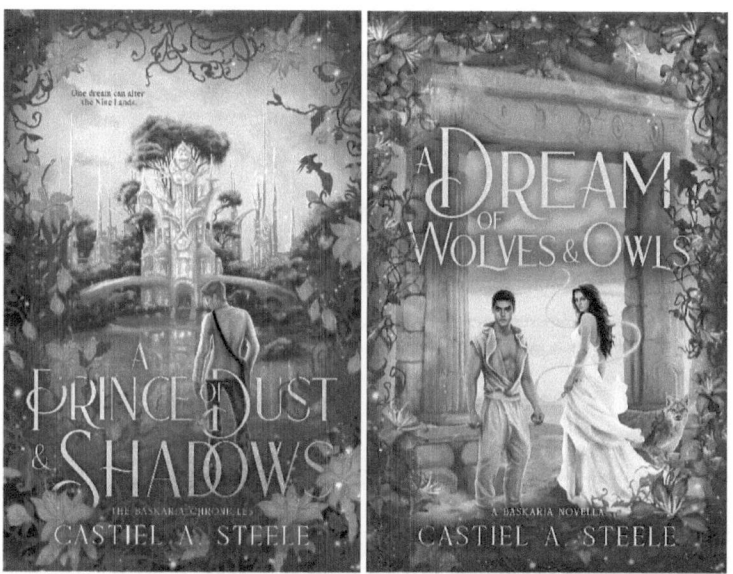

**A PRINCE OF DUST & SHADOWS: THE BASKARIA CHRONICLES**
**A DREAM OF WOLVES & OWLS: A BASKARIA NOVELLA**

www.castielsteelebooks.com